DUEL

❧ A BACKSTAGE MYSTERY ❧

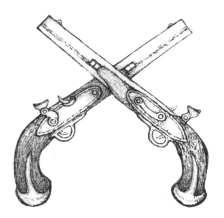

ASHLEY SARGEANT HAGAN

INKWELL
LITERARY PRESS

NASHVILLE, TN

Inkwell Literary Press
Nashville, TN

ISBN: 978-0-57856-054-0 (paperback)

Cover illustration and design by Pat Evans. Interior design by Sarah Siegand.
Headshot photography by Jon Alan Salon, Nashville, TN.

"I thoroughly disapprove of duels. I consider them unwise
and I know they are dangerous. Also, sinful. If a man should
challenge me, I would take him kindly and forgivingly by the hand
and lead him to a quiet retired spot and kill him."

—Mark Twain

PROLOGUE

The pale morning sun cowered behind the hills as two men stood with their backs to each other at fifteen paces, their dueling pistols in hand. A third man stood in between them, but out of the line of their fire. Ragged fog lay on the open field like cannon-fire after a battle, shredding across their feet and leaving a veiled mist on the men's faces.

"Do you want me to powder them?" asked a makeup artist.

"No! It's perfect!" said the director, pushing his Comteks off his ears as he rose from his chair and edged closer to the scene.

The men in the field were dressed in Regency elegance. On one side, a red-headed man was dressed almost completely in black, from his knee-length coat to his waistcoat and cravat; his white shirt stood out in stark contrast. He looked every bit the villain next to the debonair man on the other side of the field, who wore a brown coat with a multi-colored paisley waistcoat and white cravat. He pulled his free hand through his thick, blond hair. The third man wore a black coat as well, but with a simple, tan waistcoat. None of the men wore hats.

The debonair man in brown stood perfectly still, his long dueling pistol at his shoulder, pointed at the grey morning sky. The man in black seemed uneasy, dangling his pistol in his hand, the barrel pointed at the ground. The third man rolled his eyes and looked increasingly uncomfortable, his hands behind his back.

"William!" called the director. "Are you ready?"

"Ready as I'll ever be," the third man grumbled.

"What's that?"

"Yes, Sir Frederick. I'm ready."

"Good," said the director, surveying the scene.

A cameraman on a dolly track shifted impatiently in his chair.

Gathering its courage, the sun peeked above the tree line, bathing the field in red light.

"Now," said Sir Frederick to his assistant director.

"Back to one!" she shouted, then settled herself behind the video monitors.

The man in brown took a breath and stood taller. The red-headed man in black stopped fidgeting and stood rigid, his pistol still pointed at the ground, his face grim. William stared straight ahead between the two. He was carrying a large, white handkerchief, which he now brought out from behind his back.

"Rolling!" yelled the director, watching intently. "Background! Action!"

William lifted the handkerchief above his head.

"Ready!" shouted William, continuing to look straight ahead.

The two men turned toward each other.

"Aim!"

The duelers took a sideways stance, right feet toward their opponent, the pistols aimed with right arms outstretched. Their eyes locked in a death grip over their right shoulders.

There was a pause of about five seconds. The assembled cast and crew watching the performance held their collective breath.

"Fire!" shouted William, dramatically dropping the handkerchief.

Both men fired. Both men fell to the ground with a moan.

The echo of the shots rumbled against the hills, and smoke from the gun-fire lingered in the air, blending into the mist.

William stared curiously at the man in black, lying on his back in the field. He made a slight movement to go toward him, then stopped himself, realizing the scene was continuing.

A blonde woman wearing a long, blue, full-skirted dress with puffed sleeves suddenly appeared out of a stand of trees; she picked up her skirts and raced toward the scene. The sun, now higher above the trees, spun her hair into gold as her bonnet fell from her head as she ran.

"Waverly!" she screamed, falling in tears on the body of the man in brown, who groaned at her touch.

"Cut!" yelled Sir Frederick, exasperated. "Why is Peter on the ground!"

He stared angrily in the direction of the man in black.

"Something's wrong, Jake," said the blonde woman to the debonair man as she anxiously stared across the field at Peter, who still lay motionless where he had fallen.

"He's just fooling around, Corinne," the man in brown assured her as he sat up, laughing. "He's just mad that I get the girl instead of him."

William, no longer restrained by the cameras, ran over to where Peter was still lying motionless, kneeling at his side.

"He's bleeding!" he shouted, beginning to unbutton the man's collar and pull loose his cravat.

"What?" asked the stunt coordinator, running forward. "That's impossible! These were blanks!"

"Oh, come on, Pete!" Jake joked as he sauntered over. "Why do you always have to have the attention! It's me who's supposed to be injured in this scene."

He nudged at the man on the ground with his foot. William looked up at him, blood on his hands where he had opened the white, blood-stained shirt of the fallen man.

"Jake, what have you done?" asked William in a shocked voice. "Peter's dead."

Corinne screamed.

Jake stared down at Peter's open wound, then at his blank, unseeing eyes. He fell to his knees, his face as white as the dead man's.

"Oh God!" he said, staring at William. "I've killed my best friend!"

THREE WEEKS EARLIER...

CHAPTER ONE

Not quite Downton Abbey, but almost, thought Anna McKay as she slowly climbed down from the passenger van and stared in awe at the mansion in front of her. Hampstead Hall loomed above her in all its Tudor grandeur. It was three stories of dark red brick, complete with mullioned windows and a grand stone archway for an entrance. She wasn't sure, but Anna thought the carved inscription over the door was royal. She was beginning to understand why the Studio had chosen this particular house as the backdrop for *Cavendish Manor.*

Stretching her arms above her head, she filled her lungs with cool, English country air. It felt like they were expanding for the first time in a long time. The two years since graduating college had been such a flurry of activity: acting classes, auditions, bit parts. She had barely had time to breathe. Not that she wanted to breathe the LA smog, but she preferred it to the stifling atmosphere she'd left at home in Nashville.

The other passengers of the van, her fellow actors, began to spill out onto the pea-gravel, circular drive. Their astonished faces matched Anna's.

"Well!" drawled Corrine Newberry beside her. "I've never seen a house that large in all my life. Not even mine, and I'm from Atlanta. Mama will be green with envy." Corrine pretended to be a Southern belle with a grand, plantation-home pedigree, but really she was from the Atlanta suburbs and had never lived in anything larger than a one-story ranch-style house.

Anna frowned slightly as she admired Corrine's long, blond hair and large blue eyes. She certainly looked the part of a rich heiress. Which is what she had been hired to do. Anna tucked a wayward lock of her own auburn hair behind her ear and tried not to feel like the poor relation. Unfortunately, that's exactly what she had been hired to be.

Ironic, she thought.

She shook her head slightly, trying to rid herself of the feeling of unreality. Was she really here in England, about to co-star in a new historical drama? Sir Frederick Churchwood-Styles, famous writer and director, had actually seen her in a friend's short film in Hollywood and had hired her for his latest television series. It seemed almost like a dream, the kind of thing that happens to other people, but not to Anna. Yet, here she was, staring up at a Tudor mansion, her stomach in knots just thinking about all the ways this could go wrong and send her flying back across the ocean.

And she couldn't fail. Not now. It would make her parents right. And Derrick.

She stumbled slightly as someone bumped into her from behind.

"I'm so sorry!" said a deep male voice.

"No problem," replied Anna, breathlessly, giving the speaker a shy smile. He returned it with a blazing grin of his own before he continued walking and conversing with a young woman. Trying to be stealthy, Anna admired his broad shoulders and narrow waist from behind as the two walked slightly away from the rest of the group.

The young man positioned himself so Anna was in his line of vision; he slid a hand casually through his thick, blond hair and shot her an appreciative glance. Anna lowered her eyes as she felt the heat rise in her cheeks.

Corinne sidled over, a smirk turning up one corner of her sparkling lip-glossed mouth.

"I see Jake Rawlings has taken an interest in you," she drawled.

"No, he just accidentally bumped into me," assured Anna, hoping her blush wasn't obvious. "I'm sure he wouldn't think twice about me."

"Hmm. We'll see. He's awfully handsome in that young Brad Pitt, boyish kind of way. I hear he has lots of money."

Anna frowned at her mercenary friend. At least the closest thing to a friend so far.

"I know he did a recurring role in *Bandits* last year. I thought he was only just now getting some good roles?"

"Well, rumor has it he's in talks to do J.J. Abrams' next film, but he's supposedly rolling in money. He's *Rawlings*, as in Rawlings Home Furnishings." She raised her eyebrows to show Anna she should be impressed.

And Anna was.

"No way!" she whispered, trying to keep her face from making it obvious to the topic of their conversation that they were gossiping about him.

"It's true," said Corinne with a slow nod of her golden head. "He works because he wants to, not because he has to, and I hear his family is not too happy with him about it. Family name, and all that. But he's a good actor, all the same."

"Yes," agreed Anna. She had been excited to discover he was going to be part of the cast. "Who's that with him?" she asked.

Corinne wrinkled her nose. "The props master. Jaime something. Jake met her somewhere along the way. He's been doing a lot of work over here lately."

"Jaime Douglas. I remember seeing her name on something. Is she his girlfriend?" Anna asked, trying to sound casual and unconcerned.

"No way. Just look at her!" whispered Corinne. "I mean, she's so pale! No makeup on at all! She looks like some kind of ghost."

Anna glanced at Jaime, trying not to seem like she was staring. Although Corinne's assessment seemed harsh, Anna had to admit that Jaime looked like she would fade into the background if she could. She was very pale, with pale yellow hair, like she'd just wandered down from some misty Scottish mountain. She was dressed in somewhat draping, faded black clothes, the color bleeding out of the garments in an attempt to match the faded color of her skin and hair. Next to the ruddy, healthy glow of Jake, she really did look half-alive.

Jaime turned her head to look at Anna, as if she could feel she was the subject of speculation. Anna was struck by the appearance of her eyes. They were slanting, almost Asian in shape, but the color was so light grey they were almost no color at all. They were expressionless at first, but then they narrowed, and Anna sensed an intensity behind them that hadn't been there before and seemed incongruous with the rest of her faded appearance.

Jaime turned away again, her face impassive. Anna wondered if she had imagined that flicker of intensity.

Jake glanced her way with smiling eyes, and Anna noticed with giddiness that they were a beautiful brown.

"What does a props master do, exactly?" Anna asked Corinne. This was her first principal role; she was still learning all the ins and outs of the business.

Corinne shrugged; she only had slightly more experience on a set than Anna.

"In charge of all the props, I guess," she said, checking her manicure. "Making sure everything looks Regency, in our case. I wonder where Peter Mallory is?" she asked, changing the subject and fluttering her fake eyelashes. "He's Jake's best friend. He's supposed to play my love interest."

Anna suspected Corinne had hopes of making Peter her real-life love interest as well.

"I don't know," she said, "but I haven't seen any of the British cast members. Just us Americans. I haven't seen the people who are supposed to play your parents. And the woman who's going to be the Dowager Countess."

"Portia Valentine," said Corinne. "She's been around for ages. Doesn't do a lot of television anymore. I'm surprised they got her. I hope she isn't senile or anything."

Anna's mouth dropped open at Corinne's callousness. She was about to correct her rudeness when a second van pulled up and screeched to a halt. The actors either glared at it or rolled their eyes as they walked away, putting distance between themselves and the occupants.

It was the crew.

The relationship between the cast and crew of any production is strained and rocky from time immemorial, and the majority of the cast of *Cavendish Manor* was not about to end the feud. The crew, all dressed in their traditional costume—camouflage shorts, black t-shirts, black Chuck Taylors—descended on the tranquil, aristocratic scene like a swarm of gnats. They seemed to tumble out of the van with a burst of loud and boisterous laughter.

Jim Anderson, the tall, lanky cinematographer, jumped down from the passenger seat. An empty paper coffee cup tumbled out after him onto the pea-gravel drive. He glanced at it as if surprised by its presence, then continued on his way without a second thought, leaving it to roll around, unsure of itself, and hunker for safety under the van.

Anna glared at him, hoping to instill manners by sheer telepathy across the driveway. Jim was pulling an e-cigarette from under the shaggy hair that covered his ear while scratching his unkempt beard with the other hand. Anna frowned. She knew he had a reputation for being personally sloppy while requiring absolute perfection from anyone touching the gear.

He must be really good at his job for people to put up with him, she thought, grimacing while she watched his scratching move to his butt.

She decided to retrieve the cup herself, but as she headed toward the van, she watched with surprise as the cinematographer, with a sheepish expression, retraced his steps and scrabbled after the cup. Anna looked up to see the butler of Hampstead Hall glaring at Jim from the porch; he had just exited the massive oak doors to greet his guests, and Anna could tell he was not the kind of man to allow anyone to spoil the property.

The butler (at least he seemed like one to Anna) was a silvery man. His hair was a silvery-grey, parted neatly to one side, and he was wearing a silvery-grey suit. Anna hoped her fellow cast and crew members would treat the house with the respect the butler so obviously felt it deserved. Although the drama was set in a British country house, most of the actors and crew were American, and Anna knew instinctively that they would not have the same appreciation of British history as she had growing up in a home with a history professor for a mother. Even if that mother thought more of her own family history than Anna felt she should.

The butler gathered everyone into the grassy area in the middle of the circular drive, eyeing each of them sternly, as if warning them to be on their best behavior.

"I am Mr. Barnaby," the butler-like man began in his smooth, condescending voice. "I am the house manager of Hampstead Hall. You are here at the invitation of the Earl of Somerville."

Anna found his serious tone amusing, and her mouth twitched in an effort to keep from smiling.

He makes it sound like we have been invited as the Earl's weekend guests, she thought.

She knew the reason *Cavendish Manor* was being filmed at this location was because the current owner, the new Earl of Somerville, was in dire need of money. His father, the Eighth Earl, had been lavish in his tastes and had lacked good business sense. The Ninth Earl, upon the death of his father a year or two ago, had inherited a potential money pit, and if something didn't change, he could lose the house and 1,000 acres of prime Surrey farmland. She knew the house manager would be forced to put up with them.

"Lord Somerville is the Ninth Earl to reside here at Hampstead Hall, and you should consider it a great honor to be allowed the privilege of using this beautiful estate and its grounds as the backdrop for your theatrical endeavor."

There was a stifled snicker as Jim Anderson elbowed the assistant director beside him.

"Theatrical endeavor?" he whispered to her with a sneer.

The assistant director smiled smugly, her hand over her mouth. Sarah Stern was dressed to match the crew, and with her hair in a ponytail and covered by her characteristic ball cap, she could almost be mistaken for one of them.

Mr. Barnaby continued, ignoring Jim's comment.

"As you probably know, the writer and director of *Cavendish Manor*, Sir

Frederick Churchwood-Styles, was a dear friend of the current Earl's father, which is why you are being allowed the use of the estate. You are even being allowed to stay here on the property." Mr. Barnaby glared at the group from under his silver eyebrows, as if this last proclamation was contrary to his own desires. "It was the request of Sir Frederick that I give you all a little tour of the house and grounds, so as to instill in each of you the *illustrious* history and *irreplaceable* importance of Hampstead Hall, and to *ensure* that you will all value it just as highly as I do."

After a thorough glowering at each member of the group, Mr. Barnaby adjusted his gaze to the middle distance and began what Anna guessed to be a memorized speech. She found it a little amusing that he seemed to take pride in Hampstead Hall as if he had been butler on the property since the first Earl in the 1700s. He began with the acquisition of the Earldom of Somerville, and brought the history down to the present Earl. Anna noticed he skillfully forgot to mention the Eighth Earl's bad monetary choices and the current Earl's desperate attempt to hold on to his inheritance.

"I wonder what the new Earl is like?" murmured Anna to Corrine beside her.

"Probably old and fat," sneered Corrine. Plumpness was one of the worst sins in Corrine's world.

Mr. Barnaby then turned his history to the house itself, pointing out the crest of Elizabeth I carved in stone over the door.

"We will enter into the oldest part of the house, built in 1562. At one point, it was used as a hunting box for Henry VIII, although his 'box' included this first rectangle with six bedrooms, two Drawing Rooms, and a Great Hall." Mr. Barnaby snickered at his own joke. "In subsequent generations, the east and west wings were added, bringing the total number of bedrooms to forty-six. You will notice that the entryway has a double door with a foyer in between," he continued, "and the inner door is actually a wicket, which only allows one person to enter at a time. That was a safety precaution so that each guest could be assessed before entering the house, and there would be less opportunity for a large group to force the doors. We will now go into the house through the main door, but just like during the time of Henry VIII, we will have to go one by one through the wicket."

Smirking to himself, Mr. Barnaby led the cast and crew of *Cavendish Manor* through the massive outer door and through the little wicket, which looked like a child's door set into a larger one. Anna guessed it was no more than five and a half feet tall; the men and most of the women had to duck their heads.

Since it really was only possible for one person at a time to go through the wicket, the group soon found themselves forming an impromptu single-file line. Anna felt like a school child, and just like in school, she was pushed to the back of the line. A memory of plaid-skirted girls rushed to her mind, all lined up in an auditorium, waiting for the headmistress. She rolled her eyes and shrugged, content to look around her one more time before entering the darkness of the house.

"I guess we've been sent to the end of the line," teased a voice in front of her. Anna was surprised to look up into the grinning face of Jake Rawlings.

"I'm Jake," he said, sticking out his hand. "It was such a rush getting into the van, we haven't been properly introduced."

Anna felt herself blush again as she stammered her name.

"Is this your first job?" he asked.

"First real one," she admitted. "I don't really count the two lines I had on *NCIS*."

"Lines are lines," he said encouragingly. "Oh, you've got something in your hair," he said, pulling his fingers through it.

Anna's heart beat faster at his touch.

"Just a leaf," he assured her, brushing off his hands. "Ah," he said, glancing at the line steadily moving through the door. "It's almost our turn."

He caught up with the line using long strides, leaving Anna standing somewhat stunned by herself in the drive.

She sighed.

This job is getting more interesting by the minute, she thought.

She cast one final look up at the imposing edifice and the Elizabethan crest before she followed Jake into the house. As her eyes scanned the building, she was startled to see a face looking down at her from a window above the door. It was so unexpected that she got goosebumps, as if she had seen a ghost. It was a man's face, full of conflicting emotions. Anna felt she could feel those emotions emanating down through the leaded glass. She paused and stepped back again, looking up. There was no one there. She shivered, despite the brightness of the sun and darted forward through the outer door. As she squeezed quickly through the wicket to join the others, she found the darkness of the hall did little to comfort her.

CHAPTER TWO

Lord Somerville stepped back from the window. He had been staring out at the newcomers with a mixture of excitement and dread. He needed them. He really needed the money they represented. As the Ninth Earl of Somerville, he carried the weight of his forefathers on his 28-year-old shoulders. He knew that to be the landed aristocracy in the twenty-first century meant creativity. Thinking outside the box. Land was coveted in his island nation, and a massive estate was expensive to keep in habitable shape. He lived with the daily pressure to sell.

Inspired by the success that *Downton Abbey* had given to Highclere Castle, he had sought out the movie and television industry to help boost the income of the estate. He was thankful to have a friend in the industry, Sir Frederick Churchwood-Styles, an eccentric member of the aristocracy who loved to write and direct. Sir Frederick promised to film his latest creation at Hampstead Hall: five episodes, with more to come, if the show was a hit. With that and his organic farming efforts, Lord Somerville hoped to stay afloat and even to make the repairs to the house and grounds that were so desperately needed. He owed it to his ancestry. He owed it to his employees.

But having a television show on his property was not exactly convenient. He had agreed, for a price, to allow the main cast and crew to stay on the property, a decision he was quickly regretting as he stared down at them standing together on the circle drive. They looked like vultures that had come to rest on the lawn, sensing the imminent death of the estate and willing to wait for its demise so they could take their fill. He resented their presence and wished he didn't need them. But he did.

Lord Somerville's plan was to stay out of the way and allow Mr. Barnaby to handle all issues of hospitality. He had managed to be in France visiting his sister during the weeks when Sir Frederick and his staff had scouted out camera angles and worked out set design. Now that they were here in earnest, he thought he might have dinner with them once in a while and give them the thrill of fraternizing with the upper class. But mainly he wanted to stay unobtrusively out of the way. Invisible, so to speak. Unfortunately, he knew he had to live in the house with them; he didn't have the funds to go away on holiday for the autumn while the filming took over his home. And there was still the farm to run. He dreaded the noise and the cameras and the people crawling all over his privacy. But then he thought of losing Hampstead Hall, and knew it was worth the trouble.

He had been watching the line of vultures entering the wicket and decided to give the scene one last look before retiring to his rooms to hide. He noticed two stragglers at the end of the line who seemed to be flirting. He frowned, irrationally irritated by the man's gesture of pulling something out of the woman's hair.

I don't believe there was anything there at all, he thought peevishly.

Suddenly, the woman looked up, and he found himself staring down at a face that seemed at the same time familiar and yet new. Like a new beginning. Her auburn hair blew gently in the autumn breeze, and when she turned her hazel eyes up into his, it inexplicably startled him, and he caught his breath. He stepped back from view and had to steady himself for a moment.

He wasn't sure why, but Lord Somerville suddenly decided to go downstairs and join the tour. He waved the idea out of his mind that this sudden inclination to listen in on Mr. Barnaby's history lesson about the estate had anything to do with the woman he had seen below. It was his property, wasn't it? And he had every right to to join the tour of his own house.

He bounded down the oak staircase, built in the early 1600s, lovingly rubbing his hand over the intricately-carved finial that topped the newel post at the bottom of the handrail. It was a habit of his; he had always rubbed the finial, almost like a talisman, since he had first been able to reach it as a young man. It was carved to resemble a king's crown, presumably because the house had originally been one of King Henry VIII's hunting lodges before being handed off to the Earls of Somerville.

He arrived in the hall as Mr. Barnaby was beginning the tour. Lord Somerville had intended to discreetly join the party, but he had forgotten himself on the way down the stairs, and he hurtled into the room like he owned the place, which of course he did.

The assembled cast and crew of *Cavendish Manor* turned at the interruption. There were mixed reactions of interest and irritation. Corrine Newberry raked him from top to bottom with her eyes, her fluttering lashes indicating he had passed her first test. Jake Rawlings appeared amused; Jim Anderson scowled and scratched his beard, nudging Sarah Stern with a questioning elbow.

Anna was frustrated, stuck behind the large, black-clad body of the chief cameraman, who smelled suspiciously of unwashed underwear. She couldn't see the newcomer, and every time she leaned right or left, the cameraman leaned that way as well. She gave an exasperated sigh.

Mr. Barnaby eyed the new arrival with disdain. Although he was the lord of the manor, Mr. Barnaby had known Lord Somerville since he was a child, and was only just beginning to accept him as the current master. He disagreed with the young lord's ideas to increase revenue in so public a way, finding them plebeian. It was definitely not something that would have taken place during the lifetime of the former Earl. The former Earl, despite his shortcomings, always kept up appearances. He had *savoir faire*.

But it wasn't the former Earl who stood sheepishly at the back of the assembled group; it was most assuredly the new Earl, and Mr. Barnaby sniffed and scowled at the young man. Lord Somerville, feeling Mr. Barnaby's scrutiny, realized too late that he had not changed after having checked on the progress of his fields. The farmers were planting rye grass and crimson clover to prepare the soil for next year's crops. Glancing down, he noticed he was still wearing his field jacket and jeans, and his boots had dried mud clinging to the worn leather. He shrugged and gave Mr. Barnaby a quick, sideways smile.

Mr. Barnaby cleared his throat ominously and glared at his employer from under his bushy, silver eyebrows.

"I see we have a late addition to our tour group," he began. "You are all very fortunate indeed—"

"I'm Mr. Langley," Lord Somerville quickly intervened, fearing Mr. Barnaby was about to introduce him as the Earl. "William Langley."

For reasons he could not explain, Lord Somerville had a sudden desire to keep his identity to himself. He raised his eyebrows and gave Mr. Barnaby a wide-eyed look, hoping the silver-haired house manager would understand his inexplicable desire for anonymity.

"Mister…Langley," repeated Mr. Barnaby slowly while beetling his brows.

Lord Somerville, a.k.a Mr. Langley, agreed with a boyish grin. The other members of the group looked at each other, puzzled. Corinne tucked him into the back of her mind to sort out later whether he was worth her time and trouble. The others seemed to mostly dismiss him.

"Well," continued Mr. Barnaby with a sniff, "let us begin our little tour."

The group turned again to face the house manager as he began explaining about the purpose of the enormous fireplace that dominated the Hall, and pointed out the carved wooden ceiling, stained to a golden patina from centuries of smoke.

Anna was able to finally skirt around the cameraman, positioning herself so she could glance slyly at the new arrival. Her eyes took in the tall young man, hands thrust casually into his jacket pockets. His slightly mud-stained jacket pockets. Her gaze lingered on the well-worn boots, and she wondered where this man fit into the hierarchy of the *Cavendish Manor* cast and crew. She raised her eyes to his face again.

It's the man from the window, she realized, surprised.

Although she had only seen him for a few seconds, she was positive this was the same man who had gazed down at her from the window above the door. No ghost, certainly. But who was William Langley, she wondered?

She glanced his way again. He seemed happily, almost gleefully, interested in what Mr. Barnaby was saying. She noticed he had black hair that curled softly all over his head. From his profile she could tell he had a strong chin and high cheekbones, and quite a beautiful mouth. She found herself blushing slightly as she thought about that mouth, and hoped he hadn't noticed. William suddenly turned towards her and smiled. Anna sucked in her breath, and then tried to let it out slowly, as if his look hadn't affected her at all. But it had, because he had the most brilliantly blue eyes she'd ever seen, with thick black lashes that made them stand out all the more. It made him look like a movie star.

Of course, she realized, feeling silly. He *is* a movie star. Or at least he will be if *Cavendish Manor* is a success. He must be one of the actors, although she could have sworn she had met almost everyone who had a role.

Oh, God! He has dimples! she noticed suddenly, and turned her attention quickly to the blackened fireplace.

Lord Somerville, or William Langley, recognized the auburn-haired girl to his left as the girl he had seen through the window. Somewhere in the back of his mind he liked her enormous eyes and slightly turned up nose, and the way her eyebrows made her face so expressive. He also could swear he had seen her face before, or one very like it. He glanced covertly at her again with a look of concern.

Maybe there's something wrong with her head, he thought. She's turning red and she seems to take a lot of interest in the fireplace.

Mr. Barnaby moved the group along from the Great Hall to the Dining Room, explaining as he went.

"Of course, originally, the Great Hall would have been the Dining Room, but as time went on, and fashions changed, the family decided to add on this wing to incorporate a new Dining Room here, with a Butler's Pantry behind, and a secret staircase to the kitchens below."

"A secret staircase sounds exciting," Corinne whispered to Anna. She had sidled back over as they exited the Great Hall. She grabbed on to Anna's arm and slowed her down until they were nearer to William Langley.

"This is a beautiful house, don't you think?" said Corinne to William.

"It is," he agreed, resisting the urge to say thank you. "I'm William," he continued, flashing her a bewitching smile.

"Corinne Newberry," said Corinne, extending a well-manicured hand. William gallantly kissed it, causing Corinne to giggle.

"And you are?" asked William, turning his attention to Anna.

"I'm Anna McKay," she said, trying not to stare at the dimples in his cheeks.

"Scottish?" he asked.

"Oh. I guess so. On my father's side," she replied.

"I'm just plain ol' American," drawled Corinne, batting her lashes up at William.

He laughed.

"Those in the back of the group need to keep up," Mr. Barnaby barked.

The three of them scurried forward across the black and white marble floor, William giving Mr. Barnaby a mock salute.

"This room is the traditional English Drawing Room," explained Mr. Barnaby, pushing back the massive mahogany pocket doors that separated the Dining Room from the Drawing Room. "It features French windows that lead to the terrace, and the gardens beyond. You are welcome to explore the gardens at your leisure once you are guests here at Hampstead Hall."

The Drawing Room was a mix of antique and mid-century modern furniture, giving the room a theatrical, almost Hollywood, flair. Anna gazed appreciatively over the tufted dark-leather sofas and chairs, the built in cabinets filled with pieces of porcelain and silver, and the elegant, gilt-edged tables. The room was much larger than she imagined a Drawing Room to be, with several little islands of furniture dotting the thick Persian rugs. It was even larger than her parents' living room back home. A smile played around the corners of her mouth as she turned in a circle, listening to Mr. Barnaby telling a story about a famous British politician who had proclaimed one of his oft-repeated lines in that very room.

William couldn't help but watch her.

She seems so at home, he thought. Then he brushed the thought away. The last thing he needed was to be thinking romantically, especially about a red-headed American actress. He could imagine what his mother would have to say about that. But those thoughts didn't stop the twinge of jealousy he felt as he watched Jake Rawlings move close to Anna and whisper something in her ear. Especially when it made her blush so unbelievably beautifully.

"You look like you belong here," Jake whispered. Anna immediately reddened, partly because she felt he had voiced her inner thoughts, but mainly because of the admiring way he looked at her when he said it.

He quickly moved away after he spoke, as if he wanted to keep his flirtation a secret. A cloud passed over the sun for a moment, casting the room into shadow, despite the floor-to-ceiling French doors. Anna caught the faded Jaime looking her direction; instead of grey, her slanted eyes seemed black in the shadows of the room. She felt like Jaime was glaring at her, cold and menacing. Then the cloud passed, flooding the room again with bright sun. Jaime's mouth twitched in a shy smile. Anna smiled back.

Must have been my imagination, she thought, inwardly scolding herself for her silliness.

"Of course, these are the dueling pistols," said Mr. Barnaby, indicating a carved, cherrywood box on a console table. It was open, displaying a pair of pistols with unusually long barrels, the wooden handles elaborately carved and inlaid with mother-of-pearl. "This pair was commissioned by the Third Earl. As you probably know, the art of dueling was considered part of the education of a gentleman in times past. The Ninth Earl has graciously allowed the use of the family dueling pistols for this television series." His grey eyebrows lowered and he stared pointedly at William, who kept his eyes innocently on the ground. "I hope that his trust in this theatrical organization will not be a mistake. Now, moving on—"

Anna noticed William's mouth twitch in an attempt to keep from smiling, although he never looked up at Mr. Barnaby.

Odd that Mr. Barnaby would target William out of all of us for his reprimand,

Anna thought. She studied the young man out of the corner of her eye. He didn't seem threatening, or likely to steal anything. Although, those muddy boots. And the jacket. Maybe he looks too rustic for someone as put together as Mr. Barnaby.

She moved closer to the pistol display before following the rest out of the room. The guns were beautiful, like artwork. Anna wondered if they had ever been used. Until Mr. Barnaby mentioned it, she had no idea there would be a duel in the show. She hoped it would be exciting to watch. To keep the storyline a secret, the cast had only been given the script for the first episode. The other four episodes were top-secret. Anna was still getting used to the idea that there would only be five. British television series were shorter in duration, with each episode an hour and a half instead of the one-hour that American shows tended to be. Actually about forty minutes, to leave room for commercials.

On the other side of the Great Hall was a large private study and a salon or parlor that closed off from the main room with large, mahogany pocket doors. Through the Parlor Mr. Barnaby pushed open elegantly painted doors to reveal a grand Ballroom. Like the Dining Room across the way, it had black and white marble floors and delicate, though massive, chandeliers, dangling with crystal drops that sparkled like diamonds.

These wings must have been added on at the same time, Anna decided. Sometime in the eighteenth century, by the looks of them. The style reminded her of the Governor's Palace in Colonial Williamsburg, one of her family's favorite vacation spots.

Mr. Barnaby next led the group up the oak staircase that William had bounded down not so long ago. At the bottom of the staircase, Anna gazed upward through the heavy bannisters that rose three stories above her head. It was dizzying, the view and the knowledge that countless feet had trod those same stairs for centuries. Had touched this same balustrade. She lovingly caressed the newel post at the bottom of the staircase before ascending, allowing her hand to gently glide across the finial at the top. It was in the shape of a crown, she noticed, pausing to look more closely. When she did, she caught the startled expression of William Langley, who was right behind her. Afraid she had done something wrong, she withdrew her hand quickly and ran a few steps ahead.

CHAPTER THREE

"This room here at the top of the stairs is called the Tapestry Room, for obvious reasons," said Mr. Barnaby, waving his hand to indicate the antique French tapestries adorning the walls. "It is the original Drawing Room for the house, and it is still used as a private sitting room by the family, and will be off-limits during your stay."

He glared at the group from under his silver eyebrows.

Anna gasped in delight, despite Mr. Barnaby's admonishment; her attention had been immediately drawn to the window, and it was all she could do to conceal her excitement.

It was a window out of a fairy tale. It was a window out of her dreams.

In an alcove was two tiers of mullioned, stone windows reaching all the way to the ceiling; diamond panes of leaded glass sparkled in the sun and were draped on either side with red velvet curtains secured by tasseled golden ropes. In front of the windows was a window seat with a red velvet cushion that begged Anna to curl up on it and gaze out the leaded panes to the garden below.

She barely heard Mr. Barnaby point out the priceless sixteenth-century tapestry draping one wall and the ceiling carved with roses and birds. She glanced at the Queen Anne chairs and the gilt mirrors, and the Not To Be Touched For Any Reason vases and statuary on the painted tables. Her mind kept returning to those windows, and she found she couldn't keep her eyes from straying there as well.

As the rest of the group began filing out the door of the Tapestry Room, Anna purposely lagged behind. She felt she had to—simply had to—sit on that window seat and look out those panes. She lingered at one of the tapestries near the door, pretending to be enthralled by its romantic scene of lords and ladies in a garden. She felt a slight pang of annoyance as she saw, out of the corner of her eye, Corinne coyly taking William Langley's arm.

"Isn't this fun?" she heard her whisper as she squeezed his arm and he smiled warmly down into her wide, blue eyes.

Anna felt an unfamiliar knot in the pit of her stomach. *Jealousy?* she thought, and dismissed it as ridiculous. As if he would even look at me anyway, with Corinne around.

Finally alone, she crossed to the window, put one knee on the velvet cushion, and leaned forward to admire the view. The window overlooked the garden behind the house. The garden was separated into rooms by tall yew hedges and large, animal-shaped topiary. Anna could see lavender, late in the season, bushing up green and silver around a sundial, and sunny yellow dahlias still clinging to their stems despite the chill in the air. There was a pea-gravel drive between the house and the garden that continued on one side through an opening in a brick wall and disappeared into a stand of trees farther on, the leaves barely touched by autumn. Far on the other side of the garden, the drive crossed under a brick archway and became a large, square courtyard surrounded by half-timbered buildings. Anna was curious to know what their purpose was.

Focusing her attention once more on the garden in front of her, Anna reached out her hand and touched the iron handle on the nearest window. It seemed to hum with electricity under the warmth of her hand, and the handle turned, gently swinging the window open and bringing in a waft of sweet-smelling air. As she leaned forward, breathing in the fragrance of pinewood and fresh grass, she began to hear what sounded like horse's hooves in the distance. She looked toward the opening in the garden wall, and saw a horse and rider galloping toward the house from the stand of trees. It was a man in period dress, she realized with surprise. He was riding a gigantic black stallion, and he slowed as he entered the grounds through the wall, pebbles from the drive skidding out from under the horse's hooves.

Anna stared at the horse and rider as if spellbound, holding her breath.

This must be someone trying out one of the costumes, she thought. Who else would be riding a horse in that kind of an outfit?

She felt strange, like she recognized the rider just by his form, although she still couldn't see his face. She watched him intently as he approached. He rode with the grace and ease of someone who was comfortable on horseback. His clothes fit him perfectly, not like a costume, but like they had been made for him, like he wore them all the time. He was clothed in a dark suit with tight-fitting trousers tucked into tall boots; Anna could see the hint of a burgundy vest under the coat and a flutter of silk cravat at his throat. His top hat shielded his face from her view, and she waited impatiently for him to get nearer, hoping for a glimpse of it.

The rider slowed his horse even more, coming even with the window. As Anna looked down on him from above, he suddenly swept off his hat and looked up at the windows of the Tapestry Room as if he sensed her presence. Anna was startled to find a pair of brilliantly blue eyes gazing back at her. Brilliantly blue with thick black lashes, like the man who had stood looking down at her from the window earlier in the day. The same black curls and blue, blue eyes!

It can't be! she thought. He was just in this room!

Anna gasped. She let go of the handle of the window and stepped back into the room. A hand reached out and touched her shoulder, and she screamed as she found herself staring into the same pair of blue eyes she had just looked down into.

"Mr. Williams!" she breathed. She turned her head quickly to look back down at the gravel drive. The horse and rider were gone.

Why had she said *Mr. Williams*, she wondered? It had come naturally to her mind, as if she knew him.

She instinctively took a step away from the man in the room with her, but he held tightly to her upper arm.

"Are you all right?" asked William. Anna stared back into his concerned face.

"Yes," she answered mechanically. "No. I don't know."

"I didn't mean to startle you. And it's William Langley, not Mr. Williams. But please call me William." He smiled down at her, trying to soothe her obviously rattled nerves.

"I'm sorry. I don't know what happened," mumbled Anna, raising a shaking hand to her forehead.

William leaned forward. Anna began to panic. Is he going to kiss me?

He reached out and pulled the window closed. Anna relaxed, feeling a little stupid.

And a little disappointed.

"Did you feel you would fall out?" he asked, trying to understand her sudden fright.

"No, I…" she began. Then she hesitated. It suddenly sounded ridiculous. How could she tell this god-like man that she had been frightened by a waking dream about *him*. A very real-seeming dream about *him* dressed in period clothes and riding on a horse? And looking at her like…like…how did he look at her? She closed her eyes and tried to shake the dream out of her head.

"I just lost my balance, I guess," she said finally. "And then you were there suddenly and you startled me. I thought I was alone."

"Would you rather be alone?" he asked, turning toward the door.

"No!" she said, louder than she meant to. "I'm fine now. We should probably find the rest of them. I'm sure I'm missing important information from Mr. Barnaby."

William looked down at her with a twinkle in his eye.

"I mean it," she replied, dismissing his twinkle. "I love history, and I really do want to know about this house. It's so beautiful."

"Well," said William, "I can help you out in that regard. I know all there is to know about this house. And probably more than Mr. Barnaby."

"Why is that?" she asked, wrinkling her brow and trying not to drown in his clipped British accent.

"Let's just say I'm a history buff as well."

William led Anna out into the hall. At the far end, they could see the group just turning the corner as they obediently followed Mr. Barnaby. Jim Anderson, clearly bored, was lagging behind, arms folded, staring listlessly up at the ceiling.

As if by agreement, they didn't hurry to catch up. Anna noticed that along one side of the long hall were lead-paned windows that began halfway up the wall and ended at the ceiling. They flooded the hall with light, despite the dark panelling that covered the rest of the walls. On the other side of the hall were two doors, one closed and one open.

William led her to the open doorway.

"This is the Library, as you can clearly see."

Anna breathed in the fragrance of old books. They lined the walls high enough that a ladder was needed to reach the top shelves. There were also books carelessly piled on heavy, carved tables and worn leather chairs. Dust motes as old as the house itself hovered like fairies in the light from a far window. It was a magical room.

"I wonder if this room is closed to us as well," Anna sighed.

William noticed the disappointment in her face.

"No," he said. "You can come here whenever you like."

She smiled.

They moved into the hall again, rounding a jagged corner as they followed the rest of the tour.

"There's a lot of twists and turns in this house," William explained. "When an ancestor built another bit, he didn't exactly try to match the rest."

"It makes it interesting," Anna said, appreciatively. "And probably confusing."

"But great for hide-and-seek!" he said.

Door after door lined this new hall, all blending together with the walls under dark, square panelling. It was difficult to tell what was door and what was wall.

"Bedrooms," William explained, pausing. "Each one has one of these."

He pointed out a brass plate on the nearest door.

"A name card will go here, indicating whose room it is. So there's no confusion."

"Ingenious!" Anna said, running her finger over the brass plate.

"These are the rooms for the actors," William explained. "This east wing used to be the family rooms, but in the 1930s the west wing was renovated and the family moved into those rooms."

"Is the west wing still in that style?" she asked.

He laughed.

"No. There have been improvements here and there since then, although it probably needs another overhaul soon."

William frowned. His father had spent money on horses and foolish business ventures, but not Hampstead Hall.

He opened the door for Anna, revealing a spacious bedroom with a large, canopied bed, a gigantic wardrobe, several plush chairs near a fireplace, and a table near the window.

"Beautiful!" said Anna, taking it all in. "Why did the family move?"

"The loo," said William. "These rooms were last renovated during the Victorian period, so there are no private baths."

"We have to share?" asked Anna, shocked.

"I'm afraid so. But it's not so bad. There are ten rooms on this hall and three baths, so about three bedrooms to each bath."

Anna nodded.

"The bathrooms themselves are up-to-date," William added hopefully. "It's not like there are copper bathtubs and chain-flushes on the toilets!"

She smiled. "Actually, that might have been kind of cool. Are there rooms enough for all of us in this wing?" she asked.

"I think the main cast and crew members are here. There may be a few upstairs in the former servants' quarters. Sir Frederick Churchwood-Styles and Portia Valentine are in the family guest rooms in the west wing because they are personal friends."

"Of the current Earl," said Anna, guessing that's what he meant.

"Yes," agreed William, "of the current Earl."

"So which is it?" Anna asked, her curiosity getting the better of her. "Are you a member of cast or crew?"

"Oh! Um…" William racked his brain for an answer. He hadn't quite gotten that far in his deception. Obviously he couldn't pretend to be an actor, and he knew even less about the production side of things.

"I, uh, I'm…helping…" he stammered.

"Wait! Let me guess. Are you helping Mr. Churchwood-Styles? Are you his assistant?"

"You got me!" he replied, relieved. It couldn't be more of a perfect explanation, he thought. It would explain his close relationship with the director without drawing attention.

"I figured," continued Anna. "That's why you know so much about the house, isn't it? You've been here before."

"Yes," he agreed. "I've been here before."

I'll just have to convince Sir Frederick when he arrives that he needs to "hire" me, he thought.

William steered Anna down the hall of bedrooms and around another corner. This new hall had windows that faced the front lawn. In the center of the hall was an alcove with heavy brocade draperies hanging over the wide doorway. Anna peeked inside. There was a large mullioned window facing the circle drive and a few overstuffed chairs that beckoned for a quiet moment with a book. Instinctively, she went inside the alcove and leaned on the windowsill.

This is the window above the door, she realized.

William had joined her at the window, and stood staring down at the circle drive, just as he had done earlier. Anna wondered what he had been thinking about when he looked down at her. She glanced at him out of the corner of her eye. He seemed at ease now. Probably best not to pry.

She tentatively touched the handle of the lead window, but nothing happened. No humming. No Regency gentleman on horseback. She stepped back with a sigh.

"I suppose there's lots of stories associated with this house," Anna mused, half to herself. "Maybe even ghost stories or mysterious things in the night. Or day."

"Plenty, I'm sure," said William. "They say there was a murder once upon a time, but I forget the details. Oh, I hear the rest of the group. They're in the Gallery."

He indicated the closed door directly across from the alcove.

Anna wished they hadn't caught up so quickly. She tried to stall for more time with him.

"What about secret rooms or passages?" she asked, a mischievous smile curving up one side of her mouth.

William quickly looked away from her lips, hoping she hadn't noticed him staring at them.

"With a house this old, what do *you* think?" he asked.

She clapped her hands together with delight.

"Do you know where any are?" she squealed.

He laughed. "I may know a few secret places," he said mysteriously, opening the door to the Gallery.

They strolled casually into the room, still smiling and laughing. They looked up, surprised to see the entire rest of the group staring at them. They both paused, slightly embarrassed.

"Good Lord!" exclaimed Mr. Barnaby. He seemed uncharacteristically ruffled, and Anna realized to her dismay that he was staring pointedly at her. In fact, *everyone* was staring pointedly at her. Corinne, Jake, Jim Anderson. All of them. Her eyes searched their faces for some kind of explanation.

Surely we haven't broken some kind of country estate law that says you have to stay with the group at all times, she thought irritably. Or were we too loud upon entering the holiest of Galleries?

She was just about to turn to William for help (he was British, after all) when she heard his sharp intake of breath.

"Good Lord!" he said, echoing Mr. Barnaby.

Anna followed William's astonished gaze to the red damask-covered walls of the Gallery. So did the rest of the group. Anna searched for something, anything, that would explain this odd behavior. Other than the two "Good Lord's," no one had said a word.

The Gallery was more like a large hallway that spanned the center of the east wing from front to back, and it was hung thickly with paintings, mostly of

Somerville ancestors. A few were life-sized; Anna noticed that one Elizabethan male Somerville seemed to be showing off his stockinged legs in a rather absurd manner. Her eyes continued to rake the walls: men with hats, women with austere expressions, children who looked like miniature adults. And that's when she saw it, high on the wall, tucked between a larger portrait of a stern-looking couple and a painting of a fat baby. It was her own face looking down at her, except the woman in the painting was wearing a dark green, velvet dress, low on the shoulders, and her hair was pinned up in a mass of curls. She was seated on an elegant sofa with a multi-colored shawl draped across it.

Anna's mouth gaped open as she stared into her own eyes on the wall. Her mind immediately went back to the Tapestry Room window incident. The past and the present collided, and with a slight moan, Anna fell backward in a faint and was only kept from crashing to the marble black-and-white tiled floor by William's quick reflexes.

CHAPTER FOUR

When she came to, Anna found herself looking up into Jake Rawlings' concerned face, though her head was being cradled on William's knee. She immediately felt awkward and attempted to sit up.

"Slowly, now," warned William, his helpful hands sending inexplicable tingles through Anna's arms and back. Sitting up brought her in closer proximity to Jake, who was kneeling beside her on the floor and holding one of her hands. This caused her breathing to be momentarily interrupted.

"Are you all right now?" Jake asked, his large brown eyes gazing into Anna's with concern.

"Yes," Anna replied, looking away. She moved to stand. Both men assisted her, Jake holding her hand in front and William from behind with one hand at her waist and one under her elbow. Once she was upright again, the two men stood looking at each other, with Anna sandwiched in between them. She felt like a bone being fought over by two territorial dogs. She extricated herself from both men and stepped aside. This seemed to ease the tension between them.

Anna's attention returned to the portrait on the wall.

"Who is that woman?" she asked, turning to Mr. Barnaby as the most likely source of information.

"That is Lady Anna Somer, the daughter of the Third Earl of Somerville," explained Mr. Barnaby. "Before her marriage. A rather headstrong young lady, I understand." Anna could tell by his pursed lips what Mr. Barnaby's thoughts were of "headstrong young ladies."

"You look just like her," said Corinne, the first to state the obvious. There were several nods from around the group. "Maybe you're related? Maybe you're really a princess!"

Anna rolled her eyes. She could feel a slow blush creeping up her face to match the deep red of her hair. A princess. Really.

"If she were a relative, she would be an earl's daughter, not a princess," said William. "She would be Lady Anna—"

Anna had looked up into his face, and it stopped his speech. Just in time, too, he realized.

I almost gave my name away, he thought to himself. If she were my sister, she would be Lady Anna *Langley*, daughter of the Earl of Somerville. But she's not my sister.

He cast a reassuring glance over the rest of the portraits on the wall, relieved that the more recent family portraits were in the west wing in the family rooms. Here there were only the formal ones of his parents, and one of the four of them (his parents and older sister, Maria, before her marriage) when he was just a child of ten. Surely no one would recognize the man in the boy? He barely did himself.

"Well," said Mr. Barnaby, who did recognize the man in the boy, and wasn't very pleased with either, at the moment, "that concludes our tour. Tea will be served downstairs on the terrace."

He moved to exit the room.

"Wait!" Corinne said. "What about Anna? Don't you think it's weird that she looks just like that painting?"

Mr. Barnaby adjusted his tie and cleared his throat.

"A coincidence, I'm sure, Madam. Nothing that concerns me *or* the Earls of Somerville."

After a withering look in William's direction, he turned and went downstairs.

"Well, la-de-da," said Corinne, exasperated, her hand on her hip. "*Nothing that concerns me or the Earls of Somerville.* We'll see about that."

"Corinne, I'm sure it's just a coincidence, like he said," assured Anna, feeling self-conscious.

"I think this painting proves you're a princess," Corinne continued, pointing at it. "And I think we should prove it to that ol' stick-in-the-mud. I think he just doesn't like an American being up on his aristocratic wall."

She sashayed out of the Gallery, her nose in the air. Most of the cast and crew had already filed out, and more followed her down the staircase.

Anna stood gazing up at the portrait. The deep colors of the painting and the outfit the woman wore made her think of old photos her mother kept in an album in her office.

I wonder what time period the Third Earl of Somerville lived in, she thought to herself.

She sighed heavily.

I'm not a princess, she reasoned. Mother would have found that out and flaunted it.

"It really is a remarkable likeness," said William beside her.

Anna jumped. She had forgotten he was still in the room.

"Are you sure you're all right?" he asked, with a look of concern.

Anna tried to laugh it off.

"I've done nothing but jump and faint since you met me," she said. "This has been a strange day, so far. Maybe it's jet lag or something."

"Well, I'm sure tea and cakes will make it better," William said with a smile.

When they arrived on the terrace, Jake rose from an iron garden chair.

"I saved you a seat," he said to Anna.

"Oh. Thank you," she replied, with a quick glance at William, who bowed his head to her and moved on, seating himself beside Corinne on the other side of the terrace. Anna watched him go, disappointed, but when she looked up, she found Jake's kind, brown eyes smiling down into hers.

Maybe I'm not *that* disappointed, she thought, smiling back.

CHAPTER FIVE

On the ride back to the hotel, Anna stared out the van window, her thoughts flying through her mind as fast as the Surrey countryside was whizzing past her unseeing eyes. Too many things unexplained. Too many things that didn't make sense. What happened in the Tapestry Room? Was it a dream? Why did she look like a long-dead Somerville relative?

It wouldn't surprise me to be related to some earl, she thought bitterly. My mother would be thrilled.

Her mind went back to a scene in her parents' living room in Nashville the night before she left for Los Angeles two years ago.

"Anna, you are a *McKay*. He is not," her mother had said, with a look that attempted sympathy.

"Of course, he's not!" she had shouted back. "That's why I love him!"

"But obviously, he doesn't love *you*," she had continued, as Anna collapsed in tears on the sofa. "His visit here helped him realize the difference in your upbringing. I mean, a farmer from Idaho? Really, Anna."

"Well, it's over, thanks to you!"

"Thanks to me?" her mother had replied with an innocent expression. "You're the one moving to Los Angeles to try this acting thing. Even Derrick thinks it's a bad idea. If you really cared for him, would you be moving across the country?"

"This is beautiful country," Corinne said sleepily, jolting Anna back into the present. "But I can't wait to get back to the hotel." She was slumped beside Anna on the van seat, her stomach full of tea and cakes. "One more night of comfort before we have to go back to that dreary old house. And that dreary old Mr. Barnaby."

Anna turned to her in surprise. "You didn't like it?" she asked.

"Sharing a bathroom?" Corinne demanded. "All that old Victorian furniture and curtains around the bed? No, thanks. Of course, *you* would like it. You're a relative."

She yawned and stretched, her arms reaching across Anna's face.

"I'm not a relative," Anna complained, backing away from Corinne's hand,

"and besides, it's a private home, not a hotel. With this many guests, you can't expect a private bathroom for everyone."

Corinne made a face.

"Do you think we'll have to clean it ourselves?" she asked.

Jake Rawlings turned around from the row in front of her, draping his muscular arm over the back of the seat. Anna found her eyes drawn to the light-colored hairs on his forearm that curled against his tan skin.

"No," he said, "they have a large staff. I saw a couple of maids come out of one of the rooms while we were there."

Corinne gasped excitedly.

"Were they wearing those cute little black and white outfits?" she asked. "With aprons and hats? I just love the aprons and hats."

Jake laughed.

"I hate to disappoint you, but modern maid uniforms are a bit less picturesque. They were in khakis, with grey polo shirts."

Corinne pouted her disappointment.

Jake tapped Anna's arm, then leaned on his hand.

"So, who was that guy?" he asked. "The one who joined the tour? He seemed to come out of nowhere, like some sort of phantom."

And disappeared again as we were leaving, Anna thought.

Corinne turned toward her, full of interest and envy.

"Yes! Tell us more about William Langley! You two seemed cozy on the tour."

Anna shrugged. "He said he works for Mr. Churchwood-Styles."

"*Sir* Churchwood-Styles," corrected Jake with pretended seriousness.

"Sorry. I guess I'll have to learn all that British aristocracy stuff," admitted Anna.

Corinne yawned again. "I'm not going to. Too boring. They should just forgive me because I'm an American."

Jake laughed, showing perfect white teeth.

"Well, you'll have to learn some of it for this drama. You're playing Lady Margaret Pembroke, for instance. But I would call you Lady Margaret, not Lady Pembroke," Jake explained.

"And I'm just plain Miss Daphne Thomson!" said Anna.

"Exactly," agreed Jake. "A nobody. A poor relation."

Anna shrugged and rolled her eyes. She preferred it. She couldn't wait until her mother saw the show and found out she wasn't playing a member of the upper class.

"But—a very beautiful poor relation," Jake continued, "and one that I guarantee will have the audience on her side before the first episode is over." He winked at Anna, while Corinne, awakened by jealousy from her afternoon somnolence, pouted at him. Jaime, who was sitting beside Jake, stiffened at his words. At least, that's what it seemed like to Anna, although she could only see the back of her faded blond head. The props master gave the impression of being totally absorbed in her phone.

"And then there's the lady's maid," Jake continued. "I don't know why, but a lady's maid is always called by her last name, not her first. So if you were Anna's lady's maid," he said, turning to Corinne, "you would be called Newberry instead of Corinne."

Corinne squeaked.

"I would *never* be a lady's maid," she said defiantly, folding her arms over her chest, "Even if they do have cute outfits. And if I were somehow a lady's maid, I would make them call me Corinne. I don't have time for those kind of society games."

Jake laughed out loud, a good-natured laugh, full of fun, not malice. Anna laughed with him, and they shared a meaningful glance. She felt she could really like Jake.

I hope I can get to know him better, she thought. We're not that different in our upbringing, despite his well-known name. Of course, that would be playing her mother's game, wouldn't it? Someone on her social level. She shrugged it off. But she felt a momentary qualm when she thought of Jaime. She was sure the faded props master had feelings for Jake, although he didn't seem to return them.

CHAPTER SIX

The van turned into the drive of the Runnymede on Thames, a modern hotel on the banks of the River Thames. Anna felt it was more of a resort than a mere hotel, with two restaurants, a spa, and rentable boats for excursions. Like most of the modern hotels she had stayed in, the Runnymede was eccentric. Oversized deck chairs graced the front lawn, so large you had to climb to get in them, while the regular-sized garden chairs were shaped like bright flowers. Inside the hotel, you might have to dodge a slender tree trunk in the middle of the buffet restaurant, or stop to admire the display of rubber ducks that graced the main staircase.

The Studio had obviously spared no expense on accommodations, although it was only for a few days. Most of the cast and crew had arrived the day before, and wouldn't leave until the following day when they would be installed at Hampstead Hall for several weeks.

"Runnymede on Thames. Such a funny name," said Corinne, wrinkling her turned-up nose. "What's a Runnymede?"

"It's named after the area we're in," Anna explained. "Runnymede is where Magna Carta was signed by King John. You can visit the spot, and I hope to. It's in Windsor Great Park, not far from here or from Hampstead Hall."

"Magna Carta?" Corinne said questioningly.

"Surely you've heard of the Magna Carta, Corinne," said Jake with a laugh. "The document that made England a Constitutional Monarchy? The beginnings of democracy, and all that?"

Corinne waved a well-manicured hand.

"Whatever," she said.

"I'd love to visit Runnymede with you," said Jake, turning back to Anna. "If you don't mind the company."

She smiled.

"Sure," she said, shyly. "And I also hope to go to Windsor Castle."

"Now, a castle I might could do," said Corinne. "But you can have your magnum cartas. Oh! We're here. Finally! I'm definitely headed for the spa," she complained as she climbed down from the van. "I have to massage all that old stuff off me."

Jake grinned.

"Well, I'm ready for dinner," he said. "Who wants to join me?"

He turned to Anna, expectantly.

"I'll go," said Jaime quickly.

"Great!" he said with a frozen smile. "Anyone else is welcome to join us."

Anna hesitated, unsure how to answer. She wanted to have dinner with Jake, but having Jaime along might make things uncomfortable. Maybe she should just go back to her room and take a long bath. Clearly this day had proven she was not completely herself yet.

But all of their plans were interrupted when they entered the hotel lobby.

Three more cast members had arrived while they were at Hampstead Hall, along with Perry Prince, the production assistant.

Adrian Reed and Miranda Vogel, cast as Lord and Lady Pembroke, were both well-known British actors and had been specially motored down from London by Perry. Accompanying them was Peter Mallory, much to Corinne's excitement. She grabbed Anna's arm, her long, red fingernails digging into Anna's skin.

Anna noticed that Perry Prince looked exhausted. She had wondered about his absence, since he had been so very present during the audition process. Production assistants tended to do a little of everything, she knew, from copying scripts to arranging props to chauffeuring actors from London to the country.

Although she knew Perry was about her age, Anna thought he looked like he was still in high school, and it didn't help that he always smelled freshly of Axe shave lotion. He was slender, with smooth skin the color of dark roasted coffee and an endearing, slightly cockney accent that added to his boyishness.

"Dinner at seven in the Lock Restaurant," he announced to the group as they filtered through the doors. "On the terrace. That way everyone can get to know one another a little better before filming begins. Paid for by Sir Frederick," he added.

There was an audible sigh of relief from several people.

"Will Sir Frederick be joining us?" asked Peter Mallory.

"No, unfortunately, his schedule kept him in London until tomorrow," Perry explained. "You'll see him at Hampstead Hall."

Anna glanced over at Peter Mallory, curious to see why Corinne was so enamored with him. He was handsome, she conceded, with red, curly hair and a few freckles sprinkled across his nose and cheeks. He had squinty grey-blue eyes and a somewhat crooked smile. Although he wasn't as tall as Jake, he was broad-shouldered and muscular. He leaned casually against a high bar table, legs crossed, as if he expected to be admired. Corinne flashed her blue eyes at him from under her fake eyelashes, and he gave her a wink.

He seems handsome enough, thought Anna. But he's no Jake.

A thought flashed unbidden across her mind, a vision of someone sweeping off his hat while on horseback outside the Tapestry Room window. She blushed. Looking up, she caught Peter Mallory giving her a crooked smile, as if he thought the blush was for him.

Which made her blush all the more.

To cover her embarrassment, she turned her attention to the couple hired to play Corinne's parents in *Cavendish Manor*.

Adrian Reed and Miranda Vogel lounged nearby in wire basket chairs, sipping afternoon cocktails. Miranda appeared to have sipped a few already. Her wide-apart blue eyes were a bit glossy. Anna noticed that she had impossibly golden hair that she wore long, past her shoulders. She blinked at the newcomers with an air of vagueness, like her mind wasn't in the same room with the rest of her, and she had a curious way of picking at her clothes when she thought no one was looking.

Adrian Reed's eyes were more focused, Anna noticed. They were round, almost like brown buttons. His wide-eyed expression, in addition to his habit of raising his thin eyebrows while pursing up his mouth, made him look like he was in a state of perpetually happy surprise.

Jake had joined Peter and ordered a drink. Jaime was nowhere in sight.

Corinne linked arms with Anna.

"Come with me and talk to Jake," she whispered through a fake smile. "That way I can be introduced to Peter."

Anna rolled her eyes.

"Come on," she acquiesced, dragging Corinne toward the two men. "Let's get this over with. I want a bath before dinner."

Jake grinned as they approached.

"Can I get you ladies a drink?" he asked.

"Nothing for me, thanks," said Anna.

"I'll take white wine," answered Corinne, her eyes on Peter. Peter's eyes seemed to have trouble rising from the v-neck of her blouse.

"I'm Peter," he said, shaking the hand she had extended.

"Corinne," she answered, trying out a sultry voice and flipping her hair over her shoulder.

"And who's your friend?" he asked, his attention switching from one chest to the other.

Anna waited until his roving eyes found their way back up to her face.

"I'm Anna McKay," she said curtly.

"Always a pleasure to meet another ginger," he said, his smile revealing more of his thoughts than Anna cared to know.

Jake returned from the bar with Corinne's wine.

"So," he said to Peter. "How was the trip over from London? I thought you were coming in time for the tour at Hampstead Hall?"

"We were supposed to," Peter answered, "but we had a bit of car trouble along the way."

"Oh, really?" said Jake. "What happened?"

"I don't know. Something to do with the gearbox."

"The what?" asked Jake. "Oh, I remember."

He turned to the girls. "British for *transmission*," he translated with a wink.

"Yeah," replied Peter. "We met at the Studio in Hertfordshire. Perry picked us up from there and we went for lunch at some out-of-the-way pub or another that Adrian knew. Anyway, when we got back in the car, it would only go in reverse."

Corinne began to giggle.

"It was rather funny. Especially the expression on ol' Perry's face," Peter said, grinning.

"Was he angry?" asked Jake, one corner of his mouth curving upward.

"Nah," said Peter, casually rubbing his fingers across his chest in a way that drew attention to his pectorals. "I think he was embarrassed. Kinda made him look bad. First impressions and all that. Like this whole project is hurting for money."

"Is it?" asked Anna. That wasn't the impression she had at all. They were standing in a first class resort bar, for instance.

Peter shrugged, his mouth twisting scornfully as he glanced around the room.

"All I know is, Miranda and Adrian caused a fuss. They took turns chewing out Perry. Especially Miranda. She kept complaining about needing her assistant. I saw her texting, so I bet she was giving Sir Frederick a hard time."

"Why doesn't she have her assistant?" asked Anna.

Peter glanced slyly at Miranda and Adrian sitting across the room.

"I don't think she even has an assistant anymore," he said, his voice a low rumble. "I don't think she has enough work to afford it. But even so, Sir Frederick said the Studio wouldn't pay for assistants on set. Not for this long of a run."

"Plus, there's no room in the house," added Jake, nodding his head. "I would have had to pay for my assistant to stay off-site. For weeks. No need for that when there's this," he said, holding up his phone. "Everything I need in one place, including my assistant's number."

Peter nodded.

Anna nodded as well, eager to relate, although she'd never had an assistant before.

And not likely to anytime soon, she thought, awed by the status of her new-found friends.

Later, at dinner, Anna was seated between Perry Prince and Jake. Perry's usually smooth face was lined, and his jaw clenched tightly. He was silently focusing on his food, despite the frivolity of the rest of the group. Anna could hear Corinne's laugh tinkling above the rest as she sat next to Peter. A long line of patio tables had been strung together to accommodate the entire group, and Corinne and Peter were at the far end. Peter seemed to have an endless supply of funny and somewhat dirty jokes and stories and was keeping that end of the tables amused. Every now and then, Anna could feel his gaze on her, and it made her feel as grimy as the stories he was telling.

"I heard you had car trouble," Anna said politely to Perry, hoping to distract herself from Peter's voice. She also hoped it would distract Perry from whatever was weighing on his mind.

Perry's dark eyes darted across the table to Miranda before he spoke. She hadn't seemed to notice the question.

"Yes," he said tentatively.

"That must have been frustrating," Anna sympathized. "Has the car given you trouble in the past?"

Again Perry glanced toward Miranda before answering.

"No. Never. It's Sir Frederick's personal car. I often drive it to do errands for the Studio or for Sir Frederick. He keeps it in top gear."

This time Anna gazed across at Miranda. She was in her fifties, Anna guessed, but was trying for thirty with her golden blonde hair style and a few discreet surgeries. She had finished picking at her dinner and was toying with a strand of her hair, twirling it around her finger while humming softly, a vacant smile on her beautiful, if overly made up, face.

"Peter told us Miranda was upset," she ventured, speaking quietly, although Anna felt certain Miranda was oblivious to everything around her.

Perry shook his head, as if the remembrance of the day was too much to bear.

"Furious," he whispered. "They both were. She and Adrian. But she was the worst. I was glad Peter didn't join in. He understood I was doing my best, under the circumstances. I mean, I got them an Uber to the hotel as soon as I could. It just took some time. We were kind of in the middle of nowhere."

"Maybe she doesn't like to Uber," suggested Anna.

Perry rolled his eyes.

"That's an understatement. I don't think she would have done it except the alternative was to stay at the pub or go to the mechanic's. But I don't think that was the main problem," he said, glancing at Miranda again. "She kept digging through her handbag, looking for something. And she insisted that I get her suitcase from the car. Said she needed to touch up her face. I tried to explain that the Uber was too small for all the luggage, that I would bring it all in a second Uber after I got the car to the mechanic. But she wouldn't have it. That's when things got really bad."

"What happened?"

Perry shook his head and wouldn't answer. He either didn't want Miranda to overhear, or he was protecting someone: himself or the actress.

He stood up.

"Well, it's been a long day for me, lads and lassies," he said to the group. "I'm off to my room."

The cast and crew waved or said goodnight. Anna watched Miranda's pretty mouth droop as her attention finally focused on the speaker. She slowly blinked her wide-apart eyes a few times before rolling them and turning away with a sniff. She whispered something to Adrian Reed beside her, who nodded. His brown button eyes flashed angrily for a moment before returning to their usual carefree expression.

He's trying to appear younger than he is, Anna suddenly realized. As if he doesn't have a care in the world. As if everything is new and exciting. It made her feel sorry for him.

There was a spurt of loud laughter from Jim Anderson. He was clearly entertaining those sitting near him. Sarah, the assistant director, punched him playfully on the arm. Anna noticed she hadn't changed for dinner. She was still wearing her ball cap, her face free of makeup.

Just then, Miranda gathered her things, and after twiddling her fingers at Adrian, she slowly made her way into the hotel. Anna noticed that she walked strangely, swinging each foot directly in front of the other.

Walking the line, like someone accused of DUI, she thought. She remembered that Miranda's best-known role was that of an easy-going single woman in London, trying to make it on the West End. Sweet-tempered and innocent.

Her attention was drawn away again by Jake asking her a question.

"Sorry. What did you say?" she asked.

"I said, what was Perry saying about the car trouble?"

"He just said the car never broke down like that. That it was Sir Frederick's car, and he keeps it in top gear."

"Interesting," Jake commented thoughtfully. He lowered his voice. "Did he mention Miranda?"

"Yes," whispered Anna, "but he wouldn't tell me what happened. Just that she was getting more and more upset, and kept wanting her suitcase."

"Yeah," said Jake. "Peter said at one point she started yelling at poor Perry, calling him names and threatening to have him fired."

"What? Miranda? Yelling? That's awful! As if it was Perry's fault!"

Jake shrugged.

"They ended up all sitting on top of Miranda's luggage, crammed into a tiny Uber. She wouldn't leave without that luggage."

"Wow," Anna said, shaking her head at star-power. "But Miranda, yelling?" she asked again. "I can't imagine it. She seems so flighty and…I don't know…ethereal."

"Can't judge an actress by her role," said Jake with a wink. "The real Miranda is nothing like her role as Paula Parker. Peter said as soon as she was able to get into her suitcase, though, she relaxed."

"So, powdering her nose has that kind of effect on her?" Anna asked, incredulous.

Jake chuckled. "No, my naive princess. She was after more than makeup." He laughed again when her jaw dropped.

"Drugs?" she asked, lowering her voice even more, her hazel eyes wide with shock.

"I'm afraid so," said Jake, his mouth turning grim. "Peter said he saw her pull out an entire zippered pouch full of little orange bottles."

"That's so sad," said Anna, and meant it. She thought about Miranda and what she'd heard of her life. Two failed marriages so far, if the grocery store tabloids were correct. And no children from either one. And according to Peter, not enough work.

No more Paula Parker roles.

She turned her attention to Adrian Reed again. Peter had said they were both angry and giving Perry a hard time. He didn't seem upset now. He was talking animatedly to Jaime, his hands making big gestures to accentuate his story. She was laughing, a hard-edged laugh, like she was faking it. Anna wondered if it was because Adrian wasn't funny, or for some other reason of her own.

As she watched them, Jaime's silvery, no-color gaze slid from Adrian's face to her own. Once again, Anna thought she caught a sliver of malice in the depths of her eyes, like a hidden shard of glass in clear water. Then it was gone.

I'm imagining things again, Anna thought, closing her eyes. Or this wine is stronger than I think.

She decided to make it an early night. She had a lot to think about. And that bathtub was calling her.

CHAPTER SEVEN

The following morning, Sir Frederick Churchwood-Styles arrived at Hampstead Hall. William was thankful Sir Frederick was able to arrive earlier than the rest of the cast and crew, who were expected in the afternoon. He hoped to speak with the director alone.

Sir Frederick always reminded William of old pictures of Alfred Hitchcock. He was short and stocky, with a sizeable middle that rounded out over his legs, making him look like the letter "D". He was usually slightly red in the face, especially after physical activity, such as walking across the room, and he kept his sparse hair cut short. He differed from Alfred Hitchcock in that he wore round spectacles perched on the end of his hooked nose, and he tended to speak in a very clipped, fast pace rather than the slow drawl of the late director.

Sir Frederick had a not-so-secret crush on William's mother, Lady Diane, who was fortunately visiting William's sister, Maria, in France at the moment. William did not want his mother sweeping in and announcing to one and all who he was. He wanted to remain incognito, at least for a little while, and while he felt he could convince Sir Frederick to go along with the charade, he knew his mother would never do so.

Anna had seemed so at ease with him as just William Langley, he thought, remembering their walk through the halls the day before. But of course, she wasn't the reason for his wanting to keep his identity a secret. He simply didn't want things around the cast and crew to get awkward.

That's why, he thought with a decisive nod of his head as he stared into the garden through the leaded panes of the Tapestry Room window.

"Sir Frederick here to see you, my lord," announced Mr. Barnaby.

William turned with a welcoming smile.

"William, dear boy," barked Sir Frederick, crossing the room on his short legs. He brought himself up short. "Sorry. Lord Somerville, of course," he stammered.

William waved the title away with his hand.

"Call me William, like always."

"William, then," continued Sir Frederick. "So good to see you, So appreciate your allowing us the use of Hampstead Hall. The perfect setting."

"Of course. I'm delighted to have you," assured William, shaking the director's hand.

"Is your mother about?" Sir Frederick asked, vaguely glancing around the room as if expecting her to materialize out of the wallpaper.

"Unfortunately, no," said William, feeling rather fortunate. "She's in France with Maria."

"Ah," said a crestfallen Sir Frederick. "Well, I suppose she will return sometime. I think our little show would be very amusing to her."

William thought of his mother and wondered if they could be talking about the same woman. The Lady Diane he knew would find the "commoners" on the property less than amusing, which is why William had strongly suggested the trip to France in the first place. He didn't feel that the Dower House was quite far enough out of the way. Lady Diane had moved herself to the Dower House on the front of the property after the death of her husband and the subsequent inheritance of her son. Despite William's insistence that she did not have to move out of the main house, she was equally insistent that she be allowed to have her own space to "express herself," which she promptly did with way more pink than William ever thought could possibly be included into a design scheme.

"Please, have a seat, Sir Frederick," said William, indicating two chairs near the fireplace. "I have a favor to ask of you."

"Certainly, my boy," Sir Frederick said, trying out a fatherly tone.

"I have decided to remain incognito for the moment," William began.

"Ah," wheezed Sir Frederick, blinking behind his round glasses.

William realized how foolish the whole scheme sounded now that he was saying it out loud.

I wonder if I should reconsider, he thought. Then he thought of laughing hazel eyes, and plodded on.

"What I mean is, I chose not to introduce myself as Lord Somerville to the cast and crew when they were here yesterday. I don't know why. I guess I felt awkward and I didn't want to appear overly aristocratic. Anyway, I introduced myself as William Langley, and so far, no one has recognized me as anything else."

"Ah," repeated Sir Frederick.

"And I might have told someone that I was working for you."

"Ah," said Sir Frederick, still blinking.

William paused, trying to determine Sir Frederick's state of mind.

"So, you're wanting me to pretend to give you a job. Is that it?" Sir Frederick finally asked.

"Yes!" said William, relieved. "And I'll actually work for you. Whatever you need."

"Well, I could use a personal assistant," wheezed Sir Frederick, rubbing his jaw. "My last one just flew off to Hollywood to work for Christopher Nolan."

"Fantastic! I'll take the job," said William. "You don't have to pay me," he added as an afterthought.

Sir Frederick laughed, a barking, wheezing laugh that spoke of too many cigars. "You may regret that," he warned. "If a job is what you want, a job is what you'll get."

The rest of the cast and crew arrived in the afternoon, stumbling out onto the gravel drive, their eyes blinking at the sun like it was an enemy; most of their legs seemed to have lost the ability to function properly. Mr. Barnaby, who had come out to welcome them, was grim-faced and stern, like a disapproving father.

Anna was thankful she had left the dinner party early. Most had not, and the after-effects were clear.

"Sad, isn't it?" Jake whispered in her ear as he helped her pull her suitcases from the back of the van. He grinned at her good-naturedly and shrugged. "Most people don't know when to quit."

Her heart fluttered a bit. He seemed to like whispering things in her ear that no one else could hear.

Jake pulled Jaime's suitcase out next and handed it to her. She smiled at Anna, and Anna hoped her own smile seemed as genuine as Jaime's appeared to be. No shards of glass this afternoon.

I'm not jealous of her, Anna assured herself, pulling her bags off to the side to make room for others as they waited for instructions from Mr. Barnaby.

She felt a sudden urge to look toward the window above the door. Just as she suspected, William stood there, looking down as before. Looking directly at her. Only this time, he wasn't scowling.

Her heart leaped, and she couldn't stop the beaming smile that came to her lips as she waved.

He gave her a friendly salute and smiled back.

As the Studio vans approached, William had watched from the window in the alcove, thinking of Anna and the personal tour he had given her the day before. *I must remember to show her the secret passages*, he thought with a smile.

He instinctively knew she would look up at the window when she arrived, so he had purposely planned to be in the alcove.

Or maybe I just hope she'll look for me, he thought. At least Sir Frederick is already here so I have a good reason to be ahead of the rest of them.

He noticed the doughy faces and blank stares of a group of people who had enjoyed themselves too much the night before, and snickered. There were few exceptions.

The red-headed guy with his cap pulled low over his eyes definitely looked the worse for wear, as did Corinne, who was hanging on his arm for support, looking like she was going to be sick. Miranda Vogel's sunglasses were an obvious giveaway.

William recognized Adrian Reed beside her.

He doesn't look like he's in pain, he thought. That strange-eyed blonde wearing all black looks all right. So does that tall guy who is standing too close to Anna. I've seen him on TV. He seems annoyingly jovial this afternoon.

And what about Anna? he wondered. At that point she looked up at him, like he knew she would. Her clear eyes and bright smile assured him she was not suffering the fate of the others. It was enormously comforting to a young man who had endured many an evening helping his own father into bed when he returned after a "night on the town," as he liked to call it. Drinking and gambling away money that should have been spent elsewhere. William rolled his eyes and sighed before turning away from the window, taking one last look down at his last hope standing unsteadily on the circle drive below.

This time it was Sir Frederick who welcomed everyone into the Great Hall. Mr. Barnaby stood nearby, looking like a new mother who is letting someone else hold her baby.

"Come in, come in, come in!" shouted the director, waving them closer to him as he stood in front of the grand fireplace like a feudal lord. He was wearing his customary cargo shorts and short sleeves, with his favorite fishing vest thrown over it. Sir Frederick claimed the vest's innumerable pockets kept whatever he needed near at hand. The ensemble gave the impression he was leaving shortly to go on safari.

Anna pulled her jacket closer about her, astonished that Sir Frederick seemed to be warm enough in his outfit. England was much chillier than Los Angeles or Nashville at this time of the year. She watched as Sir Frederick pulled a handkerchief out of one of his vest pockets and wiped sweat from his brow.

"A little warm for a fire," he commented, darting an irritated glance at the blaze behind him.

Anna heard an amused chuckle beside her, and found that William had slipped into the room. He was grinning at his boss, arms folded casually over his chest. Today, Anna noticed, he was wearing clean jeans and a form-fitting buttoned shirt. She surreptitiously glanced down at his shoes. They were half boots with an interesting pattern in the leather, and immaculately clean. Almost new, she thought, and wondered for a moment why his outfit the other day had been so different. And how he could afford such expensive looking clothes. He looked like he had walked off a GQ magazine cover.

William noticed Anna's glances, and was secretly pleased with himself for choosing his outfit so carefully. He knew his mud-stained work clothes would never do for a man supposedly hired to be Sir Frederick's assistant, but he hadn't wanted to appear overly-dressed, either. He inwardly smiled at his expertise; he was especially pleased with his choice of footwear.

"I want to welcome you all to Cavendish Manor," began Sir Frederick. "I mean Hampstead Hall!"

He chuckled. Mr. Barnaby frowned.

"Sorry I couldn't be with you all for the tour of the house yesterday, but I hear you met my new assistant, William."

He indicated William with a gesture to the back of the room. Heads turned to acknowledge him. William smiled and gave a modest wave.

His smile froze, however, when he caught Peter Mallory squinting at him, a malicious smirk on his lips. William resisted the urge to swear out loud. He had temporarily forgotten that Peter was in the show.

Better head him off as soon as possible, he realized. This is going to be more difficult than I thought.

"Filming will commence bright and early tomorrow morning, so I hope everyone is comfortable with your scripts," Sir Frederick continued. "Mr. Barnaby and Perry have your room assignments and call sheets for tomorrow's scenes. I hope you will all feel very at home here. If there is anything you need, feel free to ask Perry or Mr. Barnaby. Or, of course, William."

He said the last comment with a wink at the Earl. William gave him a warning look.

As the actors and crew moved toward Perry and Mr. Barnaby, William strode forward and grabbed Peter Mallory's elbow.

"Assistant William, is it?" whispered Peter with a sneer. "Or should I say Lord Assistant Somerville? Or maybe it's Assistant Lord Somerville?"

William pulled him further away from any listening ears.

"Look, I don't want it known that I'm Lord Somerville. At least, not yet."

"Whatever for?" asked Peter.

"You, of all people, should know why," answered William. "Or would you like me to refer to you as 'Viscount'?"

Peter pressed his lips into a straight line.

"All right. I'll keep your secret," he said. "But I want to know why."

"Same as you," William answered. "I don't want to be seen as posh."

Peter rolled his eyes. "Come on," he said. "That works for my profession, but you're a professional aristocrat. Your job *is* this land."

"Yours would be, too, if you hadn't put cheap houses on yours," William retorted.

"Times are changing," Peter said, his face grave. "And you should keep that in mind, my friend."

He suddenly slapped William on the arm, his wicked grin returning.

"I'll be watching you," he said. "I bet there's a woman in this."

William sighed, his expression grim, as he watched Peter join the line of actors waiting for room assignments. Lord Peter Mallory, properly titled Viscount Mallory, had never been a favorite. And there was something more, a gnawing feeling that Peter was hiding something important from him. After all, he had been in Monte Carlo that day.

He shook it off. He was beginning to feel like he was in a movie himself, with all of Anna's drama from yesterday adding to the atmosphere.

Maybe this wasn't such a good idea after all, he thought. *I'll have to tell her eventually.*

Anna's eyes flicked in his direction, and she smiled.

But I don't have to tell her yet.

CHAPTER EIGHT

Anna was twirling.

She stared up at the wallpaper-covered ceiling and twirled until she was dizzy and fell on the floor, laughing.

It really does feel like a dream, being here, she thought.

She laid on the floor and allowed the flowers in the room to swirl into focus again. Every inch of the walls and ceiling were covered in flowers. Large flowered borders joined up with swaths of tiny rosebuds on the wallpaper. The ceiling was designed like inlay-work of fine furniture, all in flowered patterns and colors of rose, navy, white and green. She marveled that it was in such good condition still, and hoped the current Earl wouldn't modernize it once his finances were back in order. She imagined him, pudgy and wrinkled, sitting in his modernized west wing, drinking port and ordering his servants around. She wondered when they would get to meet him. He couldn't be that bad, she reasoned. After all, he was allowing them to stay in the house.

Her eyes had finally adjusted again. They focused on the light fixture above her head, a single chandelier in the center of the room with huge glass globes. Anna imagined it had probably originally been gas, but had been converted to electric somewhere along the way.

She sat up. Like the room William had shown her, this one contained a large four-poster bed hung with rose-covered curtains and a bedside table with a lamp. There was even a dressing table, complete with a gilded tri-fold mirror. A round table and chair by the window was for use as a desk, a large armoire stood in the corner, complete with mirrored doors, and two plush armchairs were set near the fireplace.

A fireplace in my room! She giggled, despite herself. A young woman wearing khakis and a grey polo shirt had been making up the fire when Anna first opened the door. A maid, she guessed. A real fire made the illusion of being in a storybook world even more real to her. She had a sudden urge to fling open the mirrored doors of the wardrobe. Would it be stuffed full of silk and muslin dresses? Or would there be an entryway into Narnia? She unlocked the doors using the tiny key that was in the lock.

Empty.

Well, except for a few scraps of yellowed paper, curled at the edges, lying on one of the shelves. Anna sighed, then turned to her suitcases to start unpacking.

She secretly wished she could stay in her room, like a country-house guest, but she knew she would eventually have to hang out with the others downstairs and be sociable. Local audio and video crew had already joined Jim Anderson's crew from America and was setting up cameras and equipment for the next day's shooting. She had come upstairs to avoid the grating sound of his voice as he shouted out orders.

It's probably good that the Earl isn't here, Anna thought. He would probably be upset by all the cables snaking through his home.

William sighed, his jaw clenching as he watched endless rolls of cables snaking through his home. There seemed to be a never-ending line of crew members today, crawling around Hampstead Hall like a colony of death-metal-t-shirt-clad ants. The abrasive sound of Jim Anderson's voice ricocheted like a drum rattle off the walls and ceilings, and into William's head. He closed his eyes and tried to breathe deep, cleansing breaths.

It wasn't working.

He opened his eyes again and stared out the windows of the Great Hall into the garden. He was surprised to catch a fleeting glimpse of faded black clothes and light blonde hair through the dark green leaves of the shrubbery.

That silver-eyed woman, he thought, frowning. *Jaime Douglas, the props master.* Sir Frederick had introduced them earlier. He watched, perplexed, as she glanced around her before slipping into the sunken rose garden.

William decided to follow her. As he stepped onto the terrace from the Drawing Room doors, he noticed the sky had grown darker and the wind had picked up. At the far end of his property he could see rain clouds weighing heavily on the hills, like a smudged pencil drawing. The leaves tried to trip him as they whipped by his feet. He wished he was wearing his field jacket, assistant or not. The temperature had dropped with the light.

William stepped into the rose garden. It had been planted in the 1700s and was completely circular, with tiers of flower beds that sank below the entry level to a small pond in the center, where a naked cherub spouted water out of his mouth. Circling the top tier was an arbor, an arched covered walkway smothered in rose vines, although this late in the season it sported few flowers.

Jaime Douglas was nowhere to be seen, but he did see someone else silently slipping through the arbor and heading toward the Japanese bridge that crossed the moat. Jake Rawlings, he remembered. The TV guy. Anna's admirer.

"Why does everyone seem to be sneaking around?" he wondered, following Jake over the bridge.

The bridge crossed the moat, which was Saxon, and probably the oldest part of the property, built when there was a need to protect whatever original fortress had been there before the Tudor home was built. Now it meandered serenely on one end of the garden, unneeded and unnecessary, mostly mud and water flowers, a favorite of the ducks and geese.

William remembered jumping in once as a child, convinced it would be a great place to swim, only to get his feet tangled in the roots of the water plants. He emerged, covered in slime and stinking ooze, and was forced by his ever-present and formidable Nanny to bathe immediately before his parents discovered him. He smiled inwardly, remembering the muddy footprints on the stone floors that had given him away in the end.

He entered the arbor and followed Jake at a discreet distance. He felt like he was spying. A wave of guilt washed over him. What kind of a host follows his guests around? Then he shrugged it off.

The kind who doesn't trust a bunch of actors roaming around his property.

After crossing the moat, the path continued down to the lake. William could see the dark clouds had moved across the fields toward the house, and he knew rain was imminent. The leaves on the hardwood trees near the lake had turned upside down, holding their hands out for a drink, and the wind bent the willows closer to the water, their long arms trailing along the edge of the bank. Movement caught William's eye. On the right and left of the path were a few additional garden "rooms," some large and spacious and some small and intimate. The movement William had seen was in one of the smaller rooms. A miniature gazebo was nestled in the corner of the walls of yew trees. Wisteria vines clambered up the sides, the leaves yellowed and crisp around the edges.

William paused and pulled back from immediate view. Jake and Jaime stood inside the gazebo, close together. A sickly greenish light shone down on them from the rapidly darkening sky, and the wind was whipping Jaime's hair around her head. She appeared to be agitated about something, and Jake was speaking earnestly to her, his hands gently rubbing her arms. He took her hands and leaned his head against her forehead. She seemed to relax, while the wild wind whistled through the branches of the faded wisteria.

Interesting, thought William. That seems an odd couple. Especially when he seemed to favor Anna.

William suddenly felt lighter, like a weight had lifted. He gave one last look to the couple before turning back toward the house, and froze. Jaime was staring in his direction, as if she knew he was there, although he was positive the darkening sky and the yew hedge were hiding him from her view. Her silver eyes glinted with an unearthly light that William hoped was only the remnants of the fading sun. He suddenly felt cold, and dread stole over him.

He couldn't turn away until she finally released him from her gaze and closed her eyes again. Relieved, William fled for the safety of the house. Just in time, too, he realized, as drops of water began to pepper his clothes. Shaken by what he had witnessed, he picked up his pace, thankful for the cover of the arbor as the rain began to pour. He was trying to decide which door to head toward when he saw a shadowy figure up ahead. It had suddenly appeared out of the rose garden, and his first thought was that it was Jaime again, materializing like a witch in front of him, dark and foreboding like the sky.

"William?" a voice questioned, breaking the spell.

"Anna?" he asked, relief flooding him. "What are you doing out here? It's raining!"

She laughed. "I know. We have rain in America, too!"

They met together in the center of the arbor, safe for the time being from most of the downpour's fury.

"Have you seen Jake?" she asked. "Corinne told me she thought she saw him come out here to the rose garden, but I haven't found him. Blond, kind of tall."

"Um…"

"Maybe I should keep looking. This storm is really bad."

"No, no," said William, steering her toward the house. "I don't think that's a good idea. I'm sure he can find his way back, if he's still out here." He didn't want her feelings to be hurt by seeing Jake and Jaime together. Or maybe he did want her to know. But he shouldn't. Or should he? Did she care about Jake?

"Oh," she said, allowing herself to be led by William. His hand on her arm made her feel tingly inside. But she was looking for Jake. She shouldn't give up that easily, should she? Or shouldn't she?

Looking ahead, William realized they were across from the kitchen door, which was down a flight of steps in the basement.

"We're going to make a run for it," he explained to Anna, taking her hand. She nodded.

They raced across the sodden grass and down the steps into the basement. They crashed into the warm kitchen, laughing and shaking rain from their arms and hair.

"Well!" said a surprised voice. "You like'd to scared me to death!"

"Oh, Sheila!" William said apologetically. "We got caught in the rain and this was the closest door."

Sheila, a kindly woman in her sixties, her hair a stiff helmet of perm and hairspray, gave William a motherly look.

"If I'd ha' known my lord and my lady were going to come crashing through my door, I'd ha' had your tea ready for you down here. But as it is, the girls have already taken evr'ythin' upstairs."

William laughed and gave her a kiss on her powdered cheek. She patted his arm lovingly.

"We'll just dry off and join them."

He grabbed a couple of clean tea towels and tossed one to Anna.

"Aren't you going to introduce us?" Sheila scolded.

"Sorry," said William. "Sheila, this is Anna McKay. She's one of the actresses."

"Ah," said Sheila. "A Scottish lass, I see."

Her eyes held the gleam of a matchmaker.

"Anna, this is Sheila. She's the cook here at Hampstead," William explained.

He quickly realized he was in danger of blowing his cover. Sheila was aware of his new position as Sir Frederick's assistant, but she was no actress. He wasn't sure how much direct contact with the cast and crew she could handle before she cracked and revealed his secret.

"Well, we'd better get dried off," he said, dragging Anna up the back stairs and into the Butler's Pantry above.

"So nice to make your acquaintance," said Sheila, twiddling her fingers at them. "Come visit again."

"Sheila and Mr. Barnaby are the only employees who actually live in the house," William explained as they ascended the stairs. "The others are day-people from the village."

"She called us 'my lord and my lady,'" said Anna, curiously.

William froze. He hadn't noticed. It was what Sheila usually called him. But why did she call Anna "my lady"?

"I suppose it was just her little joke," he said with a shrug.

"Hmm," said Anna, frowning.

They pushed open the swinging door from the Butler's Pantry into the Dining Room. Tea had been set up on the long mahogany buffet. Not everyone was present, but the room was full. William and Anna, still dripping with rain, quickly realized they had chosen the most dramatic entrance into the house.

"Hello, 'ello, 'ello," called Sir Frederick, a plate full of tea sandwiches in hand. "I see you two have been out on the grounds. Don't know why. Can't you see it's raining?"

Anna giggled nervously. She looked down at the director's feet and noticed he'd added a pair of gigantic galoshes to his outfit. When she looked up, she caught Corinne's questioning smirk and could feel herself blushing.

"I've been looking for you, my dear William," Sir Frederick continued. "Business and all that."

"Of course," said William. "Let me change, and I'll be right with you."

Before he and Anna could leave the room, however, there was another dramatic entrance, this time through the French doors.

Jake, with laughing eyes, was dragging a bedraggled Jaime behind him. She was not laughing. Instead, her silvery eyes were cold and pale.

"Another pair in from the rain!" shouted Sir Frederick. "There's just no accounting for young people. And none of you are dressed for it. Not even so much as an umbrella."

Anna watched Jake look questioningly from herself to William. She did the same to him and Jaime.

Peter Mallory spoke up. Anna hadn't even noticed him in the room.

"Jaime looks like she needs to get dry. Don't want her catching her death." He was eyeing the props master steadily, his arms crossed. Anna wondered why his words, which should have been polite concern, seemed more like a threat. Jaime's pale face had two spots of crimson in her cheeks as she turned away from Peter. Anna wasn't sure if she was blushing or angry.

"I'm going to change," Anna said, darting for the door. As William tried to join her, Sir Frederick grabbed his arm.

"No need to change, my boy. We'll just be a moment." William sighed and rolled his eyes to Anna. She gave him a sympathetic look.

Jaime pushed past her and up the stairs. Anna watched her retreating back, and wondered again why she had come in with Jake.

"I found her wandering around alone in the rain," said a husky voice in her ear. Anna jumped.

"Sorry," Jake apologized with a grin. "Didn't mean to scare you."

Anna smiled. Of course. They weren't together. Not *together* together.

"What were you doing out?" she asked.

"I was just taking a walk," he said sheepishly, pulling one hand through his damp hair. "I guess I didn't see the storm clouds until it was too late. You, too?"

Anna looked down at her rain-soaked clothes and shrugged. She couldn't tell him she was looking for him.

"Yeah," she agreed. "I was looking at the rose garden."

"With William?" he asked. Anna thought she heard a sharp edge to his voice. Is he jealous?

"Well, no. Not at first. He came down the path when it started to rain." Jake's face cleared.

"I wish we had found each other—out there," he said. "I would have enjoyed your company. Even in the rain."

They had arrived at her room. Anna wasn't sure what to say. Was he flirting with her? It sure felt like it.

"Well, see you in a few minutes," she said, opening her door.

He grinned and turned away toward his room at the other end of the hall.

Anna closed her door and leaned against it, her eyes seeking the solace of the roses on the wallpaper ceiling.

"Things are starting to get interesting," she said to the chandelier.

CHAPTER NINE

Dinner was in the white tent that had been set up in the large, square courtyard behind the east side of the house. Anna scanned the half-timbered brick buildings that surrounded the courtyard on three sides. One was clearly a stable, and seemed to actually still house a few horses. One had been turned into a garage for cars, though what its original purpose was, Anna couldn't guess. Maybe a guard house? Or storage building? Other buildings looked like they had once been smokehouses for storing meat long ago. There was a large greenhouse with a copper roof, green with time. On the house-side of the courtyard was an arched entrance that led to the front of Hampstead Hall and the circular driveway. Directly across from the house was another brick archway that led into the fields beyond.

It was seven o'clock, and the light was beginning to fade as Anna picked her way around the puddles that formed where the pea-gravel undulated. The rain had finally stopped, leaving a clean, fresh feeling in the air, scented with pine. There seemed to be a lot of activity in the courtyard; the crew was unloading large trucks, and there were cables stretched in long lines.

After getting her plate, Anna scanned the long plastic tables, looking for a familiar head of black curls, but she didn't see William anywhere. She settled herself at the nearest table with a slight pout.

"I guess Sir Frederick is working him extra hard because filming starts tomorrow," she thought with a sigh.

As she reached for the salt, someone suddenly sat down next to her. She turned, expecting to see William, then jumped when it was Jake.

"Hey," he said, grinning.

"Hey," she replied, hoping he hadn't noticed her surprise.

I've got to get myself under control, she thought irritably. I can't go around jumping at everything like some kind of child in a haunted house.

"Catering looks good," he said. "Hard to go wrong with chicken."

She nodded. She watched as Jaime, plate in hand, hovered uncertainly near their table. Anna gave her a tentative smile. She decided she wanted to get to know this quiet and faded girl a little better. And to study Jake and Jaime together.

"Come join us," she offered with a wave of her hand. After a slight hesitation, Jaime came over.

She sat across from Jake, who seemed pleased to see her.

Anna noticed Jaime had chosen the vegetable lasagna instead of the chicken.

"I'm glad they have a vegetarian option," Jaime commented. Her voice was quiet and lilting, although her Scottish accent wasn't very strong.

"This is a lot of food for poor Sheila to put together," commented Anna.

"Who?" asked Jaime. Jake looked at Anna questioningly as well.

"Sheila, the cook?" Anna said. "I met her in the kitchen with William before tea." She averted her eyes from Jake, whose expression had darkened somewhat.

Jaime shook her head.

"The Studio always hires a catering company," she explained, with a look that showed she thought it should have been obvious.

"Yeah," agreed Jake, "all our meals from now on will be out here. Rain or shine. I'm sure it is much easier on the Hampstead Hall staff. All they're responsible for is craft services."

"Craft services?" Anna questioned. "Oh, that's right. The snack table," she remembered. "Well, Sheila seemed nice. But I'm glad she doesn't have to be overworked."

Anna could see Jaime give her a sideways glance, like she was sizing her up. She straightened her back and plunged her fork into her food, trying to appear confident, although her obvious lack of experience felt like an albatross around her neck.

Through the open tent doors, Anna noticed a few crew members passing by, their arms loaded with equipment.

"Where are they going?" she asked, hoping to change the subject.

Jake followed her pointing finger.

"To set up base camp," he said.

Anna's face was a blank.

"You know. All the trailers," he explained. "Wardrobe, makeup and hair. Editing. And our dressing rooms."

"Oh, yes, of course," she said, as if suddenly remembering. "There's a lot going on around here," she said thoughtfully. "I hope the Earl, wherever he is, doesn't mind too much. I think it would drive me crazy to have all these people running around."

Jake shrugged. "It's money to him. I'm sure he's happy as long as the show is successful."

He flicked his eyes toward Jaime, who smiled enigmatically, like a washed out Mona Lisa.

"Did you like your room?" Jake asked Anna.

"Yes! Very much! Do you?"

"Yes. We're down the hall from each other. Jaime's upstairs."

"On the third floor?" asked Anna.

"Yes," Jaime replied. "In the former nursery. There's a small area for sleeping, and a large room for my workshop."

"Jaime is incredibly talented," bragged Jake. "A lot of the reproduction furniture are things she made herself."

"Wow!" Anna said, noticing the gleam of pride in Jake's eye. She wasn't sure what else to say, so she focused again on her plate.

Jake picked at his food a moment.

"Why were you in the kitchen with William?" he asked. The words were said nonchalantly, but Anna watched his face stiffen into a mask of polite interest, although his brown eyes were pleading with hers. She wondered why he had chosen to bring the subject up again.

"We were caught in the rain, remember," she said, trying to keep her own face a mask when her eyes met his again. "The kitchen door was the closest from that end of the garden."

"Hmmh," he said, plunging back into his dinner.

Anna couldn't tell if he was harrumphing because he didn't believe her or because he was jealous of the time she had spent with William.

She wasn't able to give it much thought, however. Sarah Stern, the assistant director, began hurrying people to finish their meals. There was to be a meeting with Sir Frederick after dinner in the Ballroom.

Although the Ballroom was the largest room in the house, Anna still felt cramped.

"Surely not all of these people are staying here!" she whispered to Corinne, who was standing beside her.

"No," she answered. "I think some of the extra crew and minor roles are staying in the village."

After a thorough scan of the room, Anna finally found William standing off to the side with Perry behind Sir Frederick. He seemed a little anxious. She caught his eye and his face relaxed as he smiled back at her.

William was thankful to see Anna standing in the crowd. She was an island in the midst of an endless sea of people, and they all represented problems in his mind. *What if they break something? What if this doesn't work and he loses the estate anyway? Can he make it through the next day of filming, not to mention the next few weeks?*

Sir Frederick cleared his throat.

"Now that I have you all together, I just want to remind you of the rules. I'm an easy-going guy, on the whole, I think, but there are some things that through the years I've come to insist upon because it makes things run more smoothly. So I've compiled a list of rules. I'll read them out to you now, but Perry has put a copy in all of your rooms. Rule number one: no drunkenness. Rule number two: no illegal drugs. These first two are important. I'm not one to get into your personal lives, but you're on my time clock now, and wasted time is wasted money. So don't get wasted!"

There was murmuring and giggling from the crowd.

"Number three: if it's not yours, don't touch it. Our props master, Jaime Douglas, takes care of all props on the set. Unless you have permission to touch something, don't touch it. Or maybe me or Sarah, or Perry or William could ask you to touch something. But otherwise, hands off."

"Does that also include personnel?" asked Peter with a leer.

Corinne let out a squeal beside him, then slapped him on the arm.

"Don't pinch my butt!" she screeched, but her laugh indicated she was more flattered than offended. Laughter erupted around the room, especially among the men.

Sir Frederick lowered his eyebrows.

"I would prefer you keep your hands to yourself *always*, if you don't mind," he clarified.

Peter gave a triumphant grin, and Corinne was still giggling like a schoolgirl. Anna was embarrassed for her friend. *Doesn't she know not to take that from jerks like him? Doesn't she want respect?* Anna caught herself glaring at Peter with contempt, and realized she probably needed to calm down. After all, filming hadn't even begun.

We're going to have to work together for weeks.

She willed her face to be pleasant, but just as she was about to shift her attention back to Sir Frederick, Peter turned toward her, his eyes raking from her face to her chest and back again.

She jerked her head forward, unconsciously looking to William. She caught her breath at the sheer anger she saw in his eyes as he glared across the room at Peter. For a moment, she thought she saw his eyes change color; a gleam of violet crossed the vivid blue.

If looks could kill, Peter would be dead right now, she thought.

William was smoldering inside. The same old Peter doing the same old things, he thought angrily. Peter smirked back at William, then shrugged, as if it was all a joke.

Watch your back mate, William thought, his eyes narrowing dangerously. *One of these days, you're going to piss off the wrong person.*

"Rule number four," continued Sir Frederick. "No running or horseplay on the set, which, as you can see, is most of the house. I know, we're all adults and I shouldn't have to say that, but we've got a lot of expensive equipment here, and if someone trips over a cable and knocks something over, someone could get hurt, and more importantly, I lose money!" He grinned to show he was joking. "Seriously though, I don't want anything toppling over. Number five—"

There was a tremendous crash that echoed through the Great Hall. Anna thought she heard glass breaking. Someone screamed; Corinne clutched Anna's arm. Everyone looked toward the open door of the Ballroom in the direction of the noise. Perry, William, and Sarah rushed into the Great Hall. Jim Anderson pushed roughly through the crowd and followed them.

The first thing William saw as he entered the Great Hall was a scattering of broken glass across the stone floor. In the corner of the room near the fireplace he could see a black metal contraption sprawled out like a dead spider.

"Tim!" shouted Jim Anderson, almost in William's ear. Tim was the lighting director, and he had followed the others into the Great Hall as well.

"Get that LD!" Jim shouted again.

"I'm right here," said an irritated, little man with a huge mustache.

"This light panel fell!" Jim continued to shout as if the lighting director were still in the other room.

William watched as Tim and Jim stood over the fallen heap of metal and broken glass. The light panel, William realized by looking at a second one in the other corner, was a flat square of lights, about three feet by three feet, and suspended at a right angle above the heads of the actors by metal poles.

"It must not have been secured!" said Jim to Tim.

Tim shook his head, causing his mustache to quiver. He pulled up his sagging, worn-out jeans.

"Impossible," he said in a low monotone. "I adjusted this one myself. There was no question of it being improperly set up."

"Then how do you explain this?" asked Jim, his large hand indicating the pile of glass on the floor.

"Now, now, now," said Sir Frederick, coming up behind them. "No need for blame. We need this cleaned up and another light brought in tonight."

"I have an extra in the truck," said Tim, still shaking his head. He gestured to a few of his guys, who headed out to the truck with bewildered looks.

Sir Frederick waved the rest of the group out of the Great Hall and back into the Ballroom.

"Nothing that can't be fixed," he said congenially. "Let's continue our rules, shall we?"

After the meeting, those who were staying on-site were asked to go directly to their rooms so as not to interfere with the cleanup efforts in the Great Hall, and the rest left through the French doors at the back of the Ballroom.

Corinne and Anna huddled together up the stairs. The crash had shaken them both for reasons they couldn't explain, even to each other. They both just looked at each other, wide-eyed, and crept to their rooms as if sudden movements and loud noises would send lighting fixtures down on their heads.

And that, Anna realized when she got to the safety of her room, was what worried her the most. That lighting panel, hanging over the heads of the actors, would be heavy enough to seriously injure anyone underneath. Fortunately, no one had been underneath when it fell.

This time.

And the lighting director had looked so bewildered. Anna remembered watching him before being pushed back into the Ballroom; he had a puzzled expression creasing his forehead and was pulling on his mustache.

If he didn't know how this one fell, could he prevent the others from falling on their heads?

She shuddered.

Then she looked around at the roses on the walls of her room, and breathed deeply.

Everything will be fine in the morning.

CHAPTER TEN

Anna awoke to the sounds of small rustlings nearby, as if someone were in the room with her, trying to be quiet. She rolled over and blinked, but couldn't see anything distinctly; the room was still dark, though she knew instinctively that it was morning already. Her brain tried to will itself back to sleep, and she closed her eyes again.

Surely I can sleep a little longer, she thought.

At her movement, a quiet voice began speaking.

"Good morning, m'lady," it said as a skirt rustled away from the bedside.

"Good morning," Anna mumbled automatically, eyes still closed.

There was a sound of curtains being pulled back, and suddenly, light filled the room. Anna groaned and burrowed further underneath the lacy sheets.

"It looks like it's going to be a lovely day!" declared the voice brightly. "They shouldn't have any trouble on the roads."

Anna's brain had begun to function now, against its will. Her brow wrinkled as she tried to think. She could smell tea nearby, and there was someone gently talking to her in the room. Where am I? Oh, yes. Hampstead Hall. In the bedroom full of roses.

Wait. Why is there someone in my bedroom?

"Who shouldn't have trouble on the roads?" she asked, trying to borrow time to fit the pieces together.

The voice laughed gently. "Have you forgotten, m'lady? Lord Mallory and his friend arrive this morning."

Anna whipped the sheets back from her face with one hand and half-raised herself in the bed. She stared at the figure in the room with her. Corinne stood in front of the window, wearing the traditional black-and-white maid's uniform she said she admired, complete with a little white apron and hat, her hair pulled back into a neat bun. She was smiling at first, but then her look changed to concern.

"M'lady?" she asked. "Are you feeling all right? You look like you've seen a ghost!"

Anna stared at her in disbelief.

"Corinne! You're freaking me out!" she scolded. "Why are you wearing a costume? I know you liked the maid's outfit and everything, but this is ridiculous. And I thought you didn't want to be a lady's maid."

Corinne's eyes filled with tears.

"I've always wanted to be a lady's maid, m'lady, ever since I was a girl," she insisted. "Have I displeased you in some way?"

"Displeased me?"

Corinne pulled a handkerchief out of a pocket and dabbed at her eyes.

"You seem that put out with me," she continued, sniffing, "and you just called me by my *Christian name!*"

"Your Christian—" Anna began, then paused. She remembered the conversation with Jake in the van on the way to the hotel.

If you were Anna's lady's maid, he had said to Corinne, *you would be called Newberry instead of Corinne.*

Anna's eyes quickly took stock of the room, and she stifled a gasp. Instead of dark roses, the room had suddenly transformed into a blue and cream wonderland, decidedly French. The bed hangings and window curtains were blue flowers on a background of cream, and the ceiling was painted with swirls of gold. The heavy Victorian furniture was gone, replaced with spindly-legged, curved pieces, painted in light colors, and the chandelier above her head was missing, replaced with a golden candelabra on the dressing table.

Like I've gone back in time.

She glanced at the puffy-sleeved, muslin dress that Corinne had hung over a chair, ready for Anna to put on. And the silver tea service steaming on the small table near the bed. And the sobbing, subservient Corinne dressed as a lady's maid and dabbing her eyes with a handkerchief.

This must be a dream, she thought. But an interesting one.

Go with it, said her brain.

"*Newberry*, I'm so sorry. I wasn't quite awake yet, I suppose."

Corinne's face relaxed in relief.

"You had me that worried, m'lady," she sighed, drying her eyes and returning the handkerchief to her pocket. She turned to tidy up the room.

"Why is Peter Mall—I mean, *Lord Mallory*, arriving today?" asked Anna, using the title Corinne had given him.

Corinne blushed.

"You and the Viscount have been getting along so well, I suppose," answered Corinne, her eyes on the floor. "His Lordship seems to be here more often than at his own estate, though it be nearby. And he's bringing his good friend this time. At least, so I understood."

Anna thought about her statement. And her accent. Corinne seemed to not only be speaking in a British accent, but a somewhat uneducated one at that.

"Abingdon Abbey," Anna replied, and almost clapped her hand over her mouth as she realized that she, too, was speaking in a British accent. And somehow knew the name of Lord Mallory's ancestral home. "It borders our land, doesn't it?"

Corinne eyed her suspiciously again.

"Yes, m'lady, you having grown up together, so to speak, and should know."

"I should, shouldn't I?" said Anna, half to herself. Somehow she did know. She knew Lord Mallory had come into his inheritance of Abingdon Abbey last year and that he had been making frequent calls on her and her father in the past few months, staying for weeks at a time. Everyone guessed he was looking to take a wife, and that she, Lady Anna, seemed to be his first choice. It would be an advantageous match. Property-wise.

She had a vision (or was it a memory?) of Lord Mallory, looking every bit like Peter Mallory dressed in Regency attire, complete with sarcastic smirk. Anna shuddered.

"It is a bit chilly this morning," said Corinne, and handed her a cup of tea. "I'll put more coal on the fire, shall I?"

"Yes, Newberry. That would be nice."

Anna took a sip of tea and closed her eyes, allowing the hot liquid to warm her throat.

When she opened her eyes, all was darkness.

"Newberry?" she cried.

There was silence in the darkened room. She could only see a slight gleam of moonlight through the gap in the heavy window curtains.

Corinne was gone, and the tea. And the morning, it seemed.

Anna rubbed her forehead.

"It really was a dream," she murmured. "But it seemed so real."

She tried to figure out what would have led to such a dream. She remembered reading for a while to try to calm her nerves after the lighting incident. She remembered switching off the light and burying herself in the lacy sheets.

Why would I dream of Corinne as a lady's maid? she wondered. This job really must be getting to me.

Slipping her feet into slippers, Anna crept out of her bedroom and down the hall to the bathroom. Fortunately, there was a small lamp shining on a table in the hall as a nightlight. As she approached the bathroom, she heard a toilet flush, and the door opened quickly afterward.

"Peter!" she said, stifling the urge to call him *Lord Mallory*.

He smirked, his gaze taking in her silky shorts and t-shirt. Anna wrapped her arms around herself, wishing she had thought to put on her robe.

"You're up late," he said, pausing in the doorway, his muscular arm leaning on the frame.

"I had a weird dream, that's all," said Anna, trying to step around him. He didn't move.

"Do you wanna tell me about it?" he asked huskily, his eyes dark in the half-light of the hall.

Anna shook her head. "No, thank you. It was nothing." She scooted past him and into the bathroom, shutting and locking the door behind her. She leaned back against the closed door and shuddered.

He creeps me out in my dreams and in real life, she thought grimly.

CHAPTER ELEVEN

It was a sleepy Anna who sat in her trailer at six o'clock the next morning, drinking tea from a paper cup and wishing she were back in bed. No Newberry to bring her tea in bed on a silver tray this morning. She sighed wistfully.

Her trailer was one of a long line of what are called honeywagons that were set up in the courtyard near the stables. To Anna, they looked like RV's with about a million doors, each room the size of a walk-in closet. Except, of course, Miranda's and Adrian's trailers. They had a bigger name, and had earned a larger trailer.

It had been dark still when Anna had followed the crowd across the courtyard. Now she watched pink fingers of sunlight stretching across the courtyard; particles of hay from the stableyard hung suspended in the morning glow. Through the trailer window she had been watching all the coming and going as actors and crew prepared for the day. She closed her heavy eyes for a moment, her script lying open on her lap. Nothing was soundproof, she noticed. The thin, metal walls couldn't keep out the sound of the other actors talking and laughing, blending together like white noise, lulling her senses. Her script began to slide toward the floor as her body relaxed.

Just as her mind began to fade into dreams, her ears picked up fragments of voices slicing like razors through the haze. Her arm stiffened and her hand caught the wayward script before it fell. Two male voices were having a discussion just outside her trailer. She recognized one voice immediately as Jim Anderson. The other one was low and rumbling.

"Like I said last night, I set the light panel up myself," it insisted.

Opening her eyes, Anna could see Tim Tremayne, the lighting director, pulling on his mustache and shaking his head.

"Then how do you explain the fall?" demanded Jim.

"I can explain how it fell," Tim complained, "but I can't tell you what happened."

"What the heck is that supposed to mean?"

Tim pulled his mustache again. "It means, I found grease on the stand. The knobs slipped because there was grease on the pole."

"Grease!" spat Jim.

"So that's *how* it happened," said Tim. "But that doesn't explain how it happened. Grease doesn't usually 'accidentally' appear on light poles."

"Yeah, I see what you mean," Jim grumbled. "Any idea who..."

"None," said Tim, still pulling his mustache. "All of my guys are top-notch. They wouldn't tamper with the equipment like that. Why would they?"

"It has to be someone's idea of a practical joke," said Jim.

"Maybe," said Tim cautiously. "It's a real mystery."

The two men walked away toward the catering tent.

Anna forced herself to relax. Her whole body had stiffened while she listened to their conversation. It hadn't made her feel any safer. Why would someone tamper with the lighting equipment? She agreed with the LD

It was a mystery.

When she stepped out of wardrobe, the scene before her was a weird mix of Regency and modern England. Actors strolled across the courtyard, their costumes forcing them to walk and move differently. Slowly and more gracefully, Anna thought. Like they were gliding. Beside them hurried tech crew members carrying cables and equipment and grumbling into walkie-talkies. The rain the evening before had brought autumn with it. Anna wrapped her arms around herself, wishing for a sweater. As she passed, Anna noticed Miranda Vogel steadying herself with a fragile white hand against the pole of the catering tent, a wisp of a smile on her lips. In an 1820's-era costume, where the waistline fell slightly higher, it was difficult to tell how emaciated her body was, though her arms were thin and bony. Anna was concerned the older actress would find the physical strain of the filming schedule too difficult.

In contrast, Jake's exceedingly healthy body came striding toward Anna, his face lit up with a welcoming grin.

"Good morning," he said genially, pausing to speak to her.

"Good morning," she replied.

"Nice hat," he complimented. Anna touched the wide-brimmed straw hat she wore, laden with silk flowers.

"Yours is very gallant," she replied, noticing the tall, top hat he wore.

"Thanks! How was your sleep?" he asked.

"Well," Anna hesitated. Should she mention the dream? Or how uncomfortable Jake's friend made her feel?

He nodded knowingly.

"It's hard to feel comfortable the first few nights in a new place," he said. "But give it a few days. It'll feel just like home."

He waved to someone, tipped his hat to Anna, and continued into the catering tent.

Anna turned to find William watching her from across the courtyard. She wondered what he was thinking. He seemed so stern.

William was thinking how irritatingly confident Jake Rawlings was, grinning and speaking to Anna as if he didn't have a care in the world. Not like a desperate landowner whose father had died of an accidental overdose in Monte Carlo, leaving him with nothing but an ancient coat of arms and a pile of debt.

She was looking at him with a puzzled expression. He shook off his dark thoughts, struck again by how much she resembled the painting in the Gallery.

"Everything all right?" asked Anna as she approached.

"Yes. In these clothes, you look even more like the Lady Anna in the Gallery," he said, then was surprised when she paled, her eyes widening, almost in fear.

"Sorry," she apologized quickly. "I had forgotten the woman in the picture was Lady Anna."

His mention of the painting had made her immediately think of her weird dream. That was what Newberry had called her. Was there a connection to the woman in the portrait?

"Excuse me," she said, hurrying past him.

William stared after her. Her response didn't make sense. But then, she was a woman, and he had never even understood his own mother or sister, let alone some random red-head from America.

Anna's first scenes were in the Great Hall by the fireplace, the very spot where the lighting panel had fallen the night before. When she arrived in the room, she saw Sir Frederick in deep consultation with Jim Anderson and Tim Tremayne. She hoped everything had been double and triple-checked for safety. The scene would film her character's entrance into Cavendish Manor: the poor relation, Daphne Thomson, coming to stay with her wealthy relatives.

Corinne, dressed immaculately as Lady Margaret, was yawning in one of the wingback chairs. Adrian Reed, as Lady Margaret's father, Lord Pembroke, was pretending to straighten his cravat but was really admiring his face in the ancient mirror that hung over the mantel. The deteriorating silver backing on the glass made the image splotchy and streaked.

Adrian turned away, masking his irritation with one of his high eyebrow looks of innocent surprise.

"The Earl should really get a new mirror," he complained, smiling like a teenager. "This old thing is warped and streaky."

Before Anna could make a comment about the historical value of the ancient glass, she was summoned to the front door by Sir Frederick. There was much discussion about whether or not she should enter the house through the wicket or if they should open the entire door. Mr. Barnaby was consulted for historical accuracy. The wicket was finally chosen because, as Sir Frederick said, it showed the cautious feelings of the family toward this poor relation.

Anna was impressed.

With insightful details like that, she thought, *this show might actually be a hit.*

CHAPTER TWELVE

The scenes were filmed without a hitch. The light panels didn't fall on their heads. They didn't even tremble ominously. Sir Frederick seemed pleased with everyone's performances and they were released for the moment while the assistant director moved on to supervise the final set-up for filming in the Drawing Room in the afternoon.

The elaborate hat was beginning to make Anna feel like she had steel pins sticking into her head, so she carefully removed it, breathing a sigh of relief. She grabbed a water bottle from craft services and headed out the Drawing Room doors to the garden. According to the call sheet, she was supposed to be at lunch, but instead of turning toward the catering tent, she found herself drawn to the garden.

She hadn't had a chance to really explore the grounds of Hampstead Hall. Her attempt yesterday afternoon had been thwarted by the rain. She entered the circular rose garden and tried to imagine what it would look like in full summer bloom. There were still a few roses lingering, but the majority of the branches were bare of flowers and leaves, and beginning to turn brown. A gardener in a straw hat was pruning the branches on the far side. Anna sidled out through one of the arches in the walkway and found herself in a kind of hallway with tall yew hedges on either side. It eventually led to a pergola-covered wooden bridge which reminded Anna of Japanese-style gardens she had visited in the past on vacations with her parents. One of her mother's favorite pastimes was visiting gardens, public and private.

She could imagine her mother right now, sitting in her own garden that had been designed by Justin Stelter himself, the landscape designer for several historic mansions in the Nashville area. Her mother loved roses, and they clambored over stone walls and up pergolas. Anna's brow wrinkled thinking about her mother. She had not been in favor of Anna's move to Los Angeles.

"I suppose she thought I would fail and come home," Anna thought, her feet making a hollow sound on the wooden planks of the bridge. She leaned her arms on the rail and gazed down into the water below. It was dark, with the occasional glint of gold from the tail of a gigantic goldfish.

But Anna hadn't come home, except on visits. Still, each time she came to Nashville, her parents acted like they expected her to stay, like this time she would come to her senses and move back. And there were times she wished she could, because rent in LA was high and jobs were few and far between.

But then there was Sir Frederick. One of her friends from acting class had made a short film and shown it in the Film Independent festival. Sir Frederick was in the audience, and called her for an audition. Unfortunately, Sir Frederick wasn't interested in her friend's film, or his career, and that friendship was at an end.

Which is probably for the best, thought Anna, remembering his unwanted advances. Sometimes it was hard to not feel like the whole industry was covered in slime. Like the water she was staring down into. Clear on the top, even flowers growing across the surface and sprouting along the edges of the bank. But underneath, where you couldn't see it, nothing but slime.

So far, nothing seemed slimy about Sir Frederick. Or *Cavendish Manor*. She hoped it would be successful. It had to be. Or she really would have to move back to Nashville.

She sighed and continued walking along the path. She could see the sparkle of sunlight on water through the trees in the distance, and guessed it was a lake or a large pond. She headed in that direction, but she hadn't gone very far before she heard the sound of voices. They sounded angry, a man and a woman, but she couldn't make out the words they were saying. The yew hedges were so tall that they formed a kind of maze of hallways, with garden rooms opening on either side. As Anna continued down the hallway, a man suddenly emerged into her path from one of the garden rooms. He seemed flustered, his face ruddy, his eyes flashing.

"Jake!" Anna cried as he almost ran into her.

Jake's face drained of color slightly before he recovered his composure and gave her his usual grin. He was still dressed in his Regency clothes.

"Anna! I didn't hear you coming," he said loudly. "I thought you would still be filming your first scene."

"Just finished," she explained, glancing around him to the garden room he had just exited. She saw a glimpse of black against the green of the yew hedge as someone slipped out the other side.

"Jaime," said Jake, running his hand through his hair. "I came out here to think, and she found me."

He shrugged, and rolled his eyes. Anna nodded, understanding.

Jaime likes him, and it makes him uncomfortable, she thought. She felt like she knew it without him saying it out loud.

"But, I'm glad to see *you*," he added with a smile. "Where are you headed?"

"Well," she said, "I don't really know. I was just exploring. I have to be back at base camp soon to go over my lines with Corinne."

"I'll walk with you," he said, heading in the direction Anna had come from, back toward the house. Anna turned and walked with him.

"What do you think about the light falling last night?" he asked, a frown creasing his brow.

"I'm not sure what to think," Anna admitted. "I was a little nervous filming underneath them today. But nothing fell."

"I'm glad," he said, giving her an admiring glance. "I wouldn't want anything to happen to you. Or anyone," he added quickly.

"No," she said, lowering her eyes to the ground.

She wondered if she should mention what she'd heard that morning, about the grease on the light pole. Was it gossiping to say anything?

"I'm sure everything will be fine from here on out," Jake continued.

Anna nodded. Of course it will. What could go wrong?

CHAPTER THIRTEEN

A week had gone by like a blur. One episode of *Cavendish Manor* was ready for final editing. Four more to go. Anna hoped she could keep up with the intensity of the schedule. Up before dawn and in bed late. Memorizing lines and learning to maneuver in the costumes. It wasn't the action that wore her out, she soon discovered; it was the waiting. It was the in-between scenes, sitting around while lighting was checked and camera angles were discussed and minor changes were added to the script.

On her walks back and forth between the house and base camp, Anna noticed the trees, which had been mostly green when she arrived, were starting to turn brilliant colors. Sometimes the sky was a dramatic grey, and sometimes, like today, the sun dominated the sky, dulling the sharp edges of the wind.

She had only had a few scenes with Jake so far, but there hadn't been much time, apart from meals, to get to know him any better. And then there was William. As Sir Frederick's assistant, he was usually present at her scenes, watching. Of course, that's part of his job, she reminded herself. To make sure everything is running smoothly for the director. She shouldn't assume that meant anything more than that. At other times, he was noticeably absent, like at meals. She found herself wanting to get to know him better, too.

There had been no more dreams or visions since the first night. Anna felt a little bit disappointed. Both the dream and the vision out the Tapestry Room window had been so real, like going back in time. At first, it had been difficult to look at Corinne without imagining her as a lady's maid. Anna had chosen not to mention the dream to her; it sounded kind of weird, especially the part about Lord Mallory coming to visit her. The way Corinne flirted with Peter, she would probably be jealous that he had been mentioned in Anna's dream.

Although she was expected on set later in the afternoon, right now there was something else Anna felt compelled to do. Something that should have been done already. She crept up the oak staircase. At the top of the stairs, she cautiously looked around. Everyone appeared to be downstairs or out on the grounds. The door to the Tapestry Room was cracked open, revealing an enticing fragment of Wedgwood blue wall and the edge of a red toile-covered chair.

It beckoned.

She hadn't been in that room since the day they toured the house and she had seen the vision of William riding a horse outside the window. She wanted to see if it would happen again, if the room itself would inspire another vision, or if it had simply been the effects of jetlag and an overactive imagination. She knew the room was off-limits, but what if no one found out? She would only be there for a minute. With one final glance around the upstairs hall, Anna surreptitiously pushed open the dark paneled door and slipped inside.

Light flooded through her favorite window and cast diamond patterns across the faded Turkish carpet. On the other side of the room was a matching window that overlooked the front entrance to the house, but it was the window overlooking the garden that still captured Anna's attention. She glided toward it, her long skirt trailing over the floor like the Regency-era occupants of the house must have done once upon a time. She seated herself gingerly on the velvet cushion.

There was no one in the garden, she noticed. The catering tent and trailers were on the far east side of the house and out of sight. At this end, it was as if there were no film crew roaming the grounds at all. As if this tranquil scene had gone undisturbed for centuries.

Anna glanced down at the window handle. It seemed an ordinary piece of curved metal, curled up at the end like the shoe of a genie. Her fingers twitched with anticipation. What if nothing happened?

"Well," she said to the French ladies and gentleman in the tapestries, "there's only one way to find out."

She grabbed the handle.

Immediately, she felt a humming sensation go through her hand and up her arm, even through the thin, silky gloves she was wearing. The scene outside the window blurred. When it cleared, she was no longer looking down at the garden. In fact, she was no longer upstairs in Hampstead Hall. She was outside, gazing at eye-level at the topiaries. As she trotted past, a blue waxwing flittered away from a nearby rowan tree, heavy with red berries.

Trotted?

"A lovely day, isn't it, Lady Anna?" asked a voice beside her.

Anna nearly fell off her horse. She grabbed the pommel for balance, noticing she was seated side-saddle. Peter Mallory trotted along beside her, dressed in his Regency finest, complete with top hat.

She smiled wanly, unable to speak.

"This must be the 'Lord Mallory' that Newberry was talking about in my dream," she thought, slyly glancing his way from underneath her hat.

He appeared completely at ease, his body rising and falling in rhythm with the motion of the horse, a satisfied smirk lifting one corner of his pale lips.

"Don't panic," Anna told herself, trying to concentrate on the scenery and not the fact that she towered above the ground on an animal she didn't know. Sitting precariously in the saddle, she began to understand just how large a horse really was. And how far away the ground was, if she were to fall. Like most dreams she'd had, she found she had the ability to do things she couldn't in real life. Like ride a horse. Side-saddle. The closest she'd come to a horse was watching the Iroquois Steeplechase, yet here she was, trotting along as if she'd done it since birth.

The gravel drive turned to a chalky dirt road dotted with milky puddles that wound slightly uphill toward the stand of trees Anna had seen from the window the first day she visited Hampstead Hall. Today she noticed there was an avenue that led to the forest. Tall maples, their bark darkened by the previous night's rain, formed a straight line on either side of the road, their branches intertwining above their heads. Their leaves were a beautiful, golden orange; the leaves that had fallen to the ground formed a carpet beneath them that glowed with a fluorescent light of their own.

Anna let out a breath and saw it form a cloudy mist in front of her. She was thankful to find she was wearing a heavy cloak, and pulled it closer around her as a chill wind sent fallen leaves scurrying across their path like a herd of animals chased by an unseen predator. She realized suddenly that she didn't know where this road led.

And that worried her.

"You're awfully quiet," said Lord Mallory, squinting in her direction.

"I'm not sure what to say," Anna replied.

He laughed.

"Let's talk about the weather," he offered. "It's a bit brisk after the rain, wouldn't you say, Lady Anna?"

"Yes," she agreed. "It is. But the colors on the trees are beautiful."

"Indeed, they are," he said. "Just like present company."

Lady Anna didn't respond.

"Your cousin seems an amiable young lady," he added after a pause.

"My cousin?" asked Lady Anna, confused.

"Miss Douglas?" he urged.

"Jaime?" she said, surprised. "Oh, yes, Miss Douglas."

"Quiet, though," he added. "But then, she's always been like that."

"Yes, she does keep to herself," she said.

"Scottish, isn't she?" he asked. "With very interesting silver eyes. Highlander eyes. Kind of makes you wonder what she's thinking."

Lady Anna was puzzled. Lord Mallory seemed more interested in this Miss Douglas than the real Peter was with Jaime. Almost as if he knew her already.

"Jake talked to her a good deal last night after dinner," he continued. "He quite enjoyed their conversation."

"Jake?"

"Sorry!" Lord Mallory apologized with a laugh. "*Sir John Rawlings, Baronet,*" he said, mockingly. "I call him Jake."

"Oh! Sir John Rawlings!" Lady Anna exclaimed, adjusting to the fact that Jake had just been added into the story, along with Jaime Douglas.

Lord Mallory raised his eyebrows.

"Did I offend you by mentioning his interest in another woman?" he asked, slyly. "I know you and Sir John have been getting along well these last few days."

Anna could feel her face reddening.

"I—we—I don't know what you're talking about," she stammered.

He laughed it off.

"No need to worry. You and I have had an understanding for a long time, haven't we? You can have friends other than me. I have friends other than you."

Lady Anna chewed on that statement for a while. What did he mean, exactly? Was he suggesting—but surely not. And what kind of an understanding did they have? Was Lady Anna engaged to Lord Mallory?

"Here we are," he said, indicating a break in the density of the trees. They had been gradually going uphill, and now found themselves overlooking Hampstead Hall and its fields below. Lord Mallory suggested they dismount and sit upon an outcropping of rock that overlooked the valley. They tied their horses to a tree branch, allowing them to munch the dry grass underneath, and seated themselves on the rocks.

Anna could make out a few farmhouses in the distance, their stone chimneys sending up wisps of smoke. A man was working one of the fields with a horse-drawn plow. In the distance was the village, with the church spire point-ing a gothic finger toward the sky.

"Do you ever grow tired of this view?" asked Lord Mallory, grinning at her. "You must have seen it a thousand times."

"No," she answered truthfully, gazing again at the tranquil scene. Somehow it was familiar, though Anna had never seen it from this vantage point before. But Lady Anna, whoever she was, must have. Hampstead Hall was her home. That was her village in the distance. It gave her a strange sense of pride.

"I know I never grow tired of it," Lord Mallory continued, his expression becoming more like a conqueror overlooking his newly-won territory.

Anna had a strange sense of peace, like this was how it should be. Lady Anna should marry a man who takes pride in her land as if it were his own. Who wanted to blend together into something larger than they would be as individuals. She had the faint impression that her parents had instilled that in her since she was a child. Responsibility. Duty. It was an honorable thing.

The sun had warmed the rocks, despite the frigid air, and Anna felt herself relaxing. Just then, an arm slid behind her and a gloved hand found its way to her waist.

"Lord Mallory," said Lady Anna, pulling away. "I don't think you should."

"There's no one around," he smirked, grabbing her waist more forcefully and pulling her body closer. "Who's going to know?"

His eyes squinted down at her. Anna caught a gleam in them that she didn't like. He leaned toward her, his hand pressing against her back. Anna tried to push him away as his freckled nose leered closer to her face.

"Lady Anna!"

They both turned suddenly. On the path behind them, an elegant-ly-dressed man on horseback stood beside their own horses, his face grim.

"Mr. Williams!" Anna breathed with relief. In that instant she knew he was her father's private secretary, a highly valued employee. But not truly a gentleman. Was he? He certainly looked like a gentleman, sitting straight and regal on his black stallion, his eyes staring cold and haughty at Lord Mallory.

Peter's face darkened as he pulled his hands away from Anna's body.

"Do you need assistance?" Mr. Williams asked Lady Anna, his gaze softening.

"No," she replied, leaping up from the rock and moving toward her horse. "But thank you."

Mr. Williams continued to stare coldly at Lord Mallory, who had also rejoined his horse. Looking up into his blue eyes, Anna was shocked to see a glint of violet. Then it passed.

"I'll accompany you back to the house," he said, dismounting to help Lady Anna back into her saddle.

"No need," said Lord Mallory curtly. He had already swung into his saddle without even a thought of helping Anna. "We know the way."

"It would be my pleasure," assured Mr. Williams, his mouth grim.

He took Lady Anna's gloved hand in his and supported her as she swung herself up. Their eyes held for a moment, and Anna felt like time stood still. She was surprised to discover sorrow in his eyes as he looked intently into hers. Then he let go of her hand.

Anna's gloved hand let go of the handle, and she gasped as she found herself back in the Tapestry Room. There was still no one in the garden: no horses, no riders. No sorrowful secretary.

Her heart pounded in her chest; she breathed deeply once or twice, trying to calm her pulse rate. This new dream or vision was going to need contemplation, something she knew she didn't have time for at the moment.

She stood up from the window seat with a sigh and glided back across the carpet. As she reached for the partially closed door, it swung open, almost hitting her, and she let out a small squeak.

Jake Rawlings jumped as well.

"I'm so sorry!" he apologized, recovering enough to grin.

"I was just taking a break," she began to explain, then paused. Before he had switched on his grin, Jake had had a guilty expression. Like someone who's caught.

"What are you doing here?" she asked.

"I was looking for you," he explained quickly. "It's almost time for our scene in the Drawing Room, and I noticed you weren't at lunch."

She smiled politely and allowed him to escort her downstairs.

"You're not supposed to be in there, you know," he teased as they descended the stairs. "Mr. Barnaby's orders."

"You won't tell on me, will you?" she asked.

"No," he said. "But you probably should steer clear. You wouldn't want Barnaby to report you to Sir F."

Anna smiled at him gratefully, but her mind raced.

Why would fun-loving Jake be so concerned about her following the rules? Did he really come to the Tapestry Room merely to look for her?

CHAPTER FOURTEEN

Anna grabbed some food quickly, then headed with Jake to the Drawing Room. It had undergone a change since Anna had first seen it. All of the furniture and objects that were post-Regency had been removed and replaced with more historically accurate pieces, much of which had been borrowed from Hampstead Hall's attics.

"Jaime really knows her stuff," she thought, amazed at all of the details that transformed the room into another century.

Corinne was seated on one of the sofas in the vast room, with Miranda Vogel beside her, picking delicately at the fringe on her shawl. Adrian Reed was standing by the fireplace, raising and lowering his eyebrows as if practicing his own interpretation of the tragedy and comedy masks.

Anna noticed William standing in a corner holding a clipboard overflowing with papers and post-it notes. It was a shock to see him in present day after so recently seeing him dressed in period clothes; she hoped he wouldn't notice her nervousness.

As he glanced over at her, his eyes twinkled.

She smiled.

He always seems to have a twinkle in his eye, thought Anna. A mischievous, I'm Up To Something twinkle.

The twinkle reminded her of something else she had seen in his eyes. Twice now. His blue eyes turning a sort-of lavender color when he was angry. She had seen it once after Peter pinched Corinne in the Ballroom, and then again in the dream she'd just had. It was curious, and deserved more thought, she decided. Then she pushed it to the back of her mind.

Anna had feared she and Jake would be late for their cues, but Jim, Sir Frederick, and Sarah were still working out camera angles with Tim, the lighting director. She watched them, fascinated by the way they considered the light in the room, both natural and artificial. They were like artists finding the perfect blend of colors and textures, the perfect play of light on the actors and objects in the room. For the first time, she realized they were using the camera's lens as a kind of character in itself; the audience would see through its eye, would know what it knew.

They had just finished filming B-roll of the elaborate dueling pistols and were moving on to film some of the other objects in the room. Perry stood at the console table, staring down at the guns as if mesmerized. Anna wondered what he was thinking. He didn't seem like the kind of guy who would be into guns. She imagined him more of a Green party member. Or whatever the equivalent was in England. Save the Planet and all that.

The next object the film crew was focusing on was a carved piece of statuary, more like a fragment of a temple, that stood on one of the built-in shelves. It was about two feet square and several inches thick, made of some kind of white stone. The carved design on the stone was of three oddly-shaped women, almost stick figures, standing close together. Anna was so deeply enthralled watching the proceedings that she didn't notice William had moved beside her until he spoke.

"It's an interesting artifact, don't you think?" he asked.

"Yes," she agreed. "It must be really old."

"Ancient Celtic," he replied. "Found on the property back in the 1700s when they were planning the gardens. They are believed to represent the three mother goddesses from Celtic beliefs."

"Interesting," Anna said, intrigued. "The way their faces are carved, it almost looks like trees. The branches in the forehead, and the trunk forming the nose and mouth. I wonder if they are supposed to represent fertility. Or life."

"Maybe," he said, considering her statement. "I never thought of that. I always thought of them as the three witches, from *Macbeth.*"

There was a deafening silence after he spoke those words. Although William had been speaking low, just to Anna, it was as if his voice echoed through the entire room. Every actor and crew member, including Anna, stopped what they were doing to stare at him.

"Did I say something wrong?" asked William.

"Out!"

Jim Anderson was the first to find his voice.

Corinne let out a snort that she quickly pretended was a cough and covered her mouth with her hand.

"Get out!" shouted Jim.

The Ninth Earl of Somerville wasn't used to being ordered around in his own home. A wave of pride and anger crossed his face before he remembered he was pretending to be William, assistant to Sir Frederick. But still, this ordering of him out of the room seemed inexplicable. He glanced toward Sir Frederick, whose grim face suggested he was in agreement with Jim.

Anna realized William was ignorant of what he had done to offend the company.

"Come," she whispered, pulling him toward the French doors.

"What is going on?" William demanded.

"William, you know you can't say that name!" Anna scolded. "This may not be a theatre, but it's the same concept. People are way too superstitious to let you get away with it."

"What name? Macbeth?" he asked.

Miranda Vogel screamed and turned away dramatically. Adrian Reed stared at William with a frozen tragedy face. Perry Prince's mouth hung open slightly.

Jake began to laugh, lowering his head.

"Out!" Jim repeated, raising his fist threateningly. "Three times in a circle, then cuss!" he yelled after him. "And you can't come back in until I say!"

Anna continued to push a bewildered William toward the terrace.

Sir Frederick shook his head at Jim Anderson.

"No, no, no. Three times in a circle, then he has to quote something from another Shakespeare play," he insisted.

"From *A Midsummer Night's Dream*," offered Sarah, also frowning.

"No, no, no. From *Hamlet*," said Sir Frederick. "It has to be *Hamlet*."

"What about spitting?" asked Adrian, recovering from his shock. "Doesn't there need to be spitting?"

"No, he has to hold his breath," corrected Miranda, suddenly coming to life.

Corinne snorted again, this time without covering it.

"How can the man quote Shakespeare if he's holding his breath?" she asked, skeptically. She got up and followed William and Anna out onto the terrace.

Jake, still laughing, followed as well.

"That was classic!" he said, slapping William on the shoulder. "The look on Adrian Reed's face was worth it."

William stared at him, still confused.

"Come on, William," teased Corinne good-naturedly. "You know better than to say Mackers on the set."

"Mackers?" he repeated.

"Surely you've heard of the curse?" Anna said. "It's unlucky to mention the name of the Scottish play while in a theatre. Or in this case, a film set."

"Why? What curse?"

Jake smiled.

"Some say Shakespeare used real incantations in the play. Others say some real witches were offended at his descriptions of them so they cursed the performance. Either way, bad things are said to happen if you say the name," warned Jake in a mocking tone.

"What kind of bad things?" William asked.

"I don't actually believe in the curse," said Anna. "But many people do. Obviously Jim Anderson does."

"What kind of bad things?" William repeated.

"Accidents," said Jake. "Death, sometimes. People fall offstage. One time, a lighting rig fell right next to Sir Laurence Olivier, almost hitting him. In John Gielgud's version of the play, three people died before opening night, and then on opening night, the lighting director committed suicide."

"That can't be true!" said Anna, shaking her head and thinking of Tim Tremayne and the fallen light panel. "Anyway, people get all upset if you mention the name. You really should have known that."

William innocently shook his head.

"First I've heard of it. So what was Jim talking about? Turn around three times?"

"Ooh, that's even more fun," laughed Corinne. "In order to break the curse, whoever said 'the name' has to turn around three times, and then quote something from Shakespeare that counteracts the curse."

"Some people think you have to cuss, but I think that's ridiculous," added Anna.

"Maybe you should try all of it, just to make them happy!" Jake suggested.

"That's the stupidest thing I've ever heard!" William said.

"I agree with you," Jake said, "but if you don't, all these people will blame you for anything that goes wrong on the set."

"Not really?"

"Yep. Happens all the time."

"It's true," Corinne offered. "Someone once told me that in a show in New York, after one of the actors said 'the name', two guys were doing a fight scene with a fake knife. But someone switched the fake knife with a real one, and the guy died! And of course, they blamed it on the person who said 'the name'."

"How is that the fault of the curse? Isn't that the prop guy's fault?" asked William.

"Maybe," countered Corinne. "But I wouldn't have wanted to be the idiot who said Mackers out loud. You can say Mackers or the Scottish play, but not—well, you know."

"This is ridiculous," grumbled William. But one glance through the French doors told him filming was at a stand-still until he complied. Jim, Sarah, Sir Frederick, and two cameramen were staring at him through the glass.

"What do I quote?" he asked, resigned.

"Try this, from Hamlet, Act I, Scene IV," Jake encouraged, thumbing around on his phone. "Angels and ministers of grace defend us."

William sighed. He looked once more at Anna's serious face, and began to turn around on the stone-flagged terrace.

"Angels and ministers of grace defend us. Angels and ministers of grace defend us. Angels and ministers of grace defend us. There, are you happy?"

He aimed that remark at Jim Anderson, whose stern face had appeared in the doorway.

"Did you cuss?" he asked, arms folded, his face grim.

William reddened, and he opened his mouth, about to let off a stream in the general direction of the cinematographer.

"Just kidding!" Jim said, uncrossing his arms. "Come on back in."

William did so, followed by Jake and Corinne, who were still whispering and laughing together.

Anna breathed a sigh of relief. She paused before re-entering the Drawing Room.

She really didn't believe in the curse of Macbeth. So why did she feel wary? Why did the atmosphere seem different now, like the ominous charge in the air before a coming storm?

William, noticing she hadn't come in yet, returned to the door.

"My lady," he said, smiling, holding out his hand.

She threw off the eery foreboding and put her hand in his.

CHAPTER FIFTEEN

Like always, the day didn't end for Anna until after ten, and she was exhausted. Just as she was drifting off to sleep, there was a knock on her door. She hesitantly answered it; she had an irrational fear that it would be Peter standing there. But it was Corinne.

She sailed into the room wearing a sequined top and skin-tight jeans, clicking as she walked in a pair of sparkly heels.

"I'm in love!" she sang.

She settled herself at the dressing table and began messing with Anna's makeup.

Anna crawled to the end of her bed and peered at Corinne.

"Are those hot rollers?" she asked, waving her hand at Corinne's head.

"Why yes, of course," she answered, surprised.

"I didn't think anyone used those anymore."

"I do. Left over from my pageant days. Hot rollers and hairspray," she said, falling into her Southern accent. "That should be a country song! Hot rollers and hairspray!"

Anna laughed. "I don't think anyone would make a country song out of that," she teased. "Except maybe Brad Paisley."

"I have to be ready, in case I get a late-night visitor," Corinne explained, digging through Anna's makeup.

"But you're not in your room," Anna reminded her.

Corinne was stricken.

"I should go back!"

"Yes, but not before you tell me who you're in love with."

Corinne smiled mysteriously.

"Peter Mallory," she admitted.

"Big surprise," Anna teased. She had been watching them all week during their scenes and could tell they were becoming very chummy between takes. Peter was playing His Grace, the Duke of Netherington, the one Lady Margaret's parents want her to marry.

She watched Corinne in the mirror as she created magically smokey eyes with a makeup brush.

"So," Corinne asked, "which one do you like better?"

Anna strained to look closer at Corinne's eyes.

"Not my makeup," Corinne clarified. "Jake or William?"

"I'm not here looking for a relationship," Anna said, putting on an innocent expression.

"Why on earth not?" asked Corinne, staring at her incredulously through the mirror with her large, blue eyes.

Anna sighed.

She tried to ignore the part of her brain that was accusing her of lying. She had attempted to push relationships to the back-burner for the last two years. But six months ago it had all come to the front of her mind again. Maybe there was a small part of her wanting to get back at—wanting to get back into the game.

"Well," said Corinne, standing and heading toward the door, "I'd better head back and take these curlers out. Wouldn't want to scare him away!"

Anna grabbed her arm as she stepped into the hall.

"Corinne," she warned, "be careful. You don't know anything about this guy."

"Pooh," replied Corinne, "men are putty in my hot little hands."

She winked as she swayed back to her room. A door closed somewhere in the house, and Corinne jumped with a squeak and ran the rest of the way on her tiptoes.

Anna snickered. But safe in her room again, she felt uneasy. Her mind went back to the dream, or was it a vision? Peter on the rock, trying to force her to kiss him. What else would he have forced if William hadn't come along?

Despite the late-night interruption, Anna awoke the next morning from an uneventful night and a dreamless sleep. She went to her trailer first, dressing quickly in her costume, then headed to breakfast. She loved the feel of the silky material of her dresses, and their little puffed sleeves. The costume design team had done an excellent job, and Anna felt like a princess, with all of the ruffles and flounces and flower designs sewn on her full skirt. A princess or an earl's daughter.

Halfway across the courtyard, she saw that her mother was calling.

She hesitated, then received it.

"Hello, Mom," she said, trying to sound cheerful.

"Hello, Anna, dear," said her mother.

Anna knew that England was six hours ahead of Nashville, and wondered that her mother had stayed up late to make the call. She could imagine her sitting in her favorite chair in the blue room, swaddled in her silk pajamas. Her hair was probably perfectly coiffed, even at midnight.

"How is it going on the set?" she asked, although Anna could detect the edge of disapproval in her voice. She could hear her mother's clenched-teeth smile. "McKays are not artists or actors or theater people," her mother had told her when she explained her intentions of moving to LA, as if that settled the question. "It's just not what McKays do."

Anna dawdled in the courtyard to keep her distance from any eavesdroppers. She absent-mindedly grabbed the arm of a life-sized statue of a draped female figure, then dropped her hand quickly as she realized the statue probably came from ancient Greece. She didn't want to break it and aggravate the Earl, whoever he was.

"Everything's going fine, Mom," she said.

"I'm glad. I've been getting all my information from the entertainment websites, since you haven't called."

"I'm sorry," Anna apologized. "It's been really busy around here, and with the time difference—"

"I know, I know. I just worry about you, with those kind of people."

"What kind of people, Mom? Actors?"

"Anyway," said her mother, ignoring her last remark. "I saw on the internet that Jake Rawlings is in your show," her mother said.

Anna groaned inwardly, knowing what that meant.

"They say he's a *Rawlings Furniture* Rawlings," her mother added with significance. "I'm sure he probably won't dabble in this acting thing for long. I wonder what his parents think about it."

"Mother, please don't."

"What? I'm merely noticing that you two would have a lot in common. A lot more than Derrick and his potato farming."

"Mom!"

"Don't tell me you're not over him yet. I thought you said he got married to someone in his hometown."

Anna sighed.

"He did, thanks to you."

"I had nothing to do with it. You're the one who moved to the West Coast. He went home to Idaho. What did you expect?"

"You know what I mean!" said Anna.

"If you are referring to the time he visited Nashville, I merely pointed out to him how different your backgrounds would be and the difficulties that would entail down the road," her mother admitted. "College tends to muddle people together a bit too much."

"You brought up my prenup!" Anna said angrily.

"Well, you will have to have one, and he needed to know that. I signed one when I married your father."

"Yes, Mother, but you know you were trying to scare him off!"

Her mother paused. "Perhaps," she agreed. "But it did. And if a little thing like a prenuptial agreement will scare a man off, then you're better off without him."

"I need to go," Anna said. "I have to eat before my scene this morning."

"Don't be angry with me, Anna," said her mother. "I was looking out for you. And it's in the past. Look to the future. I'm sure the Rawlings boy is very nice."

When the call was over, Anna took a moment beside the statue to collect herself. It had been two years since Derrick had broken things off between them, and six months since his marriage to a girl he had gone to high school with. Which is why she had been thinking about relationships again, even if it was to bemoan the fact that she didn't have one. She really didn't have romantic feelings for Derrick anymore. The subject only brought up feelings about her mother. And about herself. Her mother had just voiced what she had been unable to face head-on until now. She knew Derrick didn't care about her money. She had never been worried about that. It was the fact that her family's wealth had scared him away, had made him reconsider. Had made him go back to Idaho and never look back. Anna was forced to admit the fact that she wasn't enough. When faced with their differences, the differences meant more to him than she did.

At catering, she was just seating herself next to Jaime and Jake when Jim Anderson erupted into the tent.

"All right! Who was it?" he demanded. His eyes looked like fire and his hair gave the appearance of wanting to leap off his head to save itself.

He was greeted by blank stares.

"Who made spaghetti out of my cables?"

Anna turned to her companions for clarity.

"Cables are called spaghetti if they're messed up," whispered Jaime. "Out of order. Tumbled together."

Anna glanced back at Jim. He was clearly livid. He glared from group to group, seeking weakness.

"If I find out who is playing these practical jokes, they'll wish they'd never been born!" he growled. Sarah Stern, who was getting a cup of coffee, gave him a warning look. She took his arm and headed him toward the exit of the tent, but he stopped and turned around.

"Think it's funny, do you?" he said to no one in particular. "Messing around with my cables? There's a lot of expensive equipment in the Drawing Room right now. Spaghetti cables means time wasted while we put it all back together. It means somebody could trip and hurt themselves. It means cameras could get accidentally pulled over and broken. It's no joke! And if I find out who did it—"

He accented the statement with a clenched fist before leaving. Sarah rolled her eyes and followed after him.

Jake gave a silent whistle.

"Wouldn't want to be his enemy," he said, then shook him off like a memory and smiled his usual smile again.

CHAPTER SIXTEEN

The spaghetti cables pushed back the filming schedule for the day as Jim and the sound engineer, with their teams, put everything back in order again. William found himself free for the moment. Filming was fun, but difficult. At times, Sir Frederick seemed to forget he was the Earl and ordered him around like an actual assistant. William wondered how long he could take it before the novelty wore off. He kept reminding himself of his reason for doing it—to be near the action, of course. Also, he could keep a close eye on Peter.

Thinking of Peter brought Monte Carlo into his mind again. He would never forget that day. He was at Hampstead Hall when the call came. His mother had long ago resigned herself to the fact that her husband was an incurable gambler and had stopped going on trips with him. William had resigned himself to the fact that if he didn't step in to the farming operation, his father would gamble the estate into the ground.

His mother had called him in from the fields where he was working with the farm manager. It was early in the morning; the spring planting was going in. The birds were singing like crazy as he came across the fields.

Funny how you remember those kinds of details, he thought.

And everything changed. The sky was still blue. The birds still sang.

And Geoffrey, the Eighth Earl of Somerville, was dead.

Died of an overdose of sleeping pills, the police said.

William didn't even know his father took sleeping pills. He questioned it, even after he flew in that afternoon. But Peter had been there to verify it. He was there, in Monte Carlo, claiming he had been with the Earl that week. Saying that the Earl would stay up late gambling and drinking, then take sleeping pills at night.

"He lost that night," Peter had told him. "So he drank a lot more than usual. Maybe he forgot how many pills he had taken."

Maybe.

The birds were singing now, too, even though it was autumn instead of spring. He shoved the last piece of toast into his mouth and decided to go downstairs. He was eating most of his meals in his room instead of joining the others in the catering tent. He didn't technically work for the Studio, after all.

Downstairs, William breezed by the Drawing Room to see what "spaghetti cables" looked like. All of the neatly-laid cables had not only been unplugged, but they were thrown together in piles, audio and video together in one big mess. William sympathized with the gruff cinematographer. It was a lot of hard work undone.

And for what reason?

Out of the corner of his eye, he saw a beautiful red-head in Regency attire peeking around the corner of the doorframe. He exited the room through the hall and came around behind her.

"Did you do it?" he asked, leaning close to her ear, reminiscent of Jake.

She jumped like a startled kitten.

"William!"

Anna punched him on the arm. He laughed.

"It's a mess, isn't it?" he said.

"Yes. Do you think it was a joke?" she asked, lines forming across her forehead.

"If so, it's not very funny," said William grimly.

"No, it's not," Anna agreed, slowly and thoughtfully.

"And when did they do it? The middle of the night?" continued William.

"Had to have been," said Anna. "I didn't hear anything. Did you?"

"No, not a thing, but then I'm on the other side of the house."

"In the west wing?" she asked. "But I thought…oh, you have to be near Sir Frederick."

"Right," William answered, shaking his head at himself.

"I can't hear myself think, with all this jabbering!" Jim growled in their direction.

Sarah approached them.

"Give him some space," she said, gently pushing them out of the room. "He's a little stressed out right now."

"I would be, too," William said.

Sarah nodded, looking back at Jim. Anna was surprised to see compassion in her face. She had come to think of the assistant director as above emotion. She never really showed any. She always seemed to keep a stoic expression, very business-like and hard-edged, except when she was joking with Jim.

"He feels like it made him look unprofessional," Sarah said in a low voice. "And he desperately wants to impress Sir Frederick. Whoever did this better hope we never find out."

As they moved to the Great Hall, William and Anna exchanged glances.

"She seems protective," said William.

Anna smiled enigmatically. She would be keeping a romantic eye on those two.

They sat down on a settee that faced the grand fireplace in the Great Hall.

"This is a dark room," Anna commented as her eyes adjusted to the gloom. Despite the soaring ceilings and over-sized fireplace, the sun had trouble penetrating much past the leaded windows. Even the lamps seemed to only illuminate where the light hit directly, which accentuated rather than dispelled the darkness.

"I've always thought so," William agreed. "It's difficult to light these old rooms. Of course, back in the day, they would have used a huge amount of candles."

"Ooh, that would be pretty!" Anna said, imagining it.

"But impractical," said William.

Anna had to agree.

"They could use brighter bulbs," she suggested.

"What do you mean?"

"In the chandeliers." She pointed above their head. "And the wall sconces. They could put in a brighter lightbulb."

William glanced around the familiar room. She was right, of course. He was surprised he hadn't thought of it before. He had always felt the pressure, mainly from Mr. Barnaby, to leave things as they were. To leave things like his father before him. He covertly studied his companion and wondered again why she seemed so at home here. At home in his house. There she sat, smiling happily to herself and innocently suggesting subtle changes that would make a world of difference. A small adjustment that would bring more light into his home.

She caught his gaze.

"What?" she asked, self-conscious. "You're looking at me funny."

He shook his head.

"I was just thinking about my father," he said.

Anna's expression became serious. Although he was smiling, she could sense something beneath it, like he was holding back emotion.

"Tell me about him," she urged gently.

He bit his lip.

"He was a gambler," he said simply, looking away from her. He had never said it out loud to anyone before. Not even to his mother. He knew it. She knew it. Everyone in their acquaintance knew it. But it was understood, not spoken.

"And an alcoholic," he added, encouraged by her sympathy. "Not always, just the last fifteen years of his life. Looking back now, as an adult, I know why."

"Why?"

"He felt worthless. Like his life didn't matter. Like he wasn't doing anything that would be remembered. Like he didn't measure up to his forefathers. And I understand that feeling," said William, staring at the fire blazing in the grate. "I still feel it, if I'm not careful. After university, I knew that if I didn't return home and do something, he would leave my mother penniless. My sister was already married and out of it. So I came home. And when he passed away, I worked even harder."

"For your mother?" she asked.

"For my father," he replied. "And yes, of course, for her as well. For me. For everyone," he said, thinking of Mr. Barnaby and Sheila the cook, and all the other people the estate employed.

"How did he die?" she asked. "Sorry. That was probably too personal."

"No, it's okay. He died of an overdose of sleeping pills. But I've often wondered…"

"Wondered what?" she asked.

"Nevermind," he said, shaking his head. "It's just idle speculation."

"Well, I'm sure your mother is proud of you," Anna encouraged. "I mean, assistant to a famous director is a really good job."

He smiled at her, his blue eyes twinkling mischievously.

"So, where do you go from here?" she asked. "What are your dreams for the future?"

He sighed, his gaze straying out the windows to the front of the estate.

"My dreams for the future?" he asked. He battled within himself. Was this the time to tell her who he was?

"My dream," he began tentatively, "is farming."

"Farming?"

"Yes. Organic farming. Is that weird to you?" he asked, noticing her expression.

"No. Not weird," she said thoughtfully.

But it is weird that this is the second farmer that I'm attracted to, she thought. *I mean, second farmer I've met*, she corrected herself.

"It just seems surprising, coming from you," she said aloud. "It's a completely different field. No pun intended."

He laughed.

"I mean, how many people in the movie industry have secret dreams of farming?" she pointed out.

"True, but I'm not exactly in the movie industry."

"Of course, a friend of my dad's started a very successful Mexican restaurant in Nashville, and he used to be a professional musician for years," Anna said, overlooking his remark. "But he felt there was a lack of New Mexican cuisine in Nashville, so he decided to make it himself. It's called Sopapillas. But he stayed in music until he had everything ready to make the switch to entrepreneur."

William nodded.

"For me, there's more to it than that. I do enjoy farming, and I've learned a lot about it. But I'm not farming for farming's sake. I have a really good reason for doing it."

"For your forefathers," she said.

"Yes, for my forefathers. And for my children. If I have them."

For some reason, Anna found herself blushing.

"Well, I'm proud of you," she said. "You aren't only thinking of the past. You're thinking of what happens next."

William paused. It was a very apt description. He looked at her steadily. Something in his eyes caused Anna's breath to quicken.

"I think, from the business side of things," she said quickly, "it's not that different from going from music to starting a Mexican restaurant. You can be Sir Frederick's assistant until you're ready to take on the next challenge."

"A means to an end," he mused.

"Exactly," Anna agreed, thinking of organic farming.

"Exactly," agreed William, thinking of Anna.

There was an exasperated howl from the direction of the Drawing Room.

"Things don't sound like they're improving in there," William commented.

Anna was struck with an idea.

"Does one of those secret passages you mentioned lead to the Drawing

Room?" she asked. "Maybe someone snuck in and out that way?"

"None that I'm aware of," he answered. "But that reminds me. I promised to show you a secret passage. If we hurry, I can show you at least one before they get the cables cleaned up."

Anna clapped her hands like a little girl.

"Yes, please!"

William stood up and crossed the room. Beside the giant fireplace, he opened what looked to Anna like a tall, narrow cupboard. Inside it, instead of the expected shelving, was a set of wooden stairs.

Anna gasped, surprised at the simplicity.

"Wait!" she said, remembering she was in costume. "I can't get this outfit dirty."

"You won't," he assured her. "It's mostly stairs, not tunnels to crawl through. Shall we go up, my lady?"

She peered up into the darkness above.

"You first?" she squeaked.

William pulled a small flashlight out of his pocket, gave her a challenging look, and headed up the wooden stairs into the gloom.

"Close the door behind you," he called down. "We don't want everyone knowing about this."

Anna took a steadying breath and placed her foot on the first step.

The first set of stairs led quickly to a landing that was level with the top of the fireplace. From there, the passageway continued upward with a set of wooden spiral stairs. By the light of the flashlight app on her phone, Anna noticed that several stair treads had been repaired more recently than the 1600s.

"Hey!" she whispered loudly. "Some of these stair treads are new."

William paused and turned back to look at her.

"Yeah. I—um, I think the Earl repaired them. He used to play in these passages as a kid."

"Interesting," she replied as they continued. "This Earl is very intriguing to me. I wish we could meet him."

William thought about her statement. And about his recent confessions to her. Maybe she could handle the truth, after all.

If she likes me as William the assistant, he thought, *maybe she will still like me as William the Earl.*

He brooded as he slowly ascended the stairs. What difference does it make what she thinks? Or what my mother thinks? I'm not falling in love with her. But I think she's becoming a friend. And friends should be trusted. Shouldn't they?

William suddenly stopped and turned back toward Anna.

"I need to tell you something."

Just then, Anna, who was momentarily disoriented, dizzily crashed into him. William backed into the release latch on the door at the side of the upstairs fireplace cupboard, and they tumbled unceremoniously onto the hearthrug.

"It's the Library!" Anna exclaimed, disentangling herself from William.

"Are you hurt?" he asked.

"No," she said, sitting up. "Are you?"

He laughed.

"We always make quite an entrance into a room, don't we?" he said.

She grinned, picking herself up off the floor and adjusting her long skirt.

"That was fun," she said, reaching a hand down to help William off the ground.

"You were going to tell me something," she reminded him.

William paused. She was perilously close to him, and there was no one around. He looked down into her trusting, upturned face. The color of her dress caused her eyes to look stormy blue, he noticed. He had a strong urge to kiss her, and that scared him more than speaking the truth. The courage he had in the darkness of the staircase evaporated in the brightly-lit Library. He took a step backward. He could see in her eyes that she saw him as an equal, and he didn't want to change that. He wanted to stay plain William just a little longer.

"I wanted to tell you that this isn't the only secret passage," he said instead.

"There's more?"

"Follow me."

Anna hesitated before following him. For a moment she thought he was going to kiss her. Of course, that would have been awkward. She was a leading actress and he was merely an assistant to the director. A friend, of course, but nothing more. Right? Then why did she feel disappointed?

He led her out into the hall to the top of the oak staircase. The stairs to the third floor were slightly narrower than the main staircase because the rooms above had been built mainly for servants and children.

"This was the Nursery, once upon a time," William explained, stopping outside a wooden paneled door. "By Nursery, I mean, the children's quarters.

One big room that was playroom and bedroom, with a smaller room to the side for the Nanny. There's a passage here that leads from the Nursery down to the Tapestry Room below it, and continues down into what used to be a private chapel. Now it's more of a glorified closet."

"That's a shame," said Anna. "I bet it was beautiful."

William eyed her oddly. "It was. It is."

He pushed open the Nursery door.

"Hello?" a female voice called sharply.

William and Anna stopped at the door, surprised.

"I'm so sorry," William apologized. "I forgot this room was being occupied."

Jaime Douglas eyed him narrowly, then smiled.

"That's okay," she said. "Come on in. I don't usually get visitors. Except for my crew, who are late, as usual."

They stepped into a large room filled with furniture pieces, knick knacks, and potted palms. In the center was an over-sized table where Jaime was working on upholstering a wing-back chair.

"Welcome to my workshop," she said. "And my bedroom."

"Wow," Anna commented, looking around. She noticed a small bedroom to the side.

The Nanny's room, Anna realized from William's description. He really was a wealth of information on this house.

"Are they still working on the spaghetti cables?" Jaime asked with her Mona Lisa smile.

"Yes," said William. "I don't suppose you heard anyone moving around in the middle of the night? Anna and I didn't."

Jaime's eyes flickered a lightning glance from William to Anna and back again.

"Not that we were together last night," said Anna, catching the implication.

"No," William agreed quickly.

"I didn't hear anything up here," she replied, focusing again on her work. "But then I'm three floors up."

"Well, we won't disturb you anymore," said William, pulling Anna toward the door.

As they descended the stairs, William wondered why Anna was so quick to correct Jaime's assumption that there was something romantic between the two of them. I mean, he certainly wasn't falling in love with her. But why would the possibility be distasteful to her?

Anna wondered the same thing. Why didn't she want to think romantically about William? She remembered Corinne's irritating question from the night before. "Which one do you like better?"

Then she pushed it aside as a moot point.

I can't choose when there isn't a choice, she realized. Neither one has made a move. And even if I did like one better than the other, will anyone ever be able to get past that prenup?

I'm destined to be a nun, she told herself, sending a scowl toward Nashville.

CHAPTER SEVENTEEN

William and Anna arrived back at the Drawing Room just as the crew was ready to continue.

Anna sidled up to Corinne, who was yawning voluminously while scribbling notes in her script with a pencil.

"Good morning," said Anna.

"Whatever," Corinne replied, rolling her eyes.

"Hey, did you or Peter hear anything last night?" Anna asked, ignoring her snippy attitude. "Anything that sounded like cables being made into spaghetti?"

Corinne sniffed.

"I didn't hear anything, but I don't know if Peter did. He never showed."

"Oh!" said Anna apologetically.

"When I asked him this morning, he said he fell asleep."

"Well," said Anna, trying to be encouraging, "it was a long day."

Corinne snorted.

"Fell asleep? I hot-rolled my hair for someone who can fall asleep instead of coming to see me?"

Anna smiled wanly and backed away, leaving Corinne to gnaw angrily on the end of her pencil.

She couldn't help but be glad, though. She didn't trust Peter.

Perry Prince approached her with a handful of pink papers.

"Hey, Anna, we've made a few adjustments in the script," he said, handing her the changes. "Here's the new pages."

"Oh, thanks, Perry

"No prob."

"Weird wasn't it?" she asked. "Someone doing that with the cables?"

Perry pursed his lips.

"Jim was livid," he said. "Sir Frederick was livid. Whoever did it better hope no one figures it out."

"Yeah, that's what Sarah said. Why do you think—?"

"Don't know. There's always joking around on the set. But this is taking it a bit far. Almost like it's not a joke."

Anna glanced at his face. He seemed strangely serious.

"What else would it be, if it's not a joke?" she asked.

"Don't know," he said, walking away.

Anna sat in a director's chair while a makeup artist freshened her up and tucked wayward locks of hair back into place. Climbing through the walls hadn't been kind to her hairstyle. As she waited, she perused the new pages she had been given. She knew she had a scene with Jake on the schedule. Now she saw it included a kiss.

A kiss!

Her heart fluttered at the thought.

Then she reminded herself that this was acting. She and Jake were professionals. This was not Jake about to make a move on Anna. This was the Marquess of Waverly about to make a move on Lady Margaret's less fortunate cousin, Daphne Thomson. There is absolutely no reason to have nervous butterflies about it.

But she did.

She looked up to see Jake stepping into the Drawing Room, looking handsome and elegant in his tight-fitting, buckskin pants, dark coat, and white cravat. He gave her a wink.

She blushed.

Good Lord, Anna, she told herself. At least pretend to be a professional.

William watched Anna from across the room. With her hair piled up on her head, he was struck again by how much she looked like the woman in the Gallery portrait. It reminded him to research that subject. Why did she look so much like one of his relatives? Was it just coincidence?

Maybe that's why she seems at home here, he reasoned with himself. Not that she really belongs here, but she looks like someone who once lived here.

He glanced over at Jake, who looked regal and debonair as he stood staring at his script, a slight smile on his lips.

The golden boy, thought William. Rich, attractive to women. Certainly attractive to Anna. Perfect in all his ways. So why do I feel like it's just gilding?

William scowled down at the script in his hand.

Jake was scheduled to kiss Anna.

It's acting, he reminded himself. They're actors. Acting. It's not Jake and Anna, but Lord Waverly and Miss Thomson.

And what difference does it make? he thought, clenching his jaw. Let the golden boy have her if he wants. Or if she wants him. He wasn't interested in some American girl, anyway, he reminded himself. She's nice and all. Very pretty. But, no. Although it had never been explicitly said, he knew his family expected him to marry within his social class. Some Duke's daughter with an aristocratic upbringing. Someone like Lady Margaret in the story. Not like Daphne Thomson.

William frowned. For some reason, this story in the script was beginning to sound familiar. He wondered why.

"Miss Thomson," said Jake as Lord Waverly when the scene began filming, "you know it grieves me to hear that your cousin treats you so callously. Is there nowhere else you can go?"

"No," said Anna as Miss Thomson. "I have no money. Where can I go? Lord and Lady Pembroke have been all that is kind. I think Lady Margaret is—well, I shouldn't say it."

"You can tell me," assured Lord Waverly.

"I believe she is jealous of me."

"Jealous? Why?"

Miss Thomson crossed the room and gazed out the window at the garden. Lord Waverly came to stand right behind her.

"Lady Margaret has Lord Netherington's attention," he said.

Miss Thomson turned to face him.

"But she wants you."

He stared adoringly into her eyes.

"What if I want someone else?" he asked huskily. "What if I want—"

He leaned forward to kiss her.

"Cut!" shouted Sir Frederick.

Anna and Jake leaped apart, then laughed awkwardly. Anna hoped she wasn't blushing.

"Sorry!" said Sir Frederick. "We need to get it from the other side. Light's not right."

As the crew repositioned the cameras and equipment, Anna and Jake sat down. Anna wasn't sure what to do or how to act after being almost kissed by Jake. It was such an intimate scene. It would be awkward with anyone. But with Jake? It was like having your first date filmed in front of an audience. She knew William was in the room, watching. She wasn't sure why that made it worse, but it did. Maybe it was because he had confided in her. Maybe it was because she thought he was going to kiss her earlier. She refused to look in his direction.

"You went to high school at Harpeth Hall, didn't you?" Jake asked Anna as they sat beside each other, waiting for their cues. "The all-girls' school in Nashville?"

"Yes," Anna answered, surprised.

"Reese Witherspoon went there, too."

"She did. She was my inspiration in becoming an actress, actually."

She paused, confused.

"How did you know?"

"I looked you up," he said. "I hope you don't mind?"

She shook her head, unsure if she minded or not. Surprised that he had found the time.

"I don't really talk about the fact that I went to a private school," she said, glancing around to see if anyone was listening. "People sometimes change the way they see you if they know. But I'm sure I don't have to tell *you* that. Which school did you go to?"

"You have the most beautiful eyes," said Jake.

His eyes seemed to be drinking in hers. Anna felt like she was being drawn into him, like her soul had liquified. Her eyes widened, her tell-tale blush creeping over her face.

"They change color, depending on what you're wearing," he continued, still gazing intently into her eyes. "Right now they're blue-ish, but yesterday they were more of an amber. But I guess you know that already."

She twittered. She inwardly scolded herself for it, but there was no other way to describe the inane little laugh she had just let past her lips. It was a twitter, as if she were some kind of ridiculous bird.

"Okay, let's take it again from the window!" shouted Sir Frederick.

They both stood.

"I didn't mean to make you blush," Jake apologized with a wink.

Still speechless, Anna just shook her head as her fluid soul poured back into her body.

An impossible thought entered her mind as she watched him cross back to the window.

What if her mother was right? Jake is a nice guy, and they do have a similar upbringing. Surely he wouldn't balk at a prenuptial agreement.

She glanced at William as she got into position again. He had been watching her, but turned away when she looked his direction.

Maybe coming from a similar background is a good thing, she thought as she became Miss Thomson again, gazing out the window at the garden. *Maybe farmers should stick to marrying farm girls.*

"Back to one!" shouted Sarah from beside Sir Frederick.

"Action!" yelled Sir Frederick.

"Lady Margaret has Lord Netherington's attention," repeated Jake, leaning close to her from behind.

Miss Thomson turned to face him.

"But she wants you."

He stared adoringly into her eyes.

"What if I want someone else?" he asked huskily. "What if I want—"

He leaned forward to kiss her. And this time, there were no cuts. His mouth covered hers. She reached up and clutched his hair in her fingers.

"And—cut!" yelled Sir Frederick. "Great job. Nice touch with grabbing his hair, Anna."

Anna and Jake broke apart again. This time, Anna did blush. She walked away quickly, needing to put space between them. She knew she hadn't meant to grab his hair. It had happened unconsciously. She wondered if he knew. If everyone knew.

She seated herself on one of the window seats in the Great Hall and breathed a few cleansing breaths to clear her head. The kiss and her own thoughts about Jake and money and the future were swirling around her brain.

"Anna."

Jake sat down next to her.

She pulled her eyes away from the cupboard beside the fireplace and looked into his face.

He seemed different, serious.

"Yes?" she asked, her attention focusing.

"I, um," he stammered. "Did you feel something? In the scene?"

"What do you mean?" she asked, her breathing becoming shallow.

"I mean, when we kissed. Did you...? I'm saying this badly."

Anna remained silent, watching his face. He ran his hand through his hair.

"Let me say it another way," he said. "When we kissed, I felt something.

Something real. Not just acting. And I was wondering if you did, too?"

Anna's eyes widened. He was looking at her so earnestly.

"I just wondered, because you grabbed my hair, and I thought…but it was probably stupid of me."

This was the sign she'd been waiting for, she realized. Someone had made a move.

Anna impulsively grabbed his face and kissed him.

"Does that mean yes?" he asked, laughing with relief.

"Yes!" she said. "It means yes! I definitely felt something."

He kissed her again, wrapping his arms around her.

"They're calling for you again," said William from the doorway.

Jake laughed, standing and pulling Anna with him back toward the Drawing Room.

Anna could feel tension as she passed William, still standing in the doorway. Why did she feel embarrassed that he saw them together? Her eyes darted to his face. His mouth was a stern line, and she was startled by his expression. She turned away quickly and tried to push it to the back of her mind, but it kept creeping to the forefront.

It was the same expression that was in Mr. Williams' eyes the first time she saw him on horseback out the Tapestry Room window. He had taken off his hat and looked up at her. It was disappointment. No, more than that.

It was anguish.

CHAPTER EIGHTEEN

———◆◈◆———

That night, Anna lay awake in her rose-covered bed. The day had been another long one, and she was strangely grateful. It had left her with little time to think about things, to figure things out. Although there was a part of her that was exhilarated by Jake's newly confessed affection for her, there was another part of her that felt empty. Like something was missing. And every time she had looked at William, she had felt guilty.

And this angered her. Why should she feel guilty? William had no claim on her. He hadn't made a move or indicated any kind of feelings for her other than friendship. And that's as it should be. They were from completely different backgrounds, after all. But she couldn't get that look of anguish out of her mind, although he hadn't shown it again the rest of the day.

The next day of filming would be a lighter one for her. It was mostly going to be focused on Corinne's character. Lady Margaret was scheduled to spurn the proposal of the Duke of Netherington (a.k.a. Peter Mallory). As she drifted off to sleep, Anna wondered how Corinne would feel tomorrow, acting with the man who had stood her up. Maybe it would actually make the scene come across more real.

There was a bump against her door, and her eyes flew open.

It was morning, and Corinne entered her magically-transformed bedroom dressed again as a maid.

Anna hesitated. She hadn't had one of her weird dreams in a few days.

"Newberry?" she asked.

"Yes, m'lady? I didna think you was awake yet."

Anna sighed. She wondered where this one would take her.

"You've been summoned, m'lady," Newberry continued, setting a breakfast tray on the round table by the window.

"Summoned?"

Anna struggled to sit up.

"Your father, Lord Somer, has asked for you in the Drawing Room. Lord Mallory is also there."

She smiled then, a knowing smile, and moved toward the wardrobe to select Anna's clothes.

The smell of breakfast was too strong to ignore. That was something interesting about these dreams, Anna realized. They were fully sensory, including smells. As if she had actually time-traveled.

Anna ate some toast and tea while she thought about Newberry's statement. Her knowledge of old books reminded her that when a gentleman wished to see a lady after meeting with her father, it could only mean one thing. A proposal.

She shuddered. Even in a dream, Peter Mallory gave her the creeps. The last time she had dreamed of him, he had tried to force a kiss. Her mind tried to slip past Mr. Williams as she remembered the touch of his hand, his look.

"I think this dress will be perfect for…for whatever Lord Mallory has to say this morning," said Newberry, pursing her lips as if she were keeping in a secret. It was a robin's egg blue and showed off the red of her hair to perfection.

"It makes your eyes look blue," she added.

Anna immediately thought of Jake. In this dream-world, he was Sir John. She wondered if he would appear at long last.

On her way to the Drawing Room, Anna passed the Study. Glancing casually in, she was surprised to discover Mr. Williams sitting at a large mahogany desk, his head in his hands. Upon hearing her approach, he lifted his head, and Anna was struck by a fleeting glimpse of agony in the secretary's eyes. Then it was gone.

He stood quickly as she paused outside the doorway.

"Lady Anna," he said, bowing slightly. She acknowledged his bow with a nod of her head.

"I've been summoned by my father," she said.

His eyes slid off her face as if it hurt to look at her.

"I've heard," he said quietly.

Her odd dream-memory reminded her of a recent conversation.

"I hope you aren't sorry to have confided in me about your father's death," she said.

"No, my lady. I appreciate your concern."

"Have you been able to wrap up your father's affairs as you hoped?" she asked.

He paused.

"Not as yet, my lady," he answered, looking in the direction of the Drawing Room. "But I hope to very soon."

She wasn't sure why, but the formality of his address irritated her.

"I know it's been such a weight on your mind," she continued, brushing his formality aside. "I pray you'll let me know when you finally put it to rest."

"That may be unavoidable," he said grimly. "But it would never be my intention to cause you pain."

Puzzled, she bowed her head at him as she took her leave.

I wonder what he meant by that?

When she entered the Drawing Room, it was more populated than she had expected. Two men immediately stood; one was Lord Mallory dressed resplendently in a bright blue coat with long tails and buck-skin trousers, his hat in his hand. She noticed his ginger hair was oiled back from his forehead. The other man made her heart stand still for a moment. It was Jake, dressed like Peter, only with a burgundy coat. She caught his eye before he bowed to her. There was questioning and hurt in his expression.

Lord Mallory gave her a low, elaborate bow. She returned it with a curtsy. She noticed he had the expression of a man who has just won a fortune at cards, and thinks that somehow it was due to his own genius and not the luck of the draw.

"Here she is, here she is," said an enthusiastic voice.

Lady Anna turned with surprise to see yet another occupant of the room.

Sir Frederick stood there, beaming with paternal pride. He wore old-fashioned, gold-rimmed spectacles, and was dressed in a slightly-worn, gold brocade smoking jacket and brown breeches that ended at the knee, his legs encased in long stockings. He reminded her of Benjamin Franklin.

"Father?" she guessed.

"My dear," he said, moving forward to kiss her cheek, "That's a beautiful dress. Perfect for the occasion. It seems Lord Mallory has something he particularly wants to say to you this morning."

He patted her shoulder as he passed her on his way out of the room. He cocked his head animatedly at the others, indicating that they should leave with him. Sir John Rawlings, his head bowed, followed him from the room.

A woman rose like a phantom from the corner. Lady Anna hadn't noticed her until that moment. She was dressed in a faded black gown, high-necked, with simple lines. Her pale yellow hair was pulled sharply back from her face in a tight bun.

"Congratulations, cousin," she whispered as she passed, but the ice in her silver eyes belied a different sentiment entirely.

Lady Anna stared after Jaime Douglas until Lord Mallory, who had followed her across the room, closed the door with finality. He quickly wiped a look of disgust from his face, and smiling pleasantly, indicated with a wave of his hand that they should sit down. She sat, smoothing her skirt and keeping her eyes focused on her hands folded neatly in her lap. In her mind she had followed the others out of the room. She felt helpless and small. What was she expected to do? Was she reliving the past of this house? Would Lady Anna accept this Lord Mallory? If she refused him, would she mess something up forever?

Lord Mallory captured one of her hands and held it tightly in his.

"Lady Anna," he began, "I'm sure you know why I've asked to see you this morning."

"I'm sure I couldn't say," she replied, stalling for time.

A flicker of annoyance crossed his face, then was replaced with his pleasant expression again.

"I've just been speaking with your father, Lord Somerville, and he has given his blessing."

He moved to one knee in front of her, still holding tightly to her hand as if to keep her from running away.

"Lady Anna Somer, would you do me the great honor of becoming my wife?"

She met his eyes. She looked at him for a few seconds, searching for sincerity, searching for something yet undefined that she knew should be there. Then she shook her head. She placed her other hand on top of his.

"I am sorry, Lord Mallory. I cannot."

He stiffened, his head jerking back as if she'd slapped his face. Then he smiled again.

"Perhaps you need some time to think about what I'm offering," he said with a sharp edge to his voice and a cold gleam piercing through his pleasant facade.

She shook her head decisively.

"No," she said again. "I've quite made up my mind. I don't love you, and I cannot marry you."

He violently pulled his hand away from hers and stood up, towering over her.

"I would think again, Lady Anna," he said, threateningly. "This is a generous offer. If it's Sir John you want," he sneered, "you can have him, after we're married! I'm sure he would be quite content with that, as long as you paid off his debts."

Lady Anna stood up, shocked and offended.

"How dare you!" she spat. This time she actually did slap him across the face.

"Think carefully, Lady Anna," he warned, fingering his cheek. "I will leave today and go back to Abingdon Abbey. When I return again, I suggest that you be prepared to accept me. Good day, madam."

He stalked stiffly out of the room, leaving the door open behind him. He nearly collided with Mr. Williams, who was lingering in the hall outside the door. Lord Mallory's first reaction was anger, but as he shoved Mr. Williams out of his way, he caught his eye. The angry red color drained out of his face, and he looked startled. Lady Anna thought she also detected fear.

"Watch where you're going," Lord Mallory said gruffly, and stormed away, his footsteps echoing sharply on the stone floor.

Lady Anna released the breath she had been holding. Her eyes met those of Mr. Williams. He made a movement as if to enter the room, then noticing footsteps approaching, he bowed to her and returned across the hall to the Study.

Lady Anna's father entered the room.

"My dear," said Sir Frederick, or rather, Lord Somerville. He seated himself on the sofa; she sat down beside him.

"Father, I couldn't," she explained, turning toward him, tears in her eyes.

Instead of the sympathy she expected, Lord Somerville's expression was stern. Kind, but stern.

"My dear, you must reconsider," he said, taking her hands in his.

"He doesn't love me!" she cried. "I looked in his eyes, and he saw me only as a possession! And I don't love him!"

She wondered whether to tell him about the suggestion of keeping Sir John as a lover, but decided against it. She knew it would be shocking, especially coming from a daughter to her father.

"Anna, you will grow to love him. This marriage has all the advantages for you. Mallory has wealth and prestige, his lands border ours, and have you forgotten that he is my heir?"

"Your heir?" she asked, startled.

"You are my only child, Anna. The only thing of true value to me, since your dear mother's death. You have your dowry, of course, but this property is entailed to the next male descendent. When I'm gone, I want to know that you are taken care of. And how pleasant it would be to know you could always remain here at Hampstead Hall. It's your home."

"But," she protested, searching in her dream memory for something vague that lay just beyond her reach. "I thought someone else was your heir."

"Yes, my dear. Mallory is technically only second in line. Quite distantly related. But after the unexpected death of—what was that?"

There was a bump somewhere in the house, like someone or something had crashed into a wall.

"The unexpected death of whom?" Lady Anna prompted.

Lord Somerville opened his mouth to speak, but instead of words, he made the sound of something heavy bumping against the wall.

Anna's eyes jerked open. She was back in her darkened room. Back in the present day.

She pounded both hands on the mattress.

"Who died?" she said to the bed curtains.

Then she wondered about the bump. What if it was real? What if there was an actual bump somewhere in the house?

She crept to the door and opened it a crack. There was no one in the hall. Then suddenly, a door opened.

"I swear I heard something," said Corinne, stepping into the hall as she tied a silky robe around her.

Anna stepped out as well. She was about to speak when she saw Peter emerging from Corinne's room.

"It's nothing," he said, then stopped Corinne's response with a kiss.

Corinne pulled away playfully.

"There was a bump," she insisted, laughing softly.

Peter noticed Anna watching them and gave her a devilish grin.

This is so weird, thought Anna, raising her eyebrows in response. I just refused his proposal, yet here he is with Corinne.

Corinne noticed her as well.

"Did you hear something?" she whispered loudly to Anna.

"Yes," said Anna. "But I couldn't tell where it was coming from."

"Probably somebody rolling over in his sleep," Peter assured them. "Speaking of sleep," he said, "I need to get some. Early day tomorrow. Lady Margaret here's going to refuse to marry me."

He gave Corinne a sloppy kiss. Anna grimaced.

Peter sauntered back to his room.

"Well, good night," Anna said to Corinne, who wiggled her fingers in Anna's direction as she watched Peter with a dreamlike expression.

William stood rigidly at the door of the Tapestry Room. He had been reading. Actually, he had been pretending to read. Really he had been brooding. He was growing weary of the charade of being William the Assistant. The thrill of watching scenes filmed in front of him was rapidly becoming...irritating. That was how he felt. Irritated. He had been going over in his mind just how irritating the scene between Anna and Jake had been to watch, especially the one off-camera in the Great Hall, when there was a loud bump from somewhere in the house. He stood peering down the hall, but could see nothing. Then there was another bump. He couldn't tell where it was coming from. It could be coming from any floor. The house with all its twists and turns, he knew from experience, had a habit of throwing sounds like a ventriloquist. Then he heard voices. Moving toward the east wing hallway, he saw Anna, Corinne, and Peter talking, although he couldn't hear what they were saying. He watched as Peter kissed Corinne and saw Anna grimace.

Must have been one of them, he decided, and was secretly thankful he didn't see any signs of Jake.

He turned toward the west wing and his own bedroom.

CHAPTER NINETEEN

———◆◄►◆———

The next morning arrived before Anna was ready for it. She dressed in her regular clothes, since she wasn't needed on set until the afternoon. The first two episodes were a wrap and had been sent to the editor. Today would begin Episode Three.

She peered out her window, which had a view of the front lawn and the circle drive, to see what kind of a day had dawned. Black birds pecked languidly at the grass, searching for breakfast, while a large heron picked its way carefully toward the moat. The pale, November sun peeped through gray blankets of cloud, as if it didn't want to get up that morning, either.

Movement from the drive attracted Anna's attention. She watched as a large, black car arrived, driven by a chauffeur. The chauffeur leaped out and opened the door. An older woman stepped onto the drive, smiling up at the house as if at an old friend.

Portia Valentine, Anna knew automatically, although she had only seen pictures of the actress as a younger woman. In her prime she had been blonde, with piercing blue eyes. Now she wore her hair in a natural gray, almost white, style that fell to her shoulders. Anna felt it was a flattering look, and didn't make her seem like she was trying too hard to hold onto the past. She felt she could be friends with this woman, that she would be someone stable. And Anna desperately needed stability at Hampstead Hall, especially after last night.

Her mind went back to the dream, and then to the bump in the night. She wondered if she should tell someone what was going on. Corinne? No. Anna wasn't sure she could trust her. Jake? Maybe.

She decided to go downstairs. Maybe she could be introduced to Portia Valentine before the others? At any rate, she wanted to get a closer look. She arrived at the bottom of the oak staircase just as the front door was being opened by Mr. Barnaby himself. Anna hadn't seen him in a while. He and his almost invisible staff seemed to keep up with the cleaning and care of Hampstead Hall with very little interaction with the *Cavendish Manor* cast and crew. She decided it probably pained him to see strangers in the house, and deliberately kept out of their way.

Portia Valentine swept into the Great Hall as if the autumn wind had personally escorted her through the doors. Anna smiled to herself, knowing that even without an audience, the older actress needed to make an "entrance." She was wrapped in a pale cream cloak instead of a coat, and she glided over the flagstone floor like it was a red carpet.

Anna noticed that Mr. Barnaby had opened both of the massive oak doors, not just the wicket.

I suppose Portia Valentine gets the royal treatment, Anna thought, watching Mr. Barnaby close the door after her with something of a look of reverence on his face. The wind had also swept in a scattering of brown, crunchy leaves. Mr. Barnaby waved his fingers at the leaves on the stone floor, and a young housemaid wearing the Hampstead Hall uniform of grey polo shirt and khaki pants immediately scurried away to fetch a broom.

Mr. Barnaby turned with a smile.

"My dear Ms. Valentine! Such an honor to have you here at Hampstead Hall again."

"Thank you, Mr. Barnaby. It's been such an age!" she said as her eyes swept the room. Her voice resonated in the Hall, warm and musical. "Not since before dear Geoffrey passed away. Such a fool with money, I always thought. His son, on the other hand—"

"Yes, madam. Shall I show you to your room? I have a message for you from the Earl."

Mr. Barnaby quickly escorted her through the door to the Ballroom, and a back staircase, with a backward glance at Anna, who was standing just inside the doorway on the other side of the Great Hall.

I wonder what he's trying to hide, Anna thought, furrowing her brow. He's taking her the long way to avoid me.

Someone touched her arm from behind her. It was Jake.

"Hi," he said, kissing her lips.

"Hi," she responded. She could get used to this.

"Was that Portia Valentine?" he asked, craning his neck toward the Ballroom door.

"Yes, and Mr. Barnaby's giving her the royal treatment. William said she would be staying in the west wing because she is a personal friend of the Earl."

"Ah, the mysterious Ninth Earl of Somerville," said Jake. "I wonder if he'll ever make an appearance."

"Maybe he's really Mr. Barnaby," Anna suggested, "and he's secretly watching us while pretending to be the house manager."

Jake laughed.

"I'm keeping my eye on your theatrical endeavor," he said, standing up straight and mimicking Mr. Barnaby's accent and tone.

Anna giggled.

"Is there anything I can help you with, Mr. Rawlings?" asked Mr. Barnaby curtly from the Ballroom doorway. His grey eyes burned like laser beams across the chilly Great Hall.

Jake sucked in his breath. "No, thank you, Mr. Barnaby," he said quickly. "We were just going out for a walk."

He grabbed Anna's hand and dragged her out the front door, sidestepping the chauffeur, who was piling Portia Valentine's luggage on the drive.

"If he is the Earl," said Jake, slowing his pace, "I don't think we'll be invited to dinner."

Anna smiled.

"I think Mr. Barnaby just needs a little buttering up," she said. "He doesn't trust us because we're so different from what he's used to. But you should have seen him with Portia Valentine. She definitely has him wrapped around her finger."

"You have me wrapped around your finger," said Jake, twining their fingers together as they walked. She smiled, awkwardly looking away from him.

"Have you had breakfast, yet?" he asked. "I'm starving."

They headed toward the catering tent. Exiting out the front of the house meant they had to slip through the side yard, then wind their way through the garden and through the arched wall on the other side to get to the courtyard.

"Portia's character appears in the next few episodes," Jake commented as they walked. "She'll be fun to work with."

"I'm looking forward to it," said Anna. "Did you watch the proposal scene this morning?"

"No," said Jake. "I slept in. They had to film at the break of dawn this morning because it's getting dark so early now. Kind of an odd time of year to film. The days keep getting shorter."

"Maybe this was the best time for the Earl," Anna suggested.

As they crossed under the brick archway into the courtyard, Anna noticed a couple in serious conversation on the far side of the courtyard near the archway that led out into the fields.

"I think that's William," she said. "And Corinne."

That's puzzling, she thought. I wonder what they're talking about?

She watched as Corinne laughed and touched William's arm, while he smiled down at her. As Corinne began walking away toward the catering tent, William looked up, noticing Anna and Jake. He immediately scowled and stepped into a four-wheeler that had been waiting, unnoticed, under the archway.

"William is driving off on a four-wheeler," Anna commented, shielding her eyes from the morning sun as she watched him rumble away over a well-worn path in the field behind the stableyard.

Jake followed her gaze.

"Strange," he commented, his brow furrowed. "He's a mysterious one, isn't he? Wonder where he's going?"

He greeted Corinne, who had joined them, and turned to enter the tent, but Anna stood a moment longer, watching the vehicle bounding over the muddy ruts of the road.

Inside, Jake, Anna, and Corinne joined Peter, who was already seated.

"How did the proposal scene go?" Anna asked, turning to Corinne, and controlling her urge to question her about William.

"Great!" answered Corinne, and then began to elaborate on the scene. As she spoke, Anna couldn't help thinking about her own proposal scene from the dream the night before. She glanced up at Peter, a little unsure of how to treat him. He hadn't actually proposed to her; she had not actually refused him. Yet, it had felt so real. She found herself wanting to be careful around him so as not to arouse his animosity.

"I was all that was elegant and gracious, and she still turned me down," said Peter, one side of his mouth crooking upward.

Corinne, who was sitting very close to him, slapped his arm playfully.

"It was acting, Peter," she reminded him. "Maybe I'd say yes if you *really* asked me to marry you."

Peter sneered.

"Like that's gonna happen," he said with a snort. Jake laughed his easy-going laugh and got up to get a plate of breakfast.

Corinne's happy smile froze. Her blue eyes darted to Peter's face, but Peter had started eating again and didn't seem to notice. Anna looked away to give her friend time to recover. She could tell Corinne didn't expect so dismissive a response from Peter, especially since their relationship had appeared to be so intimate. She could feel her embarrassment from across the table. As she rose to join Jake in making a plate, Anna glanced at the two of them again. Peter was shoveling food into his mouth, and Corinne was looking down at her hands.

"You're needed in wardrobe again, Miss Newberry," Anna overheard Perry say as he paused at their table.

"Oh? Thank you, Perry," said Corinne, looking relieved as she gathered herself together. "I'd better go."

Peter nodded vaguely in her direction as he drained his coffee cup, as if her leaving meant nothing to him.

"I'm glad I turned him down," Anna thought with a scowl.

As they ate, Jake entertained Anna with stories from his previous acting jobs. He made her laugh, and Anna felt swept away by his charm. She wondered again about his friendship with Peter. They seemed so different from each other. And Peter was proving himself to be insensitive and callous. Anna couldn't imagine Jake answering that question in the same way. Even if he didn't want to marry her, Anna felt Jake would have a much more polite way of changing the subject.

"And I don't think he would lead me on," she thought as she listened to him talking. "He wouldn't pretend to have feelings for me so he could manipulate me or take advantage of me."

She felt sorry for Corinne. But she had warned her about getting involved with Peter.

Her mind shifted back to Jake. Was he a potential marriage prospect? What would a future with him be like? Then she chided herself for letting her imagination run rampant.

"So, your father's in real estate development, right?" Jake asked as they left the catering tent, hand and hand.

"My father?" Anna asked, surprised. "Yes. He builds subdivisions, stuff like that. Like his father before him."

"Sort of like the landed aristocracy of America," he volunteered.

She wrinkled her brow.

"I guess."

"And you'll inherit all that, I suppose."

"Yes," she agreed. "Some of it I already have. I have a trust fund for when

I marry or turn twenty-five, whichever comes first, but he's already put certain rental properties in my name. What about you? Do you have a trust fund?"

"Look, it's Jaime," he said, waving to the props master who had just appeared on the terrace.

As they crossed to join her, Anna peeked at Jake out of the corner of her eye. That was the second time he had changed the subject when it came to his background.

Maybe he's uncomfortable talking about his wealth, she thought. But surely he knows he can trust me. I mean, he's done all this research on me.

Seeing Jaime again reminded Anna of her part in the dream last night. The poor relation. That was Anna's role in *Cavendish Manor*. In the show, the poor relation wins the affection of Jake's character. Anna glanced from Jaime to Jake, searching for a clue to their true relationship. Why did she still feel a twinge of jealousy for the faded Scottish woman? Jake was hers, right? He was holding her hand, after all.

Clutching it, actually, so tight her fingers were going numb.

"I thought you had to dress the scene in the Drawing Room this morning?" Jake said to Jaime.

"We just finished," she said. "I thought you all might want to watch. It's Portia Valentine, Miranda, and Adrian."

"Yes, please!" agreed Anna, releasing her hand from Jake's clutch.

They joined a small group clustering behind the cameras for a view.

Portia Valentine was elegantly seated on a settee. Anna was impressed at how quickly she could change into a Regency grande dame.

Adrian Reed was standing by the fireplace, pretending to straighten his cravat in the mirror above it. Every now and then, he would gingerly touch the crow's feet at the corner of his eyes. Miranda Vogel stood just outside the Drawing Room door, ready to enter when the scene began.

"This is still just the rehearsal," explained Jaime. "To block the action."

Anna watched as Sarah Stern spoke to Miranda.

"You'll enter when Lord Pembroke says, 'I know what's best for my own daughter.' You'll cross to the wingback chair, and sit down, and then you'll say your line."

Miranda nodded vaguely. Sarah paused, a doubtful expression crossing her face. Then she returned to Sir Frederick's side.

"Isn't that the chair I saw you working on yesterday?" asked Anna to Jaime.

"It looks great."

"Yes," she said gratefully. "I'm very proud of it."

"Quiet on the set," said Sarah.

"Let the performance begin," said Jake in a low voice.

Jaime smiled her Mona Lisa smile.

"Everyone back to one," said Sarah.

"Action!" Sir Frederick shouted.

Portia Valentine was playing Lady Cassandra, the Dowager Countess, the mother of Adrian's character, Lord Pembroke. The scene would introduce Lady Cassandra's character in the show and would also reveal that Lady Margaret's parents want her to accept the proposal of the Duke of Netherington, Peter's character. Anna could tell that Portia Valentine's character was clearly intended to be comic relief, with her eccentricities and her funny one-liners.

It was time for Miranda's entrance. Fortunately, it was just a rehearsal, because Miranda missed her cue the first time. There was tension in the room; Adrian pursed his lips in an irritated manner, and Ms. Valentine's quick eyes swept over Miranda as she spent a great deal of time fluffing a scarf around her shoulders, as if she blamed it for her missed line.

The second time, Miranda entered the Drawing Room like she was supposed to, crossed the room and seated herself primly in the wingback chair. There was a cracking sound, and before Anna could figure out the source of it, she saw Miranda on the ground, the wingback chair on top of her.

"Help!" screamed the actress from under the chair. Her eyes were wild.

There was a flurry of activity as Sarah pulled the chair off and Sir Frederick bent to help Miranda to her feet.

"Get away from me!" Miranda shouted, batting his hands away.

"My dear, I am trying to help you," said an offended Sir Frederick.

"This chair hit me in the head!" screeched Miranda, turning to Jaime, who had rushed over and was examining her creation with a grim expression. Anna noticed that one of the front legs of the chair was broken off.

"What kind of a props master are you?" Miranda demanded.

Jaime stood defiantly, holding the leg of the chair. She made a shift with her hands, and Anna was afraid she would use the chair leg as a weapon.

"I'm sure there's an explanation," Jake said, stepping forward.

"The explanation is, someone is trying to make me look bad!" Miranda howled. Her enraged eyes scoured the room for the source of her embarrassment.

"Someone is trying to make *me* look bad," said Jaime, her pale face shading to pink. "This chair leg didn't break. It was sawn through."

She held up the leg, and it was clear, even to Anna, that there was a smooth cut across the leg.

"You did this!" Miranda suddenly shouted, pointing behind the cameras. Everyone turned to see the person accused.

William stood there, confused. He had entered from the terrace and had not witnessed the catastrophe. He had taken off his field jacket and slung it over his arm, but Anna noticed he had on the muddy boots he had been wearing the first time she met him.

"You did this!" Miranda repeated. "You and your Scottish curse! First the lights, then the spaghetti cables, and now this! I could have been killed!"

She broke down into dramatic sobs. Sarah, with a roll of her eyes, put her arm around the actress and walked her out of the room.

"Well!" shouted Sir Frederick, flapping his arms. "I guess we're done here, for the moment."

He glared at William through his round glasses, and stomped out of the Drawing Room.

"What did I do?" William whined.

"Sit here, Mr. Langley," purred Portia Valentine, patting the settee. "And we'll have a little chat."

CHAPTER TWENTY

William sat down obediently beside Portia Valentine, looking like a little boy who has just been given a time out. He was bewildered and irritated. He hoped Mr. Barnaby had given her the message about keeping his identity a secret.

This is beginning to get out of hand, he realized, thinking about the number of people who were having to keep his secret.

And for what, really? Especially now.

"William," began Portia in a motherly tone, "tell me what's been going on here before I arrived. I feel like I've stepped into an episode of *Coronation Street*."

William looked up at Anna, standing awkwardly behind the cameras.

Maybe she can explain this, he hoped.

"Come," invited the older actress, indicating for Anna to take a seat in one of the chairs on the set that hadn't fallen dramatically apart.

Anna sheepishly came over. Jake also pulled up a chair and joined them.

"I'm guessing," said Ms. Valentine, turning again to William, "that for some reason, you said the name of the Scottish play on the set."

"I did tell you they would blame you," said Jake.

"Yes," admitted William, coloring slightly, "but I repeated the phrase you told me to say, and I turned around three times. What more could I have done?"

"You shouldn't have said it in the first place," Jake said, shaking his head. "Actors are far too superstitious."

"And the crew, too," added Anna.

"I googled the 'Scottish curse'," William said. "Sounds like a bunch of coincidence and superstition to me. The only thing I could verify was that in New York in the 1840s, two rival theatre companies were performing the play at the same time, and there was a riot about which actor was the best Mac—leading male. People did actually die, unfortunately. Trampled to death, and so on. But that can be blamed on mob mentality, not a curse. I don't believe for a moment that my saying the name of a play will cause any tragic accidents."

"Today went a bit further than the other things," Jake reminded him.

"Maybe things are escalating."

"Jake, don't say that!" Anna warned, a superstitious shiver going through her.

"So the chair isn't the first incident that has happened?" asked Portia Valentine.

"No, Ms. Valentine," said Anna, shyly, turning toward her. "There have been other things going wrong on the set."

"Please call me Portia, my dear," said the older actress with a smile. "What *other things* are you referring to?"

"Spaghetti cables, for one. That was yesterday," Anna said.

"The lighting rig fell," added Jake.

"The lighting!" repeated Portia with concern. "Was anyone hurt?"

"No, fortunately," said William. "It was before filming began. But the light falling was probably an accident."

"No," Anna shook her head. "I overheard Jim and Tim discussing it. Someone had put grease on the lighting pole. That's why it slipped and crashed."

Jake rubbed his jaw, looking tense.

"That seems like more than a practical joke," he said seriously.

"Yes," agreed Portia, nodding thoughtfully. "These superstitious beliefs are very powerful. A few mishaps that may have happened anyway are blamed on the curse. And the curse is blamed on the person who started it, in this case, you," she said, turning to William.

"But these are more than mishaps," Anna said. "Everyone keeps referring to them as practical jokes, but these seem more serious than that."

"Practical jokes on set in my day usually centered on making the others laugh, to throw them off their game," mused Portia. "Not lights falling or chair legs sawn in two. It's almost as if someone is deliberately trying to sabotage the show."

The other three stared at her wide-eyed, then at each other.

"But why would anyone want to do that?" asked William.

Portia Valentine looked at him searchingly with her bright blue eyes, her head cocked to one side.

"I don't know," she said, thoughtfully.

Perry Prince entered the room, carrying a stack of papers.

"I have new call sheets," he said with a weary sigh.

He handed them around. A quick glance told Anna that Miranda's scene was moved to the next day. But her own scene was still set for four o'clock.

"How is Miranda?" asked Portia with concern.

Perry pursed his lips.

"She's resting. She took a sleeping pill and said she wasn't going to be doing anything until tomorrow."

"I'm surprised she didn't walk out," said Jake. Anna gave him a warning look.

"Sir Frederick was able to talk her down," Perry said. "But I have a feeling we'll be getting a visit from her agent tomorrow."

"I feel more sorry for Jaime," said Jake, staring at the broken chair. "This makes her look like the bad guy."

"I heard her having it out with her crew a little while ago," Perry said. "So far, nobody has admitted to sawing the chair leg. Not even accidentally."

"How can you accidentally saw off a chair leg?" asked William.

Perry shrugged.

"I think she was giving the guilty person an out. But there were no takers. So we're back to the mysterious, anonymous practical joker, I guess."

"Somebody needs to stop him," said William soberly.

CHAPTER TWENTY-ONE

"Who is our mysterious, anonymous practical joker?" Anna asked the canopy above her head.

She had decided to relax in her bedroom instead of her trailer. She wondered why they had to have a trailer at all, with all of their bedrooms so close by. Jake had mentioned something about Teamsters and contracts and she had zoned out on the rest of his explanation. All she wanted was to get away to think, and she knew that base camp was habitually noisy.

She lay on top of the bedspread in her clothes and stared up at the rose-covered canopy. Portia Valentine had suggested that someone was trying to sabotage the show. But why? Surely everyone here needed the work. To sabotage the show risked losing money.

Maybe the Earl wants us gone and is doing things to make us leave, she thought. But that would mean he was here on the premises. And no one has seen him.

"I wonder what he's like," she thought as she closed her eyes, her mind beginning to drift into sleep.

"Lady Anna," said a familiar voice, and Anna felt the pressure of a man's lips on the back of her outstretched hand, even through her satin glove. She opened her eyes to find William's intense gaze upon her as he looked up from kissing her hand.

"Mr. Williams," she breathed, trying not to appear moved by his touch. Or by the deep color of his lashes that made his eyes sparkle like sapphires in the candlelight.

People do this every day as a sign of courtesy, she reminded herself. Kiss a woman's hand. It means nothing. But looking into his eyes, she wondered if it did mean something.

"Williams, I'm afraid I have more work for you to do," barked Sir Frederick as her father. He was dressed in elegant evening attire: black tailcoat and white shirt, black pants that buttoned at the knee, shiny waistcoat and carefully-tied cravat at his throat, with those lovely white stockinged legs. Mr. Williams was dressed the same, Anna noticed. And it showed off his broad shoulders and trim waist, she thought, pulling her eyes up to his face again and hoping he hadn't noticed her wayward glance. Somehow his legs in white stockings looked handsome, showing off the muscles of his calves.

They were in the Drawing Room again. Her own dress was equally as formal, an emerald velvet with puffed sleeves that fell slightly off her shoulders. A quick look in the mirror across the room showed that her hair was in an updo with little sparkling gems laced through it. She stifled a gasp as she realized it was the same dress worn by the Lady Anna in the Gallery.

The mahogany pocket doors stood open to the Dining Room, which revealed signs of a recent elaborate dinner. A servant appeared, dressed as a butler, and began to close the pocket doors, his eyebrows raised and his mouth pursed. His familiar surprised expression mirrored the shock on Anna's face, and she covered her mouth with her hand to hide her smile. Adrian Reed bowed his head to her as he closed the pocket doors so he and the servants could clear the table.

"Williams, I must speak with you about the farm again," continued Lord Somerville. "I feel we need to make a change in farm managers. Wilkins is simply too much of a rustic, I'm afraid. He doesn't know anything about the new techniques. I know it's late, but I must get this off my mind."

"Of course, Lord Somerville," said William. "If you'll excuse me, Lady Anna."

He gave her a short bow and a longing, apologetic look before joining Lord Somerville, who was looking at her with an aloofness that told her he hadn't forgiven her for denying Lord Mallory. Her father nodded at her curtly, then led Mr. Williams to the Study across the hall.

Farming again, thought Anna, puzzled. Farming at Hampstead Hall? She realized she always thought of it as a place for sleeping or entertaining. Was it actually a business, as well as a house?

"That leaves us alone at last," said a voice behind her, interrupting her thoughts.

Lady Anna turned to find Jake, as Sir John, standing there. He also looked handsome in full early-1800's evening wear. Anna secretly wished men would dress for dinner in the twenty-first century.

"Well, not exactly alone," he corrected himself, grinning. "We have our chaperone."

He waved his hand at the corner, where Jaime Douglas sat, her lips a thin line, her sewing in her lap.

She smiled her enigmatic smile at them, then resumed her sewing as if it held all of her attention, although Anna noticed the red spots on her cheeks that seemed to indicate a strong emotion just under the surface. Jaime was wearing faded black again, nothing like Lady Anna's own gown.

The Drawing Room was longer than it was wide, and Sir John pulled Lady Anna to the farthest end of it. She assumed he was avoiding the prying ears of Miss Douglas.

He stopped at the very window where she and the real-life Jake had done their scene. The one where they had kissed and she had grabbed his hair. And afterward he had said he felt something real.

Lady Anna put her hand on the glass, peering into the darkness. It was cold to her touch, and she wondered again at the realness of the details of her dream. The warmth of the room, with its glowing fire in the grate and numerous candles, caused the window panes to fog around the edges.

"Lady Anna," Sir John whispered, near to her ear, "I hoped to speak to you alone. And I suppose this is as alone as we're likely to get."

He gave a backward glance at Miss Douglas sitting primly on the other side of the room.

Lady Anna turned to face him.

His expression was earnest.

"I know we aren't supposed to speak of these things," he continued, speaking quietly, "but I am aware that you refused Lord Mallory this morning."

He paused, as if unsure how to continue. He ran a nervous hand through his hair.

"You're probably wondering why I am still here, why I didn't leave with Mallory for Abingdon Abbey," he said. "I told Mallory I would stay on, as his friend, and plead his case for him."

Anna looked away with a sigh.

"The truth is," he continued, "while Mallory is my best friend, and while I should be pleading his case for him, knowing he will return in a few days for your final answer, I find that—that is to say—do you plan to accept him?"

She looked up. His usually jovial expression was serious as he gazed longingly into her eyes.

Lady Anna's eyes widened. Was she going to have a second proposal in the same day? And should she accept this one? Her mind replayed a set of sparkling, sapphire eyes, and the touch of lips on her hand.

"I'm not sure," she hesitated. "Do you think I should?"

"I could think of another alternative," he said, taking her hand and pressing it to his lips.

There was a clatter at the door. Sir John sighed and turned toward the sound, dropping her hand.

A maid entered carrying a heavily-laden tray. She seemed burdened under its weight, nearly dropping it onto a low table.

"Tea, my lady," she said contemptuously. Her wide-apart blue eyes held a barely-concealed, haughty expression.

"Miranda?" said Lady Anna. "I mean, Vogel. Thank you, Vogel. That will be all."

Miranda managed an impolite curtsy and shuffled languidly from the room, sighing audibly, her nose in the air.

Sir John turned back to Lady Anna with a look that told her he thought her servants were acting strangely. He seemed about to speak, but there was a knock at the door.

"Anna!" Perry's voice called from the other side of her bedroom door. "You're wanted in wardrobe!"

Anna's eyes focused on the rose-covered canopy again. It was afternoon in the twenty-first century.

"I've been texting you. Is your mobile off?" he asked as she opened the door.

"Sorry," she replied. "I guess I didn't hear it."

As they walked toward wardrobe, she amused herself by imagining Perry in Regency evening dress.

"Why are you smiling?" he asked.

Anna took in his dark blue skinny jeans and bright orange turtleneck and shook her head. This was definitely present day. No more stockinged legs and ball gowns.

"I just had a weird dream, that's all," she explained.

"Was I in it?" he asked.

"No," she said. "You're about the only person here who *wasn't* in it."

CHAPTER TWENTY-TWO

After a late dinner in the catering tent, Jake walked Anna back to her room. Miranda had not appeared again, but Anna had seen Perry ascending the stairs a few hours before with a plate of food. Presumably she was eating in her room.

Anna's afternoon scene had taken longer to film than anticipated, but there hadn't been any more practical jokes. If that's what they were.

"I wish we could spend more time together," Jake said, holding her in his arms at her bedroom door.

"I know," she answered, looking up into his warm, brown eyes. She remembered how he had looked at her in the dream earlier in the day, and it caused her to glance up and down the hall for Jaime lurking in some darkened corner.

"But," said Jake, pushing her hair behind her ear, "we both have lines to learn for tomorrow."

He kissed her, his lips lingering on hers.

"Goodnight," he sighed regretfully before retreating down the hall to his own room.

"Goodnight," she said, smiling to herself as she watched him go. At least *he* was a gentleman, she mused. Not like Peter.

Anna had barely glanced at her script when there was a knock at the door. She wasn't sure who to expect. Jake again? Or could it be William, wanting to talk about the anonymous practical joker? As she unlocked the door, she couldn't decide which one she hoped it would be.

But it was neither.

It was Corinne, wrapped in a silky black robe.

"I'm in love!" she announced, twirling into the room.

"You mentioned that," said Anna with a roll of her eyes.

"I was afraid I would be interrupting something," she said coyly, glancing around the room as if looking for someone.

"Like what?" Anna asked innocently.

Corinne made a pouty face.

"You and Jake, silly," she said, raising her eyebrows in a question. "Is he coming back later? Or maybe William is?" she added with a giggle.

"No," said Anna, annoyed. "Neither one. William is only a friend, and Jake and I both have lines to learn. Don't you?"

"Yes, but all work and no play makes Corinne a very grumpy girl," she said, plopping herself into a chair. "And we've been playing every night, lately. And sometimes in the day."

She giggled again.

Anna eyed her friend with concern.

"I thought—I mean, are you two getting along?" she asked.

"We're 'getting along' very well!" she answered with a sultry expression. "What do you mean by that?"

"Well," said Anna cautiously, "he sometimes seems kind of distant from you, when we're all together," she said. "And he stood you up the other day."

"Yeah," she admitted, "but he explained that. He fell asleep. You don't like him, do you?"

"I mean, I barely know him," Anna hedged. "You barely know him, either. Maybe you should slow down a little? Give yourself more time to see what he's like?"

"Barely know him!" Corinne snorted, irritated. "We've been together all day, every day, for almost two weeks!"

"Exactly!" said Anna. "Two weeks is not a very long time."

"Maybe. All I know is, some people don't know each other after two years, like me and my stupid ex-boyfriend, and for others, two weeks is more than enough time."

"It didn't work out so well for Marianne Dashwood," Anna pointed out.

"Who?"

"Nevermind. Don't you think you're jumping into things a little fast?"

"Are you calling me fast?" asked Corinne huffily, sitting up straight.

"Maybe," admitted Anna quietly.

Corinne stood.

"You're being so judgey!" she said, marching to the door. "You and your stuck up, Nashville rich-girl attitude!"

Anna stared at her, surprised. She had never told Corinne her background.

"Yeah, I know all about your fancy school, and your fancy parents," Corinne said, accusingly. "Peter told me."

She opened the door, then paused dramatically in the doorway, her eyes filled with tears.

"I deserve to be happy, too. Don't I? Why can't the poor relation be happy, too?"

Anna crossed the room to her, but Corinne slammed the door in her face. *The poor relation?*

Anna realized she'd been thinking of Corinne as her character, Lady Margaret. Beautiful and confident, without a care in the world. But maybe Corinne felt like Daphne Thomson, pushed into a corner, grabbing at anything just to survive.

"I'll give her time, and then apologize," Anna decided.

Corinne's comment about knowing someone jarred her a little. She had dated Derrick for about two years, and obviously, she hadn't really known him. If she had, maybe she would have guessed that he would go back to Idaho. Maybe she would have known they weren't right for each other.

She hadn't meant to be judgey. But what kind of person jumps in bed with a guy she barely knows? Especially a guy who gave every appearance of being someone who used women for his own gratification and nothing more. For all her claims, Anna knew Corinne couldn't really be in love with Peter. Could she? She didn't trust Peter herself, so she found it hard to believe anyone else could trust him.

But maybe she *should* trust him. Maybe he did care about Corinne. Maybe she was being too critical. He was only suspicious in her dreams, right?

After a shower and a few hours of memorizing, Anna climbed into bed. She tossed and turned, but sleep wouldn't come. And she really wanted it to. That afternoon's dream was the most interesting so far. Adrian Reed as the butler. Miranda as a pouty maid. Sir John almost proposing. Wasn't that what he was going to say? And Mr. Williams—

He was the biggest puzzle of all. Every time she met him in her dreams, he seemed on the verge of speaking, of saying something very important. Something Lady Anna needed to know. A missing piece.

After an hour of lying awake, her body almost fizzing with impatient anticipation, she made a decision.

She would go once again to the Tapestry Room.

Anna crept down the hall, thankful that the floors were thickly carpeted. It wouldn't do to awaken all of Hampstead Hall. Especially with a mysterious, anonymous practical joker roaming the house at night.

The door to the Tapestry Room was closed but unlocked. She eased it open, warily listening for sounds of movement in the house. She heard nothing but the faint ticking of a clock somewhere downstairs. The Tapestry Room was in darkness, but there were the remains of a fire in the grate, the coals barely smoldering.

"I wonder if the Earl has been here?" she thought to herself. Maybe we'll get to meet him tomorrow.

Closing the door softly behind her, Anna turned to the window. Her pulse quickened. The inexplicable call of that window caused a frisson of anticipation, but also fear. What was happening to her? Should she be concerned about her own sanity? Maybe she should confide in someone. Portia Valentine, perhaps?

She paused in the middle of the room. Despite her initial determination, she now found herself hesitant to touch the handle again, fearful that a vision would come, and yet yearning to see more. How does it work, anyway? Could she have more than one dream in a day?

She breathed in, steadying herself with that breath as if she were able to draw strength from the air of the room itself, and gently lowered herself onto the plush velvet of the window seat. The moon was full, shining intensely on the sharp outlines of the yew hedges. Everything was black and white, light shimmering off the evergreen leaves that plunged everything else into shadow. Anna closed her eyes, took a deep breath, and grabbed hold of the handle.

CHAPTER TWENTY-THREE

When she opened her eyes, she was no longer sitting on the plush velvet seat in the Tapestry Room, but on a cold, stone bench in the garden.

Lady Anna really must have been upset to come out here into the garden dressed like this, she thought, glancing down at her outfit.

She was wearing the same emerald-green, velvet gown from before, with thin, leather shoes that did little to warm her feet, and she had nothing but a thin shawl draped across her shoulders for warmth. She shivered.

The moonlight shone down like a spotlight as she gazed around her, suddenly aware of her vulnerability. A twig cracked nearby, and Anna gasped. Was someone with her in the garden? Was it Lord Mallory? He left today, didn't he? If this is the same day.

She stood up, straining her ears for movement in the dark, unsure if she should stay or run back into the safety of the house.

"I always seem to startle you," said a male voice from behind her.

Lady Anna nearly screamed, but was thankful it was only a stifled bleat when she saw it was Mr. Williams who had come up behind her in the dark. He was hatless, his dark curls blowing gently in the night wind. He was still in evening dress, but his cravat was no longer tied, as if he had violently wrenched it loose. She could see the twinkle in his eyes, even in the light of the moon, as he bowed slightly.

She giggled nervously as she bowed her head in reply. He did always seem to startle her, she realized.

I guess that's why my heart is racing like it is, she told herself as the two sat beside each other on the bench.

"Why are you out here, alone, in the middle of the night?" he asked her.

"Why are you?" she asked.

He chuckled softly.

"I asked you first, Lady Anna."

She released a long sigh, hoping to send the burdens of her mind off with it into the dark.

"I just needed some air," she replied, staring straight ahead at the sundial that loomed up like a misplaced chimney. "And to think."

He turned toward her. This agitated her more than she expected, and she drew herself to the farther end of the bench. He seemed to be studying her face, her expression, as if he could read what was there. What hadn't been said. Her eyes widened as she realized what he might be reading behind her silence. What might be hidden in her heart, even from herself.

"Lady Anna," he began, "I know we haven't known each other long, just a few months, but you have been all that is kind to me, even listening to me talk of my father's death. I hope you would regard me as a friend?"

"Of course," she said quietly, wondering where this was leading.

"Speaking as a friend, then," he continued, "I have something I feel I must say to you. I hope you will hear me, as a friend. And if not a friend, then at least a humble servant with nothing but your future happiness, and the happiness of Hampstead Hall, in mind."

Lady Anna nodded, encouraging him to go on.

"Expectations," he said, "can be a heavy weight. More, sometimes, than a person should be expected to bear."

His brow wrinkled and his expression was serious; Anna could feel an unnamed weight settle over him. He wiped his forehead with his hand, as if wiping away a memory. He pulled once more on the remains of his cravat, as if it were choking him.

"The expectations of others can sometimes cause us to do things against our own better judgement," he went on. "To do things only to please someone else. Especially those in authority over us. Or those we love. It can cause us to agree to things that would go against our future happiness."

Lady Anna's thoughts went immediately to her father. Was that who he was speaking of? Her father and his desire for her to marry Lord Mallory to keep Hampstead Hall within the family? The perfect arrangement. A most advantageous marriage.

Advantageous for whom? she thought rebelliously. Perfect? When the very thought of Lord Mallory made her inexplicably cringe?

She had lowered her eyes while those thoughts went through her mind. When she raised them, she found Mr. Williams looking at her with such genuine concern that she looked away quickly, afraid she would let loose the emotions she was feeling just under the surface. She felt trapped, she realized. Trapped like a bird in a cage. Fondly cared for, perhaps, but not free. Only there for the amusement of the owner.

She stood up. She had to get away from this man who made her think things she shouldn't. Who made her think at all.

"Mr. Williams, I appreciate your concern. You have given me a lot to think about."

She tried to return to the house, but Mr. Williams had stood as well, blocking her way.

"Lady Anna, I did not mean to overstep my bounds. But I could not watch you give in to circumstances that so obviously are against your wishes. Against your heart!"

"What do you know about my heart!" she blurted out angrily, her eyes filling with tears. "Now you have definitely overstepped your bounds."

"Have I, Anna?" he asked huskily. "Am I not reading the thoughts of your heart? Don't you want me to?"

Before she had time to consider his questions, Mr. Williams had pulled her close to him and leaned his head toward hers. His lips were soft and warm against hers, and her heart told her that he had read correctly.

Anna gasped with surprise, and as she did so, she let go of the window handle. She was suddenly back in the Tapestry Room.

"No!" she said aloud, grabbing the handle again. Nothing happened.

"Of course, right at the best part," she mumbled, turning from the window with disappointment and disgust.

"The best part of what?" asked a sleepy voice from the vicinity of the fireplace. A dark shape arose from a high-backed armchair.

"Mr. Williams!" Anna cried, exasperated. "Why do you always creep up on me?"

"Why do you keep calling me that?" asked William, stepping nearer, his face illuminated by diamond-shaped moonlight through the leaded glass.

He had fallen asleep in the Tapestry Room while staring absent-mindedly into the fire. He had been thinking of anonymous practical jokes and anonymous Earls, and wondering when the truth would come out. For both of them.

When the fire went out, it cast the tall wing-back chair into shadow, hiding him from Anna's view when she entered the room. A few moments before Anna called out, William had felt a stirring in his mind, a strange energy that filled the room and whispered things half-remembered into his subconscious.

He had awakened with a sense that he wasn't alone, and looking toward the window, had seen Anna in what seemed to him to be somewhat of a trance. She sat very still upon the window seat, her hand gripping the handle of the window and staring in a way that made William think she was looking inward instead of outward.

She must be sleepwalking, he thought, watching her as if spell-bound until she gasped and angrily turned around. She's so beautiful. Even when she's angry. And that's when he knew. He knew that it didn't matter if she wasn't nobility, that it didn't matter what his mother thought. He knew why the thought of her with Jake felt so wrong. And he knew he had to make it right.

"Why do you call me Mr. Williams?" he asked again, taking a step toward her.

Her expression was guilty.

"You wouldn't believe me if I told you," she said, covering her face with her hands.

He sat down beside her.

"Try me," he urged.

She looked up, hopeful, trying to read his intentions. Would he believe her? Would he think she was crazy?

"Why are you in here?" she asked, suddenly. "It's supposed to be off-limits."

"I see that didn't keep *you* from coming in," he teased.

She smiled.

Surely a fellow rebel can be trusted, she thought. Someone who takes her through secret passages and back doors through the kitchen. Surely he can understand something out of the ordinary, she reasoned, not bothering to check why that reasoning made sense to her.

She began at the beginning, from the vision out the Tapestry Room window when he had startled her the first time, to the dreams, to the kiss in the garden. He listened to her with shifting expressions of amusement, concern, and even dismay, but Anna never sensed that he disbelieved her.

"So, am I crazy?" she asked timidly, her story ended.

"No, not crazy," he said, thoughtfully. "But I don't know what you're experiencing. I know I've never felt it. I wonder why you seem so susceptible to these visions?"

He puzzled over all that Anna had told him. What he found fascinating was how some of what she called dreams was actual reality. Peter really was Lord Mallory, for instance.

"I wonder if what you're seeing is really the past or if it's your interpretation of it?" he suggested. "I mean, surely all of these present-day people weren't here together two hundred years ago! Not even their ancestors."

"I know," she agreed. "It doesn't really make sense."

"What if you're somehow getting a sense of the past, but you're casting your own characters? Like a play, or a movie. So Mr. Williams is me, Lord Mallory is Peter Mallory, stuff like that. And Jake."

His face stiffened when he said that name.

Anna pretended not to notice. She considered his explanation.

"Maybe," she said. "But why am I getting these visions at all? Do you think I really am a Somerville relative? Maybe the ghost of Lady Anna is trying to tell me something!"

"Maybe," agreed William. "But what I wouldn't do is worry about it. There doesn't seem to be any harm to them, other than a little stolen sleep. And maybe some good."

"What do you mean?" she asked.

"Well, I am very curious about that kiss," he said, shifting beside her. "Did you enjoy kissing me?"

Anna blushed painfully, hoping he wouldn't see it in the dark. The moonlight through the window was all that illuminated the room.

"I didn't kiss you," she insisted. "I kissed Mr. Williams. Or actually, Mr. Williams kissed me."

"One and the same, it would seem," he replied. "Mr. Williams. William Langley."

Anna was flustered.

"I—think I enjoyed it. It was interrupted when I let go of the handle."

He considered her profile, the line of her cheek in the moonlight, the curve of her neck as she bowed her head to avoid eye contact with him.

She's blushing, he knew, and smiled.

"Maybe your brain is creating what's already in your heart," he suggested.

"What do you mean?" she asked indignantly, turning to face him.

"I mean, maybe you want to kiss me, here, in real life, so you imagine situations in which you can kiss Mr. Williams."

"Oh, really?" she demanded, raising her voice. She sensed, even if she couldn't see, his eyes twinkling mischievously in the dark.

"Shh!" warned William. "Don't wake the house!"

"Why would I want to kiss you?" she whispered defiantly, balling her hands into fists.

"I don't know," he answered, leaning closer. "Don't you want to find out?"

He brushed his hand along her cheekbone and wrapped his fingers into the disheveled tresses of her auburn hair.

"No," she whispered, her eyes widening as he pulled her closer.

"No?" he asked, his lips near hers. He kissed her.

His lips were warm and soft, just like Mr. Williams' had been in the dream, Anna realized. Just like they should be, just like she knew they would be.

She reached up and touched his cheek with her hand.

Wait!

She pushed him back with a horrified expression.

"You can't kiss me!" she said.

"I just did."

"I am seeing Jake, and you know it!" she hissed.

"But is it real?" he asked. He felt emboldened by the fact that she had kissed him in her dreams. And not Jake.

Anna noticed a smile playing across his lips.

The lips that had oh-so-recently been on hers.

Stop!

"Of course it's real!" she insisted.

"Is it? Or is it just acting? You wouldn't be the first couple to confuse on-screen romance with the real thing."

"Oh, you—that's it. I thought I could trust you," she said, standing to her feet, fuming with murderous thoughts.

He grabbed her arm and stood as well.

"I'm sorry, Anna. I just—"

"Just what?" she demanded.

His eyes flicked from her rebelliously-raised eyebrow to the heaving of her chest as she tried to control her emotions.

"I thought you'd want to compare the real thing with the dream," he said.

"Well, now I have, thank you. So don't ever kiss me again!"

She marched out of the room, leaving the door open.

He watched her as she stomped down the hall in her fuzzy cat slippers.

Even her anger didn't dim his confidence. He sat back down on the window seat with a sigh.

"Red heads!" he said with a quiet chuckle.

Back in her room again, Anna still couldn't sleep. She turned on her side and punched the pillow.

It wasn't true. What she had with Jake was real.

Wasn't it?

And who is he to say anything? Who is he to kiss me and confuse me and make me doubt my own judgement?

She thought about Jake. She knew there were actors who did confuse the romance of the part they were playing with the real thing and were left with broken hearts and sometimes broken marriages and families. Surely she hadn't fallen into that trap? Two actors can fall in love for real.

She thought of kissing Jake for the first time, in the scene at the window. It had been exhilarating and passionate and…and…scripted. She was the one who had grabbed his hair. He said he felt something more. But did he? Or did he just say that because it seemed like the romantic thing to say? Was he just playing a part?

She pounded her pillow again and rolled over.

William can't be right, she thought angrily. I can tell the difference between real and acting.

Can't I?

Her mind replayed the kiss with Mr. Williams in the garden, then switched to William's kiss in the Tapestry Room. Both the same. Warm and sweet and wonderful. Dream and reality matched.

Stop!

That was playing into his plan. She was not going to compare Jake's kiss to the real thing.

"I mean, compare Jake's kiss to William's! Ugh!" she said out loud, realizing William had already gotten into her head.

CHAPTER TWENTY-FOUR

"I wish I could get inside her head," thought William with a sigh. Looking across the room at Anna, he could see the exhaustion that was beginning to become obvious, at least to him. Her tired eyes, the slight hollowness beneath them still showing despite carefully applied makeup. The way she started at every sound.

What did she really think of him? Did she think of him?

He felt sorry for her, knowing her dreams must be the primary source of her stress, although he hoped that maybe a sliver of it was caused by last night's kiss. He hoped she had begun to question the reality of her relationship with Jake. Reality over fantasy.

His mind replayed what she had told him the night before. What must it be like to be swept up into a story that's not your own? To see things in a dream-world that happened long ago? At least, he assumed they actually happened. And why did he? Why didn't he assume that it was just a dream? A world of make-believe from a very creative and over-worked mind. But there was something to the stories she was telling, something real and tangible, something that sparked a memory in his own mind that he couldn't quite put his finger on yet.

And then there was the portrait in the Gallery, hanging like an accusation among the Somerville relatives.

He glanced her way again as she sat unobtrusively behind the cameras in a chair in one of the darkened bedrooms. Their eyes met, and he tried to pour all his sympathy for her into his gaze, wanting to somehow strengthen her with a look.

Anna pulled her eyes away from William's.

"He feels sorry for me," she realized, feeling the color rising in her cheeks. Why?

He probably thinks I'm pathetic, following after an actor who doesn't really care about me.

"Yes, he does!" she inwardly corrected herself. She turned her head and caught the sweet smile of Jake as he stood near the door of the room, waiting for the scene to begin.

There, he does care about me, she reassured herself. I don't care what Sir Frederick's assistant thinks.

The scene being filmed was an attempted rape scene between Corinne's character and Peter's, or Lady Margaret and Lord Netherington. Only Corinne, Peter, and Jake were in it, but most of the cast and crew had squeezed themselves into various corners of the room or were crowded around the monitors to watch the dramatic scene unfold.

Anna could see Adrian Reed's vacant smile from his squished position in a corner. Miranda wasn't in the room; Perry said she hadn't left her own bedroom since the incident yesterday, despite the rescheduling. Which meant more rescheduling. Her agent had arrived and left again without incident, but Anna still wondered if Sir Frederick would have to recast the part. Which would be very inconvenient for everyone. All of the previous scenes would have to be reshot.

"Portia Valentine met with the agent first," Perry had told her. She must have talked them all down, Anna reasoned.

Portia Valentine sat primly near the fireplace in a chair someone had brought in for her.

She's the kind of person people bring chairs in for, thought Anna. Not because she's old, but because she's Portia Valentine. A benevolent queen. She watched as the older actress's quick eyes took in the scene. The whole scene, not just the one in front of the camera. Their eyes met, and Anna once again wondered if she should confide in someone. Someone other than Sir Frederick's assistant.

She sighed deeply and focused again on the set.

Corinne, wearing a voluminous nightdress, complete with lacy nightcap pinned to her blonde hair, sat propped up in the bed looking bored.

Their eyes met, and Corinne gave Anna a flicker of a smile.

Earlier in the day, Anna had apologized.

"I know you were just looking out for me," Corinne had said, almost as if she meant it.

Anna knew it would take a little work to get back to normal, but at least they weren't enemies. She glanced over at Corinne again. She was surprisingly calm.

At lunch, Anna had asked her how she felt about filming the scene.

"It's no big deal," she had told her with a nonchalant shrug of her shoulder.

"It's not like Peter's really gonna rape me. It's just a scene."

Anna's eyes strayed to where Peter stood leaning against the bedpost, arms folded across his chest. He was talking with Alan Potts, the script supervisor, a silent little man Anna had seen every day but never met. He was short and grizzled, in his early fifties, with sharp, black eyes that missed nothing. His job was to keep track of details: start and stop times for scenes, camera angles, what characters are wearing or holding in their hands. He controlled continuity from scene to scene so that the editor back in base camp could do his job piecing the various scenes together to form the completed episode. He was quiet, but very, very important, and revered by the crew in a weird, silent kind of way, like he was a voodoo priest lurking behind the scenes.

Anna had never seen Peter speak to Alan before. She watched them, vainly trying to read their lips.

Across the room, she noticed Jaime Douglas hiding in the shadows, also watching. Her silver eyes were fastened on Peter and Alan with an intensity Anna couldn't place. Was it anger? or fear? or something else entirely?

Because of the nature of the scene, there had not been much rehearsing. The scene had been blocked and Sir Frederick had discussed the general direction. Peter's character, a drunk Lord Netherington, angered by Lady Margaret's second and final snub of his proposal, was going to attempt to rape her, in the hopes that nineteenth-century morality would dictate a marriage to the man who had taken Lady Margaret's virginity. Jake's character, Lord Waverly, was to rush in at the last minute and save Lady Margaret from Lord Netherington. He would then challenge him to a duel to defend her honor.

Anna was thankful she was not playing Lady Margaret. She knew it would be a difficult scene to film, despite Corinne's confidence.

"And, action!" said Sir Frederick, his body rigid with intensity. He seemed as nervous as Corinne should be.

The scene began at the door, with Lord Netherington forcing his way into Lady Margaret's bedroom when she innocently opened to his knock.

Anna had a perfect view of the two actors. She shook her head as if to clear her mind when Peter, as Lord Netherington, pushed his way into the room. She sucked in her breath, then stifled herself, realizing the people around her had glanced her way. She didn't want to be thrown from the room by Sir Frederick for disturbing the action. But, dressed in his costume, Peter looked so much like Lord Mallory in her dreams, even partially undone as he was, with no coat or cravat, and his shirt unbuttoned slightly.

"Lord Netherington, what are you doing?" said a startled Lady Margaret, glancing toward the bell rope, her call for help to the servants.

Peter as Lord Netherington grabbed her arms and pinned them behind her back.

"You're hurting me!" cried Lady Margaret.

"I always get my way," sneered Lord Netherington through clenched teeth, leaning close to her face. "It's a privilege to marry me, and you will do it."

"I already told you, no," said Lady Margaret with defiance. "Twice, if I remember correctly."

"No one tells me no," Lord Netherington continued. "Certainly no woman."

He pushed her toward the bed. Lady Margaret began fighting him off, but he was too powerful.

As Anna watched Corinne's face, she saw a flicker of fear in her eyes that seemed real, not acting. The look in Peter's eyes was dark and sinister, with a determination Anna hadn't seen before. It was like a switch had been turned on in him. Or turned off.

Suddenly, the room itself began to flicker, in and out, darkness and light. Anna grabbed the sides of her chair, thinking she was about to faint, but it was no longer there. Instead, her hands grabbed handfuls of lacy sheets.

Peter's face was up against hers, his alcohol-laced breath acrid in her nostrils. She pushed against him, but the weight of his body was forcing her back against the bed. Looking into his eyes, she saw that same, dark, determined look, and she knew he was going to do what he came to do.

"But I'm not going to make it easy for him!" her brain screamed.

"If you won't marry me willingly, Lady Anna," said Lord Mallory, his lips at her ear, "then I'll take you by force. I think your father will gladly give you to me, then! Nobody else will want a de-flowered woman!"

She could feel his desperate hands groping with her nightclothes. She kicked at him, and pounded him with her fists, but nothing was stopping his single-minded onslaught.

Lady Anna desperately pushed his face back from hers with both her hands and screamed as loud as she could.

The door crashed open, and Sir John rushed into the room. He pulled

Lord Mallory's body off of hers.

"Mallory, what are you doing?" shouted Sir John, his face enraged.

Lord Mallory laughed, stumbling to stand, and looked haughtily at his friend.

"Taking her in whatever way I have to," he sneered.

Sir John pointed his finger at him.

"I demand satisfaction for this affront to Lady Anna's reputation!"

Lord Mallory shook his head in disbelief.

"You're challenging me to a duel?" he asked contemptuously.

"Name your second!" demanded Sir John.

"Anna!" Mr. Williams cried out from the doorway. Lady Anna saw a mixture of anger and concern in his face as he quickly took in the scene. He ran to her side.

Sir John, noticing his action, turned to her as well, grabbing her hand before Mr. Williams could.

"Are you all right?" asked Sir John.

She switched her glance from Mr. William's eyes to Sir John's, and something in them surprised her.

"Yes," she said, pulling her hand away. "He didn't hurt me."

"Who didn't hurt you?" asked Jake.

He was kneeling in front of her, and Anna realized she had just pulled her hand out of his grasp. William was hovering beside her, his face full of concern. Filming had stopped, and all eyes were on her instead.

"No one," she whispered, horrified by all the attention.

"Was it another dream?" asked William in a low voice.

"I need to get out of here," she said, rising to her feet.

"I think that would be best," grumbled Sir Frederick, exasperated at the interruption, his round glasses glinting. "Get some sleep or something. Just don't come back in here."

He rolled his eyes and grabbed the sides of his balding head with his hands.

"What next?" he asked Sarah, who shook her head sympathetically.

Anna could feel the annoyance of the crew. She avoided eye contact with everyone, especially Peter, even though he was safely across the room from her.

"What dream?" asked Jake, looking from Anna to William for an explanation as they left the room together.

A black back-drop had been placed outside the door to block the light in the hall while filming the scenes at the door.

"Back to one!" announced Sarah from inside the bedroom.

"I have to stay here at the door," Jake explained, stepping in front of the back-drop. "For my entrance. But I want to know what's going on, Anna. I want to know you're all right."

Anna nodded as she moved away from the door and down the hall.

"Later," she promised.

William followed her, and so did Portia Valentine, who slipped out the door before it was shut on the scene inside.

"Anna, what happened?" William asked, grabbing her arm as she tried to escape down the hall, away from the filming.

"Nothing. I don't want to talk about it."

"It was another dream, wasn't it?" he asked. "You know you can tell me."

"No!" she said angrily. "I especially can't tell you, after last night! I can't trust you!"

She pulled her arm out of his grasp and ran toward her own room.

"Let me talk to her," said Portia, giving William's arm a motherly pat.

Safely in her bedroom, Anna burst into tears. She wasn't sure if she was crying because she felt violated by her dream or because she had embarrassed herself in front of the cast and crew.

How would she explain it? She wasn't even sure she could explain it to herself. Would she lose her job for this? She knew Sir Frederick was angry with her for the interruption.

There was a low knock on the door.

"Go away!" she said, expecting it to be William.

"It's Portia, my dear," said a kindly voice.

Anna swiped at her tears and tentatively opened the door.

Portia Valentine stood there, looking sympathetic, and Mr. Barnaby stood just behind her carrying a tea tray.

"May I come in?" asked Portia.

Anna reluctantly opened the door wider. Mr. Barnaby set the tea tray on the table by the window, then slipped from the room without even glancing at her. No sympathy, but no reproach. Anna appreciated it, taking it as an act of kindness.

"A nice cup of tea can solve so many things, I always say," said the older woman, taking a seat at the table and fiddling with the tea things. "When my son, Edwin, gets stressed, even now, all grown up, I make him a pot of tea. It soothes the soul."

Anna joined her and allowed herself to be served. There were a few scones on a dish, with clotted cream and jam. Anna suddenly felt hungry, and was thankful for the buttery goodness.

"Now," Portia began after Anna had eaten and was on her second cup of tea. "It sounds like you need a friend to confide in."

Anna's tears began again. She told her story, starting at the beginning, when she first saw William in the window above the door, and ending with the attempted rape. She told her about the picture in the Gallery, and her theory that Lady Anna Somer was trying to communicate through her.

Portia frowned.

"An interesting theory. I don't know much about ghosts myself. What I do remember, vaguely, is that Lady Anna Somer was the last Somer to live in this house. She was an only child. After her father's death, the title changed to the next male heir, who had a different surname."

"Did she move away?" asked Anna.

"For some reason, I believe she died here, in this house."

Anna's breathing quickened. *Died?*

"Everyone dies at some point, Anna," Portia assured her. "It doesn't necessarily mean anything sinister."

"No, of course not," Anna said, pushing back the panic that had been rising in her mind. "Did she ever get married? Have a family?"

If she got married, perhaps she didn't die an untimely death, she reasoned with herself.

Maybe she wasn't—killed.

"I don't know for sure," answered Portia, "but I believe she married the person next in line to be Earl of Somerville."

"She couldn't have married Lord Mallory!" Anna declared with a burst of passion. "She just couldn't! I refuse!"

"You refuse?" asked Portia, her head to one side.

"I mean, she refused him," Anna corrected herself. "At least, in my dream, she did."

"And it would seem Lord Mallory wasn't willing to take no for an answer."

"Yes," agreed Anna with a shudder. "Isn't it odd that *Cavendish Manor* is so similar to my dreams? It makes everything so unreal, like I'm living in a movie or something."

"It is curious," Portia agreed. "It reminds me of a story dear Geoffrey told me once. The Eighth Earl of Somerville."

She looked thoughtful, as if reliving something from long ago.

"Ah, well," she said, shaking herself back into the present-day. "Perhaps, before long, we can ask the Ninth Earl. Your dreams do remind me of stories I was told as a girl. We had a Scottish housekeeper when I was growing up, and she would tell us the most amazing stories about *an da shealladh*."

"What's that?"

"Second sight. The ability to see what others don't. To see past what's obvious in the material world. The Scottish Highlanders are known for it, and it's said to pass down through the generations."

Anna gasped.

"Jaime Douglas is Scottish!" she exclaimed. "With her weird, silver eyes and faraway smile that isn't really a smile. Maybe she's doing this, causing these dreams! Like some kind of Scottish witch! Maybe she hates me."

Portia Valentine laughed. It bubbled up from the depths of her, like a benevolent tea kettle.

"My dear, aren't *you* Scottish?" she asked.

"Oh," said Anna, stunned. "I suppose I am. On my father's side."

Portia patted Anna's hand.

"Just something to think about. Normally, second sight refers to seeing the future. But still," she said with a shrug of her shoulder, "perhaps you're seeing something in the past that will show us something in the present, or warn us of the future. It will all work itself out, I believe. In the meantime, I think you should get some sleep."

Anna's brow furrowed at the thought.

"Sleep is what I don't seem able to have," she confessed. "Every time I sleep, lately, I dream. Sometimes the dreams come even when I'm not sleeping. Like today."

"But you must try, nevertheless," said Portia, comfortingly. "I have a feeling you won't have another dream tonight."

"I hope not," said Anna, glancing tentatively at the canopied bed as if it were an enemy.

CHAPTER TWENTY-FIVE

Anna awoke to the sounds of birds chirping merrily in the ivy outside her window. It was morning, and Portia Valentine had been right. No dreams. She sighed with relief when her newly-awakened brain remembered it was Sunday, their only official day off in more than two weeks.

Sir Frederick had informed those staying at the house that since catering would also have the day off, the Hampstead Hall staff would be attending to meals. Breakfast would be a buffet in the dining room. Anna wondered how many people would still be on the premises. She had heard several talking about taking an Uber into some of the surrounding villages for a change of scene. A few of those who lived in London, or its vicinity, had gone home the night before, including Adrian and Miranda.

As she descended the oak staircase, Anna's hand rubbed over the crown-shaped finial at the bottom. It immediately brought William to her mind.

I wonder if he will still be around today, she thought. She had never asked him where he lived. She had almost determined that she would ask him the next time she saw him, until she remembered she wasn't speaking to him.

He had texted her, as had Jake, the night before, but Anna had turned her phone to silent and had slept through it. She was thankful to have missed them. She didn't want to talk about the dream attack.

The attack had left her so mentally and physically drained that she had fallen asleep last night before she had time to think about what Portia Valentine had said about second sight. *An da shealladh.* Was it real? Could some people see what others couldn't? It had never happened to her before.

It all started here, she realized. In this house. In the Tapestry Room, to be exact. But why was it happening to her? Why was she experiencing what no one else was? Did it have anything to do with the picture in the Gallery?

She hadn't been in the Gallery since the tour.

"Maybe I'll make a little visit today," she thought.

But not before breakfast.

She had fallen asleep without dinner, and her stomach was less than happy with her. It complained in an aggressive and audible manner.

From the Great Hall, she couldn't see anyone in the Dining Room. She checked her phone. Just after nine. Maybe everyone is sleeping in. Or already gone. At any rate, she was glad to be alone with her thoughts and her increasingly loud stomach.

"Try the Eggs Benedict," said Jake as she entered the Dining Room. "Just what you need to tame the beast."

He was just standing up from his breakfast at the far end of the dining room table, unobservable from Anna's point of view until she was in the room. There were no other occupants. Anna noticed a neat row of heated dishes arranged on a sideboard, as well as urns of tea and coffee.

Jake gave her an exuberant smile, followed by a quick look of concern, as if he had just remembered her ordeal from the day before.

"You heard my stomach growling, I guess," said Anna. "How embarrassing."

He dismissed her noisy stomach.

"How are you this morning?" he asked, wrapping her in his arms, his brown eyes full of compassion. "I texted you, but you didn't answer. And you didn't come to dinner."

"Portia Valentine brought me tea and scones, and sent me to bed," she explained, wondering why she felt cautious. She forced herself not to stiffen in his embrace. Was it the look she had seen in his eyes when he took her hand after the attack? Or was the look in Sir John's eyes? It was so hard to tell the difference anymore. They blended into each other, like William had said. One and the same.

She shook her head slightly, as if to clear her disloyalty.

"Have you already eaten?" she asked, gently pulling away.

"Yes, afraid so," he replied. "We're going into Windsor, and we wanted to get an early start."

"We?" she asked.

"Oh, um, Peter and Jaime and I," he said, trying to appear nonchalant. He shifted his weight, running a hand through his hair.

"Would you like to come?" he asked. "We're not going to the castle today. We've all been. But it's a quaint little British village."

Anna felt a reluctance in his question, like he was merely being polite. It was odd behavior for a man who was supposed to be her boyfriend. She weighed her two curiosities against each other: to see what Jake was up to, or to stay and figure out what Scottish second sight had to do with the picture in the Gallery and her plague of dreams and visions.

"No," she answered. "I think I'll take it easy today."

He pulled her in again and kissed her. He smelled of balsam wood and cool winter streams.

"Well, get some rest. See you when we get back?"

She nodded.

He paused at the door.

"You still haven't told me what happened," he said. "Something about a dream?"

Anna waved him on.

"We'll talk when you get back," she said. "It was nothing."

After he left, it occurred to her that spending a day with Peter would have been more than she could have borne. Even if it wasn't really Peter who had attacked her. It was Lord Mallory. But still. One and the same.

Of course, that's ridiculous, she scolded herself. They're all starting to blend together. Like one story. Peter, Jake, William.

And Jaime. Scottish, witchy Jaime. Was there something to those silver eyes? Something she was seeing or doing that was causing these dreams and visions? And why does she seem to have it out for Peter? Maybe they used to date or something.

Nasty, she thought, cringing, but not impossible. It was odd, though, that she would agree to go to Windsor with him.

After an undisturbed breakfast, Anna wandered up the stairs to the Gallery. The door was closed, as it usually was. She wondered if it was to protect the Somerville ancestors from prying, un-aristocratic eyes. Like hers.

She defiantly pushed open the door, which made a soft creak in the silent stillness of the almost-vacant house. The room was dimly lit by two lamps on a long table against the wall.

William turned at her entrance.

He had been staring at the portrait of Lady Anna.

Who was she? He racked his memory for stories told to him by relatives or servants. He remembered that she was the last Somer. But there was something more. Something sinister. A shadow in the annals of the family history, tucked away in the vaults. Something hidden behind those hazel eyes. A story that had been buried with the last of the Somer ancestry.

When the door opened, the bright light from the windows in the hall beyond momentarily blinded him, giving him an impression of red hair and a pale face floating between two worlds, the material and the spirit realm. He blinked the thought away, and saw, to his relief, a real red-head standing in front of him. A real, not-very-happy-to-see-him woman, whose hazel eyes flashed fire at him beneath her beautiful, long lashes. And her lips—

"Sorry. I didn't mean to disturb you," said Anna curtly, turning back. "I'll come another time."

"No! Stay," he said quickly, moving forward.

She paused.

"I have a feeling we are here for the same reason," he added.

"And what is that?" she demanded coldly, her hands on her hips.

"To answer the question. Who is Lady Anna Somer? And why do you look just like her?"

"And what, if anything, does it have to do with my dreams?" Anna added, overlooking her animosity for the sake of intrigue.

William settled himself on a toile-covered bench across from the portrait. Anna stood nearby.

"What happened yesterday?" he asked, a note of true sympathy in his voice.

Anna sighed. He was doing it again, she realized. He sounded like he was actually interested, like he was legitimately concerned for her well-being. She thought of Jake's fleeting, almost indifferent questions, and realized that she did want to talk about it. To someone who was willing to listen. She welcomed the feeling of being taken care of, even if he was only an assistant who overstepped his bounds.

She reluctantly sat down beside him. Glancing into his face, she could read his genuine sympathy.

At least I don't have to question whether or not he's acting, she told herself, relieved.

"I was watching the scene," she explained, shivering despite herself, "and then suddenly, I was in it. Only it wasn't the scene. I mean, it wasn't acting. It was the characters from my dream again. Peter became Lord Mallory. I could smell the alcohol on his breath, and if Jake hadn't—I mean Sir John. If he hadn't come in, Lord Mallory would have raped me. I couldn't stop him, and believe me, I was trying."

Tears sprang to her eyes. William put a comforting arm around her.

"I'm sorry," he said. "I wish I knew why this was happening to you."

"Me, too," she said, wiping the tear that threatened at the rim of her lower lid.

"He challenged Lord Mallory to a duel, just like the scene for *Cavendish Manor,*" she continued. "And then he—Sir John, that is—took my hand. And you were there beside me, too. I mean, Mr. Williams."

She stopped speaking, remembering the scene. Sir John was concerned about appearances, she thought. That's why he challenged Lord Mallory to a duel.

"Sir John only became concerned about me when he saw that Mr. Williams had come in and was at my side," she said aloud. "He took my hand, and when I looked into his eyes…"

"Yes?" encouraged William.

"Nothing," said Anna. "It was nothing."

William pulled his arm back from her shoulders.

"What did you see, Anna?" he asked. "Were you afraid of him?"

"No!" she answered, irritated. "Nothing like that."

"Why aren't you with him this morning?" he asked. "I mean Jake, not Sir John. He told me at breakfast that he was going to Windsor. I assumed you were going as well."

Anna bit her lip.

"He invited me this morning, but I declined," she said.

"I believe he was taking Jaime with him," William continued, with a sly look out of the corner of his eye.

"Yes, he mentioned that," she said, staring straight ahead.

"Hmm," he said.

"What's that supposed to mean?" she demanded.

"Nothing," said William innocently. "I'm just surprised you would let your boyfriend go off with another woman."

"He's not my—I mean, she's not—there's nothing between them!" said Anna, flustered.

Why is he so irritating! she complained to herself. Why do I let him do this to me?

She rose abruptly and stood in front of the painting, distancing herself from him. As she calmed her thoughts, she gazed up into the face of Lady Anna. It was still an eerie feeling to look at the image of an unknown woman but feel like she was looking in a mirror. There was even the slight scattering of freckles across the nose, so like the ones that Anna covered every morning with makeup.

"I'm sorry, Anna," William apologized, rising to his feet.

He wondered if he should tell her about what he had seen in the garden when the cast first arrived. Jake and Jaime, looking very much like they were together. Maybe he had misread the situation, but it had certainly looked intimate at the time.

William stood just behind Anna, looking down at her flushed face and the line of her jaw. He couldn't tell her about Jake. Not right now. He didn't want to give her any more stress than she was already feeling. He longed to pull her in his arms and comfort her. To tell her it was all going to be okay. Somehow.

He ran his fingers gently down the sides of her arms, and Anna could feel the warmth of his breath in her ear, his lips nearly touching her earlobe. She closed her eyes, relaxing into his embrace, her back leaning gently against his chest. She felt his lips brush her hair just above her ear.

She jerked away from him.

"I told you!" she said angrily, pulling her sweater closer around her. "I'm with Jake!"

"*She's so irritating!*" thought William as she rushed from the room. Why do I let her do this to me?

CHAPTER TWENTY-SIX

Afraid that William would follow her to her bedroom, Anna slipped quickly into the room next door to the Gallery and closed the door noiselessly.

Entering the Library, with its dark panelling and heavy curtains pulled almost shut against the day, was like entering an ancient church; she instantly felt the necessity of silence.

But not everyone felt the same.

"Oh! Anna, my dear!" shouted Sir Frederick from a corner of the room. He was standing in front of a heavily-carved table, scattered with books and papers. She was relieved to detect the hint of a smile beneath his glasses.

"Sir Frederick, please forgive me—" she began, but he put up a protesting hand.

"No need, my dear," said the director kindly. "Ms. Valentine has told me all."

"She has?" squeaked Anna.

"Yes. That you've been having some bad dreams lately, and so you were overly tired yesterday. It's easy to fall asleep in a darkened room like that. I hope your nightmare wasn't too scary? You seem recovered now."

"Yes," Anna said, breathing a sigh of relief. Portia must not have told him *everything*. Just what would pacify the eccentric director. "Yes, I'm all better now. It won't happen again."

I hope.

"Good to hear," he muttered, returning to his pile of papers.

Anna curled up in a leather armchair near the fire. It crackled and popped in a conversational tone, blending with Sir Frederick's rustling papers. Her eyes examined the fireplace surround; it was made of dark wood and was elaborately carved. She was amazed to discover she couldn't see the outline of the secret door within it, even though she knew it was there. But with the comforting heat and a faint aroma of hickory, it wasn't long before Anna's eyes began to droop.

"It's just got to be here somewhere!" growled Sir Frederick suddenly.

Anna jerked awake.

I'd better not fall asleep in front of Sir Frederick again, she thought, thankful no dream had come.

"Is there anything I can help you with?" she asked.

"No," he answered, flipping through what seemed to be a leather-bound, handwritten journal. "I'm just looking for something. When I was here, years ago, visiting Geoffrey—that is, Lord Somerville—he showed me a journal, a diary of sorts. Someone had written down the story of the duel."

"The duel?" questioned Anna.

"The one that happened here, long ago. I wrote *Cavendish Manor* because of that story. I mean, it was so perfect. Romance. Intrigue. Murder. It couldn't be more perfect."

Romance was perfect, thought Anna. But intrigue? And murder? Not something she considered in as favorable a way as clearly Sir Frederick did, with the happy smile that was currently lighting up his face.

"Of course, I did adjust the story a bit," he continued. "Poetic license and all that. Anyway, I just wanted to have another glance at it. But I can't seem to find it anywhere. Ah well. Perhaps William knows where it is."

Anna stared at the door after Sir Frederick had bustled himself through it.

Why would William know where an old journal was in Hampstead Hall's Library? She had a vague memory of something he had said when they first met. Something about a murder happening in this house. He had also told her he was an expert in the history of Hampstead Hall. The son of a gambling, alcoholic farmer? Why would he know anything about this aristocratic estate? He puzzled her more everyday.

Then she realized Sir Frederick was probably going to fetch him, and she slipped from the room before they could return.

CHAPTER TWENTY-SEVEN

"My dear, William, you really must try again."

Portia Valentine was strolling through the garden, one graceful hand resting on William's arm. William was proving a difficult escort. Every few feet he whacked at an unsuspecting plant or flowerbed with the switch he had pulled off of a hazel bush.

"She doesn't want anything to do with me," he said, swatting at a clump of nearly-dead lavender. "She's with Jake."

"Oh, poo," said Portia. "As if that should stop you. She barely knows Jake. He's a closed book if ever I saw one. Secretive, I would say, despite all his smiles and laughs."

"Yes," agreed William, glancing admiringly at her out of the corner of his eye. Then his face clouded.

"She barely knows me, either," he said.

"I wouldn't say that," said Portia, patting his arm. "You have an open heart. Everything you do is in the light, not in the darkness. You've always been that way, even as a child. I remember you broke a vase once, when we were visiting, and your mother tried to blame it on the dog. But you confessed. You said you couldn't sleep until you had admitted it was you. My son, who is several years older than you, was appalled. He was afraid he would have to measure up to your truthfulness!"

William laughed.

"I remember. I couldn't let Wags get the blame. He was always in enough trouble."

He whacked at a nearby dahlia plant, decapitating three stems.

"I'm not in the light right now, though, am I? Pretending to be Sir Frederick's assistant. I told myself it was to make things easier with the cast and crew. But that's a lie. It was for her. I wanted us to be equals."

"How do you know you're not?" Portia asked. "And equal in what ways? We have royalty marrying commoners these days. Why should you feel some hereditary pressure?"

"I don't know. I don't, but I do. I want to steal her from Jake, and then I don't want to take another man's girl. I want to tell her who I am, but then I don't want her to look at me in the way I know she'll look at me."

"And how is that?"

"Like an imposter," he growled, whipping his hazel switch at an animal-shaped yew hedge.

"Don't decapitate the peacock, William!" scolded Portia, grabbing his arm.

The older actress saw Anna approaching them from another path.

"Perhaps you should have that conversation now," she suggested, nodding her head toward Anna.

William's face darkened. The memory of her rejection of him in the Gallery was still fresh in his mind.

"I have farm work to attend to," he grumbled, and stalked off in the opposite direction.

"Why was William whacking at that peacock bush?" asked Anna as she joined Portia. Her eyes strayed to where he had just disappeared beyond the garden wall.

"Oh, I think you know," she said.

Anna pouted as she fell into step beside Portia. She did know. But how manipulative of William to try to steal her from Jake! Or was it sweet? Was it really wrong for him to have feelings for her just because Jake made a move first? And how did she feel about him? She had allowed herself to relax against him in the Gallery. It had felt so natural, like coming home.

"No!" she said aloud, then blushed. "I mean, I understand why William is mad at me," she explained to her surprised companion. "But he knows I'm with Jake."

"I see," answered Portia, nodding. "You're very protective of that relationship."

"Shouldn't I be?" asked Anna. "When people are trying to tear it apart before it's really begun?"

"What about Jake Rawlings appeals to you?" asked Portia.

Anna frowned.

"Well, he's handsome," she admitted. "And talented. And we have so much in common."

"Like what, my dear?"

"Like similar backgrounds," she said. "People don't always understand what it's like when—when their lives are different from yours. Jake and I grew up the same way. We understand each other. And I've learned the hard way that having too many differences doesn't work."

Anna wished she had a hazel switch to swat at a nearby patch of purple coneflowers. She gave them a hateful stare instead.

"My dear, Anna," said Portia, patting her arm. "Things are not always what they seem. We have to learn how to see past what's on the surface to the motivation behind it. The *why* is often more important than the *what*."

"So I should question my motivation?" Anna asked. "*Why* I want a relationship with Jake?"

Her mind went immediately to her mother.

But she has nothing to do with this, Anna reminded herself.

"And coming from the same background isn't always necessary," said Portia, seating herself on a garden seat and adjusting the wool hat she had put on to ward off the chilly wind. "My own husband, Sir Thomas, is a peer. He had a whole career in the foreign office before he met me. I come from a middle-class family. I worked hard to get ahead in my career, even forsaking a family, for a time. But when the time was right, Sir Thomas saw me in a play at the National Theatre and insisted on meeting me backstage. And the rest is history. People speculated that it would never work. But we can't imagine life without each other!"

She smiled, looking off into the distance. Anna felt a twinge of jealousy. She wanted to feel that way about someone. But more than that, she wanted someone to feel that way about her.

Dinner that night was in the Dining Room for those staying on the property. Not everyone had returned yet, but those who had were gathered in the Drawing Room having cocktails, like traditional English country house guests. Mr. Barnaby had arranged it, and had even joined them, hovering around Portia Valentine like her personal footman.

"Just a reminder," said Sir Frederick, raising his glass to the assembled group. "No drunkenness. It's in the rules."

There was light laughter, and Peter rolled his eyes as he grabbed another glass off the tray of a passing waiter.

Although William usually took his meals with only Sheila the cook as his not-very-formal server, he had arranged for day-off dinners for the cast to be served by extra wait-staff dressed in white tuxedo shirts, black pants, and bowties. After all, these were his guests, even if they were paying ones. He had decided to eat with the cast. It was his home, after all. And this wasn't technically catering.

The cast and crew had not been asked to dress up for dinner, and there was a wide variety of fashion represented. Miranda, back from London, had taken on the role of traditional, country-house matron, and was dressed in a sequined cocktail dress with a flowing scarf around her neck that trailed over her shoulder. Adrian matched her in a coat and tie. Portia Valentine looked elegant in a simple dress and pearls.

Jim Anderson was still wearing the same jeans he had worn for the past two days; Tim Tremayne had at least changed into a clean, plaid shirt. Sarah was wearing jeans, as usual, but her face looked scrupulously clean and shiny, and she had brushed out her hair and wore it long. Jake, Jaime, and Peter had just returned from Windsor, and had not changed for dinner. Sir Frederick, despite his hereditary title, was wearing shorts, although he had temporarily dispensed with his fishing vest for the evening.

William had put a lot of thought into his evening clothes. As the host, known or unknown, he felt a certain responsibility to look the part. But, on the other hand, he didn't want to stick out as more than just Sir Frederick's assistant. He opted for a tweed blazer over a wool sweater, with a pair of tight-fitting black jeans. He caught Mr. Barnaby's eye across the room, and could feel that gentleman's disapprobation. The house manager was impeccably dressed in his traditional silver suit, and clearly felt that William was shirking his aristocratic responsibilities. His father, the Eighth Earl, had been rarely seen in anything less casual than what William was currently wearing, and certainly would have dressed with more aplomb for his guests.

But I'm not my father, William reminded himself, and sent that thought telepathically across the room to Mr. Barnaby, who ignored it.

Precisely at seven, the mahogany pocket doors were drawn back. People began to filter into the Dining Room, and since there were no seating arrangements, they crowded uncertainly around the massive dining table, looking at each other as if unsure where to sit.

William gave one more despondent look at the Drawing Room door that led to the Great Hall, hoping for Anna to come. He knew he would have to apologize. He had spent the afternoon supervising the baling of hay in the North field, and it had given him plenty of time to think. He was giving her unwanted attention. It really didn't matter how he felt about her relationship with Jake. If she wanted things that way, he shouldn't interfere. The one thing he wanted to keep was her friendship. He didn't think he could live without that.

She must not be coming, he thought, turning away to join the others. Just then, Anna appeared in the doorway, out of breath. Her sudden appearance nearly took his own breath away.

She also had dressed with particular care. Not because of William, she told herself. Or to show up Jaime to Jake. Of course not. That would be childish. But something about the house made her feel that wearing her jeans that night would be inappropriate. Somehow she knew that more was expected of her. She finally settled on a simple cotton skirt that ruffled at the knee and a soft turtleneck sweater. She had even taken the time to do her hair and makeup.

She tried not to notice how handsome William looked, standing there gaping at her. Or how his gaping at her made her heart flutter.

After William began breathing again, he reached for her hand.

"I'm sorry," he said, and she knew what he meant. She nodded and gave him the ghost of a smile.

It was enough. He squeezed her hand, then dropped it, remembering Jake was in the next room.

When they entered the Dining Room, William automatically went to his chair at the head of the table, then stopped himself, glancing toward Mr. Barnaby for help. Although the house manager would not be eating with them, he had not yet left the room. He made his mouth into a stern line.

"You may sit where you like," Mr. Barnaby said to the group. "No assigned seating. Sir Frederick, would you care to take the head of the table?"

"Certainly, certainly," said Sir Frederick, with a wink to William.

"Oops," whispered Peter to William with a smirk as everyone scrambled and rearranged themselves around the table. William glared at him.

"I'd like a word later, if you have the time," said Peter quietly.

William nodded, puzzled.

Jake managed to secure a seat next to Anna, and William seated himself across from her. Anna noticed that Corinne was sitting between Peter and Perry Prince. Perry was dressed in his fashionable best, as usual, and Corinne looked like a true Southern belle in a red and white polka-dot wrap-around dress and big, white hoop earrings.

Anna realized she hadn't seen Corinne all day. Or Perry, either, for that matter. She watched them surreptitiously, but they seemed almost to ignore each other. At one point, she noticed Corinne sending some sort of eye-signals to William, who shook his head. Corinne frowned.

"What's going on with those two?" Anna wondered. Not that it makes any difference to me, she reminded herself.

Instead, she focused on her surroundings. She still marveled at the Dining Room itself, although she had filmed several scenes in it, and eaten in it once or twice already. It was larger than her parents' dining room at home, which was quite an accomplishment, since her parents entertained large groups often, and had specifically expanded their dining room to accommodate three dining room tables. Hampstead Hall's dining table sat thirty people easily, with sideboards against the walls. Anna was sure at least one more table the same size could fit in the room, even with the extra furniture and the marble fireplace on one wall. A gigantic chandelier hung above them, each crystal teardrop sending sparks of light around the room. Anna guessed it to be from the eighteenth century, and was probably originally used with candles. It reflected the ornately-painted ceiling, with its octagon shapes and scrollwork.

When she pulled her attention away from the chandelier, her eyes met William's across the table. She wondered what he was thinking, but he blinked away the enigmatic look she had surprised in his eyes before she could understand its meaning.

"I love that she appreciates my house," William had been thinking. "Really appreciates it. The history and the legacy of it."

Then her eyes had met his, and he froze his thoughts. It wouldn't do to let her know how much she was still in his mind.

Conversation began with stories of everyone's day off, but eventually led back to work. Sir Frederick had dueling on his mind, and couldn't wait to work out the details of the upcoming scenes. A professional stunt coordinator was arriving the next day and would be teaching those involved in the scene.

"Oh, Sarah, I need to make sure we have seconds," said Sir Frederick to the assistant director. "You know, the 'friends of the duelers' and all that."

"We didn't cast any, yet," Sarah reminded him.

"I know. I was hoping to just grab a couple of likely candidates from the extras. What do you think?"

Sarah looked dubious.

"You know we have to follow the firearm guidelines," she reminded him. "We can't have just *anyone* involved in those scenes. We have to trust them. We don't want any accidents."

Sir Frederick was clearly irritated.

"You sound like you're channeling Julia," he said.

"Well," said Sarah, "you know my job is to be the voice of the producer on the set. And Julia is very concerned about safety."

"Yes, yes. Of course, we're all concerned about safety," agreed Sir Frederick, waving away his safety concerns with a flapping arm. "But these regulations are very limiting. And costly. Julia should care about that as well."

"We don't want another Jason Lee," said Adrian sternly from his end of the table.

"Terrible," agreed Miranda, with an appropriately concerned face. "Just awful. Accidentally shot on set, the poor boy. You can't let Sir Frederick put us in danger, Sarah!"

Anna wondered if Miranda's fears were real, or if she was playing the part of "motherly concern" for her fellow actors. Miranda wouldn't even be in the dueling scenes, so it wasn't self-preservation.

"Why don't we use one of us," suggested Peter with his sideways smile. "If it's 'friends of the duelers' you want, I choose Alan for mine. He's trustworthy."

Alan Potts looked up from his intense study of the food on his plate. It was clear by his expression that this was unexpected and unwelcome. He stared at Peter with a mix of caution and animosity.

Peter laughed.

"Come on, Alan, *my friend*," he said, "this is your chance to be on the other side of the camera. No speaking parts, no risk."

"But who will do my job during the scene?" asked Alan quietly.

"I'm sure they can find someone," said Peter. "You're not the only one who pays attention to details and has a good memory."

Anna felt the tension between the two men. Why did it feel like Peter was challenging Alan? She watched as the older man dropped his eyes back to his plate.

"Then you don't have to hire an extra to do it," said Peter to Sarah. "Problem solved. Surely Julia would be good with Alan in the dueling scene."

Sarah seemed unsure. She looked to Sir Frederick, who sat motionless, his brow furrowed.

"I choose William," added Jake, grinning at him across the table, joining in the joke.

At least, William hoped it was a joke.

"What?" he asked, nearly choking on his dinner. "No, that would be quite impossible."

"To redeem yourself for saying the name of the Scottish play," said Jake with a wink at Anna.

"I thought I already redeemed myself for that!" William retorted. "I really have to say no this time."

"Yes!" Sir Frederick exclaimed suddenly, nearly jumping out of his chair, but remembering at the last minute that he was at a dining room table and not in a catering tent.

"Yes! Perfect!" he continued. "Just the thing. Alan, you can second for Peter, and William for Jake."

"But, Sir Frederick—" William protested.

"William, my boy, you asked for this," said the director, smiling. "You can add 'acting' to your list of accomplishments. Sarah, make it happen. I'm sure Julia will be thrilled. Tell her in particular that William Langley will be involved."

"Yes, sir," said Sarah. She pulled her phone out of her pocket and typed a note.

"It will be fun, boys," Sir Frederick said to Alan and William, who both eyed him dubiously.

"Seems like just another example of cutting corners," mumbled Miranda to Adrian in a low voice intended to be heard.

He nodded.

Sir Frederick's face took on a purple hue.

"This is not cutting corners!" he exclaimed. "It's simplifying. And it's abiding by Julia's rules. I haven't been cutting corners for this show. Is that what you think? That these little incidents have been because I've cut corners?"

He stood up, throwing his napkin onto his chair in disgust.

"Cutting corners!" he repeated, glaring at Miranda. He marched from the room.

There was an awkward silence. Miranda pouted and tried to look innocent, and Adrian resumed his high-eyebrow, youthful look.

"I guess he's sensitive about it," he said smilingly to the group.

Sarah glowered at him across the table.

"You don't know what you're talking about," she said icily. "There have been no 'cut corners.' If you want to know why weird things have been happening, there's another explanation."

She shoved her chair back and left the room.

"All I'm saying is, maybe Julia needs to pay us a visit," continued Miranda, her eyes seeking camaraderie from the others at the table. "Maybe Sarah isn't a very good 'voice of the producer.'"

"Miranda! Really!" scolded Portia Valentine.

"It's just a suggestion," said Miranda, delicately shrugging her shoulders and continuing her dinner.

William cleared his throat in an authoritative manner, effectively quelling any other comments on the subject.

Anna looked up, surprised. It seemed so out-of-character for him. She assumed he was sticking up for his boss. She followed his gaze to Miranda and Adrian. This was the first she'd heard of that accusation. Sir Frederick cutting corners? She just couldn't imagine it. But then, Peter had said, when the car broke down, that maybe this whole project was hurting for money. She glanced across the table and found William's eyes on her.

Surely William knows. He's Sir Frederick's assistant. Wouldn't he tell her if things weren't going well?

Maybe not now, she thought, remembering that she ran away from him that morning.

William watched Anna's face, trying to read her mind.

I wish I could talk to her about all this, he thought as a shroud of responsibility settled down on him like a weight. He felt responsible for the success of *Cavendish Manor*. He wasn't sure why. Maybe it was because the success of the show seemed irrevocably linked to the success of Hampstead Hall. To *his* success. As a landholder. As a landlord.

As a man.

He swallowed hard and attempted to ignore the hollow feeling in his stomach. The dread that was creeping into his soul. This show *can't* fail. *He* couldn't fail. And if being a second in the dueling scene would help it, then that's what he would do, however unwillingly. He pulled his eyes back down to his plate, not wanting to show any of his thoughts to Anna. He was sure she would be able to read them.

Anna's own stomach began to knot. Before he dropped his eyes, Anna had seen something in William's face that hadn't consoled her.

He knows something, she thought.

Or fears something.

CHAPTER TWENTY-EIGHT

"Hey! Can we talk?" Jake looked wistfully into Anna's eyes as they were exiting the Dining Room. "We haven't seen each other all day."

Anna paused.

"Of course," she said, nodding.

Of course I should say "of course," she thought, realizing she had almost declined. What's wrong with me?

"We'll go out to the rose garden," he said. "It's a nice night. A bit chilly, maybe."

"Let me go upstairs and grab my coat," she said.

"I'll go with you and get mine," he agreed.

Anna had hoped to escape back to her room after dinner. She had a lot to think about, Jake being one of those things. It surprised her that she had hesitated about spending time with him. She wondered what it meant. Or if it meant anything at all.

As they passed the Tapestry Room door at the top of the stairs, Peter was just closing it. He looked suspicious, like he was up to something. Behind him, Anna caught a glimpse of William leaning on one hand against the mantelpiece, staring into the fire, his body rigid and tense. She wondered what they could possibly have to talk about. Peter had chosen Alan for his second, not William, so it wouldn't be about the scene.

"Why did you choose William for your second?" she asked Jake.

Jake grinned.

"No reason," he said with a shrug. "Peter was egging on Alan, so I joined in the joke. I half-expected Sir Frederick to shoot it down."

They grabbed their coats and headed back downstairs.

"Did you miss me today?" Jake asked, draping his arm over Anna's shoulder as he led her out into the rose garden.

She smiled and nodded.

Did she miss him? She should have.

"Did you get some rest while I was gone?" he asked.

"Yes," she said. "And I talked with Portia Valentine."

"Ah, yes. You did yesterday as well."

"She's a good listener," Anna explained.

"So am I," he said, looking at her tenderly. "What's going on, Anna?"

They sat on a bench under an archway covered with ancient, climbing roses, whose flowerless branches sprawled and tangled together over their heads.

She sighed. There were limitations with Jake. She saw sincerity in his eyes. She believed he truly cared about her and wanted to know about her odd outburst the day before. But there was something behind that. Something she had seen when he took her hand after the dream of Lord Mallory's attempted rape. Not so much something there, she realized as she looked at him in the moonlight, but something not there.

Something missing.

"I think I was just over-tired," she said, using the excuse Portia Valentine had given Sir Frederick. "I've been having some bad dreams the past few nights, and it all caught up with me."

"It was pretty scary," he said, wrapping his arm around her shoulder and pulling her close to him. "I was outside the door at first, you know, waiting for my cue. The scene sounded like it was going along fine, and then I could hear someone else yelling. I went in at my cue, and everyone was staring at you instead of at Corinne and Peter."

"I guess I put the scene into my dream, and I thought it was happening to me," Anna said.

Jake nodded.

"I wondered if that's what happened."

He kissed the side of her head.

"I'm glad you're all right now," he said. "I got something for you."

"You did?"

"Yes," he said, reaching into his pocket. He looked at her with a self-conscious expression as he pulled out a flat, square box.

"You may have wondered why I didn't ask you to go into Windsor with us," he said. "For one thing, I knew you needed the rest, but also, I wanted to get something for you."

He held it out to her.

Anna opened the box. Inside was a silver bracelet with a heart charm.

"Oh, Jake!" she cried. "It's beautiful!"

She held it up, and it sparkled in the light of the moon.

"Put it on," he suggested, helping her with the clasp.

Anna admired it on her wrist. She looked up into his face. His brown eyes melted into hers.

He wasn't up to something, Anna reasoned. He just wanted to surprise me.

"Do you like it?" Jake asked.

"Oh, yes."

He leaned in and kissed her.

Jake was a good kisser, she had to admit. His lips were cold from the night air, and there was a faint tang of mint on his breath.

Maybe whatever was missing in his eyes wasn't that important, anyway, Anna reasoned, kissing him back. Or maybe there was nothing missing. Maybe she just imagined that part.

There was a buzzing sound. They broke apart.

"Sorry," mumbled Jake, fumbling with his phone.

He glanced at the message on the screen. His face hardened slightly, then relaxed again.

He sighed deeply.

"I hate this, Anna," he apologized, brushing his thumb over her lips. "I've got this thing I'm working on. A business thing, and unfortunately, I've got to deal with it right now. I'm so sorry."

Anna shook her head.

"It's okay," she told him. "We can talk tomorrow."

He kissed her again.

"I'd like that," he said. "Maybe after the dueling demonstration. Are you coming to it?"

"I'm not sure," she said. "I'm not actually in that scene."

"You don't want to watch me get shot?" he asked with a grin. "It may not be a death scene, but I plan on making the most of it."

"I'll think about it," she said, laughing. "Jake!"

"Yes?" he turned back toward her.

"Thank you for the bracelet. I love it."

He smiled a million-dollar smile.

"You're welcome. See you tomorrow. At some point." He strode quickly out of the rose garden and back into the house.

Anna watched him, sorry to see him go. She sighed and shook her head, clearing all her silly fears that there was something going on between him and Jaime. Would he have given her a gift if he didn't care about her? Would he have kissed her like that? She sighed again, smiling to herself as she fiddled with the bracelet around her wrist.

She looked up into the clear, night sky. Stars were everywhere, scattered like sparkling fairy dust. The light of the moon, almost full, made the fountain in the center of the garden seem like it was bubbling up light itself. She watched, mesmerized, until a door opened and disturbed the magic.

Through the intertwining rose branches on the other side of the circular garden, Anna could just make out a man's form stomping over the terrace.

It was Peter.

He stormed across the grass and into the area of garden to Anna's right. She held her breath and backed herself into the shadow of the bench, hoping he wouldn't see her. He didn't seem aware of anything else except his own thoughts. A glimpse of his face as he crossed the path near her told her it was best to keep out of his way. After he passed out of sight, she quickly crossed the rose garden and slipped back into the Drawing Room.

On her way to her room, she paused on the stair landing between floors. The Tapestry Room was just ahead, at the top of the stairs. She knew Peter had left the room, but had William? As if in answer to her question, she caught a glimpse of him at the open door, right before he slammed it shut. He hadn't seen her.

I guess he doesn't want to be disturbed, either, she thought.

She caught movement above her on the third floor and, looking up, saw Perry looking down at her over the balustrade. He shook his head in answer to her questioning look.

"Big row," he whispered before heading down the hall to his room.

From her love of British television, Anna remembered that a "row" was an argument. She tiptoed up the rest of the stairs and past the Tapestry Room door, wondering what William and Peter had to fight about.

She hadn't been in her room long when she heard someone stomp up the stairs and down the hall. Then she heard loud knocking on the door next to hers.

"Corinne!" she heard Peter say. "Corinne, let me in. Why aren't you answering your mobile?"

Anna heard Corinne's muffled voice say something through her closed door.

"Come on, Corinne," Peter demanded, angrily. "I know you're not ill."

More muffled talking from Corinne. Peter swore loudly.

Anna jumped when she heard a loud slam. It was Peter banging his hand against Corinne's door, she guessed. Then she heard him stomp back down the hall to his own room.

All was quiet in the house again.

Anna shivered. That feeling of pressure, of the charge of a coming storm, was tangible again. As if nature itself were listening, lightning flashed outside her window, accompanied by a crack of thunder. Anna pulled her heavy draperies closed as rain began pelting against the glass.

CHAPTER TWENTY-NINE

"Come with me," begged Corinne a second time.

Anna let out an exasperated sigh.

"You're the one required to be there. Not me," she reasoned. "Besides, it rained last night. It will be muddy."

Anna was thankful that Corinne still wanted her around. This morning, she seemed especially friendly, like her old self.

Corinne, seated at Anna's dressing table, twirled a lock of hair around her finger.

"Wear your rain boots," she suggested. "Anyway, you're the history girl. I thought you'd be interested in hearing about dueling. Especially if it happened here, in your house."

Anna gave her friend a smirk.

"You know it's not my house," she said.

"Maybe," said Corinne coyly. "Besides, both Jake and William will be there."

Anna sighed. That was what she was worried about. Jake and William. Jake said he wanted her to be there, to watch him get shot. But she wasn't sure where she was with William. He had apologized for getting too close. Would watching him act in the scene with Jake be weird?

Things are beginning to overlap, she thought. In real life and in my dreams. She frowned, realizing she hadn't had a dream last night. That reminded her of something.

"I heard Peter banging on your door last night," she said, glancing at her friend.

Corinne gave a short laugh and picked up a brush at random.

"Did you? I was tired, so I told him I'd see him tomorrow."

"He didn't seem happy about it," Anna said. "But maybe he was already mad about something else."

Anna hoped Corinne could enlighten her about Peter's argument with William.

Corinne put down the brush again.

"I wouldn't know," she said. "So are you going, or not?"

Anna gave in. Truthfully, she *was* interested in hearing about the history of dueling. It was a subject that had always fascinated her. Why seemingly sane men would stoop to shooting at each other for the sake of their "honor" was something of a mystery. Brian Elliston, the stunt coordinator, had arrived that morning and would be doing a crash course on dueling for those in the upcoming scene. The actors and crew members directly involved were required to attend, but Anna had secretly hoped to listen in, even before Jake had invited her and Corinne had insisted on her attendance.

The field behind base camp was separated from the stableyard by a line of trees. A few days ago, she had overheard William refer to it as a hedgerow, which sounded familiar to Anna. She remembered reading about hedgerows in Jane Austen novels. She thought they had something to do with keeping cows and sheep where they belonged, although there were currently no animals in the fields of Hampstead Hall. There was a narrow path through the trees, and a gap in the fence where there used to be a stile once upon a time. It felt a little like going back in time.

When Anna and Corinne arrived in the field, a small crowd had already assembled. Sarah and Jim were there, speaking with a man Anna guessed was the stunt coordinator. Jaime was there in her role as props master, standing to one side like a shadow. Jake and Peter were leaning over the props table that held the box of dueling pistols from the Drawing Room.

Perry and Alan Potts were talking with Sir Frederick who, despite the chilly air, continued to wear his shorts and fishing vest. Perry, Anna noticed, had wisely donned a quilted jacket and a hat. She shook her head at his ability to out-fashion everyone around him. He smiled when they arrived, like he'd been waiting for them. He strolled over and stood beside them, waiting for the demonstration to begin. Corinne fiddled with her hair.

Glancing around, Anna noticed the absence of William.

He has to come to this, she reasoned. Now that he's a character in the scene. She rolled her eyes and sighed.

"What?" asked Corinne. "Why are you rolling your eyes? It's Sir Frederick's pink legs, isn't it?"

Anna giggled.

"Maybe he should wear knee-socks, like the actors," Perry commented, and Corinne playfully slapped his arm. Anna's mind played a vision of Sir Frederick as her father in her dreams, in complete Regency attire, stockinged legs and all.

Just then, a four-wheeler rumbled into view. Anna wasn't surprised to see William driving it; she had seen him doing so before. But she did wonder where he was coming from. And he was wearing that mud-stained jacket again. And those boots. She smiled, despite herself, as she watched him step down from the vehicle.

He looks so—manly, she thought, then blushed at her own thoughts.

Well-worn boots don't make a man, she reminded herself, glancing across the field at Jake's sparkling-clean running shoes.

"Ah! William!" said Sir Frederick, congenially. "Glad you could make it. You're just in time."

"Well, if it isn't the Lord Assistant," said Peter, eyeing William up and down.

William gave him a cold stare. Anna's eyes flicked between the two of them; she was still puzzled by the animosity between them. They hadn't seemed to get along from Day One, but this was one step further. Last night's conversation must have been intense; both had allowed it to carry over into the morning. The rain overnight hadn't washed any of the pressure away. Instead, there was a heaviness in the air, and the clouds moved low over the hills.

"Come stand next to us, William," said Corinne. William gave her a meaningful glance before coming to stand beside Anna. Corinne smiled smugly. Anna tried not to interpret the meaning behind the glance. One look at Peter told her he was trying to read it as well.

Sir Frederick made a gesture as if to bring everyone closer. Alan moved to join the rest of the group. He had his clipboard out and was taking notes.

"This is Brian Elliston, our stunt coordinator," Sir Frederick explained, indicating the man standing beside him. "Brian is an expert on the art of dueling, and I asked him to give us a little history and demonstration before tomorrow morning's shoot."

The stunt coordinator smiled graciously and cleared his throat. He was in his mid-forties, fit but not overly-muscular. And American, Anna realized once he started speaking.

"I'll start my history lesson with where you left off in the script," he began, smiling. "'I demand the satisfaction of a gentleman!' said by Jake's character to Peter's."

Peter cocked a challenging look at Jake, who laughed.

"What does that mean, exactly?" Brian Elliston continued. "The satisfaction of a gentleman? I think I would begin by saying that honor is measured in different ways in different places and time periods. In times past, a man's ability to fight, either in battle or as an individual, was a direct implication of his ability to lead well. The best fighters, the best warriors, were chosen as kings or chiefs. As time went on, fights between individuals became common, and a kind of code was developed to make it 'fair.' It started among the elite, with sword fighting. Sword fighting required training, and training cost money and time, so it was only able to be mastered by the aristocracy. It was a gentleman's fight, because only gentlemen could afford to be trained. When pistols came along, dueling became much more democratic. Anyone who owned a gun could learn to shoot at very little cost. But dueling was still considered a 'gentleman's' fight. Why do you think that was?"

He looked across the group after asking the question. There were uncomfortable shiftings.

"Because gentlemen are the only ones stupid enough to fall for it?" suggested Jim with a snort.

"You won't find a woman doing it," Sarah commented smugly.

The stunt coordinator gave them both a patient smile.

"No. *Not stupid enough* isn't the answer, and actually there have been a few cases of women fighting duels. But gentlemen were the ones who felt they had something to protect. And that something was called *honor*. Honor to a man in the 1800s was everything. And there were a lot of reasons a man might feel his honor was in jeopardy. Most of the time, it actually wasn't over a woman, although that definitely could be an incentive. But a man's honor could be at stake because he was accused of lying, or cheating in business, or two men could argue about politics and end up saying something personal that would lead to a duel. Nowadays we might say *saving face*, or saving our dignity, but to a gentleman in the seventeen and eighteen hundreds, preserving your honor—not looking like a coward, not running from a battle—was the equivalent of the ancient idea of the best warrior is king. If you lose your honor, you lose your manhood. It was unthinkable. And dueling became the way to fight those battles and preserve your reputation."

"So, you're dead, but you still have your honor?" asked an incredulous Corinne.

"Yes, but only one out of five duels ended in death. So your chances were pretty good at coming out alive."

"Were they just not good shots?" asked Perry.

"It partly had to do with the dueling pistols themselves," said Brian, "and it also had to do with the fact that shooting at your opponent was the goal, not killing him. In other words, as long as you came and fired a shot, you got honor credit; it wasn't as important as the death of your opponent. Now, you couldn't always predict that a duel wouldn't end in death, and yes, many times people were angry enough to kill each other. But the code of dueling attempted to prevent the kind of Wild West shootouts that you might be thinking of. These duels were usually scheduled weeks, or at least days, in advance, and there were rules in place to get people to reconcile ahead of time through what we call *seconds*."

Anna glanced in William's direction. His mouth had formed a straight line. She guessed he was still unhappy about his new role in the show. Her eyes then fell on Peter. His eyes were hard and glassy, but he wasn't looking at William, or even Alan. He was looking at Corinne.

"Seconds held a crucial role in a duel," continued Brian. "When a man chose a second, he was choosing a negotiator. All communication between the primary parties ended after a second was chosen. The person who was challenged chose the weapons and the location—usually a field somewhere outside of town—but it was the seconds who carried messages back and forth and made the arrangements. If the seconds couldn't get the two parties to agree to some kind of truce, then the duel would proceed.

"The principals, those who were about to fight, would go home and write their will, get their affairs in order. Just in case. Also, dueling was never legalized, so if you did happen to kill your opponent, you became a wanted man. Another risk."

"How is any of that worth it?" Corinne whispered to Anna. "Even if they were fighting over me. What if the guy I *didn't* want killed the guy I *did* want?"

Anna nodded in agreement.

"Now here's where things get really interesting, as far as we are all concerned," Brian continued, rubbing his hands together. "And I'll need a couple of volunteers. Why don't we have you," he said, pointing to William, "and you. Red hair. Peter, isn't it?"

William's face was inscrutable as he moved toward Brian Elliston. Peter swaggered over with his thumbs tucked into his belt loops, his head cocked to the side like a gunslinger approaching his noon meeting.

"One of the things I want to point out," said the stunt coordinator, "is the differences between actual dueling practices and what you may have seen on TV or in the movies. What is the first thing you think of when you think of a duel?" he asked, moving the two men so that their backs were up against each other.

"They both walk ten paces while someone counts," Jim volunteered. "I love Westerns," he said, nudging Sarah.

"Exactly," agreed the stunt coordinator. "So, gentlemen, please walk ten paces in the direction you're facing."

William and Peter began walking, using wide steps. Peter counted out loud as he walked.

"Nine, ten!" he said, turning around. William kept his back to Peter.

"No, no, Pete!" said Sir Frederick. "You have to wait for someone to say, 'Ready, aim, fire,' and then you turn around."

"Well, you're getting ahead of me," said Brian with a smile. "Why don't you both turn around for a moment."

William swiveled, keeping his eyes on Brian Elliston and not Peter.

"Who sees the problem with this scenario?" asked Brian to the crowd.

Perry raised his hand as if he were in a classroom.

"Yes?" asked Brian.

"If they both walk ten paces apart," said Perry, "then they end up being twenty paces apart. Ten in each direction."

"Precisely," agreed Brian. "In the movies, it seems more dramatic to have the principals walk away from each other. But in reality, it was the seconds who marked the distance for them, and ten paces was the usual distance. So, each one of you, please walk back five paces."

William's eyes met Peter's as they moved closer together. It was all he could do to keep a civil expression on his face. Did Brian Elliston sense the animosity between them? Is that why he chose them for this demonstration?

Peter's mouth curved upward on one side in what William considered a villainous sneer.

I should have punched him, William thought. When I had the chance.

"So this is the actual distance apart that most duels were fought," explained Brian.

"That's so close!" said Sarah, her eyes wide.

"How could they possibly miss?" commented Jake.

"No rifling," said Perry, shaking his head. "Of course. I should have remembered that."

"Yes. Dueling pistols have smooth barrels," said Brian. "Rifling is the groove pattern on the inside of a gun barrel. It spins the bullet, making the shot more accurate. Dueling pistols had no rifling."

"So they weren't as accurate. I get it," said Corinne, nodding.

"It was considered unsportsmanlike," said Brian. "That's how it was possible to miss, even at such close range. You still had to be an awfully good shot. Also, like I said, often times the opponents didn't really want to kill each other, so they aimed to wound. But they weren't allowed to miss on purpose. No shooting at trees or anything. That was considered cowardly."

Anna shivered. It all seemed so barbaric, even explained in terms like "code" and "gentlemen". She was thankful the practice had gone out of fashion. *Now we just use the internet to kill reputations*, she thought maliciously.

"Another difference between movies and real-life is the stance," Brian continued. "How many have seen dueling scenes in which the opponents stand facing one another, head-on?"

Most hands were raised.

"A proper dueling stance is sideways, to make yourself as little of a target as possible."

He arranged Peter and William into proper dueling stances. They stood sideways, right foot closest to the opponent, feet wide, head turned to the right, looking straight across the right shoulder at the person ten paces away.

William raised his right arm, his hand forming a gun aimed directly at Peter.

"This keeps the left side protected," explained Brian, adjusting Peter's arm to aim at William. "Protects the heart. Each man gets one shot, so usually they shot at the same time, though not always. In President Andrew Jackson's famous duel with Charles Dickinson, Jackson knew he wasn't as good of a shot as his opponent, so he took his chances and withheld his fire. Dickinson shot him in the chest. Jackson pressed the wound to stop the bleeding, and made his shot, while Dickinson had to stand still and take it. Jackson killed him."

"Did Jackson die, too?" asked Corinne, horrified.

"Almost forty years later. With the bullet still in his chest."

The group laughed, releasing the tension that had been building. William and Peter dropped their arms.

"This is excellent information," commented Sir Frederick, scribbling in a notebook he had scavenged from one of the pockets in his fishing vest. "Are they ready to shoot each other now?"

"Almost," said Brian, smiling. "The principals are in position. It's time for the seconds. The seconds have loaded the guns and each principal has chosen a weapon. Now comes the actual duel. Sir Frederick was correct about ready, aim, and fire. That would be said by the second who had been chosen to officiate. He would stand about here," he said, moving to the center between William and Peter, "and he would be holding a handkerchief as a signal."

Jaime grabbed a handkerchief off the props table and handed it to him.

"Thank you," he said, holding it over his head. "Now, gentlemen, turn your backs to each other again. When I say, 'Ready,' you turn around, but don't aim yet."

"Ready!" said Brian.

Both men turned.

"Aim!"

William and Peter took their dueling stances, their pistol hands aimed at each other. Anna held her breath. Peter's head was slightly tilted and his eyes squinted, as if he were looking down an actual gun barrel at William. William's jaw was clenched tightly. His eyes blazed across the short expanse. Anna gasped, recognizing the familiar violet flicker.

"Fire!" shouted Brian.

William's finger twitched as if he had pulled a trigger, and his hand jerked with a pretend recoil. His face hadn't moved a muscle and his eyes never flinched from his opponent.

Peter moved his head as if the bullet had whizzed past his ear. Anna thought she saw fear in his eyes for a moment. But then he let out a mocking laugh.

The audience clapped enthusiastically.

"Thank you, volunteers," said Brian, waving them back to the others. "I hope that helps give some context. Obviously, Sir Frederick may choose, for dramatic purposes, to do things a little differently."

"Yes," Sir Frederick agreed. "I believe we need to be at least fifteen paces apart. Ten is just too close together."

"As you wish," said Brian. "Now, I'll need the principals and seconds to stay with me and practice with the actual dueling pistols. We'll try shooting a few times with blanks, as well, so you can get a feel for what it will feel like and sound like tomorrow morning."

Jake, Peter, William, and Alan gathered around the stunt coordinator. Sir Frederick, Sarah, Jim, Jaime and various crew members grouped themselves to discuss camera angles and prop needs.

"So, if I remember correctly," said Brian, "we have Mr. Waverly shooting at—"

"*Lord* Waverly," corrected Jake with a grin.

"Yes, *Lord* Waverly. And you are shooting at—"

"Lord Netherington," said Peter, bowing with a flourish of his hand.

"And Lord Netherington over here will wound Lord Waverly," Brian clarified. "So, Jake—we're going to learn to fall."

Jake's face lit up with a grin.

"Not as much fun as a death scene," he said, "but I'll give it my everything."

"Just don't upstage me," Peter teased. He winked at Corinne, who pretended not to notice, and Peter's face darkened.

Anna eyed Corinne curiously. She had been acting strangely of late. The fact that she didn't let Peter in the night before was suggestive, especially since she didn't want to talk about it. She wondered if it had anything to do with the rape scene. Or were her amorous intentions shifting to William? Not that it matters.

"Corinne," called Sir Frederick. "Stick around. We're going to put you in that stand of trees over there. You'll need to rehearse running across the field when Jake gets shot."

"In the mud?" Corinne asked, wrinkling her nose.

"It's not that muddy," Sarah assured her. "Just a little wet."

Corinne sighed. She waved goodbye to Anna and joined the others in the group around Sir Frederick.

Anna watched the proceedings for a few minutes. Alan, as Peter's second, had been chosen to hold the box of pistols while each man chose his weapon. William, as Jake's second, had been chosen to drop the handkerchief during the duel. She could tell he was still unhappy about being forced into the role.

How did I let this happen? William grumbled silently to himself. How did I go from host to assistant to actor?

"William!" barked Sir Frederick, near at hand. "After you're through here,

I need you to go to wardrobe for your fitting."

"Wardrobe?" William asked, surprised. "For my fitting?"

"Of course," said Sir Frederick. "You don't suppose I'd let you be in my film dressed in your farm clothes, do you?"

William's eyes quickly shifted to where Anna was just turning away to go back toward the house. She paused, glancing back at him questioningly. Their eyes met.

I'm going to have to tell her, William realized, seeing the confusion on her face.

He found himself trying to answer her with a look, wishing she could understand his motives, that he wasn't a crazy, lying aristocrat.

His thoughts were interrupted by a horrible scream.

"Waverly!" Corinne shouted.

William turned to see Corinne running across the field toward them.

"No, no, no!" shouted Sir Frederick. "Don't run like a rugby player! Run like a lady! Like this!"

The director skipped toward Corinne, his arms extended like a ballerina.

"No. Way," said Corinne. They began to argue good-naturedly together.

William, grinning, turned back to where Anna had been standing, hoping to share the moment, but she was no longer there. He sighed, watching her as she made her way back to Hampstead Hall.

I'll tell her today, he decided.

CHAPTER THIRTY

Anna sat in her trailer in her Regency attire, waiting to be called for the short scene she had to film with Portia Valentine. Behind her, the dueling practice was continuing; every now and then, a shot rang out. She jumped every time, though she knew it was blanks.

Outside her window, she could hear voices through the thin trailer walls. She picked out Sir Frederick's voice, and he didn't sound happy. She moved closer to the window and peered down through the blinds. They were closed, but if she held her head just right, she could see through them without being seen.

It's not really eavesdropping, Anna reasoned. I mean, if they didn't want to be heard, they wouldn't have their conversation in front of my trailer. Plus, she had questions about *Cavendish Manor*. Were there any money problems? Was there more to Miranda's accusations than spite?

"What do you mean, the dailies are missing?" she heard Sir Frederick say.

Peering down through the blinds, she watched Sarah Stern biting her lip and glancing at Alan, whose only show of emotion was the redness of his face. Jim was standing stoically beside Sarah, as well as another man. The editor, Anna recognized, although she had rarely seen him. He wasn't staying on-site. His expression was also serious.

"George says he can't find them," said Sarah, indicating the editor, who nodded somberly. He had exited his usual home of the editing trailer at base camp, a rare occurrence. He was pale and anemic-looking, with thick glasses and even thicker hair that stood up on his head like one of those toy trolls. He was Irish, Anna guessed by his accent.

The dailies, Anna had learned quickly upon arrival in England, were the day's film footage. Everything that had been recorded was sent to the editor in daily files. Part of Alan's job, she knew, was to go over the dailies looking for any mistakes, looking for continuity.

"I know I sent the files," growled Jim.

"I know you did," whined the editor in his lilting voice. "I'm not saying you didn't! All I'm saying is, they're not there now!"

"But where did they go?" asked Sir Frederick, turning slightly purple.

"Were they misnamed?"

"I've looked through everything," said George. "They're just gone."

"Who was the last person to use them?" asked Sir Frederick.

George turned to Alan.

"Me, Sir Frederick," admitted Alan quietly. "I looked at them last night, verified everything was okay. They were there last night before I went to bed."

"These were Saturday's dailies," complained Sir Frederick. "Why did you wait until Sunday night to look them over?"

"You gave us the day off," Alan reminded him. "I went out to base camp last night after dinner."

"So sometime between last night and this morning, they just disappeared?" asked Sir Frederick, incredulous. "Just gone. Everything from Saturday. Gone. The whole rape scene."

The entire group seemed to simultaneously take a deep and grievous sigh. So did Anna inside her trailer.

The whole rape scene? Gone?

"Just what I need," grumbled Sir Frederick, holding the sides of his head. "More for Miranda to complain about. And more for Julia to question. Well, there's nothing to be done," he said, resignedly. "We'll have to shoot everything again. Sarah, make it happen. And George—keep looking!"

The group parted ways.

Anna's eyes widened. What would Corinne think of this? They would have to re-film the rape scene, and even though she hadn't said so, Anna could sense that Corinne had been weirded out by it in some way. She didn't envy her at all.

Putting on her winter coat over her gown, Anna stepped out of her honey-wagon. A text from Perry told her the scene she was waiting to film would be delayed, so after grabbing a cup of tea from catering, Anna headed out behind the tent to the field, where Peter and Jake were still shooting at each other.

The scenario had changed somewhat since the morning. Brian Elliston was still there, but instead of dueling practice, Peter and Jake were filming closeup shots. They had changed into wardrobe, and Anna couldn't help but think of them as little boys playing dress-up. They looked so excited to be handling the weapons.

Sarah was in charge of directing the scenes, and Alan was back in his role as script supervisor. She looked around for William, but he wasn't there. She guessed he was with Sir Frederick, setting up for the scene she would film with Portia Valentine. She checked her phone. Still no message from Perry saying she was needed.

"Okay, now we need one of Peter's hand pulling the trigger," Sarah said, looking up from the schedule. "Gun loaded?"

"Loaded and standing by," said Brian.

"We're ready," said Sarah with a nod.

Brian handed the loaded gun, barrel pointed down, to Peter, who moved into position. Anna noticed he was wearing safety glasses.

"Remember," warned Sarah. "Don't point that thing at *anyone*. Keep it aimed at the ground unless you're shooting it."

Peter rolled his eyes at her.

"I've shot a gun before," he complained.

"Aim at those trees in the distance," said Brian. "And don't forget there will be more recoil on this one."

Peter nodded. He squinted his eyes toward the distant trees, his brow furrowed with concentration.

"That's a lot of safety instructions for shooting blanks," Anna commented to Jake, who had come to stand by her side.

"Those aren't blanks," he told her.

"What?"

"They wanted some closeup shots of the pistols firing, and they wanted to use live ammunition. But don't worry," he assured her, "tomorrow's duel will definitely be blanks!"

"Stand by to fire!" shouted Sarah.

Anna and Jake went silent, watching. Jake indicated for Anna to close her ears.

"Standing by," said Brian.

"Standing by," said Peter.

"We need more bounce, Tim," said Jim to the LD, who adjusted a foam board he was holding just out of range of the camera. It was intended to bounce some of the harsh sunlight off the actor.

"Perfect," Jim said.

"Cameras rolling," Sarah said to Jim.

"Rolling," he said.

"Action."

Peter pulled the trigger. There was a flash of fire from the back end of the pistol; the sound of the shot reverberated like rolling thunder against the hills.

"Did we get it?" asked Sarah.

"Got it," said Jim.

"Whoo, that's some kinda kick!" Peter cried, obviously exhilarated. He and Jake laughed.

"Told you it would feel different," said Brian, grinning and taking the pistol from his hand.

"Okay, we need another one of Jake," said Sarah to Brian.

"Let me get it loaded," said Brian. "Jaime? I need another live round."

The props table looked like a booth in a gun show. The elaborately-carved pistol box was there, lying open, one pistol nestled into its bed of green baize. Next to it were boxes of bullets, some brass and some made of what Anna guessed to be cardboard. There was a metal box of what looked like lead marbles, and also a bottle labeled "gunpowder." Jamie assembled a few things on a tray for Brian, who picked up a cloth to wipe down the barrel.

Anna was fascinated. She moved closer to the table to watch the loading. Jaime gave her one of her enigmatic smiles, then moved away to speak to Jake. Anna subdued the twinge of jealousy that went through her as she watched the two of them laughing together. She wondered for a moment if they were laughing at her, but she shrugged it off.

Don't be silly, Anna, she told herself as she turned her attention back to Brian and the props table.

Brian smiled at her.

"Fun to watch, isn't it?" he asked.

"Yes," Anna agreed. "I've shot rifles before, but never pistols."

"Really?" he asked, surprised.

Anna shrugged.

"I *am* from Tennessee."

Brian laughed.

"Well, the modern pistol would be similar to the rifle," he said. "They both have rifling in the barrel for accuracy and speed. But like we talked about earlier, these dueling pistols don't have the rifling."

He pulled a long, metal rod from the bottom of the pistol barrel.

"This is used to make sure there is nothing obstructing the barrel," he explained, poking the barrel with the metal rod. "Once I know everything is clear, I put the blank cartridge in the barrel. Or in this case, I add gunpowder and lead balls."

"Directly into the barrel?" asked Anna, shocked. "I didn't realize that."

"Have to," he explained. "There's no chamber to open and close, like on a rifle. These guns are muzzleloading, meaning they are loaded from the barrel. They were intended to use gunpowder and lead balls. See, look here."

He opened a corner compartment in the original wooden box that held the pistols. It contained a vial of gunpowder. Another compartment contained lead balls to be used as bullets.

"We aren't using these. They're original. But the concept is the same," Brian explained. "This is a regular bullet, like you would use in a modern pistol," he said, picking up one of the brass cartridges from a box. "You have four parts: the cartridge, the projectile, the propellant, and the primer. The cartridge, of course, is the metal tube that holds everything, the gunpowder is the propellant, the projectile is the metal bullet—this pointy part at the top of the cartridge—and the primer is a small brass cap in the base of the cartridge that ignites on impact and expels the bullet."

Anna nodded. It was a refresher course for her, but she hated to interrupt. Brian seemed to enjoy teaching.

"In a blank cartridge, like this one," Brian continued, picking up a cartridge from another box, "you only have primer and a reduced amount of propellant, or gunpowder. No projectile. See? It's crimped at the top. No point."

"Oh, I see," Anna said, touching the crimped top of the brass blank. "There's nothing for the gunpowder to expel from the barrel."

"Only gas," agreed Brian. "And maybe some wadding. It can still be fatal, though, at close range, as everyone now knows. From the heat and fire of the gunpowder. Also, some blanks actually shoot wax projectiles, and at close range, they can do damage. Nothing to play around with."

Anna thought of the couple of cases she had heard of where actors had been accidentally killed by blanks. She shuddered.

"In our case," continued Brian, "I've made my own blanks, basically, using these paper cartridges." He held up one of the cardboard cartridges. "Jaime had a few different cartridges for me to try, both for live and blank ammunition, but I was concerned about ruining these fine antiques." Brian gave a final, loving rub to the pistol with his cleaning cloth. "Blank gunpowder is super-fine, so I sealed the cartridge with wax to keep it from spilling out. For blanks, we just won't be using the lead balls as projectiles. Right now, though, we're loading in the traditional way. Gunpowder, followed by lead ball, followed by cotton wadding to pack it tight."

Anna watched, mesmerized, as he loaded the pistol, carefully packing everything into the barrel with the metal rod.

"Then I add a percussion cap here, under the hammer. That's the primer that sparks the gunpowder."

"So that was the spark I saw when the gun went off," realized Anna. "The percussion cap."

"That's right," agreed Brian.

Anna noticed his pleased smile. He obviously loved his job.

"Is the history lesson over?" asked Sarah sarcastically, her hand on her hip.

"Come on, man, time's a wastin'," complained Jim. "Save your speeches for the Historical Society."

"All right, all right," said Brian. "Gun's loaded. Standing by."

Brian handed Jake the loaded pistol. Jake grinned and winked at Anna from behind his safety glasses as he moved away and into position to fire. Jim moved his camera closer in toward him and readied himself for the shot.

It was just after noon, and the sun was bright and hot, despite the temperature of the air. As Anna watched Jake aiming the pistol, she suddenly felt dizzy, and held on to the props table for support.

"Are you all right?"

"Yes," she said with a slight giggle, feeling silly. Then she gasped. The speaker was Jake, and he was right at her elbow. She glanced quickly at the field. It was empty. No Jake. No Peter. No Brian Elliston. And no props table or camera crew.

She stared at the Jake beside her. He was dressed in Regency attire, like a costume, she noticed, but his clothes were different. He was wearing the same brown coat, but his waistcoat wasn't the same as it had been a moment ago. Instead of paisley, it was striped, and green instead of multi-colored. Anna looked up into his worried eyes.

"Lady Anna?" he asked.

She swallowed hard. This must be a dream, she realized. It had been a while since she'd had one. She should have expected it. But out here, in the bright sunlight? She took a deep breath.

"Sir John?" she asked, just to be sure.

"Yes? Is everything all right?" he asked. "You look pale. Perhaps I shouldn't have brought you here, to the scene of tomorrow's duel."

"It all seems so unreal," she replied, hesitantly. She wasn't sure what to say. She noticed she was wearing a different dress, with a cloak around her shoulders and a bonnet that forced her to turn her head entirely toward Sir John when he spoke. Otherwise, the sides of the bonnet got in the way of her peripheral vision.

"Well, the reality is, it *will* be unreal," Sir John said, with a slight curve of his lips.

"What do you mean?"

He glanced around the empty field.

"Do you promise to keep my secret?" he asked.

She nodded.

"I don't intend to kill Lord Mallory tomorrow. How can I? No matter how angry I may be at his actions, he's still my best friend."

"So you've called off the duel?" she asked, surprised.

"Of course not," he said, indignantly. "That would be cowardly. And he should be publicly punished for his insult to your character. No, the duel will go on, as planned, but I've given my second specific instructions."

"Mr. Williams?"

"Yes. The seconds load the weapons, so I've instructed Mr. Williams, and Mr. Potts, not to put the lead into the pistol. Only the powder."

"Blanks!" said Lady Anna.

"Pardon?"

"Nothing. Please, go on."

"The gun will fire the same," Sir John resumed, "but there won't be a bullet. It will seem like we both missed. He'll go back to Abingdon Abbey, alive and well, and sorry for his actions against you, I hope. And I, also, will be alive and well."

He looked earnestly at Lady Anna, who dropped her eyes.

"And Lord Mallory will never know," she said, amazed at Sir John's plan.

"No. Nor will anyone else who happens to be watching. Only the seconds, and they don't want to see bloodshed tomorrow, either. Promise me you won't come to the field!" he said suddenly, as if just realizing the possibility.

"But—"

"Promise me. It's no place for a lady. And there's no reason to stop us. There's no danger."

"Is that why you told me?" she asked.

He smiled indulgently as he swept his hand through his hair.

"Nothing escapes you, my dear one," he said, then laughed self-consciously, realizing what he had said.

"I promise I'll stay away," Lady Anna said, blushing up at him.

"Are you all right?"

Anna snapped her head toward the speaker.

William had suddenly appeared by her side, and there was no bonnet to prevent a perfect view of him.

Anna glanced again at the field. Jake was preparing to fire, with Brian giving him a few final instructions.

"Anna?" asked William again, stepping closer.

"Yes!" she said quickly, steadying herself, her hand on the props table. "I'm fine. I was—"

"You were what?" he asked, concerned.

"Nothing. I'm fine. Just a little dizzy. It passed."

Anna took a deep breath. She hadn't lied. Jumping from the past to the present was definitely dizzying.

So the past Jake is also using blanks, she thought to herself. Is he who Lady Anna marries? Not Lord Mallory?

"Stand by to fire," said Sarah. William and Anna put their fingers in their ears.

"Standing by," said Brian, stepping out of the camera-range.

"Standing by," said Jake, aiming his weapon.

"Camera rolling," said Sarah.

"Rolling," said Jim.

"And, action," Sarah said.

Jake's shot rang out, just like Peter's, and echoed against the hills.

"Good thing we let the police know we were doing this," said William, "or I'd have the local constabulary down on me."

"Why on you?" asked Anna.

William froze.

"Was it your job to call them for Sir Frederick?" she asked.

"Um…"

"We're going to have to do that one again," said Alan.

"What do you mean?" asked Sarah, turning to Alan.

So did everyone else.

William breathed a sigh of relief. He was glad for the interruption. Now was not the time to explain who he was, but slip-ups like that were becoming too frequent. He had to tell her.

Alan cleared his throat, clearly uncomfortable being the center of attention.

"It's the wrong angle. It should be here, not here," he explained, pointing out the inconsistency.

Jim nodded his head.

"Easy fix," he said. "Should have caught that myself. Thanks, Alan. Good eye."

Brian took the pistol back from Jake.

"Reloading time," he said as he returned to the props table. Jaime joined him.

Anna looked back at Alan. She was remembering the conversation she had overheard outside her trailer. Alan was the last person to see Saturday's dailies. And now they were gone. Was this cyber-sabotage? Was this an escalation of the practical jokes, or something unrelated? Just a coincidence? Could it be put down as a technology glitch?

"I came to tell you that they're almost ready for you," said William to Anna.

"Oh. Thank you," she said. Her thoughts had been so focused on Alan and the dailies, she had forgotten he was there. "I guess I better get going."

"William!" Sarah barked. "You better get into costume. We need some footage of you and Alan as the seconds."

William groaned.

Anna snickered. She smiled up into his eyes before she turned to make her way to the house.

William's heart leaped. Did that smile mean something? Was it more than just amusement at his ridiculous predicament?

Jake laughed from across the field. William watched him as he threw his head back and swept his hand through his hair, clearly amused at something Peter was saying. He looked so confident and bold and perfect.

William shook his head at himself and moved off toward the wardrobe trailer.

How can I compete with that? he thought miserably.

CHAPTER THIRTY-ONE

"What is your relationship to Lord Netherington?"

"I don't know what you mean, Lady Cassandra."

Anna, as Daphne Thomson, sat primly across the tea table from Portia Valentine as the Dowager Countess.

"I believe you know exactly what I mean," said Lady Cassandra, her mouth pruned up, her eyes cold and haughty.

"I only know Lord Netherington as Lady Margaret's suitor," explained Miss Thomson, her eyes wide and innocent. "Beyond that—"

"Beyond that, I have seen you having whispered arguments together in the hall," snapped Lady Cassandra. "I believe you knew each other before you arrived here at Cavendish Manor."

Miss Thomson pouted prettily.

"Are you suggesting there's something romantic between us?" she asked.

Lady Cassandra's look asked the question.

Miss Thomson put down her cup and saucer primly, as if offended.

"I'm surprised you would even suggest such a thing," she said with pained dignity. "What would Lord Netherington have to gain? I have no dowry."

"You have other things a man may want, and accept without marriage," Lady Cassandra said saucily.

"Lady Cassandra!" said Miss Thomson, with feigned astonishment.

"Stay away from Lord Netherington, Miss Thomson," Lady Cassandra warned. "I'll not have you luring him away from Lady Margaret."

Miss Thomson's face darkened.

"You can rest assured, I have no intention of luring him anywhere," she said with quiet resolve. "If Lord Netherington is who Lady Margaret wants, she is welcome to him."

"Of course he's who she wants," snapped Lady Cassandra.

"I wouldn't be too sure," said Miss Thomson, rising and leaving the room.

"You're a feisty one," said Portia Valentine to Anna after the filming was over.

Anna grinned.

"So are you!"

They laughed.

"I'm going to catering. Care to join me?" asked Anna.

"Thank you, my dear," said Portia, "but I think I'll go up to my room. Even with the heaters they've added, it's a bit cold in the tent. Besides, I'm supposed to call my husband this afternoon."

When Anna entered the catering tent, she saw Sarah seated at a table with Corinne, Peter, and Jake. She guessed by their expressions that they were hearing the bad news about the dailies. Corinne's face was ashen, and she kept blinking her eyes, as if she was blinking back tears.

Jake saw Anna and beckoned her over.

"Did you hear?" he asked. "We have to reshoot the rape scene!"

"That's terrible," she said, giving Corinne a sympathetic look.

Peter shrugged his shoulders.

"I guess that happens sometimes," he said, leaning back in his chair and scratching his chest. "Part of the Scottish curse, maybe."

"No, it doesn't just happen," snapped Sarah, standing up to leave. "Curse or not, this kind of thing, and all the other 'jokes', they don't just happen. *Someone* has to do it on purpose."

She glared at Peter, who returned her look with a challenging one of his own. Sarah stomped away.

"Guess she's taking it personally," Jake said, looking at his friend.

Peter brushed it off with a laugh. He leaned forward, wrapping his arm around Corinne's shoulders, and leaning into her ear.

"Maybe we can practice our scene later on," he said in a gravelly voice, giving her a sloppy kiss on the cheek.

Corinne stiffened and pulled away. Anna tried to keep herself from cringing.

"What?" Peter asked, offended. His nostrils flared and his face reddened under his freckles. He tried to pull her close again, edging his chair up next to hers.

"Peter, don't!" Corinne said, standing up and brushing his arms away.

"Miss Newberry?"

Perry had just entered the tent and was paused in the doorway.

"Do you need any assistance?" he asked, looking only at her. There was an awkward silence for a few seconds.

"No, thank you, Perry. I'm fine," Corinne finally answered. "And I told you to call me Corinne."

Anna noticed her face had softened, and her eyes were glowing.

Perry nodded curtly and continued on his way to get food. Peter stood angrily, glaring intently at Perry, whose back was turned. He shoved a chair out of his way as he left the tent; the production assistant didn't seem to notice. Jake stood up and followed his friend.

"I'm going to my trailer," said Corinne before Anna could speak. Perry's eyes strayed after her, a look of concern creasing his usually smooth face.

"Please, join me," said Portia to William as he pushed open the door of the Tapestry Room. "I decided to take tea in here. It's gotten a bit chilly for the terrace, or the catering tent. And Mr. Barnaby is always so accommodating."

William gave her a smile which quickly vanished as his mind continued its reverie. He had hoped to have the Tapestry Room to himself. He had a lot on his mind. Instead of taking the seat she offered him, he went to the window and stared out over the garden, his hands in his pockets. Winter was creeping in like an unwanted guest. The sky was slate grey; another impending storm threatened from across the fields. The leafless branches of the hardwood trees on the hills looked like ghosts, ethereal and otherworldly against the cold reality of the dark evergreens.

That's what this feels like, he realized. Like ghosts of my past flitting in and out. Here but not here. And Anna. In and out. Here and not here. He released a restless sigh.

Portia gave him a motherly glance as she poured him a cup of tea.

"I see that Sir Frederick has brought in a dueling expert," she said lightly. "Sugar?"

"Yes, whatever," William said with a distracted wave of his hand. He had changed back into his normal clothes, but the reminder of how he had spent the morning and part of the afternoon chafed him.

"What's his name?" she asked, adding sugar to his tea.

"Whose name?"

"The stunt coordinator."

"Oh. Um," he irritatedly gathered his thoughts. "Brian Elliston. I've put him in the bedroom next to yours."

"Yes, I noticed," she said. "Milk?"

He didn't answer. He stared unseeingly at the sun dial in the garden.

"I think I'll go to the set tomorrow morning," she prattled on, adding milk. "I've never seen a duel before. That must seem surprising to you, considering my age. You probably expect that dozens of men fought over me when I was young."

William turned, focusing his attention on his companion, his blue eyes twinkling. He gave her a half-smile.

"Dueling ended well before you were born, Ms. Valentine," he reminded her.

Her blue eyes twinkled back merrily.

"I'm glad to see you're paying attention to what I'm saying," she said, crossing to him and handing him his cup.

"I apologize," he said, reaching for it. "My mind is elsewhere today."

Portia nodded.

"I hear Saturday's dailies have magically disappeared. Do you think it has anything to do with the other practical jokes?"

"I'm not sure," said William thoughtfully. "And I don't know that I'd call them jokes. Miranda and Adrian are under the impression the whole show is going under before it's even begun."

"Yes," Portia agreed, eyeing him curiously. "It does seem like sabotage."

She seated herself on the red velvet cushion of the window seat. William sat down as well. He absent-mindedly brushed his fingers against the curled ironwork of the window handle. It felt cold to his touch, but nothing hummed or changed as Anna had described.

Movement caught his eye. A lone figure in a navy-blue peacoat wandered into the garden, her red hair showing brightly above the soft knitted scarf she wore around her neck. He watched her threading her way along the path, past the topiary peacock he had nearly killed yesterday, and into the rose-covered arbor. There were no roses now, only brown branches, twisted and gnarled together.

Like spaghetti cables, William thought.

She was walking slowly, her hands shoved into her pockets, like there was a lot on her mind. He watched her disappear from his line of vision.

He turned back to Portia and shifted impatiently. She turned her head from the direction he had been looking and smiled at him, a slow, knowing smile.

"Well," she said, rising with a graceful movement and stifling a yawn, "I

think I'll just go to my room for a little nap. Little old ladies need their rest."
She moved toward the door. Turning back, she caught his wistful eyes straying
out the window to the rose arbor.

"Perhaps you should take a walk," she suggested, the hint of a smile on
her lips. "Exercise on a brisk November evening is very bracing for the soul."

William stood suddenly without taking his eyes off the arbor, nearly dropping his cup and saucer.

"Yes," he agreed, setting it down on the tea tray. "I believe I will."

William strode off down the garden path and into the arbor, finding it difficult
to keep himself from breaking into a run. It was nearly sunset, though it was
barely four o'clock. It would be dark soon, and the rain still threatened in the
distance. The air was full of the scent of it, and also the pungent odor, almost
like cinnamon, of the decaying leaves he was crushing beneath his feet.

He came to the end of the rose arbor but didn't see Anna anywhere. Just
ahead was the Japanese bridge crossing the moat, and beyond it, he knew, was
the ornamental lake, hidden from his view by tall yew hedges.

She must have gone that way, he thought, and then slowed his pace as if
to convince himself that he was merely out in the garden to get a breath of air
before dinner. Brisk exercise, like Portia Valentine suggested. It certainly wasn't
because he wanted to see her again. To be alone with her again.

But maybe this was his best chance to explain himself. It was inevitable; he
had to tell her his real identity. Maybe she had already guessed?

As he walked, he reminded himself that he could make no romantic moves.
She had made it clear she didn't want anything to do with him beyond friendship. She was seeing Jake. He had apologized for his actions in the Gallery,
and she had graciously accepted. His next move needed to be brotherly. Non-
threatening. Completely unromantic.

As he passed through an arch of yew, he saw her at the bottom of an
incline of terraced garden. The canopy of trees shadowed rocky steps that led
to a stone-flagged terrace overlooking the lake. Anna stood still and remote,
staring out at the lake, her gloved hands resting lightly on the stone balustrade
while her auburn hair blew gently around her face. William watched her tuck a
wayward strand behind her ear. The storm was edging closer, and the wind was
picking up. Matted leaves slid clumsily over the terrace stones.

William's feet thudded on the rocky path as he descended toward her; he desperately hoped she wouldn't run away at his approach.

Anna turned sharply when she heard his footsteps. Her cheeks, already pink from the chill of the air, deepened with a slow blush. She had been thinking of him as she stared out at the lake, of his lips against hers, of the gentle caress of his hand across her cheek. She had a ridiculous feeling that she had somehow summoned him.

William paused as she turned; their eyes held and locked. Something in her expression told him his presence wasn't unexpected.

Was she waiting for me? he wondered to himself, daring to hope. He continued slowly down the steps toward her as she watched him in silence.

She took a steadying breath as he drew near, her lips parting slightly, and she watched his gaze dip to her mouth before raising again to her eyes.

All his unromantic intentions were forgotten as he cupped her face in both his hands and kissed her, slowly and passionately, while she unconsciously crumpled his sweater in her fists. Their kiss deepened, and Anna sagged against him while William's hands moved from her face to her back, pressing her body against his. A sudden gust of wind swept across the lake and blew Anna's hair over her head and across both their faces.

The cold air brought Anna to her senses again. She pushed back gently, taking in a deep breath, her eyes wide as she looked up into his.

"I told you not to kiss me again!" she half-whispered when she caught her breath, her hands nervously smoothing the wrinkles she had inflicted on his sweater.

"Then why did you let me?" he asked, his voice soft and low. His arms were still around her.

"I didn't! I—" then she stopped herself as it dawned on her that she had. And what's more, she knew with a sudden and perfect clarity that she would let him again. And again.

The realization caused her to clap her hand over her mouth and break free from his embrace. She ran away up the stone steps and into the garden.

"Anna!" William called after her, but she had already disappeared into the yew hedge.

CHAPTER THIRTY-TWO

William ate dinner by himself in his bedroom. He scowled at his wine. He ripped his bread with his teeth.

Women! he growled to himself between bites.

Outside, the rain pelted the house; the wind whistled through the chimney like a ghost story, causing the fire in the grate to flare and spit with an angry light.

Anna stood at the window in the alcove above the front door, staring out into the gloom. Her coat and gloves were in a heap on the floor at her feet. She felt a text come through and gazed at it thoughtfully. It was Jake, asking where she was. She had skipped dinner to avoid being around people. All filming was done for the day, due to the rain, and especially the lightning, and even catering moved dinner for the cast and crew indoors in an impromptu, picnic-like fashion. People were strewn about, sitting on the floor around the fireplace in the Great Hall or crowding around the dining room table.

Anna looked back out into the night, a slight smile on her face as she tucked her phone back into the pocket of her jeans without answering. Lightning lit the sky, and for a moment, she saw herself reflected in the window pane, a grin spreading uncontrollably across her face.

Because now she knew.

She finally knew the *why*, not just the *what*. She knew why she was so protective of her relationship with Jake. She had been fiercely protecting it because she was afraid someone would reveal it for what it truly was. Not real. Acting. She didn't love Jake, and the look in his eyes that had caused her to pull her hand away proved his feelings as well. It wasn't what was there, it was what wasn't. No love. Kindness, maybe. Attraction, maybe. But nothing more. Not even the hint of the possibility of more.

And now she knew for sure what was real: her feelings for William. They had always been there, since the day he had looked down at her from this very window. If her dreams were revealing her true feelings, like William had said, then her true feelings were for him. Always for him. Mr. Williams or William Langley. One and the same.

William Langley, leaving the remains of his dinner on the table, stood glaring at the storm through windows that faced the front of the house. A huge oak tree outside groaned ominously in the wind, its branches casting claw-like shadows on the walls of the room. He was unknowingly staring at the same view as Anna.

"I don't know what I was thinking," he said aloud to the lightning that crashed once again overhead. "She's not right for me, anyway. An American actress? How would I explain her to my mother?"

"How am I going to explain him to my mother?" Anna wondered. "Another farmer? She'll disown me." She frowned thoughtfully. Maybe that wouldn't be a bad thing. No prenup.

She contemplated the farm subject a bit more. What had Sir Frederick said today? *I can't have you in my film wearing your farm clothes.* So those are William's farm clothes. If so, then he was dressed in his farm clothes the day she met him.

"He must be going back and forth from his farm to Hampstead Hall," she reasoned. It made sense. It would account for the vast difference in the way he dressed from day to day. But if so, then his farm must be close by. Close enough to get there by four-wheeler.

"He must be a local boy," she thought, surprised that she hadn't thought of that before. She imagined the farm: small and quaint, with a little farmhouse, maybe with a thatched roof, like in the movies. Sheep in the pasture. Smoke in the chimney. His rosy, plump, little mother making him breakfast.

"Mother would have eaten her alive," William said aloud. He gave a brief snort when he thought of the two women encountering one another. Anna would have probably held her own, he thought, and regretted that he wouldn't get to see her go toe-to-toe with Lady Diane.

He felt his anger begin to subside and be replaced with melancholy as he leaned his shoulder against the cold stone of the windowframe. The wind was beginning to die down as well. Only the steady drumming of the rain continued, wearying and monotonous, like white noise.

William turned from the window and plunged himself into a chair by the fire, daring it to rouse him from his reverie with its brightness. Behind him, Sheila tiptoed in and began to remove his tray.

"Sheila?"

"My lord?" she said, pausing.

"You've met Anna."

"I have, my lord."

"She's an American," he said, picking at the fringe on the arm of his chair.

"Yes, my lord," answered Sheila, cautiously.

"Certainly not the kind of woman a man of my stature should consider, don't you think? Romantically, I mean."

Sheila paused, setting down the tray.

"I'm not exactly sure what you're asking," she said. "She's a fine young lady, and you two seem to get along well. Mr. Barnaby and I were just saying so the other day."

William turned astonished eyes to her.

"You and Mr. Barnaby were discussing us?"

"Now, don't you get upset. We weren't matchmaking. Only noticing things, so to speak."

William stared at her.

"What things?" he asked.

"Well, the way you get along with each other. We haven't seen that before. Not with any of the girls you brought home from university, though there were only two, as I recall. Not even with the young ladies Lady Diane has brought in for you to meet."

William cringed.

"And I can tell you that she sneaks into the kitchen every chance she gets to give me a hug and a how-do-you-do," added the cook.

"She does?" William was incredulous.

"Yes, and she's always extra careful around the house. Respectful. Some of them aren't, like that Jim Anderson. Always sitting down hard on things. I'm afraid he'll break a chair, one of these days."

William returned his gaze to the fire.

"But if she weren't here as an actress," he said, frowning. "If she were here as a guest, and she knew I was the Ninth Earl. What about then? Would she fit? Would she blend in with all the young ladies my mother likes? Wouldn't it be obvious that she didn't belong?"

"I would hope she would stand out!" said Sheila with emphasis. Her face softened as she looked down at him. She smoothed his dark curls like a mother patting her child.

"I know what you're trying to do, and it won't work," she crooned. "You're trying to convince yourself that she isn't worth it. Did she turn you down? Is that it?"

William sighed.

"I kissed her, and she ran away," he pouted.

Sheila chuckled softly.

"Did you ask her why?" she asked.

"No! And I'm not going to," he said, folding his arms.

"Well, then," she said, "That's on you, isn't it? The only way to know the answer is to ask."

She picked up the tray again and exited the room.

William continued to glare at the fire.

His mobile buzzed. He had plugged it in across the room.

He closed his eyes and didn't move from his chair.

Anna stared at her phone for the hundredth time.

No reply.

"Why doesn't he answer?" she wondered.

She had texted William, asking to meet. She wanted to explain why she ran away. She wanted to tell him he no longer had kissing restrictions. He could kiss her whenever he wanted, as far as she was concerned. The more, the better.

But his silence was puzzling.

I mean, I know I told him I was with Jake, she reasoned. He probably thinks I ran away because I don't like him. If he'd just let me explain.

She toyed idly with the bracelet around her wrist. It reminded her that she would have to also have a conversation with Jake, one she did not look forward to having.

Her stomach growled audibly.

Probably better sneak down to the kitchen and see if I can scrounge something up, she thought. Sheila won't mind.

The sounds of people heading to their beds began to die away. The local talent and crew had already left in a string of cars Anna watched from the window. She was hoping the coast would be clear soon. She still didn't want to face anyone, especially Jake. What would she say to him?

She peeked out from the curtained alcove. No one was in sight. She tip-toed down the stairs. There were no lights on downstairs, and even the fires had been put out. Outside, the rain still drummed its fingers on the window panes, but the lightning had moved over the hills.

Anna carefully maneuvered through the darkened Great Hall to the Dining Room. As she crossed to the Butler's Pantry, she froze. She could see through the open pocket doors into the Drawing Room. One lamp was lit, on a table by a wingback chair. Peter was slouched in the chair, facing her, but his eyes were closed, and she could hear a faint snoring. In one hand he held a glass that was tipping precariously. Anna quickly disappeared into the Butler's Pantry and out of his line of sight.

"Well, now," said Sheila when she emerged into the kitchen below. "I wondered if I would see you tonight."

"You did?" Anna asked, surprised.

"I stayed down here late, just in case," answered Sheila. "I was helping the caterers and didn't see you in with the others at dinner."

"I had a lot to think about," Anna admitted. "But I'm hungry now."

"Lucky for you, I saved you a plate." Sheila pulled one out of the warming oven.

She seated Anna at the kitchen table.

"Now then," said the cook, settling herself down across from Anna. "What did you have to think about, that kept you from eating?"

Anna looked up into her kind, brown eyes.

"I was thinking about farming," she said, smiling. "And truthfulness. It's good to be honest with someone, don't you think? And with yourself?"

"Ye-es," said Sheila, hesitantly. "Of course, sometimes, people have reasons for not being completely truthful."

"But generally speaking," said Anna. "Farmers tend to be truthful, right? I mean, more truthful than actors, for instance. A farmer wouldn't pretend to be something that he's not. He wouldn't pretend to care about you when he doesn't. When you look into his eyes, you know what he's thinking, and you see the real man."

She continued eating, a dreamy look in her eyes.

Sheila shifted uncomfortably in her chair.

"Are you thinking of farmers in general, or a particular farmer?" asked Sheila, perplexed.

Anna reached out and squeezed her hand.

"I'll tell you my secret," she said. "I was thinking of William."

"Ah," said the cook, nodding. "Yes, I suppose William *could* be considered a farmer. But my dear—"

"Yes?"

"If someone were to have hidden something from you, and he had what he thought were good reasons for it…innocent reasons…you could forgive that, couldn't you?"

Anna smiled.

"Of course," she said, "but William wouldn't hide anything from me. He's always been completely above-board. That's why I lo—that's why I like him so much."

Sheila nodded and smiled, but her smile faded once Anna's eyes left her face.

CHAPTER THIRTY-THREE

———————◆━◀━▶◆———————

Anna returned to her bedroom after her meal. When she tiptoed back across the Dining Room, Peter was still in the same chair, snoring. At some point, he must have awakened, because his glass, now refilled, was sitting on the floor at his side, and his phone was the object in a precarious position in his hand. It looked to Anna like he had fallen asleep in the very act of texting.

It still puzzled her that William hadn't returned any of her texts. She hadn't mentioned any explanations as to why she ran away from him; she preferred a face-to-face conversation.

"At this point," she thought as she got ready for bed, "I'll have to corner him in the morning."

Preferably before filming starts.

She had already decided to be there to watch; most of the cast and crew would be. It was the most exciting thing to happen since the rape scene.

She climbed into bed and stared up at the rose-covered canopy.

Today has been monumental, she thought dreamily, wondering what tomorrow would bring to top it. She felt a surge of anticipation when she thought about the duel. She hoped William had reconciled himself to his role as actor. She smiled, thinking of how handsome he looked in his period clothes.

"But then, I've already seen him wearing them," she thought.

In my dreams.

William closed his laptop with an irritated snap. He had tried to watch one of his favorite shows, but couldn't keep his attention on the plot line. Solitaire had failed to entertain him. It was now nearing midnight, and he knew he had to get up before dawn. He had to be in wardrobe first, then the scene was scheduled so that it could be filmed "just as the sun peeped from behind the hills," as Sir Frederick described it. Fortunately, sunrise for that time of year was seven o'clock. Even so, he should have been in bed hours ago. At least he had very few lines.

As he got ready for bed, he wondered for a moment if Anna would come to watch the scene, but then he angrily pushed the thought from his mind.

What difference does it make? he thought angrily. She won't be watching *me.* She'll be watching *him.*

He was glad he hadn't answered her texts.

She just wants to spell it all out for me, that she doesn't want me, he thought bitterly. What could she possibly have to say that she hadn't already made perfectly clear?

He laughed cynically, wondering if she wanted to talk to him so she could have closure and go to bed in peace.

Well, I didn't give it to you, did I?

Sleep well, Lady Anna.

"You called, Lady Anna?" said a whispered voice as someone shook Anna's arm.

"Yes, Newberry," said Anna, blinking herself awake.

Another dream. She wasn't surprised. Another chapter was inevitable.

"Is it about the duel tomorrow, m'lady?"

"Yes," said Lady Anna, taking hold of Newberry's hand. "I need you to go to it."

Newberry squeaked in horror.

"M'lady, I can't!" she cried, pulling her hand away and covering her face.

"Yes, you can. You have to go and see what happens!"

Newberry shook her head, staring at her mistress with terrified eyes.

"Newberry," said Lady Anna, taking a stern tone, "I can't go. You know I can't. It would be the height of embarrassment to both men if I were found there. But you can. You must. You have to go and hide in the stand of trees on the other side of the field."

"M'lady!"

"Hide there before anyone comes. When it's still dark. No one will know you're there. And if you're caught, tell them you were out picking flowers."

"In November?"

"Just make something up, then," said Lady Anna impatiently. "Hide there and wait for the duel to happen. And when—" Lady Anna swallowed her fear. "When it's all over—you must come back and tell me what happened. Tell me—who won."

Although Sir John had assured her they would be using blanks, she still had an uneasiness in her mind.

"M'lady, do I have to?" asked Newberry, shaking all over.

"Yes, Newberry. It's an order. I have to know the outcome. And I can't go myself. Please, Newberry. Do it for me."

Newberry sighed in resignation.

"Yes, m'lady. I will do it—for you."

"Now, go!" said Lady Anna. "Quietly, before anyone sees you."

She squeezed her maid's hands in hers before shooing her to the door.

Newberry paused in the doorway and looked back. Then she nodded, and left the room.

But instead of the door closing quietly behind her, it slammed.

Then it slammed again.

Anna sat up in bed and stared at the door.

"Corinne!" said Peter's voice from the hallway.

There was another bang.

"Corinne, talk to me. Tell me what's going on!"

Anna crept to her door and opened it a crack. Peter was standing outside Corinne's door. He was clearly drunk; he swayed a little as he leaned his muscular arm against the doorframe. He was staring intently at the wooden door as if he believed he could see through it eventually if he concentrated hard enough.

He's not allowed to be drunk, thought Anna. It's against Sir Frederick's rules. That must have been what was in the glass downstairs. She wondered where he got the stuff. Maybe he bought it in town when they went on Sunday.

"I need a drink," mumbled William to himself, throwing on his robe. Sleep was still far from him. He convinced himself that a glass of whiskey was what he needed to get through the night. He knew there was some in the antique lacquered Chinese cabinet in the Drawing Room. The key was always kept on top of the cabinet for convenience.

"At least the rain has stopped," he grumbled to himself.

As he shuffled toward the stairs, he heard what sounded like shouting in the east wing hall. He stopped to listen.

Peter!

Yelling for his girlfriend to let him in.

He headed down the stairs, shaking his head and wondering how soon this whole *Cavendish Manor* thing would be over.

"Is it Perry? Is he in there?" yelled Peter.

"No! He's not, so leave him out of this!" Corinne shouted from behind her closed door.

"I don't know if I can leave him out of this," said Peter with a sneer. "He's pushing in where he doesn't belong."

"I don't belong to you!" shouted Corinne.

Good girl, thought Anna, peering out at Peter through her cracked door. For a brief moment, Anna had the sinking fear that someone else was in Corinne's room instead of Perry. Someone like William. Then she shook it off.

"Go away, Peter," Corinne said wearily. "I'm not letting you in tonight."

"Not tonight, not tonight," said Peter in a mocking voice. "That's what you always say these days. What am I supposed to think, Corinne?"

He turned to leave, then thought better of his sudden movement and leaned heavily against the wall. His body sagged, as if he were falling asleep for a moment, standing up. Then he suddenly sprang to life and slammed his hand against the door again; both Corinne and Anna made involuntary squeaks.

Peter's cloudy gaze cleared as his head snapped in Anna's direction.

"Hey!" he said, his face nearly purple with rage as he noticed Anna's face at the crack in her door.

She pushed the door closed and tried to lock it, but Peter was faster than she expected. He lunged at the door, pushing it open.

Once inside, he shoved her hard across the room; she stumbled, but didn't fall.

"It's you, isn't it?" he asked.

"I don't know what you're talking about," answered Anna, pretending to be unafraid. "Get out of my room."

"You and your fancy high school and your morals!" he shouted, moving closer. "You've got Corinne keeping me out, now, don'tcha? Following in your footsteps, Miss High and Mighty?"

Anna shook her head through his speech, incredulous. She hadn't done anything, and told him so.

He twisted her arm in front of her and leered into her face. The acrid stench of his breath was so familiar that Anna almost fainted with fear. Instead, she pushed back against him.

"Get away from me, Peter!" she shouted. "You're drunk!"

William turned on the lights in the Drawing Room and crossed to the Chinese cabinet. Then he paused. He had thought he heard Anna's voice cry out from the darkness, but now all was silent. He dismissed it as an illusion.

He reached for the key on the top of the cabinet, but his fingers slipped over empty space. Then his eyes focused on the cabinet doors. The key was in the lock. William opened the doors and saw that someone had been helping himself to the contents. Someone who obviously knew where the key was kept.

Peter!

No longer thirsty, William relocked the cabinet and pocketed the key. He would address this in the morning. It angered him that Peter would take advantage of his hospitality and not even bother to ask permission. Then he remembered Sir Frederick's rules, and was even more determined to make an issue of it.

As he headed back up the stairs, he could hear Peter's voice.

No wonder he's so angry, he thought. He's drunk. Peter had always had the reputation of being an angry drunk.

He heard Anna's voice again, distinctly this time, and a chill went through him. Was she in danger? Why would Peter bother Anna?

Then he steeled himself, purposely slowing his steps.

If she's in trouble, Jake can save her, he thought icily, determined to pass the east wing hall without a second glance.

Peter pressed his face against Anna's, his strong body pushing her against the side of the bed.

"Girls like you need to be taught a lesson," he growled in her ear. "You think you're better'n anyone! You think you're better'n Corinne, even."

"No!" said Anna, shaking her head at him. "I don't think that. You're just drunk and angry. Please let me go!"

She pushed against him, but he wouldn't budge.

He lunged his face toward hers and planted a sloppy kiss on her mouth.

When William reached the upper landing, he couldn't resist glancing down the east wing hall. He was surprised to see Jake running toward Anna's room, with a frightened Corinne following behind.

"What is going on tonight?" he said aloud, but Jake and Corinne didn't hear him.

Jake burst through the open door of Anna's room.

"Peter, my God, what are you doing?" William heard him say, and his heart plunged to his feet.

"Oh, no!" he whispered as he ran toward Anna's bedroom.

Standing in the doorway, he surveyed the scene.

Jake had pulled Peter off of Anna and was glaring at him in disbelief. His fists clenched and unclenched at his sides. Peter swayed his way to one of the chairs near the fireplace and sat down heavily, laughing in a mocking way.

"I wasn't gonna do anything," he said, wiping at his eyes to keep them open.

Corinne was consoling Anna, who had slid to the floor, unable to stay standing once she was out of danger.

Anna looked up to see William in the doorway, a mingled look of sorrow and relief on his face. Their eyes met, and she knew that he knew what she was thinking. She knew he was thinking it, too.

This is just like the dream.

Only this time, nobody called for a duel.

"Anna?" William asked, and she knew what he wanted to know.

"She's fine," Jake answered before she could. "He was just fooling around."

Jake's usually jovial face was serious.

"Fooling around?" William asked skeptically.

"Look," said Jake, pulling William into the room and closing the door. "Pete could get fired for this. We need to keep this to ourselves." He looked at Anna. "I mean, what did he actually do?"

"He pushed me," whispered Anna, with a nervous glance at Peter, who leaned his head against the wing of the chair and began to snore loudly. "And he was kissing me. I thought he was going to—"

"He was just fooling around, Anna," Jake interrupted. "No harm done, right?"

"You've got to press charges, Anna!" Corinne said, ignoring Jake.

"No!" said Jake. Then he lowered his voice. "He's drunk, and that's against the rules, number one. And if you press charges, not only will he be fired, his whole life will be over. He'll never live down the scandal. Is that what you want, Anna? To ruin someone's life because he got a little tipsy?"

Anna and Corinne stared at Jake in disbelief.

"He's more than a little tipsy!" said William icily. "How can you defend him?"

"He didn't mean to scare you," Jake said, ignoring William and addressing Anna.

"Well, he did," she said, tearily. "He said he was going to teach me a lesson!"

"All talk, don't you see? He wouldn't have actually done anything."

"It's sexual harassment," said William. "At the least."

"Can't we wait to deal with this until after the duel?" asked Jake. "Do we really need one more set-back?"

"It's not your decision!" William reminded him. "It's Anna's! Anna, what would *you* like to do about this?"

He turned to look at her. She was still crouched on the floor; she seemed to be in shock. Her face was pale, and her breathing shallow. She looked up at him with hollow eyes.

William sighed heavily, wiping his brow.

"We can deal with this tomorrow," he said to Jake. "Anna needs to get some sleep. And he needs to get out of here." William nodded toward Peter, who shifted sleepily in the chair. "But we *will* deal with this," he said pointedly to Jake, his eyes flickering violet.

"I'm sorry, Anna. It's my fault," said Corinne, tears streaming down her face. "If I'd just let him in—"

"Don't say that!" said Anna. "It's not your fault. And what more would he have done if you'd opened your door?"

"Come, Corinne," said Jake. "Let's leave Anna so she can sleep. We all have an early call in the morning."

He reached out a hand and pulled her up. Then he pulled Anna to her feet.

"Get some sleep," he whispered to her, kissing her forehead. "He didn't mean anything. It will all be fine in the morning."

He ran his fingers along her jawline and looked intently into her eyes, as if willing her to see things the way he wanted.

Anna kept silent, her eyes wide and grey as she looked into his.

Jake heaved Peter up from the chair, and assisted him out of the room. Peter didn't protest, but allowed himself to be led like a child, almost as if he were sleepwalking.

Corinne tearfully hugged Anna.

"I'm sorry," she said again. "Are you sure you'll be all right? I could stay."

"No, don't be silly," said Anna, hoping her voice was steady. "I'll be fine. Get some sleep. You have a scene tomorrow."

Corinne hesitated in the doorway, looking back at her, then went out. It reminded Anna of the dream she'd just had. Corinne had looked just like that as her lady's maid, fearful and unsure of herself.

William was the only one remaining in the room, just inside the door.

Now is not the time to tell him how I feel, she thought as she watched him shift uncomfortably. But oh, how I wish he would hold me right now.

I wish I could hold her right now, thought William, his arms aching. But she wants Jake to do that.

"I'm glad you're all right," he said gruffly, almost afraid to look at her.

Anna nodded, holding back her tears.

"We'll deal with this in the morning," he said as he turned toward the door. Then he paused, looking back at her.

"Anna?"

"Yes?" she said, hopefully.

"Lock the door."

He left. She collapsed on the floor in tears.

CHAPTER THIRTY-FOUR

It was still dark when Anna came downstairs the next morning. She had barely slept. When she finally crawled out of bed, she merely pulled on leggings and a sweatshirt under her heavy coat and threw her hair up in a messy bun. Downstairs, the whole place was bustling with activity; it was as if everyone in the house had been up for hours.

Which they probably have, she thought. Especially the crew.

Everyone, it seemed, was awake to see the duel. Anna even caught a glimpse of Miranda, whom she hadn't seen in days, wrapped in a heavy overcoat as she crossed the courtyard and disappeared into the fog. Last night's rain brought a blanket of fog, thick and low to the ground, stealing over the grass from the river and the lake. Anna watched as people disappeared and reappeared in it as they went about their business. It reminded her of all the stories she'd read of Victorian London, and Sherlock Holmes.

And Jack the Ripper.

She shuddered.

She felt like she was in a dream, only instead of dreaming of the past, she was dreaming in the twenty-first century.

Would anything feel normal again? she wondered.

She carefully crossed the courtyard, stopping at catering for a cup of tea. It was still too early to think about breakfast; her stomach revolted at the thought of it. She could always eat later.

There was a part of her that had wanted to stay in bed, or to run away, or to do anything but see Peter Mallory again. She wondered if he would even remember what happened, and if he did, how he would feel about it. She figured he would justify it. Like Jake.

Why had Jake justified it? It seemed so out of character, especially for a man who thought he was still her boyfriend.

"He obviously cares a lot about his best friend's career," she reasoned. She had heard about things like this. Movie industry people protecting their own. Overlooking clear violations against women.

She didn't really know what to do. Part of her wanted to forget the whole thing. If she hadn't been so nosy, peeking into the hall, this wouldn't have happened. If Peter hadn't been drunk. But he'd overstepped before, crossed lines. Forced himself on her. Or was that only in her dreams?

She shook her head, then stopped walking suddenly, realizing she had almost walked into a cameraman who was crossing in front of her. He gave her an annoyed glance as he kept his fast pace.

"Sorry," mumbled Anna, but the cameraman had already disappeared in the mist.

She looked around the field. It was transformed into a movie set. There were cameras set up on tracks like weird train cars. There were tall lights casting an eerie glow over the scene while the fog left streaky smears of cloud hanging in the air.

Sir Frederick, wearing long pants this time instead of shorts, was barking orders to whomever would listen. There was a line of director's chairs for the actors to sit in. Anna noticed Peter slumped in one, and a knot formed in her stomach. He looked somewhat pale and haggard, despite his makeup, but otherwise awake. He was listening to Jake, who was standing beside him, without making any facial expression. Jake wasn't smiling for once, and his eyes were sharp. Anna wasn't sure why that made her uncomfortable, but it did.

Jake had said Peter didn't mean anything by what he did. That he wouldn't have gone too far.

What did he really do, anyway? Anna thought. Pushed me. Got in my face. Kissed me with bad breath. Accused me of influencing Corinne. She didn't want to be responsible for ruining someone's career. For making more of something than she should.

Corinne caught her eye from across the field. Anna gave her a half-smile, and Corinne returned her greeting with a small wave, a signal of solidarity. "We're in this together," she seemed to be saying. Anna wondered what her advice would be today, after having time to think about it. She was dressed in a long, blue dress with a puffy black ski jacket over it. Anna assumed she would take that off when filming began. Corinne turned and crossed the field to a stand of trees, her mark until Jake was injured in the duel.

"Where are the pistols?"

Sir Frederick stood at the props table, confronting Jaime.

"I took them back to the Drawing Room yesterday, Sir Frederick," William called out before she could answer. "They're antiques, and I didn't want anything to happen to them."

"I assumed you had asked him to," Jaime answered, her flared nostrils the only sign that she was feeling Sir Frederick's accusations.

"Well, we need them back," barked Sir Frederick with a wave of his arms. "Brian needs to load them with blanks, and the sun is not going to wait for us."

Anna noticed the darkness had already turned to a monochrome grey. She was glad William hadn't seen her yet in the darkness. It gave her more time before she would have to deal with last night.

Jaime turned to head back to the house, but Sir Frederick stopped her.

"Send Perry," he said impatiently. "We need you here. Where is Perry?"

Anna glanced around her. Perry wasn't anywhere, and she realized she hadn't seen him yet that morning.

"I'll go," William volunteered. "I have the four-wheeler with me. It will be faster than walking."

"Thank you, William," said Sir Frederick. "But hurry. Don't think you can get out of this scene by being late."

When William arrived at the house, Perry was emerging with the box of pistols.

"I was just sent to retrieve those," said William, a little puzzled.

"Yeah," said Perry. "I remembered you brought them back, and when I saw they weren't on the props table, I thought I'd better run get them so Mr. Elliston can load them. Is Sir Frederick losing it, yet?"

"No, not yet," said William, "but if we don't hurry, he will. I'll give you a ride back."

As he drove, William glanced at Perry, who held the pistol box with great care on his lap, almost protectively. It brought to his remembrance the day of Brian Elliston's dueling demonstration. Perry had seemed to have a keen interest in the pistols and how they were used.

"Was Corinne asking for me?" Perry asked suddenly.

"I don't know," answered William, with a sly peek in his direction. "I didn't speak with her."

Perry nodded, his face serious.

"Do you know Peter Mallory very well?" he asked William.

"Fairly well," William admitted carefully.

"I don't trust him," said Perry with a scowl. "I don't like the way he treats her. And she lets him, because I don't think she knows how special she is. She thinks he's the best she can get. But she deserves better."

William nodded. He was surprised by Perry's candor, and suspected he had someone specific in mind as Peter's replacement.

"Have you told her that?" he asked.

"Nah," said Perry. "Do you think I should?"

"Can't hurt," William replied. "She might feel honored that someone is looking out for her."

"Or she might feel like I should mind my own business," answered Perry, shaking his head.

Brian Elliston was relieved when they arrived back at base camp.

"Got to get these things loaded before the sun rises!" he said, taking the box gingerly out of Perry's hands. He brought the box to the props table, and William watched as he and Jaime went to work loading the weapons.

The fog was beginning to dissipate, but it still hung in wisps, leaving beads of cold mist on faces and cameras with its icy fingers. William shivered. He hadn't worn anything more than the costume, thinking that his black, Regency-period coat would cut the chill of the morning air. He pounded his arms to get the blood flowing.

He felt eyes on him, and looking over, saw that Peter and Jake were turned his direction. Jake appeared stern, his mouth a thin line, but Peter stared at him with an expression William couldn't read. In the half-light that reflected off the mist, Peter's eyes looked black and soul-less, the dark circles underneath giving the impression of hollow space where eyes should be. William set his jaw; he wasn't going to buckle under the force of Peter's personality. Or Jake's.

Peter needs to pay for his crimes, he thought grimly before turning away.

His gaze fell on Anna, lost and alone on the edge of the set. He was surprised to see her. He thought she would want to stay away, after last night. His heart plummeted as he watched her; what if Jake hadn't pulled Peter off in time? What if no one had come to her rescue, and he had gone on about his business, ignoring her cries like he had intended? He shuddered at the thought.

"How are you this morning?" he asked her gently as he approached.

Anna took a deep breath. William had slipped in beside her while she was still thinking of Corinne and the events of last night. He looked just like Mr. Williams in her dreams, dressed in his Regency clothes. The weird lighting in the field made his blue eyes look dark, and it reminded her of the dream in the garden when he had kissed her.

"Fine," she said, looking back at the action in front of her.

"Have you made a decision?" he asked in a low voice. "About last night?" She didn't answer.

"Anna," he said with a note of frustration, dropping his voice even more, "something has to be done. You have to press charges against Peter. He can't get away with—"

"I don't want to think about it right now!" she whispered fiercely. "I'm not even sure what happened, anyway. It wasn't rape. He didn't actually do anything to me."

William was surprised.

"He threatened you!" he reminded her. "Jake pulled him off of you! Who knows what he would have done had we not come in at that moment!"

"He was drunk," Anna said, facing him. "Shouldn't I give him a break for that? If he'd been sober—"

"That is never an excuse, Anna," said William, his voice like a razor. "That was his decision, to drink too much, and he should be held responsible for his actions, drunk or not."

Anna stepped back from him. His whole body was tense, like he was holding himself together by sheer willpower.

"I need time to think about it," she said quietly, her face paling under his intensity. "You have a scene to film."

He sighed, looking over at Peter. Then he turned back to her, grabbing her arm and leaning into her face so close she thought for a moment he would kiss her.

"Something needs to be done about Peter Mallory," he said, his eyes boring into hers. "And if you choose not to press charges, I will take matters into my own hands."

Anna's eyes widened as he spoke. He dropped her arm and strode away from her, back toward base camp instead of toward the set.

"What was that about?" asked Portia Valentine as she approached her. "Is everything all right, Anna?"

Anna turned a pale face toward her.

Portia will know what to do, she thought, feeling peace for the first time since the incident.

She squeezed the older woman's hand.

"Can we talk later?" she asked.

"Of course, my dear," said Portia, concerned.

Anna felt a stir of excitement run through the camp. It was almost time to film, and the attention turned to the props table. Brian and Jamie were there, as well as Peter and Jake. She was surprised to see William there, as well. Perry had also joined the props master and the stunt coordinator at the table. As Anna watched, Brian Elliston reverently handed over the pistols to Peter and Jake, barrels pointing toward the ground.

Everyone began to move into their positions, cast as well as crew. Anna noticed Alan sitting huddled up in a director's chair, a large scarf over the lower half of his face. Yesterday, Sarah had filmed him holding the box of pistols while Jake and Peter chose them, so he wasn't in costume this morning and was free to do his job without distraction. Corinne peeked out from the trees, then hid again, shedding her big coat as she did so. One of the props people took it from her and ran back behind the camera line.

"She must be cold," thought Anna, pulling her own coat closer around her.

"Standing by to fire!" she heard Sarah shout.

"Standing by," answered Brian, as did Peter and Jake, who moved into their positions in the field, fifteen paces away from each other. The mist shredded across their feet as if it had read all of the nineteenth-century novels and was heightening the melodrama.

"Where's William?" asked Sir Frederick in an irritated tone. "The sun is about to rise above the hills."

"Right here, Sir Frederick," William answered, jogging into place between the two men with guns.

He searched for Anna in the watching crowd, and their eyes met.

William looked determined, Anna thought. And protective. Her own eyes filled unexpectedly with tears, and she swallowed hard.

There was a sudden crash that sounded like metal clanging together, and someone cried out.

Anna turned toward the sound.

It was Jaime. She looked up apologetically, her usually pale face crimson.

"I'm so sorry," she said to Sir Frederick. "I lifted up this box of bullets to pack it away, and the bottom fell apart."

She was hurriedly scooping the brass cartridges off the table and back into a box. Perry helped by retrieving the ones that had fallen to the ground.

Sir Frederick sighed, shaking his head, then turned his attention back to the scene.

The mist was giving the duelers a slight sheen. Peter wiped his forehead with his spare hand.

"Do you want me to powder them?" asked a makeup artist.

"No! It's perfect!" said Sir Frederick. Anna could feel his excitement as he rose from his chair and edged closer to the scene, pulling his Comteks off his ears as he did so.

Anna watched Jake pull his free hand through his hair. It was a habit of his, she knew. She wondered if it was to hide nervousness. Otherwise, he appeared tranquil, his dueling pistol leaned against his shoulder, pointed at the sky.

She glanced at his opponent. If anyone was nervous, it was Peter. He dangled his pistol in his hand, the barrel pointed at the ground.

She looked at William again. He sighed heavily, his hands behind his back.

"William!" called Sir Frederick, shrilly. "Are you ready?"

"Ready as I'll ever be," William grumbled.

"What's that?"

"Yes, Sir Frederick. I'm ready."

"Good."

Sir Frederick's eyes roved the scene, taking in every detail. Sarah and Alan sat in their director's chairs behind the monitors like statues, waiting for the action to begin. The first scene being filmed would be a wide shot. Sir Frederick was hoping to capture the light of daybreak as it broke from behind the hills.

Jim shifted impatiently in his chair behind the camera. He was exalted on a moving dolly track, and Anna thought he looked proud of his position above the others.

There was a flash of light from the hills. The sun had finally answered its cue.

"Now," said Sir Frederick.

"Back to one!" Sarah shouted.

The three actors in the field readied themselves. Willam pulled a white handkerchief out from behind his back.

"Rolling," said Sir Frederick, watching intently as he rose from his chair.

"Action!"

William lifted the handkerchief above his head.

"Ready!" he shouted, continuing to look straight ahead.

Peter and Jake turned toward each other.

"Aim!"

The duelers took their sideways stance, just like Brian had taught them. Anna was riveted to the scene. It felt so real; it reminded her of her dreams. She held her breath, amazed at how much animosity was being expressed between the two men. For a moment she was fearful that someone would get hurt, until she remembered that this was a scene.

"Just actors," she reminded herself.

There was a pause of about five seconds after William spoke his second line. Sir Frederick had directed William to pause for dramatic effect. It was working; William could feel the tension as everyone watching held their breath.

"Fire!" he shouted finally, dramatically dropping the handkerchief.

There were flashes from the pistols, and a deafening sound that rumbled through the air and reverberated through Anna's ribcage.

Both Peter and Jake fell to the ground. Jake groaned, but Peter gave more of a strangled cry, like someone had punched him in the gut and taken his breath away.

William, hearing Peter's cry, immediately looked in his direction.

"Peter shouldn't be on the ground," he thought. He almost went to him, but stopped himself. The scene was continuing, and he didn't want to risk Sir Frederick's wrath.

"Waverly!" Corinne screamed as she ran across the field toward Jake. She fell, wailing, on top of him.

"Cut!" yelled Sir Frederick, exasperated. "Why is Peter on the ground?"

Anna could tell Sir Frederick was angry, and wondered why Peter didn't get up. If he was joking, he was taking it too far.

"Something's wrong, Jake," she could hear Corinne say, and Anna had to agree. Prickles went up her spine as she continued to stare at Peter, sprawled on the ground.

"He's just fooling around, Corinne," Jake said, laughing as he sat up. "He's just mad that I get the girl instead of him."

"No," thought William. "This is more than a joke."

He ran to Peter, and kneeling down, began to unbutton his collar and untie his cravat.

"He's bleeding!" he shouted over his shoulder.

"What?" said Brian, rushing over. "That's impossible. These were blanks!"

"Maybe he hit his head?" suggested Sarah to Jim, who had dismounted from his camera.

"Oh, come on, Pete!" said Jake, sauntering to his friend. "Why do you always have to have the attention! It's me who's supposed to be injured in this scene."

He nudged Peter with his foot.

William had blood on his hands where he had opened Peter's shirt, looking for signs of life, and a source of the wound. Death was looking up at him through Peter's lifeless eyes. He remembered his shadowed stare from earlier, and shuddered, realizing it was a premonition. He looked up at Jake. What had he done? How had he done it? Who else could have?

"Jake, what have you done?" he asked. "Peter's dead," he said, watching him. Searching for guilt. Or remorse.

Corinne screamed.

Jake stared down at Peter's open wound, then at his blank, unseeing eyes. William watched as the reality of Peter's death hit home. Jake's face physically paled; he looked horror-stricken. He fell to his knees beside William and Brian.

"Oh God!" he said, staring at William, his breath coming in short gasps. "I've killed my best friend!"

CHAPTER THIRTY-FIVE

"The curse has come upon us!"

Miranda put a dramatic arm across her forehead and collapsed against Adrian in her best Lady of Shallot pose. Adrian staggered under her unexpected weight.

"It's the curse!" she whimpered. "The Scottish curse! Who will be next?"

"Miranda! Stop it!" Portia hissed. "Now is not the time!"

William could feel Miranda's accusing eyes from across the field. He ignored her; there were more pressing matters to deal with than a superstitious actress. He pressed Peter's wound with his hands, but even as he did so, he knew it was futile.

Peter was gone.

William flicked his eyes to Jake, still kneeling beside him. He looked like a ghost himself.

"I don't understand," Brian kept repeating, as if everything would become clear if he said the words enough. "Those were blanks."

He had picked up Peter's pistol and was examining it. His eyes turned toward Jake's pistol where it had dropped fifteen paces away.

"Don't," warned William. "Don't touch the other pistol. It will be evidence."

Brian nodded, glancing at Jake, then looking away, as if concerned the other man would guess his suspicions.

Anna was also staring at Jake. The brightness of the sun, now unhindered by the mist, brought out every color in the field with dazzling clarity. Jake's paisley waistcoat glimmered in the light, and she noticed there was gold piping on the edges of his brown coat.

Jaime ran to the field, kneeling down beside Jake and rubbing his back. He looked at her as if from a great distance. Anna could see that Jaime was whispering something to him. Words of comfort, she guessed.

I should be there, instead of her, she realized. I'm supposed to be his girlfriend.

But her legs wouldn't move.

William stood up, holding his hands out stiffly in front of him. Anna could see blood on his hands and on his clothes. Bright red and sticky. He was yelling something about calling 999. Somewhere in the back of her mind, she registered that 999 was the British equivalent of 911.

"Already on it!" Sarah called out to William. She was talking rapidly into her phone.

"And Portia," said William. "Call Mr. Barnaby. Let him know to expect the police."

Portia nodded and pulled out her phone.

Black spots began to form across Anna's vision, and her stomach felt hollow. Her body began to sway slightly.

"Don't faint," whispered Perry reassuringly beside her. He wrapped an arm around her shoulders and led her to a director's chair.

"Perry?"

It was Corinne. He opened his arms and she fell into them, blubbering and shaking.

"It's gonna be all right," Anna heard him say.

Will it be all right? she wondered. Peter was dead. Jake had shot him. Filming would have to stop.

She shook the last thought from her mind. Someone's life is over. This is not the time to be concerned about a TV show.

For the first time, Anna noticed Sir Frederick standing absolutely still at the edge of the field. Portia Valentine was standing next to him, speaking to him, but he didn't seem to hear.

"Stay with Anna," Perry told Corinne. He joined Portia, and together they led Sir Frederick to a chair.

He's in shock, she realized, watching the director's stiff movements.

Anna wrapped her arms around Corinne, who was still weeping.

"I'm so sorry," she said, but Corinne only sobbed harder.

"Oh, why is this happening to me?"

Miranda's wail quivered on the breeze. Adrian's face wore the perfect look of concern.

"Perry!" he called sharply, waving to the production assistant.

Someone had brought Sir Frederick a cup of tea from the craft services table, and Perry was attempting to get him to take a sip.

"Perry! Help me with Miranda!" demanded Adrian, scowling. "Can't you see she needs help?"

Perry sighed, furrowing his brow. He handed the paper cup to Portia, who nodded at him, then joined Adrian, who had allowed Miranda to drop unceremoniously to the ground. Anna was amazed at the actress' commitment to the role of damsel in distress.

Anna breathed deeply. She didn't want to faint, to become Miranda, a burden to be taken care of, focusing the attention away from what was important.

"Focus," William told himself. He felt an urgent need to pay close attention to details, to make sure nothing was touched that shouldn't be. If it was an accident, then Jake would need to be proven innocent without a shadow of doubt. And if it was otherwise—

"I'm so sorry, Pete," said Jake, grabbing his friend's hand, tears falling from his eyes. "It was an accident. I didn't mean to—please believe me, Pete! I didn't mean to!"

"Shh," said Jaime soothingly. "Come away. Let's get a cup of tea."

"No!" he shouted at her. "I'm not leaving him. He's my best friend." He looked at her, shaking his head. "He's my best friend."

She nodded, biting her lip.

William turned away. The emotion of the moment was catching up to him. He had been so focused on trying to help, he hadn't fully acknowledged the reality of Peter's death. He suddenly felt sick, and realized he had skipped breakfast because of the early call. He should eat something. His thoughts went to Anna. How was she handling this? He searched the field for her and found her sitting in a director's chair, clinging to Corinne. It seemed all wrong.

Why isn't she here? he wondered. Why isn't she comforting Jake?

She looked his way, and the sympathy he read in her eyes soothed his soul like a warm embrace.

"The paramedics are here," announced Perry, gazing in the direction of base camp. An ambulance was bounding across the field toward them. When the ambulance reached them, a team of paramedics spilled out, surrounding Peter and pushing Jake and Jaime out of the way. They stood nearby, looking helpless. Brian moved away and joined Sarah and Jim at the side of the field. William knelt beside the paramedics, who were checking for vital signs.

Anna felt a surge of sympathy for Jake. He was her friend, after all, even if she didn't love him. She untangled herself from Corinne and went to him, touching his back gently with her hand.

He had his arm around Jaime, but turned at Anna's touch.

He clutched her to him, and Anna found herself unexpectedly crying in his arms.

"Sir Frederick! The police are here," said Sarah, rousing the director from his stupor.

"The police," he repeated in a monotone, nodding his head, his round glasses reflecting the sun. "Of course. The police."

He stood up, like a prisoner preparing himself for the firing squad. There were two uniformed officers and two plain-clothes detectives being led by Mr. Barnaby through the hedgerow from the direction of base camp. Perry and Sarah joined Sir Frederick, waiting for them to arrive. Anna lifted her head from Jake's chest. She could feel him take a deep breath, steeling himself for the inevitable questions that would come with the arrival of the police.

"This is Sir Frederick Churchwood-Styles," Mr. Barnaby said as the group approached the director. "Sir Frederick is the director of the show being filmed on the property."

Mr. Barnaby appeared to be unruffled, despite the fact that he had been awakened to the news that an accidental shooting had occurred at Hampstead Hall and the police were on their way. But Anna detected a slight strain in his eyes as he made the introduction.

"Sir Frederick," acknowledged the plain-clothes detective, giving the director a nod. "I'm DCI Ferguson, Surrey Police, and this is Sergeant Patel." He indicated a woman standing beside him, of Indian ethnicity. She was also in plain clothes, and was carrying a notebook.

Detective Chief inspector Ferguson was a sturdily-built man, not overly tall, but with wide shoulders and a square-shaped head covered by graying hair in a side-part. His eyes, Anna noticed, were dark and sharp, like he never missed a detail. He had a habit of squinting, as if the narrowing of his eyelids gave him greater insight. He was wearing a plain black suit with a white shirt and black tie that was tied crookedly. He squinted at Sir Frederick, then addressed Mr. Barnaby.

"I'm going to need to speak to the Earl," he said, glancing around, searching for someone.

"Of course, Inspector Ferguson," said Mr. Barnaby with a conciliatory nod. He also searched the field. "The Inspector needs to speak with the Earl of Somerville," he said, raising his voice.

William looked over at the mention of his title. He had been speaking quietly with the paramedics, who had determined their services were unnecessary and were awaiting instructions from the police. A sheet was now draped over Peter's lifeless body.

"Oh, dear," mumbled Sir Frederick to the Inspector. "Of course, you'll need the Earl."

"But the Earl's not here," said Sarah, reminding Sir Frederick of the obvious.

"Oh, ah, I'm not sure," replied Sir Frederick, turning toward the field and William. "I think he might be here after all."

Inspector Ferguson frowned at Sir Frederick.

"Is Lord Somerville on the property, or not?" he asked, raising his voice.

"Yes, Inspector," said William approaching him, his hands still covered in Peter's dried blood. "I'm here."

CHAPTER THIRTY-SIX

"A word, if you will, my lord," said the Inspector, leading William away from the group.

There were surprised murmurings among the cast and crew as Sir Frederick's assistant drew himself up to his full height; he seemed to metamorphosize into a member of the aristocracy before their eyes. His posture changed, and his face took on an authority that hadn't been there a moment before.

Anna stared at him. She detached herself from Jake, which proved to be difficult because his arm suddenly felt vice-like, holding her tightly against his side. She followed William with her eyes as he spoke to the Inspector, daring him to look at her. Finally, he gave her one fleeting, apologetic glance. She clenched her teeth and turned away, walking rapidly toward base camp, but was stopped by one of the uniformed constables at the edge of the hedgerow.

"Everyone needs to stay here, ma'am," he explained politely.

She stopped, but didn't turn around. She folded her arms, keeping her back to the Ninth Earl of Somerville.

Jake approached her.

"What's the matter?" he asked. "You seem angry with William."

"*Lord Somerville*, apparently," she said haughtily.

"What difference does it make who he is?" said Jake impatiently. "It's weird, I admit, that he would pretend to be an assistant, but why does it matter to you? Why should it matter to us?"

He was pleading with her with his dark brown eyes.

She closed her own eyes for a moment.

"It doesn't," she said, hugging him. "It means nothing to us."

Through his coat and waistcoat, she could hear Jake's heart beating rapidly. She didn't think he could bear the stress of one more thing.

"Uh-oh," said Jake quietly as they pulled apart. "Everyone's heard now."

He jerked his chin in the direction of base camp, where a stream of worried-looking actors and crew members was making its way toward them.

The constable stretched his arms out like a barrier.

"No one is allowed to go any further," he announced to the first of the arrivals. "This area is off-limits."

"I can't talk to people," whispered Jake to Anna. "I can't face the questions."

"Let's go back to the others," she suggested. They walked back toward the field, their arms around each other. Perry passed them on the way.

"Filming is canceled for today," he announced to the group assembling in front of the constable. "Until further notice, actually."

Anna glanced back at Perry. He had really proven himself to be invaluable in a crisis. He was calm, yet compassionate, a good combination.

In the distance, she could see more police on the way, some in uniform and some not. She wondered how long it would be before she would be allowed to go to her room. She was suddenly very, very tired.

Inspector Ferguson was making an announcement.

"My constables will be taking statements from each of you," he said. "We would appreciate your cooperation. Just a formality, to write our reports." He nodded at Jake. "Mr. Rawlings? If you don't mind, I have a few questions for you."

Jake nodded, his face serious and his mouth a tight line. Anna gave him a squeeze.

"It's going to be all right," she heard herself tell him.

She hoped it was true.

She looked up to find William staring in her direction. She almost felt sorry for him, standing there, alone and exposed. But she glanced away.

"May I ask you a few questions, ma'am?" asked Sergeant Patel.

"Yes," Anna said, "of course."

William sighed as he watched her. He made a movement to rub his face with his hands, but stopped himself, realizing they were still covered with Peter's blood. He flung them to his sides, exasperated. Now she knew. And what he feared would happen had happened. The final look she had given him before joining Sergeant Patel showed him how she felt about him: disappointed. Surprise he could have handled. Of course she would be surprised. Maybe even angry. He could take that. But disappointed? He shook his head.

The sun rose higher in the sky. The fog had evaporated, but the brightness of the fall morning did little to illuminate what had occurred at the break of day. Forensics came and went; the coroner pronounced death, and the body was taken away; the weapons were confiscated for further investigation. Questions were asked, but no answers were given.

All of the witnesses had been questioned, with Jake and Brian taking the longest. Anna assumed they were being considered as the most at fault in the accident. After the questioning, Brian had gone immediately back to the house. Anna could only imagine what must be going through his mind with a death on his conscience.

I hope it wasn't negligence, she thought. For his sake.

Yellow caution tape had been erected around the perimeter where the duel had taken place. The cast and crew were allowed to go back to the house, except for those responsible for putting away the filming equipment. So far, there was no word from Sir Frederick as to whether or not filming of *Cavendish Manor* was cancelled for good. Everyone walked around with anxious expressions; it was disconcerting to not know.

It was disconcerting to not know a lot of things, thought Anna, walking hand-in-hand with Jake across the courtyard.

As they entered the house, they could hear Miranda's voice raised to a high pitch.

"I don't understand how you can keep me here!" she was saying to Sir Frederick in the Great Hall.

"Miranda, there are so many unknowns at this point," the director was insisting. "We could be filming again by tomorrow."

"One of your principals is dead!" she shrieked. "How can you even think about continuing? And in the meantime, you expect me to just stay here, waiting for another practical joke to be played on me?"

"It was an accident," Sir Frederick said, his eyeglasses flashing.

"She makes a good point," added Adrian, his arm around Miranda. "Can you guarantee our safety? I have a wife and children at home to support."

"If you don't mind, Ms. Vogel," said Inspector Ferguson, stepping up from the shadows, "I would prefer you to stay here for a bit longer. Until we hear back from forensics."

"Oh?" said Miranda haughtily. "You would prefer I stay here, in danger? Can *you* guarantee my safety? I'm sure my agent would *love* to hear about what happened. As well as the public."

"Not the public!" grimaced Sir Frederick.

The Inspector squinted his eyes.

"This seems like an accidental shooting," he said. "What makes you feel you're in danger, Ms. Vogel?"

Miranda's wild-eyed expression sobered, as she realized her audience was the police.

"Well, Inspector, if you have one accident, you could have another one," she said non-committally.

The Inspector gave her a brief nod. Anna couldn't tell if he was satisfied with her answer or not.

"It would just make me feel safer if we had someone here to protect us," Miranda went on.

"I'm sure the Earl has security," Inspector Ferguson suggested.

"He has a security *system*," she admitted reluctantly, "but that's all. No guards or anything. I know, because I had my agent check security before I agreed to come to this place. It wouldn't do to have any crazy fans sneaking onto the property. Not after what happened to Edwin Sterling at Kensington Gardens."

Anna remembered the recent news story Miranda was referring to, in which a famous actor and his girlfriend were attacked by a knife-wielding fan over the summer. Fortunately, all had ended well.

"I will leave some of my men here," the Inspector assured her. "They will be on guard, if you feel you need them. That, and the Earl's security system, should make you feel safe while we wait to hear from forensics. It makes it a lot easier to have you all here, in one place. Just in case."

"Just in case what, Inspector?" asked Adrian. "Are you saying it may not have been an accident?"

Anna and Jake, who had paused at the door to the Great Hall to eavesdrop, waited eagerly for the Inspector's response.

"We should have a more complete picture of what happened in a few hours," the Inspector said, non-committally. His sharp eyes flicked in Jake's direction as he spoke.

Adrian and Miranda turned to stare at them, as well.

"Come on," said Jake, pulling Anna by the hand toward the stairs.

When they got to Jake's bedroom door, he pulled Anna into his arms, leaning his forehead against hers.

"They suspect me," he whispered. "I could see it in their faces."

"Who?" asked Anna. "The police?"

"Maybe. But Miranda and Adrian. They think I killed Peter on purpose."

Tears ran slowly down his cheeks, and his body shuddered in a heart-wrenching sigh.

Anna gently wiped his tears.

"Don't worry about what they think," she said gently.

"Do you believe me?" he asked suddenly, pulling back to look her full in the face. "You believe it was an accident, don't you?"

"Of course, I believe you," she said. He visibly relaxed.

"You didn't tell the police about Peter, did you?" he asked. "About last night?"

She shook her head.

"Good," he said, nodding. "No point, now, is there? No need to destroy his reputation, now that he's—"

He swallowed hard, closing his eyes.

Anna hugged him tightly. When he pulled back, he smiled weakly.

"I think I'd like to be alone for a little while," he apologized. "I hope you understand?"

"I understand," Anna said, kissing his cheek. It was what she wanted, as well.

Back in her bedroom, Anna sat down in the chair by the fire that was cheerfully crackling away, as if nothing tragic had happened. As if everything was just as usual, and at any moment, Peter would come pounding on Corinne's door.

But it wasn't just as usual anymore. Everything had changed. Peter was dead. And the truth was, Anna didn't know what she believed.

CHAPTER THIRTY-SEVEN

"What do I believe?"

Anna asked the question out loud in the rose-covered bedroom. She had answered Jake out of pity for him, out of a desire to comfort him. But did she believe him?

How could she not? How disloyal would that be? She was supposed to be his girlfriend, even though yesterday she was planning to break things off. Of course, she believed him. Didn't she? How could Jake have killed Peter on purpose?

But that was just it. How *could* Jake have killed Peter? Blanks wouldn't have killed him, not at that distance. In order for Peter to be dead, there had to have been a projectile. So who put it there?

Brian? He seemed baffled. He kept saying the bullets were blanks.

Jake? He wouldn't have purposely killed his best friend. Fragments of the night before flitted through Anna's brain. Surely he wouldn't have actually dueled with Peter to defend her honor?

That's ridiculous, Anna told herself sternly. That was just in the dream. And even the dream Jake had asked his seconds to put in blanks. Besides, she reminded herself, how could Jake have loaded a live bullet in the gun this morning? She had watched Brian hand it to him, already loaded.

But who else could have loaded live ammunition into that pistol?

Her exhausted mind shuddered at the possibility that had sneaked in from the dark.

A sudden knock at the door caused her to jump.

"Anna?"

William, thought Anna, resisting the thrill his voice sent through her. *I mean, the Ninth Earl of Somerville*, she corrected herself.

"Please let me in," he pleaded. "We need to talk."

She reluctantly opened the door.

"You look terrible!" she exclaimed.

William glanced distractedly at his costume. He had managed to wash Peter's blood off his hands, but he hadn't changed his clothes, so intent was he on speaking with Anna. There were bloodstains on his waistcoat, and the cuffs of his coat were stiff with dried blood.

"I don't care," he said, stepping into the room. "I'll change later. I wanted to talk to you about—my deception."

"So who are you then?" she asked querulously, shutting the door behind him. "Lord William? Or is that even your real name?"

"My real name *is* William Langley," he explained, leaning against the footboard of her bed, putting space between them. "My *title*, that goes with the Earldom, is Lord Somerville."

"Well, sorry, *Your Highness,*" she answered spitefully. "I guess I don't know all the rules!"

"It would be *Your Lordship,*" he corrected, then bit his lip. He was not there to quibble over his title. "It's okay to be angry with me," he said. "I get it. I deceived you. You have every right to be angry."

"I just feel so stupid," she admitted. "I should have known. No wonder you knew everything about this house. The history. The secret passages. It was *your* house!"

She glared at him, amazed at his audacity. William dropped his eyes.

"But why?" she asked, leaning against the dressing table to face him. "Why did you pretend to be Sir Frederick's assistant? Were you trying to impress me?"

"No, actually, I was trying to un-impress you. I didn't want you to like me for my house, and my title, and my alcoholic father."

He smiled weakly at her, searching her face for signs of forgiveness.

The corners of her mouth twitched despite her attempts to stay angry with him.

"I'm sorry, Anna," he said, his blue eyes rimmed with red. "I didn't mean for it to go so far. Every day, I told myself I would tell you. I almost told you in the chimney passage, only I chickened out. We felt like equals, and I didn't want to ruin it."

"So you don't think we're equals?" she asked.

"I, um…" he stammered. He watched as her eyes widened, and changed from amber to dark grey.

The door crashed open. They both turned, surprised. William was on the verge of sending a string of curses in the direction of whoever was disturbing them when he saw who it was standing in the doorway. He stared in disbelief, his shock keeping him silent.

"There you are!" said a woman from the doorway. She was tall, blonde, and beautiful, dressed in clothes that screamed expensive. A cloud of French perfume wafted across the open space between them. "Mr. Barnaby told me you were speaking with one of the actresses, so I came to look for you myself, since you weren't answering your mobile. Close your mouth, William."

"Yes, Mother," William answered mechanically.

Mother?

Anna felt her own jaw drop. This spectacle of beauty looked thirty-five, and William had just called her *Mother*. Then Anna looked a little closer. Her skin might be smooth as a baby's bottom, but there was something about her cheekbones and chin that didn't seem natural. She was older than she looked. But *Mother?* Anna's dream of the plump, farmer's wife vanished in a cloud of expensive perfume.

"Mother, may I introduce Anna McKay," William said, overcoming his initial shock of finding his maternal parent in the same country, not to mention the same house. "Anna, this is my mother, Lady Diane Langley."

"It's so nice to meet you," said Anna, resisting the urge to curtsy. She felt horribly ill-prepared to meet a Countess. Under-dressed and under-makeup-ed.

"Charmed," said Lady Diane, dismissing Anna with a glance. "We must talk, William. Apparently, things are not going well this morning. There are police everywhere, and Mr. Barnaby says there is some kind of investigation. Is that blood on your clothes? And what are you wearing?"

William sighed. None of this was going as he planned. Anna's finding out his true identity; her first introduction to his mother. He had imagined it all going much differently. In his dreams, Anna fell into his arms, murmuring something romantic about always wanting to marry an earl. He had secretly hoped his mother would have been so struck by Anna's beauty and wit that she would have overlooked the fact that she was an American actress. Everything was against him today, he realized. Then he remembered there were actually more important things to deal with than romantic misunderstandings. Someone had lost his life, and it was on his property.

He noticed Mr. Barnaby standing apologetically in the hall.

"Let's go to the Tapestry Room, shall we?" William said, nodding at Mr. Barnaby.

"We'll have to continue this conversation later," he said to Anna. "Please?"

She nodded.

When he left the room, Anna dropped herself onto the dressing table chair and stared at her reflection in the mirror. Pale. The unmistakeable path of mascara-tears down her cheeks. Her hair, which had already been in a messy bun, was in a worse state than it had started. No wonder William's mother had been unimpressed.

Grabbing a tissue, she dabbed at the mascara streaks.

She remembered William's last comment before they were interrupted. He hadn't answered her question. Did he actually think they weren't equals? Her parents were wealthy landowners in Nashville. She had an expensive education and expensive friends.

She crumpled the used tissue in her hand.

How dare he consider her beneath him?

CHAPTER THIRTY-EIGHT

"Well, William," began Lady Diane, taking a seat in the Tapestry Room as if it were a throne. "What do you have to say for yourself?"

"I'm not sure what you mean," answered William, irritated by her insinuating tone.

Sir Frederick arrived, and Mr. Barnaby discreetly left the room, closing the door behind him.

"Lady Diane!" Sir Frederick said, smiling.

"Sir Frederick!" she replied, crossing one shapely leg over the other and extending her hand toward him.

He kissed it gallantly, then seated himself near her throne.

"I'm so glad you could come," he said. "Of course, the circumstances have changed a bit."

"What are you talking about?" asked William.

"Oh, didn't I tell you?" asked the director. "I told Lady Diane you were going to be in the film, and that she should pop 'round and watch your performance."

Lady Diane raised her manicured eyebrows at her son.

"I crossed the channel right away," she explained. "To find out what was going on in my absence. And I find everything in upheaval."

"Everything was going fine until this morning," William replied curtly. "There's been an accident on set, but the police are taking care of things."

"More than an accident," his mother replied. "Peter Mallory is dead. It certainly looks bad, especially knowing the way you feel about him. I'm surprised you even let him on the property."

"It wasn't my decision to hire him. It was Sir Frederick's," said her son, his eyes flicking toward the director. "And we have no proof that he had anything to do with—Monte Carlo. You know that."

His mother's eyes met his. Then she glanced away.

"If you were here to watch me in the film," William continued. "why didn't we see you earlier?"

"I got in to my little cottage last night, but I never get up before dawn. I need my beauty rest, after all," she said, batting her eyes at Sir Frederick.

"Of course, you need your rest," he murmured, patting her hand.

"And by the time I was up and dressed, there were policemen swarming all over the place. I could hardly venture out. I might have been interviewed."

"They'll probably get to you anyway," said her son. He had moved to the window and was looking out into the garden.

"Speaking of dressed, William, you really must change. What is this outfit of yours?"

"This is my costume, Mother," William replied. "And this is Peter Mallory's blood."

He turned back toward her, holding out his arms.

"Oh," she said, pulling her hands in to protect herself. "Did you shoot him?"

William rolled his eyes toward the ceiling.

"William was merely standing nearby," Sir Frederick explained. "He tried to save Peter's life."

"Did you, dear? How very altruistic of you," commented Lady Diane. She rose from her throne and crossed the room to him. She rubbed her thumb across the creases in his forehead.

"There now," she said kindly, softening her voice. "We'll get through this."

He sighed and looked at her gratefully. She smiled.

"Now, go and change."

There was a knock on Anna's bedroom door. It opened quietly, and Corinne, dressed as a lady's maid, crept in.

Anna sat up in her chair. Another dream.

"My lady," said Newberry, breathing in gulps.

"Newberry, what is it?" asked Lady Anna. "What happened?"

Her maid knelt at her feet and collected her thoughts. It seemed an eternity to Lady Anna, who bit her lip to keep from screaming.

"I was behind the trees, like you said," she began, her breathing coming more regular now.

"Yes?"

"And they come out, all of them. Lord Mallory and Sir John. And Mr. Williams and Mr. Potts." Newberry's eyes stared into the fire, as if she were seeing it all again in her mind. "Mr. Potts held the box of pistols, and the gentlemen each picked one. Then they went and stood on the marks in the grass, and Mr. Williams stood in the middle. He had a white handkerchief. I could see it in his hand, though his back was to me. I could see Lord Mallory's face from where I was hiding. I was closer to Sir John, but I could only see him from the side."

"Then what happened?" asked Lady Anna, leaning forward.

Newberry thought back.

"Then there was a strange sound. Like a scream. It was coming from the hedgerow in front of me. The trees that separate the field from the stableyard."

"What was it?"

"I don't know, m'lady. Mr. Potts went to look, but he didn't find anything. Sir John said it must ha' been a fox or somethin'. They do make strange sounds, m'lady. Otherworldly, sometimes."

Anna nodded.

"And did they duel?" she asked.

"Yes. Oh, m'lady! It was horrible!"

"Horrible?" asked Lady Anna, surprised.

Newberry's face was pallid.

"And he's dead," she said, breathlessly.

"Who's dead?" asked Lady Anna, scarcely breathing.

"Lord Mallory, m'lady. Mr. Williams tried to save him, but he couldn't. And Sir John was so upset."

Lady Anna covered her mouth with her hand.

"Lord Mallory is dead?"

"Yes, mum. And poor Mr. Williams with his blood all over him. He kept saying it was impossible. I suppose he didna think Sir John a good enough shot."

"Yes," said Lady Anna thoughtfully, remembering her conversation with Sir John about using blanks. "Perhaps that was it."

"And Sir John! I never seen anyone so sorrowful. He kept sayin' as how he never meant to shoot him. Which is strange, 'cause he was dueling. He looked terrible bad. I rushed back here as soon as I could, without being seen," Newberry went on. "'Cause I knew you would be waiting, but I had to wait for the doctor to take Lord Mallory away. But when I sneaked in through the kitchen, Mr. Reed, the butler, told me the constable was sent for! I hope he doesn't try to question you, m'lady! Or me!"

"He won't question you, Newberry," Lady Anna reassured her. "He doesn't know you were there."

There was a knock at the door.

Newberry squeaked.

"It's him now!" she whispered.

Lady Anna gave her a stern look as she rose to answer the door.

Anna jerked awake. She had fallen asleep in her chair by the fire.

"So, the duel had the same result in the dream as in real life," she thought as she fully came to consciousness. "Peter Mallory is dead. The blanks failed. And Mr. Williams—William—tried to save his life."

She crossed the room to the door, assuming the knock she heard was a real one.

"It must be William," she told herself, "coming back to finish the conversation."

She opened the door, ready to reprimand him for thinking she was beneath him. Then she stepped back in surprise.

"Am I disturbing you, dear?" asked Portia.

"No. Of course not," Anna replied. "I was just expecting someone else."

The older actress entered and took the chair by the fire opposite to Anna's.

"How are you feeling?" she asked as Anna settled down in front of her.

Anna sighed.

"I'm not sure how I feel," she said, tears welling up in her eyes.

Portia nodded.

"A man is dead, and that is a heavy thing, regardless of how you felt about the person," she said.

"Oh, Portia!" Anna cried. "What I was going to talk to you about doesn't even matter anymore," she explained. "Because it had to do with something Peter did last night. And now he's dead. So it doesn't matter. Does it?"

"Well, my dear, how can I possibly know unless you tell me about it?"

Anna explained everything that had happened the night before, from her kiss with William to her realization that she loved him to Peter's drunkenness and attempted rape.

"This morning, William was pressuring me to turn Peter in," she explained. "He said, if I didn't—"

"Yes?" asked Portia.

"He was just very insistent," she said. "All I could think of was how much

Jake didn't want me to end Peter's career. I wanted to ask your advice about it. But now, it doesn't matter, does it?"

"So you haven't told the police?" asked Portia.

"No. And Jake said there's no point destroying a man's reputation, now that he's dead."

Portia sat still, gazing into the fire.

"Thank you for telling me, Anna," she said seriously, her brow furrowed. "This sheds some light on a few things."

"What do you think?" Anna asked. "Should I have mentioned it to the police?"

Portia looked at her thoughtfully.

"If it comes up during the investigation, you have every right to mention it, dead man or not," she said.

"Investigation?" asked Anna. "You think there will be one?"

"Oh, I think it is inevitable," said Portia. "Especially now that you've told me this."

She stood, and so did Anna. The older woman embraced her.

"I'm sorry that happened to you," she said sincerely. "You are fortunate it only went as far as it did. I hope it never happens again, but if it does, don't keep silent."

She pulled back and looked Anna sternly in the face.

"Do you hear me?" she asked. "Don't keep silent, no matter who it is."

Anna nodded. Portia kissed Anna's forehead, then headed for the door.

"I am going to text my son," she explained as she went. "He loves it when I do that. Especially when I add little smiley faces."

She gave Anna a wink as she left the room.

It was lunchtime, and Anna was ravenous. She had never eaten the breakfast she had had no stomach for before dawn, and she was regretting it now. After redoing her hair and makeup, she ventured down into the Dining Room. She wanted to look a little more presentable, in case she ran into Lady Diane again.

Sir Frederick had sent the catering staff home, and asked William to arrange meals through Hampstead Hall for the resident cast and crew members. Anna passed Corinne and Perry, who were seated in the Great Hall. They told her they'd already eaten. Corinne was still a mess of tears; Anna was surprised she hadn't come to her room for comfort.

Through the front window, Anna could see a police vehicle parked in the circle drive.

"I guess that's our protection," she said aloud.

"Protection from what?" scoffed Corinne. "Can they really protect us from accidents? From life?"

"Maybe they think it was more than an accident," Perry suggested.

Corinne stared at him with horrified eyes.

"How can you even suggest that!" she said.

"I don't know," he said, shaking his head. "Don't listen to me."

Anna sat down next to Corinne.

"If you need anything, just ask," she said.

Corinne nodded, pressing her lips together and staring at her hands.

Anna exchanged a concerned look with Perry before moving to join the others in the Dining Room.

When she entered the room, all conversation stopped. She knew it was because of Jake. They were speculating, and didn't want her to know. She didn't blame Jake for wanting to eat in his room, alone. He didn't want to face the scrutiny.

Miranda and Adrian were at one end of the table. They started chatting again while she filled her plate.

They don't seem worried about anything, including their safety, Anna thought, annoyed by their self-centeredness.

Jim, Sarah, and Alan were seated at the opposite end of the table.

His Lordship, William, must be eating in the throne room, Anna thought sarcastically.

And where's Peter? Oh.

It still didn't seem real.

She sat down in the center between the two groups.

In a few minutes, Sir Frederick sailed in. He seemed to have recovered somewhat. Anna remembered thinking that morning that he was going into shock, but he wasn't in shock now. He filled his plate and sat across from Anna, his back to the door that led to the Great Hall.

"Where's Brian?" he asked, his mouth full of food.

"He went to his room after the police were through," said Sarah. "I guess he's still there."

Sir Frederick nodded.

"Don't blame him," he said. "It must be difficult for him. It could ruin his reputation as a stunt coordinator if—well, depending on what happened."

The room was silent.

Sir Frederick continued to eat busily. He seemed more serious than he usually did, but he didn't look like he would crumple to the ground. Anna once again wondered what the future held for *Cavendish Manor*. How could they continue, even if Peter's death was indeed an accident, and not—

"Hello, Freddie."

Anna watched Sir Frederick freeze, his fork in mid-air, his mouth hanging open. He recovered after a few seconds, and turned with a smile toward the doorway behind him. A woman stood there, not quite as regal-looking as Lady Diane, but just as intimidating. She had dark, wiry hair and a wide, attractive face.

No facelifts there, thought Anna.

"Julia!" Sir Frederick said, smiling with all of his teeth.

"I've been looking all over for you, Freddie," said Julia. "I was beginning to think you were avoiding me."

She gave him a look that suggested that, if he was avoiding her, it would behoove him to keep that information to himself.

Sir Frederick rose from the table.

"How wonderful to see you," he said, kissing her on the cheek. "Why don't we go somewhere private and have a chat?"

After they left, there was a stifled snort from Jim's end of the table. From the other end, Miranda let out a low whistle.

"This can't be good," said Sarah.

"Why?" asked Anna. "Who is she?"

"The producer," said Miranda, her lips pursing in an "I told you so" kind of way.

"Worse than that," said Sarah somberly, staring at the door. "She's Sir Frederick's ex-wife."

CHAPTER THIRTY-NINE

———◆-◀-◉-▶-◆———

In the Tapestry Room, Sir Frederick closed the door. William had been summoned for moral support.

I'm earning my title today, thought William bitterly. Acting as a professional mediator.

"It's always good to see you, Julia," Sir Frederick began, "but there was really no need for you to have come all this way." Sir Frederick wrung his hands, his eyes blinking rapidly behind his glasses. "Everything's in hand. No need to worry."

"One of your actors is dead, Freddie!" Julia exclaimed. "You call that 'in hand?'"

"The police are here, dealing with things. I'm sure it will be no time before we're up and running again."

"Up and running again!" Julia repeated sharply. She was pacing back and forth across the carpet. William attempted to fade into the background. The last thing he wanted was to be in the middle of a domestic.

"One of your principal actors is dead, and you're three episodes into the series," Julia reminded the director. "You would have to reshoot from the beginning!"

"Not necessarily," said Sir Frederick, raising his finger for emphasis. "I've been thinking…"

"This is no time for you to be thinking, Freddie," Julia snapped. "That's what I'm here to do."

Sir Frederick's mouth closed with a clicking sound.

"It's your thinking that got you into this mess in the first place," she continued. "Why did you house them here? In the house? All together, like a college dormitory?"

"William gave me a good deal," Sir Frederick whined, looking to the Earl for help. "It's expensive to house all these people, as you very well know, and the Studio wasn't doing me any favors…"

"You should have known better, Freddie. You know what actors are like! These artistic types, all cooped up together? No offense, Lord Somerville. I'm sure you were only being kind. But someone was bound to lose their mind."

"Well, if I'd had a bit more budget," said Sir Frederick in an irritated tone, "perhaps I could have housed them more to your liking."

"I hope you are not blaming this death on my budget cuts!" said the producer sharply, stopping in front of him. She stood a good four inches taller than he did.

"Well, I hope you're not blaming it on my housing options!" countered Sir Frederick. "You can't blame Peter's death on artistic temperaments thrown together. It's more likely to be caused by money. Money always makes people do crazy things!"

"It's not the only thing that drives people crazy!" Julia retorted, her eyes blazing.

"Hold on, Julia," said William, holding up his hand. "You're assuming Peter's death wasn't an accident. We were working with pistols. Accidents can happen, even in the best of circumstances."

"You were supposed to be working with blanks," Julia said curtly. "I'll have Brian's head on a platter before the night is out."

"Don't blame Brian prematurely," said William. "We haven't heard from forensics, yet. And besides, we were using blanks today. But not yesterday," he reminded her. "Perhaps, somehow, a live bullet was left in the pistol, and the blank cartridge was loaded on top of it. It *can* happen."

Julia pursed her lips.

"I'll believe it when I hear it from the police," she said. "I know what Peter Mallory was like. Any number of people would have loved to have murdered him. Including me."

"Lady Churchwood-Styles," called Mr. Barnaby in his silvery voice. He had appeared silently in the doorway. "Your room is ready."

"Thank you, Mr. Barnaby," she replied, taking a calming breath while keeping her gaze sharpened on Sir Frederick. "Lead the way."

"I wish Mr. Barnaby wouldn't use that name," whimpered Sir Frederick after Julia left the room. "Isn't there a way to take my title back from her, since we're divorced?"

His eyes appealed to William, who shrugged.

"She doesn't use it, does she?" he asked.

"No, thank God," said Sir Frederick. "She goes by her maiden name, Julia Shrewsbury. But Mr. Barnaby is all that is correct. Can't blame him, I suppose. But I do blame *her* for coming and spoiling everything."

"I think things were already spoiled before she arrived," murmured William.

In the afternoon, Julia called an impromptu, though required, meeting of all resident cast and crew. Even Jake and Brian were expected to be there. They met in the Drawing Room. When Anna entered, she saw Corinne cuddled up in a corner of a sofa. Her eyes were still puffy and red from crying. She kept her attention on her lap, not looking at anybody else, including Anna.

Strange, Anna thought. It seemed so out of character for Corinne to distance herself. She would have expected her to crave the comfort and sympathy of others, instead. And the attention.

Jake was seated on another sofa next to Jaime, but when he saw Anna, he indicated the open seat on his other side. She joined him and sat down. Looking up, she caught William watching her from where he was standing across the room in front of the fireplace.

William looked away.

She seems to be recovering, he thought, *from all she's been through.* He told himself he was glad she was being a comfort to Jake. He looked to William like a man who was coming unraveled around the edges. He glanced over again, and watched Anna take Jake's hand. She was looking up into his face, like she was giving him strength. On Jake's other side, William noticed Jaime watching as well. Her pale eyes seemed to flash, although her face hadn't changed expressions. She looked up, catching William in her gaze. William was surprised to read hatred in her eyes, and wondered if she applied it generally to everyone in the room, or to him in particular. Then she gave him a half-smile and turned away.

Maybe I imagined it, he thought.

At the front of the room, Julia cleared her throat.

"This has been a sad day for our *Cavendish Manor* family," she began. "We have lost a fellow actor, and a friend."

There was a stifled sob from Corinne.

"I wanted to personally offer my condolences to all of you," Julia continued, "especially those who were particularly close with Peter. The police have asked that we remain here for the time being, and I appreciate your patience as we decide how we are going to proceed in the future."

"Can I say something?" asked Brian.

Julia hesitated.

"Of course," she said, smiling stiffly.

Brian stood and faced the group. Anna was immediately sorry for him. He looked like a man searching for forgiveness.

"I just wanted to say," he began, "that I did everything in my power to make this duel as safe as possible. I loaded the pistols," he said, addressing Jake, "and I swear there was nothing in the barrels when I loaded the blank cartridges. If there had been, I would have felt it with the metal rod. This whole thing is—well, it's impossible!"

"And yet," said Julia icily, "it happened."

"Julia!" warned Sir Frederick, standing beside her.

"I just wanted to apologize," Brian continued, "first to Jake, and then to all of you, for what happened. Because, even though I can swear there was nothing in the barrel, the fact is, like Julia pointed out, something was. And it ultimately falls on me, as stunt coordinator, to take the blame."

Jake stood up.

"No one is blaming you, Brian," he said, his voice hoarse. "Especially me. If it's anyone's fault, it's mine. I'm the one who pulled the trigger."

The two men shook hands, then pulled in for a brief hug.

"It's still my responsibility," Brian said, but Anna could tell a weight lifted from his shoulders.

"So," Julia said, returning the attention to herself, "if everyone will just be patient, we should know more by tomorrow morning."

"Do the police really think it's murder?" asked Miranda.

"No one has said anything about murder, Miranda," said Julia.

"Actually, you did, earlier," Sir Frederick volunteered.

Julia gave him a withering glance.

"The police will tell us their findings," Julia continued, "and until then, we will not discuss it. Especially with anyone *outside*," she emphasized. "And that means the press. I remind you that you all signed confidentiality agreements. Do I make myself clear?"

"I don't see why we can't discuss things with *each other*," Miranda complained. "I mean, if the gun had a real bullet in it, then someone put it there. Maybe the props master. The jilted lover."

Miranda let out a tinkling laugh that fell like glass breaking in the silence that followed.

William watched as Jaime's face reddened. Her eyes stared daggers at Miranda. The older actress was snickering like a schoolgirl behind an elaborately decorated scarf.

Portia Valentine strode forward and took Miranda's hand.

"Come, Miranda," she said. "We've all had a stressful day."

Miranda pulled her hand away.

"I feel fine," she insisted. "I was merely pointing out that Jaime and Peter used to date. I remember. It was a couple of years ago, when we were doing *Love and Loss*." She turned to Adrian. "Anyone can see they hate each other, now. I've been pointing out to Adrian how she's always glaring at Peter when his back is turned. Or *was* turned, I guess I should say, now."

"Yes, well…" Adrian mumbled, clearly embarrassed to be included. He raised his eyebrows toward the ceiling.

Corinne looked up, horrified.

"How can you say things like that?" she asked tearfully. "Peter's dead!"

"So much happened to me today," Miranda said, waving her arm, as if to clear the air. "Everything's just a blur right now. It's hard to believe it was only this morning."

"Happened to *you?*" Corinne fumed.

"All I'm saying is that if anyone had the opportunity or motivation to put a bullet in the gun, it was the props master," Miranda said, giving Jaime a challenging look.

Jaime rose slowly from her seat, her silver eyes locked on Miranda's, and silently left the room, pushing past Jim and Sarah, who happened to be standing in front of the doorway.

"That's enough!" shouted Jake, standing up and glaring back at Miranda. His fists were clenched. Anna had never seen Jake angry, and the sight of it was alarming.

He chased after Jaime.

"Well, that was interesting," Miranda commented with a giggle, eyeing Anna slyly. "Are *you* going to follow after *him?*"

Anna didn't answer. She couldn't believe Miranda could be so callous.

She must be on something, she realized. The older actress's eyes, she noticed, had pinpoint pupils.

"Miranda, be quiet!" demanded Julia, attempting to regain control of the room. "You're not helping."

"I'm not helping?" Miranda asked, suddenly angry. "Our lives are in danger. We need all the help we can get. It's that stupid curse!" she said, glaring at William. "And all along, you were the Earl. No wonder you made such a blunder about the Scottish play. You're not one of us. You can't say this one was a practical joke!"

"What curse?" asked Julia, confused. "What is she talking about? What practical jokes?"

She turned to Sir Frederick, who spread his hands wide, pretending to be clueless.

"Yes, what curse are you accusing my son of causing?" demanded an authoritative voice from the doorway. Lady Diane had entered the room and struck a statuesque pose. She stared frigidly at Miranda.

"The curse has come upon us," Miranda quoted like she had earlier in the day, widening her eyes dramatically at her new audience. "And I'm not taking any chances. I'll be in my room until further notice."

She rose imperially, and swept past Lady Diane and out of the room, dragging her scarf along the floor behind her.

There was something that sounded like a sniff from Lady Diane as Miranda passed.

Adrian gave one of his surprise faces, his eyebrows nearly disappearing into his hairline.

"What did I tell you, Freddie?" Julia said to Sir Frederick in a loud whisper. "Too much drama!"

"Why, Julia, I didn't see you there," said Lady Diane with a smile that said she wished she hadn't. She sauntered across the room toward her.

Julia smiled back. Or, at least, the edges of her mouth curved upward.

"Lady Diane. How pleasant to see you again," she said in a less-than-enthusiastic voice. "You are all free to go," she said to the rest of the group, waving her hand dismissively. "Meeting adjourned."

"But you haven't told us if we still have jobs," called Jim from the back of the room.

"No decisions will be made until we hear from the police," said Julia curtly.

Jim grumbled something to Sarah as they left, followed by Alan.

Corinne left the room quickly as well, holding a kleenex to her nose and mouth. Perry followed her.

Anna remained stunned on the sofa.

"The Studio would like to apologize, Lady Diane, that this has happened on your estate," said Julia.

"It's not my estate anymore," said Lady Diane, waving her arm toward her son. "It's William's."

"Thank you, Julia," said William politely, giving his mother a warning glance as he joined the group. "We appreciate your condolences."

"Frederick, this whole business makes me feel so confined," said Lady Diane, wrapping her well-manicured hand around Sir Frederick's arm. "I simply *must* go for a walk and get some fresh air."

Sir Frederick chuckled nervously, turning a rebellious shoulder toward his ex-wife.

"Would you like some company?" he asked.

"Oh, yes! You're a darling!" cooed Lady Diane.

"Such a darling," sneered Julia under her breath as she watched them exit through the French doors. She sighed audibly and headed to the Great Hall, where she was accosted by Jim, Sarah, and Alan, who were clearly not finished with their questions.

William and Anna found themselves alone in the Drawing Room.

Anna stood up from the sofa, feeling awkward and out-of-place.

"Well…I guess…" she stammered, turning toward the door.

"No, sit," said William, motioning her back.

Anna obediently sat down again.

"I didn't mean…that wasn't a command," said William, frustrated that their relationship was so strained now. He sat down on the sofa, leaving space between them.

Anna eyed him warily.

He looked like the same William she had known from the beginning, the one wearing muddy boots and a stained field jacket. The one whose eyes twinkled when he was joking or up to something. And yet, he was different now. She wasn't sure if the difference was in him, or in her perception of him.

William could read the mistrust in her eyes and body language.

"How are you doing?" he asked sincerely.

"I'm fine," she snapped, annoyed still about the "equals" comment he had made earlier.

Her arms were wrapped around herself, as if she were giving herself a hug. William longed to pull her close, to tell her it would all be okay. But there was

Jake. It was as if he were sitting on the sofa between them.

"What are you going to do?" he asked. "Now that your attacker is… dead?"

She shook her head.

"I spoke with Portia about it," she began.

"Good!" he said, nodding.

"She said to only bring it up if it came up in the investigation."

"Does she think there will be an investigation?"

Anna nodded.

William was thoughtful.

"I didn't see the actual shot," he said. "I was so focused on my one line, not messing it up. What did *you* see? Anything unusual?"

She shook her head.

"No," she answered. "I've gone over it and over it in my mind, but everything looked just like it should have. Except that Peter yelled out and fell, and he wasn't supposed to. I thought it was just pretend. Until he didn't get up."

"I think we all did," William agreed. "What if—but I suppose we have to wait for ballistics. But what if there was a second shooter? What if there really was only a blank cartridge in the pistol?"

"Someone else, not involved in the duel?" she asked, whirling the new possibility in her mind. "But that would be—murder!"

She whispered the word, glancing around to make sure they were still alone in the room.

He leaned forward conspiratorially.

"It would be murder, either way," he said quietly. "If someone put live ammo in the gun, it would have to have been on purpose. I can't imagine Brian Elliston, or even Jaime, accidentally leaving a bullet in the barrel. They aren't careless people. And I believe Brian. He says he would have noticed that something was in the barrel when he loaded the blanks."

"Yes," Anna agreed, remembering the loading lesson Brian had given her. "He would have felt something with the rod. Unless he's lying."

Their eyes met.

"But if it was another shooter, how could they have done it?" she asked. "They would have to have been hidden somewhere. Are you thinking of some kind of outsider? Like a crazy person?"

"No, although I suppose that's not impossible," said William. "No, I was thinking maybe from the trees along the edge of the field. It's the only cover. His wound was from the front, not from the side, so someone shooting long-distance from base camp, or even from the hedgerow, is out of the question."

"But that would be Corinne!" Anna said. "William, how could you? You can't suspect Corinne!"

"Anna, we have to keep an open mind about this," he said, checking the room again to make sure there was no one listening. "I know she's your friend, but she is the only one who could take a shot without anyone seeing her. And it would be the right angle. From her vantage point, she would be looking at Peter's face and Jake's back."

Anna knew he was right, even as he said it. But he couldn't be right! Corinne?

"She couldn't have done it," Anna said, refusing to believe it. "She and Peter were—well, I don't know what they were, but they were sleeping together."

"Not lately."

Anna closed her eyes.

"Do you really think she could do that?" she asked, looking up at him with a horrified expression. "To kill her former lover?"

William shrugged.

"People do it all the time," he said. "Or don't you read the news?"

She sighed.

"I'm surprised you would accuse her. You two seem to be—close," she said, gauging his reaction.

He gave her a puzzled look.

"What do you mean?" he asked. "I barely know her."

"I've seen you talking together," she said, nonchalantly. "I thought maybe she liked you or something. Shifting from Peter to you, maybe."

He shook his head, incredulous.

"No way," he assured her, one side of his mouth curving in a smile. "I can tell you that for certain."

"Oh," said Anna, wondering why he could.

"Look, it's just a theory," he said, dismissively. "I'm sure Corinne is innocent. I'm sorry I brought it up. The police will probably tell us it was an accident. End of story."

Anna nodded, biting her lip.

"What about Jaime?" she asked, remembering Miranda's accusation. "Do you think she and Peter used to be together?"

"I wouldn't know," he replied. "Peter didn't confide in me. They definitely weren't chummy."

"No," Anna agreed. "But it reminds me of the script, for some reason."

"What about in your dreams?" asked William. "Does the Jaime in your dreams know Peter?"

Anna thought back.

"I don't think so," she said slowly. "In my dreams, my *Cavendish Manor* character is played by Jaime. I mean, she's the poor relation. She hasn't shown any interest in Peter, or Lord Mallory. Wait! He said something that struck me as odd. Right at the beginning!"

She closed her eyes, her mind returning to the first few dreams.

"We were riding horses through the park, and Lord Mallory asked about her, my Scottish cousin. He said she was quiet, and that she'd always been that way. And I was surprised, because he wasn't supposed to have known her before."

"That's interesting," said William. "What else do you remember?"

"He told me she was talking a lot to Jake. To Sir John. And he wondered if I was jealous."

"Were you?"

Anna's answer was a long exhale. The dream had been early on, she remembered. When Jake had been foremost in her mind.

"Sorry," William apologized. "It's none of my business."

The picture of Jaime and Jake in the garden when they first arrived went through his mind. He wondered again if he should tell her.

"Jake is taking this hard," he said instead. "I'm sure you're very comforting to him."

"Yes," she answered, her eyes downcast. "I suppose so."

Things are so complicated now, she thought. If only William had answered her text last night. Then she could have told him how she felt about him. They would be in this together, instead of sitting here, miles apart.

"I wonder what he thinks now about you mentioning Peter's attack to the police?" William asked.

"He was glad I didn't say anything," she replied. "No need to ruin his reputation."

She closed her eyes. Peter's drunken face rose up before her mind's eye, and she shuddered.

"You're safe, Anna," William said, reaching across the divide and taking her hand, as if he could read her thoughts. "Peter's dead. There are no more threats."

She looked at him steadily.

Oh, how I wish I could believe that, she thought.

CHAPTER FORTY

Dinner was a silent affair. The only member of the cast who was absent was Miranda, who, true to her word, stayed in her room. Even William joined them at the table, and this time, he sat at the head.

Lady Diane, making the excuse of a headache, retired to her cottage.

William was thankful. It was one less actor in the drama that had become his life.

Julia Shrewsbury had seated herself across from Sir Frederick. William amused himself by watching the two of them. Sir Frederick was smiling at everything and everybody, as if willing them to be cheerful in spite of tragedy; Julia's face clearly reflected her distaste for his jollity.

"I feel sorry for Brian Elliston," William thought to himself, watching Julia's contemptible glances in the direction of the stunt coordinator. She clearly blamed him for the accident.

There was almost zero conversation. When anyone did speak, it was impeccably polite, even regarding minor things, like passing the salt.

Too polite, Anna thought. She couldn't help examining every move and word her fellow cast-members made. And the crew. Peter wasn't well-liked by them, either.

"Stop it, Anna," she told herself. It was an accident. She had to keep believing that, until—well, until she knew otherwise.

She glanced at Corinne, across the table and down several seats, who was keeping up her silent misery. She barely raised her eyes from her plate, and she chewed slowly, like she even lacked the energy to eat. Anna was surprised she had come to the table at all. Like Miranda, she could have asked for a tray to be brought to her room. Anna prayed the police would give them an answer soon. It would be so much better to know *something*.

Finally, Brian broached the forbidden subject.

"Have we heard anything more from the police?" he asked cautiously, turning toward the producer.

Julia pressed her lips together and glanced away.

"No," she said. "Nothing yet."

Anna felt Jake's fingers touch her hand under the table. She looked up into his face and saw the expression of a lost child. She wrapped her fingers around his. He gave her a tight smile.

"I'm sure it won't be long, now," interjected Sir Frederick, jovially. "There's bound to be some kind of news soon."

Julia's gaze shriveled his grin.

Mr. Barnaby entered discreetly from the Great Hall and whispered something in William's ear. Although no one had dressed up for dinner, the house manager was impeccable in his silver suit. As she watched him, Anna decided he probably had a whole closet full of silver suits.

William nodded in answer to Mr. Barnaby. The house manager exited the room and returned a short time later with Inspector Ferguson.

Anna could feel the tension in the room as all eyes turned to the Inspector. William rose.

"Inspector Ferguson," he said, greeting the man with a handshake.

"My lord," the Inspector answered courteously. He turned to address the table. Anna's eyes focused involuntarily on his still-crooked tie.

"I am sorry to interrupt your meal," he began, "but we have the results back from the preliminary autopsy."

Jake's grip tightened on Anna's hand, and she squeezed it back.

"Peter Mallory died of a gunshot wound to the heart," the Inspector continued. "The projectile was a lead ball, approximately half an inch in diameter. Fired from a muzzle-loading pistol," he said, as if it needed clarification. His sharp eyes roved around the faces in the room.

"That's impossible!" said Brian Elliston. "Those were only used yesterday, when we filmed with live ammunition."

Jaime laid her hand on Brian's arm, as if to warn him to keep quiet.

"Nevertheless," the Inspector said, "that is how he died."

"But it was an accident, right?" asked Corinne, her eyes filled with tears.

"That has yet to be determined," Inspector Ferguson answered non-committally. "It's an on-going investigation."

"I swear, Inspector," Jake insisted, squeezing Anna's hand even tighter, "I didn't—"

"No need for that right now," the Inspector assured him, waving him back with his hand. "We'll go through it all again tomorrow."

Anna noticed Jake's brow had broken out in a sweat. He looked like he was going to regurgitate.

"Are you going to take us down to the station and interrogate us?" Corinne asked, her eyes wide and dramatic.

"We will need to conduct further interviews," said the Inspector.

"But the press can't hear of this!" stammered Sir Frederick nervously, with no hint of his previous smiles. "If you haul us all down to the station, how will we keep things quiet? We can't have the paparazzi descending down on us!"

Inspector Ferguson squinted at the director.

"You could do your interviews here," William suggested. "You can use my Study as an office. It would be much more convenient for you to keep everyone here in one place. And no publicity."

The Inspector appeared to consider it.

"We wouldn't need to re-interview everyone," he clarified. "There are many who have been cleared already, like Mr. Barnaby. Yes, perhaps doing the interviews here would be for the best. If you don't mind, my lord?"

"Not at all," answered William.

"Thank you, my boy," said Sir Frederick to William, gratefully.

Julia sniffed from across the table.

"The Studio appreciates this, Lord Somerville," she said, attempting to show who was actually in charge. "And Inspector, you have our full coopera- tion. We want to know the truth of what happened in this dreadful tragedy."

"Thank you, Miss—?"

"Shrewsbury," Julia answered. "Julia Shrewsbury. I'm the producer for the show."

"Ah," he said. "I'm afraid we didn't meet earlier."

"No, I only arrived around one o'clock. After it happened."

"I see."

The Inspector gave another brief, squint-eyed look around the table of faces before landing once again on William.

"We'll begin tomorrow, then," he confirmed. "and I don't have to tell you all not to leave the premises?"

CHAPTER FORTY-ONE

———◆◂◦▸◆———

The Inspector's announcement left a chill in the air, and most of the cast and crew sneaked up to their rooms after dinner. Anna accompanied a haggard-looking Jake.

His bedroom is a disaster, Anna thought, trying not to be obvious as she glanced at the discarded clothes strewn over chairs. There was a messy pile of papers on the desk.

"Sorry," he mumbled self-consciously, tidying the papers, then leaning against the desk as if to hide them from her sight. He smiled sheepishly. "I'm not good at keeping my room clean."

"Doesn't the maid come in?" Anna asked.

"Well, I like my privacy, so I told her not to," he explained. "I thought I'd do a better job. Guess I better start letting her do hers."

Anna nodded.

"What do you think will happen?" he asked, his face growing serious as he changed the subject.

"You mean, with this investigation?" she asked. "I don't know."

It was a truthful answer. She wasn't sure what an investigation would find.

There was a knock at his door. It was Jaime.

"I was just checking on Jake," she explained, her pale eyes withholding emotion when she noticed Anna in the room.

"Thank you Jaime," he said, giving her a hug. "I was just asking Anna what she thinks will happen. Tomorrow, I mean."

Jaime shrugged.

"Hard to know," she answered. "I know the three of us are in the hot seat, of course. You, me, and Brian."

Anna noticed Jaime's eyes were tired. She was tempted to feel sorry for her. But something about the props master's aloof manner held back her sympathy.

"How could he have been killed by a lead ball?" asked Anna. "It would have to have been in the gun."

"But Brian says it wasn't," said Jake. "He checked before he loaded the blanks, and I believe him."

Jaime shook her head.

"It's a mystery," she said. "You don't think…no, nevermind."

"What?" asked Jake.

She grimaced.

"You don't think this was one of the practical jokes that have been going on, do you?" she asked, looking from Jake to Anna. "Maybe someone meant for it to only scare Peter, but it went too far."

"I really hope not," Anna answered.

Jake rubbed his face with his hands. Jaime gave him a sympathetic look.

"You need to get some sleep," she ordered, pushing him toward his bed. "Maybe we should borrow some sleeping pills from Miranda."

The corner of her mouth turned up to show she was joking.

"That's the last thing I need," Jake said with a sigh. "I want to think clearly. To figure this out."

He laid down wearily on top of the bedcovers, throwing an arm over his eyes to block the light. He let out another deep exhale, and his body appeared to relax.

Jaime shook her head.

"Go to sleep, Jake," she said. "We can figure all this out tomorrow."

As she and Anna tiptoed out of the room, Jaime's eyes strayed over the papers on the desk, and her jaw clenched.

"He said he doesn't let the maid in," whispered Anna.

Jaime rolled her eyes and shook her head, quickly shutting off the light and closing the door softly behind them.

"I'm worried about him," Jaime admitted as they stood in the hall. Anna believed that to be true. It was the first candid thing she had heard from Jaime, and it surprised her.

"He's taking it very hard," Anna agreed. "Understandably."

Jaime nodded, pursing her lips.

"I'm sure there's a rational explanation," she said, peering at Anna with her other-worldly eyes.

"The Inspector will figure it out," Anna said.

Jaime tilted her head to the side like a doubtful bird.

"Good night, Anna," she said, heading for the stairs and her room on the third floor.

"Good night," Anna replied, watching her go.

Anna was more tired than she'd been in all the weeks of filming. With an almost sleepless night after Peter's attack, followed by a long, hard day full of death and police and suspicion, she should have been asleep in minutes. But her brain simply wouldn't shut off. Sleep would not come.

She knew what she had to do, what was calling her, but she resisted as long as she could. Finally, she could resist no longer.

Wrapping her robe around her, she tiptoed out into the darkened hall, shaking the irrational thought to listen for Peter sneaking around, ready to pound on Corinne's door.

"Peter is dead," she reminded herself. "Then why don't I feel any safer?"

The stairwell was dark with shadows, and no light came in through the leaded windows. The moon was in hiding.

I don't blame it, Anna thought with a shudder.

The door to the Tapestry Room was closed. Anna hesitated. Should she knock? Or should she give up and go back to her room and her sleepless, dreamless night?

Determined, she held her breath, slowly turned the antique door handle, and stepped into the room.

A fire crackled in the hearth, but no other lights were lit. Anna froze; last time, she remembered, William was asleep in one of the chairs.

"Anna, is that you?"

William had been waiting for her to come. Hoping she would, anyway. He knew the lure the Tapestry Room window had for her, and he had bargained that she would want to gain any information from the past that she could, after today's events. After last night's events, as well—the attack that was so similar to her dream. And to the script. That was something he thought they should explore more fully. Truthfully, he just wanted to talk with her again, about anything. Maybe now, with his identity no longer an issue, the tension between them could be resolved. Maybe, if he could be alone with her. Without Jake.

She and Jake had left together after dinner, he noticed. But something about the way she was treating him had given William hope instead of melancholy. It was motherly, like Jake was a child who needed her care.

He had drifted into sleep a time or two, sitting in his chair by the fire, but he jerked himself out of it. It was late, and he was about to give up and go to his rooms to bed when he heard the furtive opening of the door. He asked the question without turning in his chair; he already knew the answer.

"William?" Anna asked in a whisper, then felt foolish. Why did she feel the need to whisper? Maybe it was the darkness.

Maybe it was death.

William rose from his chair and beckoned her to the chair beside him. She sat down tentatively, keeping to the edge, ready for flight. The firelight flickered over William's face, sparking in his eyes, and revealing the hollows underneath them. A surge of sympathy washed over her as she realized how much he had been through in the last twenty-four hours. An early-morning call-time, an unexpected death. The police coming, forcing him to reveal his secret identity. And before that, Peter's attack. He had been there then, as well.

He must be just as exhausted as I am, she thought. She felt her eyes begin to fill with tears, but William's voice arrested their progress.

"You've come to dream, haven't you?"

She suddenly felt exposed. She fiddled with her fingers in her lap.

"That isn't an accusation," he added. "I want you to. I want you to find out what you can, if there's any connection between the past and…and this."

"There has to be, doesn't there?" she asked, leaning forward, her body tense. "There are too many similarities." She hesitated. "I had another dream this afternoon."

He leaned toward her.

"What was it?"

Anna could smell the clean scent of soap, combined with something sharp and sweet. Maybe a hint of cologne? Or aftershave?

She focused her mind again on his question. Why did his very presence cause her mind to unravel?

"Apparently, Lady Anna sent her maid to watch the duel, so she could know the results."

"Which would be Corinne, right?" he asked.

"Yes," answered Anna. "And she hid in the trees, just like Corinne did today."

He gave her a knowing look.

"You can't assume her guilt, just because she was hidden in the trees in both situations," she scolded. "And we don't know it was murder, anyway."

"You're right," he admitted. "What happened? In the dream-duel?"

"The outcome was the same," she said solemnly. "Peter Mallory died."

They paused, staring at each other, as if the mention of Peter's death required a moment of silence.

"Something else interesting," added Anna. "In both duels, they used blanks."

"Even in the past?" asked William, surprised.

"Yes. Sir John told me before the duel. He said that he had asked you, I mean, Mr. Williams, to use gunpowder but no lead ball when he loaded the pistols. Blanks."

"Why?"

"He said he didn't want to kill his best friend. That even though Peter had done wrong by attacking me, or Lady Anna, he couldn't kill him. He said that Peter would never know. He would think they both missed."

"Clever," murmured William, thoughtfully. "If it had worked."

"Yes," Anna agreed. "If it had worked."

"I've been thinking about something," said William. "Some of these things that have been happening, Peter's attack, the duel. It's similar to your dreams, but it's also similar to the script. Sometimes I think your mind is replaying the script, but then sometimes—"

"Things happen in the dream before I get the script," Anna finished for him, nodding.

"Exactly," he agreed.

"Last Sunday, after I left the Gallery, I went to the Library," said Anna, leaving out the fact that it was to avoid him. "Sir Frederick was there looking for a book. Some kind of journal he said Lord Somerville, your father, had let him read. He said he based *Cavendish Manor* on a story from that book. He was going to ask you if you knew where it was."

William was thoughtful.

"He did ask me about that book. It's a kind of family history, stories written down by previous Earls. He told me my father had let him read it, and he was looking for it, but he didn't tell me why he wanted it."

"Maybe he didn't want you to know he put your actual family into a television series," suggested Anna. "But that would explain why the script and the dreams are alike. If my dreams are some kind of reliving of the past, and Sir Frederick used stories from the past to write the script, then there would be similarities. Did you give it to him?"

"No," said William. "I couldn't find it, either. I've never read it myself. I'm not sure where my father would have put it. Maybe I should give it another search."

"If we found it, we might be able to know what's going to happen in the future," Anna said, shivering. "Maybe we can prevent something."

She fidgeted with her fingers again.

"I'm afraid, William," she said honestly, looking up into his face.

"Afraid of what?" he asked. "Of a murderer on the loose?"

"No. I mean, maybe," she admitted. "But I'm more afraid of what I'll find out. In my dreams, I mean. Maybe there's still bad things coming."

William rubbed the stubble on his chin and looked toward the fire.

"I think," he said finally, looking steadily into her eyes, "that this is a time for bravery."

He took her hand in his and brought it to his lips. Her stomach fluttered as he kissed it.

"Touch the window handle, Lady Anna," he said quietly, releasing her hand. "Be brave. I'll be here with you."

It was bright day in the garden. Lady Anna whirled around at the sound of someone approaching on the gravel path.

It was Mr. Williams. Or rather, as she had so recently learned from her father, William Langley.

She scowled at him as he drew near.

"Lady Anna, you have every right to be angry with me," said Mr. Langley, opening his arms wide. "I deceived you. But you must allow me to explain."

"You have blood on you!" she exclaimed, drawing back.

He glanced down at his clothes.

"It's Lord Mallory's," he admitted. "I tried to stop the bleeding, but I couldn't. Sorry, I should have changed, but I wanted to speak with you. The doctor just left, or I would have come before. Are you—all right?" he asked. "Lord Mallory's death must be a shock to you. And Sir John—"

"If you are asking if I mourn for Lord Mallory, I do not," she said bluntly. "I don't have to explain to you why."

Mr. Williams nodded grimly.

"But I am sorry for Sir John," she said. "It must have been a shock."

Mr. Williams gave her a puzzled glance before changing the subject.

"I wanted to speak to you about my identity," he said. "I almost revealed myself to you so many times. But it was imperative that I keep my identity a secret while I was here at Hampstead Hall. After the duel, I no longer needed the deception, so I told Lord Somerville my identity. I see he has told you. It was a relief to him. I hoped it would be to you, as well."

He looked at her earnestly.

"I don't even know what to call you," she complained, pouting. "Lord Langley?"

"My name is William Langley," he said. "but I'm not a member of the aristocracy, as yet, so—"

"Well, *Mr. Langley*, what did you hope to gain from this deception?" she asked. "Were you trying to trick me into falling in love with my father's secretary?"

"*Did* you fall in love with your father's secretary?" he asked, taking a step toward her.

Her eyes widened and she took a step back.

"Shall we sit down?" he asked, sweeping his arm toward a nearby bench.

She wrapped her shawl more tightly around her and sat on the stone seat. He sat as well, keeping a space between them.

"So, are we related, then?" she asked, trying to sound casual. "Since you're the heir to my father's estate? Father's over the moon to have found you."

"Distantly related," he said, nodding. "Lord Somerville and my father were second cousins. But not so close that—"

She looked up at him. He took a deep breath and continued.

"Do you remember when I told you about my father's death?"

She nodded.

"You said you had details that still had to be dealt with," she said.

"Yes. Well, those details were that I didn't believe his death was an accident."

"Oh," she said, taken aback.

"Believe me, my father was no saint," he added grimly. "He was known for being a gambler and a drunk. It was why I sailed to America."

"To get away from him?" she asked.

"No. To make my own way in the world. He was gambling away every penny. I knew there would be nothing left. I was sending money to my mother, when she was alive. After her death, apparently, my father went from bad to worse. He died in a gambling house in France. I wasn't surprised by that, but when I returned, I visited the gambling house, to find out what happened in his last days, and the stories I was told caused me to suspect his death wasn't accidental. He had been befriended by a man, an evil man, though well thought of by many."

"And you think this man killed your father?" Lady Anna whispered, breathlessly.

Mr. Langley paused.

"I wish it were that straight-forward," he answered finally. "It was his influence. He took an avid interest in my father, although he was a younger man. He took advantage of a gentleman already gripped by drink and cards and suggested other degradations. Opium dens. Things like that. He was as responsible for my father's untimely death as if he gave him the drugs himself."

Lady Anna reached out and touched his arm. He covered her hand with his.

"I began to suspect there was a reason behind it, that he wanted my father to die, although it was nothing I could prove. So, I made the decision to get closer to this man without him knowing my true identity. It meant deceiving your father, though I knew he was searching for me, as the next heir. I arranged for my solicitor to introduce me to Lord Somerville as a young man who needed employment, and he was kind enough to take me on. It seemed the perfect way to accomplish my purposes, and it would have little negative effects on the household. I knew your father would understand, when the time came. The man in question was a neighbor, and visited Hampstead Hall frequently. Everything was going according to plan, until you returned from your visit with your friends in Derbyshire."

"What happened then?" she asked.

He turned toward her, his hand still firmly on hers.

"Then I met you."

Lady Anna's breath lodged in her throat. She drew her hand away.

"I was still gathering evidence against the man," Mr. Langley explained, turning away. "But now my deception was—interfering. At least with my peace of mind. I wanted to tell you my true identity, but it could have exposed me to the one I was spying on. And every blot I found against his character was a stain against the man your father wanted you to marry, against the man I was afraid you loved. My investigation was ruining your future happiness. But now," he said, his blue eyes piercing with meaning, "I no longer need the disguise. The man is dead."

"Mr. Langley," called Lord Somerville as he approached from the house.

Lady Anna jumped like a frightened kitten.

She and Mr. Langley both stood, waiting for her father to approach. He was accompanied by a man who looked vaguely familiar. As he got nearer, Lady Anna gasped.

"Mr. Langley, this is Mr. Ferguson," said Lord Somerville. "The constable felt it was best to call him in from Bow Street."

"A Bow Street Runner?" Lady Anna clarified. She had heard of them, of course. The detective force developed by the writer, Henry Fielding, to help solve crimes.

It's way before Scotland Yard, she remembered.

"Mr. Ferguson says he has a few questions for you," Lord Somerville continued, "about—the unfortunate incident this morning."

"Of course," Mr. Langley said with a slight bow.

Mr. Ferguson squinted at him, then turned his attention to Lady Anna.

"My daughter, Lady Anna," Lord Somerville introduced.

Lady Anna nodded her head as the detective bowed.

"Mr. Langley, I understand you were one of the seconds in this duel," Mr. Ferguson began.

"Yes, sir. I was."

"I have come to interview Sir John, who, surprisingly, is still here at the house and not halfway to France," said Mr. Ferguson. "Unusual, considering he is now wanted for murder."

"Murder!" Lady Anna repeated.

"All duels ending in death are considered murder," Mr. Langley explained, his face serious. He turned to the detective. "Sir John expressed his intentions of staying to prove his innocence, Mr. Ferguson. He did not intend to kill Lord Mallory."

Mr. Ferguson squinted in his direction.

"It was a duel, Mr. Langley."

"I understand that, but Sir John—"

"Shot blanks," Lady Anna interjected, then clapped her hand over her mouth.

The three men stared at her questioningly.

"Sir John told me he asked the seconds to load only gunpowder," she explained nervously. "No lead balls. He wanted to teach Lord Mallory a lesson, not kill him."

"You knew about this?" Lord Somerville asked, shocked.

"It's true, Mr. Ferguson," Mr. Langley agreed. "He asked me to ensure the pistols were loaded with gunpowder only."

"Then how do you explain Lord Mallory's death?" asked the detective.

"I can't," Mr. Langley answered.

"Well," Mr. Ferguson said, bowing again to Lady Anna, "if I could have a word with you in private, then, Mr. Langley?"

The two men headed back toward the Drawing Room.

Lord Somerville turned toward his daughter.

"Anna?" he said, dismayed. "Are you all right?"

Lady Anna was swaying on her feet.

"I don't know," she answered before crumpling into her father's arms.

"Anna!"

William cradled her in his arms.

He had watched her dream-like state from his chair by the fire, concerned that his nearness would mess something up in the supernatural dreamworld she was entering. But when she had suddenly cried out, eyes wide with horror, he had leaped to her side, just in time to catch her as she dropped off the windowseat in a faint.

When she came to, she pulled back from him, scrambling over the floor.

"Anna! Are you all right?" he asked. "It's William. It's present-day."

She clambored to her feet. He rose as well.

"What happened?" he asked, concerned. "What did your dream tell you?"

She swallowed hard, then looked him in the face.

"Peter Mallory killed your father!" she said.

CHAPTER FORTY-TWO

William stared at Anna in disbelief. She had just voiced his secret thoughts. He recoiled away from her, as if she were a witch.

How could she know?

"Why do you say that?" he asked, keeping his voice calm, hoping it would keep the rest of him calm, as well. He couldn't read her feelings; he saw in her eyes a mixture of doubt and pity.

"It's true, isn't it?" she asked. "It was in my dream just now. Mr. Williams was hiding his identity, just like you. He's the heir to Lord Somerville, Lady Anna's father, but he was pretending to be his secretary so he could spy on Lord Mallory."

William sat down heavily on the windowseat. Anna sat beside him. He noticed, vaguely, that she didn't leave a space between them.

He leaned forward, his arms on his knees.

"My father was an alcoholic and a gambler. I already told you that," he said wearily.

She nodded.

"And he died of an overdose of sleeping pills. In Monte Carlo," he continued. "One of the maids found him dead in his room. We didn't think anything was out of the ordinary, my mother and sister and I. It was the kind of call we had expected for a long time, that he would drink himself to death. I volunteered to go and…collect the body. And when I got there, Peter Mallory was there."

"Why?" Anna asked.

William shrugged, sitting up.

"He said he had been vacationing there at the same hotel and casino. He told me that he and my father had been hanging out together. Gambling together. Drinking together. He's the one who told me Father had been taking sleeping pills, suggested he must have taken too many that night because he was drunk, upset about his losses. It was the first I'd heard of him taking sleeping pills at all."

"Do you think Peter gave them to him?"

"I can't prove it," he said.

"But why?" she asked. "Why would he want your father dead?"

William didn't answer.

"He must have known who you were, then," Anna continued. "Peter had met you before. He knew you weren't Sir Frederick's assistant."

"We've known each other a long time," William said. "He owned the property adjacent to mine."

"What? Peter?"

"Oddly enough, he is actually Lord Mallory," said William, giving her a wry smile. "Imagine my astonishment when you told me you dreamed he was a viscount."

"I can't believe it," said Anna.

"I asked him, when he got here, to go along with my deception."

"I'm surprised he agreed," she said.

William shrugged.

"He likes to keep his title a secret," he said. "Thinks it makes him sound posh. But also, Peter enjoyed having power over other people."

"Does he inherit?" Anna asked suddenly.

"What?"

"Does he inherit Hampstead Hall?"

"No. Why do you ask?"

"In my dream, Lord Mallory was next in line to inherit, after dream-William and his father," she explained.

"But he had only gotten rid of the father," William pointed out. "Dream-William would still have inherited."

"Which means," said Anna, thinking aloud, "if his intention was to inherit the Earldom, he would have had to get rid of dream-William, as well."

Their eyes met.

"It's fortunate that dream-Lord Mallory died in a duel before he could accomplish his goal," said William, holding her gaze.

"Yes," she answered, her breath quickening. "I should go to bed," she added, shaking her head slightly, as if she were still dizzy.

"I'll walk you to your room," he offered as they stood.

"No, thank you," she said quickly. "I know the way."

After she left, William stood staring at the closed door, his mind in a million directions.

CHAPTER FORTY-THREE

Anna awoke from a fitful sleep. She had not had any more dreams, at least, not the kind she had become accustomed to. Fleeting images, yes. And she had the vague impression that she had wandered through an old house, searching for something, but not finding it. But those dreams were nothing to her. She dismissed them. Now that she was awake, her thoughts returned to her dream from the Tapestry Room. To William and Viscount Mallory.

A glance out her window told her the day was sunny, though she couldn't tell if there was actual warmth, or if it was merely a trick of the light, giving the false impression of heat. She touched the icy glass of the window before turning away. Dressing quickly, she headed downstairs to see what the day would bring.

As she passed through the Great Hall, she was startled to hear the sound of a car door slamming in the circle drive and the unmistakeable crunch of footsteps approaching the house. The oak door was wide open, despite the chill of the day, and the bright sunlight caused the wicket to glow like a giant keyhole. Anna paused, wondering who was arriving.

Probably the Inspector, she thought.

There was a flickering of light as a man entered through the door, bending his head as he passed through the wicket and into the dark somberness of the Great Hall. Standing to his full, six-foot height, Anna could still only see the man in silhouette; the light shining through the wicket onto the back of his curly head gave the aura of a golden halo, like a medieval painting.

"Mr. Sterling! My apologies," said a distraught Mr. Barnaby, materializing out of nowhere and scurrying across to the door. "I didn't realize you had arrived."

"Edwin!" said Portia Valentine, breezing into the room from the Drawing Room. "Finally."

She kissed the newcomer on both cheeks, then pulled him further into the Great Hall. The gloom that engulfed the visitor finally dissipated as he moved under one of the lofty chandeliers.

Anna gasped, staring at the man. It was…but it couldn't be…

"Oh, Anna," said Portia, noticing her. "This is my son. Edwin Sterling."

The room spun slightly.

Anna had always prided herself on the fact that she wasn't star-struck. When she met celebrities, either music people in Nashville or actors in LA, she treated them as she would anyone else. No nervous twitters in her stomach. No silly stammerings or goofy grins.

But not today.

Today, she was a silly fangirl who couldn't make her lips move correctly. A ridiculous fool who realized, too late, that her mouth was literally hanging open, and that she had stopped breathing about half an hour ago.

Edwin Sterling!

The movie star!

Edwin Sterling! Action hero!

It was Dr. Hanover himself, the doctor who solves crimes, standing in front of her, looking exactly like he did on the *Dr. Hanover* TV show. She had watched every episode, multiple times. Light-brown curls. Electric-blue eyes. Eyes like his mother, Anna realized, and wondered why that should surprise her.

Edwin Sterling, in the flesh, was standing in front of her in the Great Hall.

And she was speechless. Staring at him like a child stares at Santa Claus in the mall.

He smiled politely at her, and Anna shook her head, trying to recover her dignity.

He held out his hand.

"I'm Edwin," he said, as if it were a perfectly normal thing to say. As if the sound of his oh-so-familiar voice didn't cause her legs to threaten to collapse and throw her to the ground.

Anna took his hand and smiled, but speech was still beyond her. A noise passed out of her throat, but failed to form into a word.

"This is Anna McKay," said his mother, coming to the rescue.

"A pleasure," said Edwin.

Anna giggled.

"You haven't breakfasted yet, have you, Anna?" asked Portia.

She shook her head, unable to tear her eyes away from Edwin's face.

"Mr. Barnaby? Would you mind if Anna had her breakfast in the Tapestry Room?" requested Portia. "We have some things to discuss."

"Of course, Ms. Valentine. I shall send up a plate right away," said Mr.

Barnaby with a slight bow. "Mr. Sterling, I'll have your luggage put in your room in the west wing."

"Thank you, Mr. Barnaby," said Edwin, pleasantly, as he gently disengaged his hand from Anna's grasp.

In the Tapestry Room, Anna quietly ate her eggs and bacon, attempting to calm herself while she watched the famous mother and son in front of her.

"How is dear Adrianna?" Portia asked Edwin.

"Stunning, as usual," he answered, a smile lighting up his face. "Still in America for now, but she'll be back for a visit at Christmas."

"Such a charming girl," said Portia, smiling indulgently.

"She's perfect," he agreed. "Perfect—for me," he added, smiling broadly at his mother, who had given him a warning glance.

Anna had heard vague rumors that Edwin Sterling had a mystery girlfriend who had recently been revealed. She'd been so caught up getting ready to move to England that she'd missed any real gossip on the subject. All the information she had was from reading the headlines of the tabloids while standing in line at the grocery store.

"Mother, why am I here?" Edwin asked, giving his parent a stern look.

"You know why, darling," answered his mother, gazing at him with innocent blue eyes. "Are you forgetting that Sir Frederick asked you to consider a role in *Cavendish Manor*?"

"I'm not forgetting that," he said with a roll of his eyes. "Are you forgetting that I already turned him down? I don't have time for another series right now."

"Hmm," answered Portia, pouring a cup of tea for herself.

"I'm sure it wouldn't have anything to do with the accident on the set you mentioned on the phone, now would it?" he asked, eyeing her suspiciously. "Because I don't believe for a moment the 'mother in distress' act you gave me."

"Yet you came anyway," she said, her eyes twinkling. "This is the opportunity you've been waiting for. To be a real-life hero."

Edwin sighed.

"If there's foul play involved, the police will take care of that," he said.

"Perhaps they will," his mother agreed, handing him a cup. "If they know all they need to know."

Anna interrupted.

"All they need to know?" she asked. "What do you mean?"

Portia turned her innocent look in her direction.

"The police deal in facts, my dear," she said. "But sometimes you need more than facts to solve a crime. So, I've called in an expert."

"Oh, Lord," exclaimed Edwin, setting his cup down on the table at his elbow. "Me? How am I an expert?"

"You're a detective," she said.

His eyes narrowed.

"I'm an actor, who plays a detective on television. That's hardly the same thing."

"Don't you remember anything they've taught you on the show? Besides, it's in your blood," said his mother matter-of-factly.

"You're an actress!" he exclaimed, exasperated, "Who has never played a detective!"

"You have more than one parent, Edwin," his mother reminded him. "How do you think your father became so successful in the foreign office?"

Edwin sighed heavily.

"You handled yourself so well in Istanbul," she continued.

He snorted.

"You make it sound like it was some kind of test run," he said, shaking his head.

His mother focused her attention on the tea table, rearranging the tray of scones.

Edwin's gaze sharpened. He opened his mouth to ask a question, but before he could speak, the door opened, and William strode in.

"Edwin!" he said, grabbing the man's hand when the actor rose to meet him. "Mr. Barnaby told me you arrived."

William glanced tentatively at Anna, who quickly lowered her eyes.

"Yes," said Edwin. "My mother was attempting to explain why I'm here."

The two men looked at Portia Valentine, who smiled benignantly on them.

"Tea, William?" she asked.

"Yes, please," he answered, seating himself in a chair near Anna. He pretended not to notice the fact that she shifted herself away from him.

"You're here, Edwin, because we need your brain and observational skills," said his mother. "There was plenty of excitement here *before* the duel. There's been a—what would Agatha Christie call it? An atmosphere."

"I have to agree with you," said William.

"And we've had practical jokes," Portia continued. "At least, that's what we've been calling them."

"Practical jokes?" asked her son. "Do they have something to do with Peter's death?"

"That is yet to be determined," said Portia, glancing at Anna. "Perhaps we'd better begin at the beginning and explain everything to him."

Between the two of them, with the occasional addition of William, Edwin was told all the happenings at Hampstead Hall, from the collapse of the lighting rig to the duel.

"So, Miranda Vogel thinks all of this was caused by William's curse?" Edwin clarified, his brow wrinkled.

The two women nodded.

"According to her, it's all my fault," William said dryly.

"Of course, the first accident happened before there ever was a curse," Edwin said matter-of-factly.

"What?" asked Anna, stunned.

"The lighting panel," he said. "You said it fell the first night, before filming began. And William didn't make his silly blunder until a week of filming had gone by. Am I getting the timing wrong?"

"No," Anna answered, thoughtfully.

He was right, she realized. The first "practical joke" had happened before William had said Macbeth.

"So it's *not* all my fault," said William. "Not that I ever thought it was."

"Wait," said Anna. "That wasn't even the first practical joke. There was one before that. At least, it could have been a practical joke. The car that was bringing Miranda and Adrian to Hampstead Hall. It broke down and would only go in reverse. They had to call an Uber, and Miranda had a fit about it."

She explained all that Perry and Jake had told her about the breakdown and the Uber ride.

Edwin narrowed his eyes.

"That could fit in with the other practical jokes," he said, considering.

"And it shows that Miranda—" she began, then stopped herself. "But I guess that doesn't have anything to do with it."

"That Miranda has a drug problem?" finished Portia, nodding. "Yes, I'm afraid she does, poor girl. And it's yet to be seen what details are important."

"So," continued Edwin, "if we consider the car as the first practical joke, who could have done it?"

"Only the people who were there, right?" said William. "I mean, none of the rest of us were near the car. We were all here, at Hampstead Hall. I was touring the house with the rest of the cast and crew."

He glanced furtively at Anna, who looked away.

"Which leaves Peter, Miranda, Adrian, or Perry," said Edwin. "Why would any of them sabotage the car?"

"Miranda has been saying she thinks Sir Frederick is cutting corners," suggested William. "Could it have simply been neglect? The car just needed servicing?"

"No," said Anna. "Perry said it had never done that before, and that Sir Frederick keeps it in good condition."

"Maybe he was lying?" William offered weakly.

"I don't think so," Anna said, shaking her head. "Portia said she thought someone was trying to sabotage the whole show. Maybe it was part of a larger plan to make *Cavendish Manor* seem unsafe."

"It definitely worked," Edwin agreed.

"But which one of those four would want to sabotage the show?" asked William. "And also, who would have the knowledge to actually mess up the car in the first place?"

"I can't see Miranda getting her hands dirty," said Portia.

"It makes Perry look bad," said Anna. "It was his responsibility to bring the actors to Hampstead Hall. They were supposed to join the tour. Why would he do something that could put his own job in jeopardy?"

"That leaves Peter and Adrian," said Edwin. "Either one could have the knowledge to do it. But what about the motivation?"

Anna shrugged.

William furrowed his brow and stared into his tea cup.

"We're forgetting something," said Edwin suddenly. "The car came from the Studio. It could have been sabotaged before it ever left."

"By Sir Frederick?" asked Anna, incredulous.

"Or Julia," offered Edwin.

"Oh, no. Not Julia," said his mother, pursing her lips. "Producers are such angelic creatures."

She beamed an innocent smile on the group, then winked.

"But why would they want to sabotage their own show?" asked William.

"That seems counter-productive."

"Well, let's move on," said Edwin. "The next practical joke was the lighting panel falling. Thankfully, no one was hurt. Probably on purpose. Up until the duel, none of the practical jokes seem to have been intended for actual bodily harm."

"True," agreed his mother. "If someone had wanted to harm one of the actors, he—or she—would have caused the light panel to fall during a scene, not when there was no one in the room."

Anna shuddered.

"It certainly kept me watchful for my own safety, though," she said.

"But it's true," said William. "Until Peter, there was no physical damage to people, only to property, with the exception of Miranda and the chair, but I think her injuries were manufactured. What's our list of 'jokes'? The car, the light panel, the spaghetti cables, the chair leg breaking. The damage was financial, including lost time."

"Which makes a show more costly," said Edwin, nodding.

"You forgot about the missing dailies," added Anna. "That is time and money, too. We'll have to reshoot all of those scenes. Oh!" she cried, putting her hand over her mouth. "We can't now! Peter's dead!"

"Maybe that completes the sabotage," Edwin murmured. "How can the show go on without a principal character?"

"But no one would be that heartless!" cried Anna. "To kill someone merely to stop a show from filming!"

There was a knock at the door, then Mr. Barnaby entered the room.

"Sorry to disturb you, my lord, but the Inspector is here to begin his interviews," he said. "I've put him in the ground-floor Study, as you advised."

"Thank you, Mr. Barnaby," said William. "I'll be down in a moment."

The house manager nodded, and closed the door.

"Well," said William, standing. "I'm afraid duty calls. It's showtime."

CHAPTER FORTY-FOUR

In the Study, William found Inspector Ferguson and Sergeant Patel waiting for him. After shaking hands all around, William asked the question that he had been pondering since he woke up that morning.

"Inspector, would you mind if I stayed in on the interviews?"

Inspector Ferguson didn't immediately answer. He squinted at William as if summing him up.

"So, asserting the ancient right of judgement in your shire?" he asked finally, giving William a wink.

"Something like that," said William, smiling. "I feel responsible, with it happening on my estate. If I could sit in, it would make me feel like I was doing something to help. Maybe I could be of some assistance?"

There was restless movement from the direction of Sergeant Patel. Inspector Ferguson ignored it.

"Yes, I would be glad to have your observations, my lord," he said.

He circled behind the large, mahogany desk.

"Do you mind if I use your desk?" the Inspector asked.

"Not at all," said William.

"And if you could stay quietly in the corner, there, your lordship. Sergeant? After you set up the camera, I think we'll get these interviews started."

"The camera?" asked William.

"Digital camera to record the interviews," the Inspector explained. "We already experimented with angles while we were waiting for you. I think we've chosen the best spot."

William watched as Sergeant Patel adjusted a small camera on the book shelf behind the desk. She was able to monitor it from her laptop.

"Ready, Inspector," she said.

"Please bring in Jake Rawlings first," he said, settling into the leather chair behind the desk.

Sergeant Patel opened the door and motioned to someone. Jake had obviously been waiting nearby. He greeted William with a surprised glance, but said nothing. He seated himself in a leather armchair in front of the desk.

Sergeant Patel closed the Study door and positioned herself in a chair against the wall, facing William, her laptop open on her knees. Her sharp, black eyes failed to hide her obvious dislike as she glared at him. She was dressed in pressed black dress pants and a starched white blouse. Her thick, black hair was pulled into a tight knot at the back of her neck. She gave the appearance of a tightly-laced cobra, ready to spring. William gave her a brief smile, hoping to warm the air between them. She pressed her lips together and narrowed her eyes before rolling them and looking away.

"The Ice Queen," William thought, and focused on Jake, who ran a nervous tongue over his lips as he waited for the Inspector to look up from a sheaf of papers he was glancing through.

"Mr. Rawlings," said the Inspector, finally looking up. "Thank you for meeting with us this morning. I know this has been a particularly difficult business, with it being a personal friend who was killed."

"Whatever will help, Inspector," said Jake.

The Inspector consulted his notes.

"Your full name is John Samuel Rawlings, of Little Rock, Arkansas, in the United States?" he asked.

Jake nodded.

"Jake, for short," he said.

"And your social media account shows that you like to go deer hunting."

"Yes," said Jake, caught off-guard. "Though I haven't been in a long time. I've been living in LA"

"Do you currently own a gun, Mr. Rawlings?" asked Inspector Ferguson.

"No," said Jake. "Not currently."

"But you are a good shot?"

Jake paused.

"Not really," he said, running a hand through his hair. "I wouldn't say that. But what has hunting got to do with Peter's death?"

"We have record of you and Peter Mallory both frequenting a shooting range in the Los Angeles area. Would that be accurate?"

"Yes," Jake answered, "we were practicing, in case we were asked to do it for a role. We were hoping for action roles, and wanted to be believable."

"I see," said the Inspector, looking down again at his notes.

"Turns out it was an advantage for our current roles," Jake said, then his face clouded over. "At least, we thought it was an advantage at the time."

After William left the Tapestry Room, Anna began to feel awkward. Edwin Sterling, sitting in an armchair, sipping tea, was a little too surreal for her. She wondered if she should leave mother and son alone. Maybe they wanted her to, but were just being polite.

"Anna," said Portia Valentine, "I'd like you to tell Edwin about your dreams."

Anna blushed painfully. It was one thing to tell William, or even Portia, but to tell Edwin Sterling, the famous Dr. Hanover, that she was having constant dreams about the past, peopled by the present? She felt foolish.

Edwin turned toward her, expectantly. He was looking at her as if she were a completely normal human being. But he hadn't heard the dreams, yet. She sighed heavily.

"Whatever those dreams are," said Portia, "whether your active imagination, or *an da shealladh,* or the ghost of Lady Anna Somer, they are interesting, and I think they have a bearing on what's been going on. You can trust Edwin."

Her son gave a questioning, sideways glance at his mother, then focused again on Anna in front of him. Anna could read sympathy in his piercing blue eyes. He looked to her like a man who would believe her, not make fun of her or dismiss her. She bit her lip, then she began to tell him about all of the dreams and visions she had been experiencing since arriving at Hampstead Hall. Edwin listened attentively, asking a clarifying question every now and then. She ended her tale with the dream from the night before, when she had learned of Peter Mallory's possible involvement in the death of William's father.

"Your mother said that maybe it was second-sight. *An da shealladh,"* said Anna. "But it never happened to me before I came here."

Edwin was silent for a few moments, staring into space. Anna and Portia watched him expectantly. He furrowed his brow.

"It is amazing how many things are the same in your dreams and in real life," he said. "And sometimes, your dreams seem to come before the actual event takes place. Almost like a premonition. Other times it clarifies what's going on in present day."

"It's also similar to the script," added Anna. "William and I were talking about it last night."

"And what conclusions did you come to?" asked Portia, encouragingly.

"Well, I remembered that Sir Frederick was looking for some kind of journal or book that William's father let him read. He told me it was where he got the idea for *Cavendish Manor*. He said it was a kind of history of the house. So maybe that's why the script is similar to my dreams. Maybe Lady Anna is trying to tell me something about what happened, to warn me, and Sir Frederick happened to write a script that is based on what really happened long ago, when she was alive."

She looked from Portia to Edwin to see what they thought of her theory.

"Perhaps," said Edwin, thoughtfully. "But what is especially intriguing to me is the differences. The stories don't always match. I mean, for one thing, you are not cast as the wealthy daughter in *Cavendish Manor*. You're the poor relation."

"That's true," she said.

"And you cast Jaime Douglas in the role of poor relation in your dreams," he continued. "And Corinne as the maid."

"But Corinne was in the trees in the dream and in the script," Portia added.

"What other differences stand out to you, Anna?" asked Edwin, leaning back in his chair and crossing one ankle over his knee like he was settling back to watch a movie.

"Well," said Anna, thinking. "Mr. Williams and William were the same in my dream and in real life, although I didn't realize it at the time. I mean, I knew they were both William, but I didn't know William was the Earl until yesterday. In the dream he was my father's secretary, and in real life he was pretending to be Sir Frederick's assistant. But in reality, in both cases, he was the Earl. Or the heir to the Earl."

"William wasn't originally in the script for *Cavendish Manor*," Portia reminded him, "but he was written in as Jake's second. Which places him in the same role in the duel in both real life and the dream."

"But those are similarities," reminded her son, impatiently. "I'm asking about differences."

"Jake's character is the same in both," Anna continued, thinking aloud. "And Peter's. As for differences, Adrian and Miranda are servants in the dream, like Corinne. But Perry hasn't appeared at all."

"I wonder if that's significant," said Edwin.

"I'm not sure," Anna said. "I hadn't really thought about it. Sir Frederick plays my father in the dream. That's different."

"What about storyline?" asked Edwin. "How does the storyline match with real life?"

"Let's see," said Anna, her eyes staring at the intricately-carved ceiling above her. "Lord Mallory wants to marry Lady Anna in the dreams, but it's Corinne in the script, as Lady Margaret. In both, she doesn't want to marry him because she doesn't love him. Or trust him. But in both, the parents want her to marry him. She seems to like Jake's character in both, but then there's William."

"Yes," agreed Edwin. "What about William? Lady Anna seems to like him best, but keeps pushing him away. But William isn't in the script. At least, not as a major role."

"No," Anna agreed, avoiding his eyes.

"How does the love story play out in the script?" he asked.

"I don't know, yet," Anna admitted. "We haven't gotten that far. The duel is the end of the third episode, and Sir Frederick keeps each episode a secret until the last minute."

"Hmm," Edwin grunted. "And what about real life? What does Anna think of William in real life? Does she prefer Jake to William?"

Anna's eyes widened.

"Does it really matter what I think about them?" she asked, indignant.

"Sorry," Edwin apologized, waving his hand as if to wipe away the question. "Perhaps it's unimportant."

CHAPTER FORTY-FIVE

"Is any of this important?" asked Jake, shifting in his chair. "Why does it matter if I've shot a gun before? Even if I hadn't, we were trained by Brian Elliston on Monday."

"Perhaps it's unimportant," said Inspector Ferguson, giving him a tight smile that failed to reach his eyes. "Your mother must be proud," he said, changing the subject. "A single mom, raising her son on her own. It couldn't have been easy. And now, here you are. Successful."

Jake flicked an uneasy glance at William, who gazed at him curiously.

"She *was* proud," Jake admitted, setting his jaw. "When she was alive. She died of cancer before my career really took off."

"I see," said the Inspector, squinting at him. "So, you say you learned to shoot the dueling pistols. Were you taught to load them?"

Jake shook his head.

"No. That was Brian's job. I mean, maybe Jaime learned because she's the props master."

"So, you wouldn't be able to tell if your gun was loaded with a blank cartridge or a live one?"

"No. Can anyone?" asked Jake. "Wouldn't it all be inside the barrel?"

The Inspector ignored the question.

"When was the first time you handled the gun on Tuesday morning?" he asked.

"Right before we shot the scene," said Jake, taking a deep breath and closing his eyes, as if to jog his memory. "Brian loaded the pistols, and handed one to each of us. To me and Pete." He opened his eyes, revealing a hollow expression. "We didn't rehearse then. We'd already done that the day before. It was supposed to be simple," he said, wiping his brow. "Just like we rehearsed. It should have gone perfectly. I don't understand what went wrong."

"After the gun was fired, did you notice anything unusual?"

"There was more kickback," said Jake thoughtfully. "I should have realized something was wrong because of that. The blanks didn't cause as much kickback."

"You said in your earlier statement that you didn't notice anything was wrong, even when Peter Mallory was lying on the ground," said the Inspector.

Jake nodded.

"Shouldn't you have?" continued the Inspector. "I understand that Peter Mallory wasn't supposed to be the victim in the scene."

"Well," Jake explained with a shrug, "Pete was always joking. I thought he was just playing around. Pretending to be shot."

"You are reported to have said, 'You're just jealous because I get the girl instead of you.' What did you mean by that?"

Jake looked up, surprised. The Inspector squinted at him, waiting.

"I meant in the script," he said quickly. "Pete's character and my character were after the same girl. That's why they're fighting the duel. I was joking. I thought—I didn't know he was actually—"

Jake put his hand over his mouth, looking like he was going to be sick.

The Inspector's lip twitched slightly.

"So there was no basis in fact?" he asked. "You weren't fighting over the same girl in real life?"

"No!" said Jake emphatically. "Peter wasn't fighting with *me*."

Jake clenched his jaw shut, as if he had said more than he intended.

"But he was fighting with *someone*?" Inspector Ferguson asked. "Over a girl?"

Jake sighed. He glanced at William, who kept his face impassive.

"Pete and Corinne were a thing," Jake admitted. "And recently, things had shifted a bit. I don't know exactly what was going on, but they weren't hanging out like they used to. Peter was convinced she was into someone else."

"Any idea who?"

Jake pressed his lips together.

"I have no evidence that Peter was right," he said, shaking his head, "but he thought it was Perry."

"Perry Prince, the production assistant?" Inspector Ferguson clarified, making a note.

Jake nodded apologetically.

"It's what Peter thought," he said. "But he tended to be the jealous type."

After the interview, Sergeant Patel went in search of Brian Elliston. William followed Jake to the bottom of the oak staircase.

"A bit rough, these interviews," he said.

"Yes," said Jake, pausing impatiently at the foot of the stairs. "But he's just doing his job. And I want to do all I can to get to the bottom of this."

William nodded.

"I thought you were the son of wealthy parents?" he asked, giving Jake a quizzical look. "Didn't I hear you were the heir to a furniture empire or something?"

Jake's face reddened.

"Is it my fault people make assumptions?" he asked with an irritated shrug. "It can be our little secret." He slapped William confidentially on the shoulder, but when he turned to climb the stairs, he came face to face with Anna, descending from the Tapestry Room. Jake froze, the knuckles on the hand that gripped the stairwell turning white.

"Excuse us a moment, Lord Somerville," said Anna, her body stiff and formal, and her eyes never straying from Jake's shocked face.

William gave her a nod.

"I have to go back to the interviews," he said, and returned to the Study.

I don't envy Jake a bit, he thought, shaking his head, and wondering what Anna's reaction would be to yet another deception.

"Anna, I can explain," Jake began, his arms outstretched.

"You'd better," she said, folding her arms over her chest.

"But not here," he said, glancing around. "Let's go to my room. For privacy."

Anna stood in Jake's bedroom, although he had offered her a chair. She made a mental note that he had cleaned up since she'd last been there. There were no more piles of clothes. Even the papers on the desk were gone, presumably swept into a drawer.

He must have let the maid in, finally, she thought.

Jake shut the door and leaned against it.

"Now we can talk," he said.

Anna raised her eyebrows in answer.

"You're angry with me," he said.

"I don't know how I feel!" she said. "All I know is, I've been made a fool of by two men in as many days."

"I don't think you're a fool," said Jake, reaching for her hands.

Anna pulled them out of his reach and backed away.

"So I'm guessing you're not a *Rawlings Furniture* Rawlings," she said.

He bowed his head.

"No. I'm a Little Rock, Arkansas, Rawlings. My dad left us when I was a kid. It was just me and my mom, until she passed away."

"Then why did you say you were?"

"I never said I was," Jake insisted. "People made assumptions early on in my career, and I just didn't correct them."

"Which is the same as lying," Anna pointed out.

Jake shrugged one shoulder and gave her a half-smile.

"All actors are liars, aren't we?" he asked.

She folded her arms.

"When it seemed to work in my favor, to get me jobs and notoriety, my publicist told me to just be vague. He said as long as I wasn't actually claiming to be one of the Rawlings Furniture people, I could always laugh it off and say how funny I thought it was that people thought that."

"It still feels like deception to me," said Anna, thawing.

"Maybe so," said Jake. "I know it will end eventually, and someone will out me, but until then, maybe it can be our little secret?"

"And William's," she reminded him.

"And the Inspector's," he admitted, grimly.

"William was in your interview?" asked Anna, surprised.

"Yeah. I don't know why."

"I'm surprised the Inspector allowed it," she said thoughtfully. "It seems like it would be against protocol."

Jake shrugged.

"Maybe earls get special privileges," he suggested.

"Maybe," she said.

He moved closer to her and she allowed him to put his arms around her.

"Do you forgive me?" he asked.

She rolled her eyes.

"I guess. But why didn't you tell me? You knew all about me, but you weren't honest about yourself."

He leaned his forehead against hers.

"I guess I felt a little intimidated," he admitted, his warm breath brushing against her lips. "You had the perfect background, from the perfect family. I wanted you to think I was worth your time."

"Oh, Jake," said Anna, shaking her head. "My life isn't perfect. No one's is. Money doesn't solve all your problems!"

"It solves a lot of them," he said, grinning his million-dollar smile.

She giggled.

"Okay, maybe it solves some things," she conceded, "but don't ever think you're beneath me just because we come from different worlds."

He kissed her.

"Thank you, Anna," he whispered in her ear. "I don't know how I would get through this without you."

Anna frowned.

Rawlings Furniture Rawlings or not, she knew she didn't love him. But how could she leave him now? It would be the height of cruelty.

CHAPTER FORTY-SIX

———◆◦◆———

Brian Elliston was next to be interviewed. William noticed his face looked strained, but otherwise he was calm. He sat on the edge of the chair in front of the Inspector, who remained seated at the desk.

"Mr. Elliston," Inspector Ferguson began, "as the stunt coordinator, it's your job to ensure the safety of all those handling the weaponry, is that correct?"

"Yes," said Brian, leaning forward, "which is why—"

The Inspector held out a hand to stop his explanation.

"I'm just clarifying your responsibilities," he said. "When was the first time you handled the pistols on Tuesday morning?"

"Before dawn," answered Brian. "I'm not sure of the exact time, but it was as soon as William and Perry handed me the box. The sun hadn't come up yet, I know, because Sir Frederick was adamant about shooting the scene just as the sun rose above the tree-line."

Inspector Ferguson shot an interested, but fleeting, glance in William's direction, but William could feel the direct gaze of Sergeant Patel, and it felt like some kind of accusation.

"I understood that the stunt coordinator would be in charge of all weapons during the duration of the filming of those scenes?" said the Inspector. "You're saying they were out of your possession?"

Brian swallowed hard, giving William a quick look.

"Under ordinary circumstances, yes, I would be in charge of the weapons. But these were antiques, owned by the Earl, and William said…of course, we didn't know he was the Earl at the time. But he said Sir Frederick told him the Earl wanted the weapons kept in the house instead of in my possession or with Jaime. She's the props master."

"Isn't it typical, Mr. Elliston, to use replicas in films? Why were you using antique guns in the first place?"

"Well," said Brian. "Yes, replicas are usually preferred. They're cheaper, for one thing, if you have to buy them. But Sir Frederick loved the idea of using the original weapons, and it saved money because we already had access to them. The Earl—William—I was told that the Earl had given us permission to use them. And I wasn't complaining. I mean, how often do I get the opportunity to handle actual dueling pistols from the early 1800s?"

The Inspector seemed satisfied with his answer and moved on to his next question.

"So, the pistols were out of your sight for how long?"

"Um…we used them the day before and finished up about three o'clock. William took the box with him to the house after I cleaned them. After that, I didn't see them again until the next morning, like I said."

The Inspector grunted, causing his stomach to bounce.

"Were the pistols locked when they were in the house?"

Brian turned questioningly toward William.

"The pistols themselves weren't locked, Inspector," explained William, "but the house was, of course."

"Hmfph," the Inspector responded, as if he felt William's security measures were inadequate. "So anyone could have had access to them while they were in the house."

"Yes, I suppose so," said William, "but—"

The Inspector ignored him and turned his questions back to Brian.

"And you say Perry Prince, the production assistant, and William—Lord Somerville," he said with a slight nod in William's direction, "brought the pistols to you from the house?"

"Yes."

"Were they already loaded?"

"No, sir. I can guarantee that," said Brian emphatically. "The method for loading a dueling pistol begins by prodding a metal rod into the barrel to make sure it's clear. I always do this. I never skip a step. And I can tell you, without a doubt, there was nothing in either barrel before I loaded the guns with blanks."

Inspector Ferguson nodded. He consulted his notes.

"You said in your earlier statement that you make your own blank cartridges."

"Yes, sir."

"Is it possible you mixed up your cartridges that morning?"

"No," Brian explained. "The blank cartridges are made of cardboard, and the live ammunition is metal. Hard to mix up."

"Is it possible that someone else substituted a live cartridge disguised as a blank cartridge, and that you mistakenly loaded that into the pistol?"

Brian appeared doubtful.

"The live ammunition is heavier. I think I would have noticed. And it would be all but impossible to add a lead ball into one of my blank cartridges without my noticing. Not to mention, the expertise that would be needed to do so."

"But not impossible," clarified the Inspector.

Brian twisted his face.

"I guess I can't rule out the possibility entirely," he said. "I just don't think it very likely. Plus, how would they know which cartridge I would choose?"

"Were the guns out of your sight after you loaded them and before you handed them to the actors?"

"No. As I said, I was in a hurry to beat the sun. As soon as they were loaded, I handed them to Peter and Jake, just before they stepped into their places."

"And at that point, the actors were in full view of the entire group, is that correct?"

"Yes."

"Jake didn't, for instance, leave the field for any reason?"

"No, Inspector. Both actors were in place, and filming began very shortly after I handed them the weapons."

"I see. When the shots were fired," continued the Inspector, "did you hear any sounds other than the two shots?"

Brian furrowed his brow.

"I don't think so. What do you mean?"

Inspector Ferguson flipped his hands nonchalantly.

"I mean, did you only hear two shots? Or did you, perhaps, hear a third?"

William shifted in his chair. It was the very theory he had posed to Anna.

"Another shooter?" asked Brian, surprised. "I don't think so," he said after some reflection. "But I can't say for certain. I wasn't listening for that at the time, and with all the excitement, I don't know if I would have heard that. Positionally," he went on, as if imagining the scene, "If there were a third shooter, he would have to have been in the trees. Maybe Corinne heard something."

"Perhaps," said the Inspector, looking down at his notes.

"I didn't hear anything," said Corinne, her blue eyes wide. "There was no one in the trees except me. But of course, you have the film footage, right? You could just watch it and see."

The Inspector ignored her remark.

"I understand you have experience with guns," he said, looking up blandly from his notes.

Corinne stared at him.

"I...took a self-defense course once," she stammered. "My cousin taught it."

William rubbed his chin as he attempted to guess the Inspector's thoughts. Did he suspect Corinne? Or was he just being thorough?

"We were also able to retrieve photographs of you deer hunting with your father," the Inspector volunteered.

Corinne's expression was furious.

"From Instagram," the Inspector explained mildly.

"You were spying on me?" she asked, incredulous.

"It's all public information," the Inspector answered placidly. "I'm merely suggesting that you are familiar with using a gun."

"Maybe," admitted Corinne, sulkily, "but not a dueling pistol."

"So, you didn't see or hear anything unusual during the duel?" Inspector Ferguson asked, returning to his original subject.

Corinne hesitated before replying.

"I didn't hear anything unusual," she said. "And there was no one in the trees with me."

The Inspector consulted his notes.

"Were you close with Peter Mallory?"

"I suppose so," she said, looking down.

"Would you say your relationship was a romantic one?"

William watched Corinne closely.

How will she answer? he wondered.

Corinne swallowed hard, closing her eyes, as if bracing herself.

"We had been in a romantic relationship," she admitted.

"Had been?" asked the Inspector.

She sighed heavily.

"I had recently realized that Peter and I weren't a good match," she said.

"And what made you decide this?"

"Nothing in particular," she said, shrugging and giving the Inspector a weak smile. "He just wasn't the one for me."

"I was given to understand that he was the jealous type," he said, squinting at her. "That he thought you were seeing someone else."

She scowled.

"I wasn't seeing someone else," she said angrily. "And even if I was, he doesn't own me!"

"So, if he thought you were interested in Perry Prince, for instance, that would be incorrect?"

Corinne clenched her jaw.

"Perry had nothing to do with my decision," she said.

"And what decision was that, Miss Newberry?"

She sighed again.

"To—cool things off," she said.

"To break things off?" the Inspector clarified.

"I hadn't gotten that far yet," she admitted. "I hadn't actually broken up with him."

"But you were going to?"

"Yes," she said, with tears in her eyes. "I was. But it doesn't matter now, does it? And my last words to him were angry." She sobbed.

Sergeant Patel grabbed a tissue out of a small package beside her and handed it to Corinne. William was surprised to see compassion in the Ice Queen's eyes.

Inspector Ferguson waited until Corinne had her emotions under control again.

"How long have you known Peter Mallory?" he asked after she dried her eyes.

"We met on the set," Corinne explained. "So about three weeks, I guess."

"That isn't long," he said, "to have already formed and broken off a relationship."

"Everything gets, I don't know, speeded up when you're on set," she said. "It's kind of like camp. You're with each other all day, every day. And sometimes there's filming all night, too. Things are on a faster speed than in normal life."

"I see," he replied, scratching his neck. "You mentioned your last words to him were angry," he said. "Did you have a row—an argument?"

Corinne reddened, but didn't look William's direction.

"I wouldn't let him in my bedroom the night before the duel," she explained. "He was drunk, and he was pounding on the door. He thought Perry was in my room, but he wasn't. I told Peter to go away."

"And did he?"

"Yes," she answered simply.

William was surprised Corinne didn't mention the attempted rape.

Maybe she and Anna talked about not bringing it up, he thought. Or she and Jake.

"Was Peter in the habit of getting drunk?" asked the Inspector with a squint.

Corinne hesitated.

"I don't know," she said. "Sir Frederick had a rule against being drunk on set. I'm not sure how Peter got alcohol that night. It's not served in catering, and he had run out—"

She stopped herself.

"I'm guessing Peter was in the habit of taking a drink now and then behind closed doors," the Inspector prodded. "Is that correct?"

"Sir Frederick has a rule against drunkenness on set," Corinne explained. "But he didn't say we couldn't drink *at all*. Peter had brought a stash of whiskey with him, and sometimes, when we were alone, he brought it out. I didn't see the harm in it at first. It was kind of like being underaged and getting someone to buy you beer."

"Exciting," the Inspector suggested. "A secret thrill."

"Yes," she said. "And at first, it was just a glass or two. But after awhile, he wouldn't stop at one or two. He would get angry if I tried to get him to cut back. He would get angry at almost anything."

"Do you think he had a drinking problem?" asked the Inspector. "Was he an alcoholic?"

"I didn't at first," she admitted. "But then he kept drinking more, as time went on. He seemed to need more, just to relax. That's what he called it."

"Was Mr. Mallory ever violent with you?"

Corinne stiffened.

"What do you mean?" she asked cautiously.

"Did he ever push you, or hit you? Threaten you in any way?"

She took a deep breath.

"I mean, sometimes he was a little rough, if he'd been drinking. But he never hit me."

"Rough in what way?" asked the Inspector.

"I don't know," said Corinne, clearly uncomfortable. "Just rough.

Grabbing my arm, sometimes, to move me out of the way. Stuff like that."

"Did he rape you?"

Corinne's eyes darted to the Inspector's face, then down into her lap.

"No," she whispered.

"You seem unsure."

"He was my boyfriend," she explained, defensively. "It's not rape if he's my boyfriend, is it?"

The Inspector made a note on his pad, then leaned forward over the desk.

"The definition of rape is not restricted to whether or not you have had sex with the person consensually before," he said, his squinting eyes penetrating hers. "It's rape if it's against your current wishes. Would you say Peter Mallory raped you?"

"I don't know!" she blurted out. "You're confusing me!"

Sergeant Patel shifted uncomfortably in her chair, and the Inspector relaxed, leaning back. Corinne accepted a kleenex from the Sergeant, and dabbed at her eyes.

William felt sorry for her. No wonder she wanted out of her relationship with Peter.

"Did you speak to him the following day?" asked the Inspector, trying to use a soothing tone. "After you refused to let him in your room? That would be the morning of the duel."

Corinne shook her head.

"I was trying to avoid him," she said, covering her mouth with her hand, her tears springing fresh. "I thought we'd talk later, but…"

"Later never came," Inspector Ferguson said quietly.

CHAPTER FORTY-SEVEN

Jake and Anna joined the nervous group that was gathered in the Drawing Room. Jim and Sarah sat on a sofa together, their worn jeans looking out-of-place in the Regency setting. Jim had his dirty Chuck Taylors up on a round, marble-topped coffee table. Tim, the lighting director, sat slumped in a corner, his mustache frowning as he thumbed through his phone. Alan Potts was standing at the window overlooking the garden; his shoulders seemed pinched and stiff. Perry was pacing the length of the room, his hands thrust into his pockets.

"How'd it go?" Jim asked of Jake.

"As expected, I guess," he answered with a sigh, plopping himself down on an empty settee. He pulled his hand through his hair, then threw his arm over the back of the sofa.

"Jaime's in now," volunteered Sarah. "We don't know who's next."

"Have you been interviewed?" Perry asked, pausing in front of Anna.

She shook her head. She positioned herself on the edge of a chair. She could feel Jake's questioning glance. He had left space for her on the settee, but she would have to start distancing herself at some point.

"Did you see Edwin Sterling?" asked Sarah, her eyebrows raised, obviously pleased with herself for having gossip to share.

"Yes!" Anna said, hoping her voice sounded calm. "I saw him arrive."

"What's he doing here?" asked Jake, surprised. "Surely he's not taking Peter's place already!"

Sarah shook her head, and Jake relaxed somewhat.

"We don't even know if the show is continuing," said Sarah with a serious expression. "I know Sir Frederick didn't call him in. Unless he had Perry do it."

"No," answered Perry from across the room. He was looking at the empty space on the console table where the box of pistols had been displayed.

"I think his Mama called him," grumbled Jim. "Guess she wanted him to comfort her. Bet she won't be yelled at for breaking confidentiality."

"I had no idea until this morning that Edwin Sterling was Portia Valentine's son!" said Anna, her eyes shining.

"Everyone knows that," said Sarah, shrugging. "They have the same eyes.

His are so blue and sexy. Makes you want to melt right into them."

She smiled a dreamy smile. Jim grumbled something under his breath and folded his arms, scowling.

Anna tried not to be embarrassed by her lack of Hollywood inside knowledge. She hoped no one had seen her silly scene in the Great Hall that morning.

"I can see why you wouldn't guess," offered Jake, coming to her rescue. "They have different last names. Portia's is a stage name."

She smiled gratefully at him.

"I'm not sure I can continue here," Jake added, "even if the show does."

There was an uncomfortable silence.

"Totally understandable, mate," said Perry, moving forward and taking a seat near the others. He gave Jake a sympathetic nod.

"Yes, it is understandable," Anna agreed. The others remained silent. Anna wondered if it was because losing another lead actor was bad for the show, or because they suspected Jake of murder. She wondered how it made Jake feel.

Tim Tremayne looked up from his phone, oblivious to the previous conversation.

"Hey, Jim," he rasped. "Are we going to mention the pranks to the Inspector?"

Jim gave him a warning look, like he didn't want to discuss it in present company. Alan turned abruptly toward the group from the window.

"What do you mean?" asked Perry. "What do the pranks have to do with Peter getting shot?"

Jim and Sarah exchanged a glance. Jim growled.

"We figured out it was Peter who was doing all the practical jokes," he admitted reluctantly.

"What?" Jake cried. "No. You must be mistaken."

Sarah shook her head.

"We confronted him about it after dinner Monday night."

"You and Jim?" asked Jake, glancing at Alan.

"Yes," she said, "and Tim."

"Did he admit to it?" asked Jake, eyeing them sharply.

"Might as well have," Jim said angrily.

"He didn't go so far as to admit it," Sarah clarified, "but he didn't deny it. He said, 'What's the harm in a little joke now and then?' and he laughed that annoying laugh he has when he's trying to get under your skin."

"He did it," said Jim. "I'm sure of it."

Jake shook his head, bewildered.

"He didn't say anything to me," he said, leaning his head against the hand that was outstretched on the sofa. Anna watched as he gripped his hair.

He's stressing out, she thought sympathetically. Maybe Peter isn't who he thought he was.

Alan sighed and turned back to the window.

"So, shouldn't we tell the police about it?" Tim asked again.

"Why would you?" asked Jake.

"Maybe the person who killed him did it because of the practical jokes," Jim suggested. "I mean, it wasted a lot of time and money."

"Yeah," said Sarah, thoughtfully. "But maybe that would put suspicion on us!"

CHAPTER FORTY-EIGHT

When Jaime Douglas entered the Study, she cast a curious look in William's direction. He was struck once again by the other-worldliness of her eyes. The image of she and Jake in the garden on the first evening they arrived came immediately to William's mind. He remembered the way she had looked through him, even though he was convinced she couldn't have actually seen him. A dark foreboding stole over him, even now, in the Study, surrounded by the police. Like a spell was being put on him.

That's ridiculous, he told himself sternly. Witchcraft is a thing of the past.

"Tell us about your past relationship with Peter Mallory," Inspector Ferguson began.

Jaime's silver eyes narrowed.

"Why is that important?" she asked.

"The man is dead," he answered bluntly. "Shot by a prop. And you're the props master."

William was surprised. The Inspector was taking a very different approach with Jaime. No subtlety at all.

Jaime's jaw tightened, then released. She seemed to be making her mind up about something, all the time staring unblinkingly at the Inspector, as if they were competing in a staring contest. Finally, she lowered her eyes.

"We were together for awhile," she said, looking back up at him. "About two years ago."

"Care to elaborate?" he asked.

She shrugged and rolled her eyes.

"It was temporary. We met on the set. We had fun while we were filming. We moved on after."

"So there were no hard feelings between you?" the Inspector asked. "You weren't jealous, for instance, of his relationship with Corinne Newberry?"

She snorted.

"Jealous of that airhead?" she asked. "No. Peter and I were over long ago. I wasn't pining away for him. Besides, I'm a professional. I'm here to do my job, not worry about old boyfriends."

"So you're not mourning his loss?"

Jaime dropped her eyes momentarily.

"Peter and I may not have been friends anymore," she said quietly, "but I'm sorry he had to die."

"Was Peter ever violent when you were together?" asked the Inspector, squinting across the desk at her.

"Violent toward me?" she asked. "He didn't hurt me, if that's what you're asking."

"Do you feel he had a temper?"

"Doesn't everyone?" she asked.

Inspector Ferguson waited in silence.

"Yes, he could get angry sometimes," she admitted. "Maybe it's the red hair."

Her eyes flicked toward William.

"Do you feel Peter had a drinking problem?"

Jaime shrugged.

"No more than anyone else on the set," she said. "There weren't any rules against drunkenness under that director. It was one big party."

"So, you never felt threatened by Peter?" he asked. "Particularly in a sexual capacity?"

"You mean, did he rape me?" she asked, scoffing. "No. Anything we did was consensual."

The Inspector consulted his notes, apparently satisfied with her answers.

For now, thought William. But here was proof of Miranda's accusation. If Jaime really did have a past relationship with Peter, maybe she had a motive for murder after all? He couldn't wait to tell Anna about it. Then he remembered her odd way of leaving the night before, and he furrowed his brow.

"You said in your statement earlier that it was Brian Elliston who loaded the pistols on the morning of the duel," the Inspector continued.

"Yes."

"But you also know how to load the pistols. Is that correct?"

"I watched Brian load them, so I could probably do it in a pinch. But there are safety regulations about those things. You have to be certified."

The Inspector nodded.

"You have to be certified to be legal," he agreed. "Did you notice anything unusual about the guns that morning? Did Brian vary at all from his usual method of loading?"

"No, everything seemed the same," she said.

"Was anything missing from the props table?"

"Other than the pistols, you mean?"

Jaime glanced slyly in William's direction.

"Nothing was missing, as far as I know," she continued. "It's hard to tell exactly, with boxes of bullets. I wasn't counting them."

"I notice you had both live and blank cartridges on the table," said the Inspector. "Why is that, when you were only using blanks for the duel? Couldn't that have led to a mixup?"

"I had both because it was supposed to be a long day of filming," Jaime explained. "Close ups as well as long shots, like the scene when Peter was shot. And it would be hard to mix them up. They look completely different. Only a fool wouldn't know the difference."

"A fool or a murderer," said Inspector Ferguson matter-of-factly.

Jaime's silver eyes narrowed.

"Tell me, Miss Douglas," said the Inspector, "did Peter Mallory have any enemies?"

She smiled her enigmatic smile.

"It might be easier to name his friends," she said.

"He wasn't well-liked?"

She shrugged.

"He tended to rub people the wrong way. Just ask William."

Inspector Ferguson's eyes didn't leave Jaime's face, but William looked up to find the haughty, black eyes of Sergeant Patel on him. He glanced at Jaime, but she was looking smugly at the Inspector, as if William wasn't even in the room.

"What do you mean by that?" the Inspector asked, casually.

Jaime cocked her head to one side.

"He and Peter had an argument a few nights ago. My bedroom is just above the Tapestry Room where they were having it out."

"What was their disagreement?"

She shook her head.

"I could only hear raised voices," she explained. "One thing I heard for sure was at the end. Peter said, 'Oh? You think you're tough, eh? Going to punch me? I'm your bread and butter, mate!'"

"What do you think he meant by that?" asked the Inspector.

William shifted uneasily in his chair. It was awkward to sit quietly while someone else discussed his own conversation.

Jaime shrugged her thin shoulders.

"Maybe they were doing business together," she suggested. "Peter always had some kind of scheme going."

After she was dismissed, Inspector Ferguson turned to William.

"Care to elaborate?" he asked. "Did you and Peter Mallory have an argument?"

William sighed.

"Yes, we did," he admitted. "As I'm sure you're aware, Peter Mallory is Viscount Mallory, whose property used to adjoin to mine, until he sold it off piece by piece for housing developments."

"You were arguing about housing developments?"

"In a manner of speaking," said William. "He was making me an offer. He wanted to buy my estate. I think he thought I'd be desperate because I had resorted to allowing a film crew on my property."

"And are you desperate?"

William hesitated.

"No," he said. "Not completely. I would be lying if I said I didn't need the money Sir Frederick offered me. It's the reason *Cavendish Manor* is filming here in the first place."

The Inspector nodded.

"Do you think he had the money to buy you out? Was it a serious offer?"

William nodded.

"He claimed he'd been investing the money from his land sales," he said. "I have no reason to doubt him. We live on an island, after all. Land is a precious commodity, and people pay top dollar for a piece of it."

"Is that all you were fighting about?" the Inspector asked, squinting. "What *did* Peter mean by his last remark?"

William rolled his eyes.

"Peter really knew what buttons to push," he said. "Always did. Always tried to hold things over your head. He wasn't taking no for an answer. He made me so angry, I wanted to punch him, and he must have seen my hand form a fist. He said what he said, meaning he was the one with the money to get me out of debt 'the easy way,' as he put it. But the easy way was never for me, I guess. And I'm not as desperate as he thought. Certainly not desperate enough to sell my family's history to someone like him."

"Was he holding anything over your head?" Inspector Ferguson asked. William could feel the eyes of Sergeant Patel burning into him from across the room.

He shrugged.

"My father had gambled away our family money," he said.

"That's no secret," said the Inspector, jotting something on a pad in front of him.

"No, it's not," William agreed.

The two men eyed each other. Finally, the Inspector rose to his feet.

"Time for a lunch break," he announced. A faint, irritated sound came from Sergeant Patel, but the Inspector ignored it. William looked up to find her glaring at him, as if he were a juvenile delinquent who had wiggled his way out of punishment.

"You are both welcome to have lunch here at Hampstead," William offered.

"Thank you, but I think we'll go into the village, if you don't mind," the Inspector said pleasantly. "We'll finish up interviews in the afternoon."

CHAPTER FORTY-NINE

William was disappointed the Inspector turned down his invitation for lunch; he knew it meant they would discuss the case without him. But, he was thankful for being included in the interviews, and he hoped he would be allowed to continue that role in the afternoon.

What did they think, he wondered, about his argument with Peter? Did the Inspector suspect him of killing a man over a real estate offer? Sergeant Patel seemed eager to convict him without any evidence.

He headed for the Dining Room, hoping to find Anna. It was always so easy to talk to her, and he needed to process things. The interviews had revealed a lot.

A buffet had been set up again across the long sideboard. When William entered the room, he saw Jaime standing in front of it, plate in hand. She was talking with Jake and Anna. When they noticed him, they stopped speaking. Jaime smiled her eerie smile at him, and turned back to filling her plate. Jake gave him a nod and joined her.

"Probably telling them about the argument I had with Peter," he surmised.

Adrian, seated at the head of the table, gave him one of his customary, surprised expressions that turned into a high-eyebrow smile that William wasn't sure how to interpret.

Anna approached William cautiously, still holding her empty plate.

"How are the interviews going?" she asked. "Jaime was just telling us a little of hers."

"Fine," he answered. He wasn't sure how the Inspector would feel about revealing the details he now knew. Even if he did decide to share them with Anna, it wouldn't do to let the entire cast and crew know. They wouldn't speak freely, otherwise.

Edwin and Portia's arrival caused a stir that relieved William from any more awkward questions.

"Edwin Sterling! What are *you* doing here?" asked Miranda, who arrived as well, making a dramatic entrance through the pocket doors from the Drawing Room.

"Miranda!" said Edwin, kissing her cheek. "Looking as radiant as ever."

"Even in the middle of a murder investigation," Miranda pouted.

Anna noticed Miranda was dressed as if she were going to a photoshoot. Out of the corner of her eye, she saw Jake and Jaime move out of the Dining Room with their plates. She couldn't blame them. Miranda had been horrible to Jaime the night before. Miranda had been horrible, period.

"You must be feeling better today, Miranda," said Portia.

Miranda scowled.

"How can I feel better when there's a murderer after me?" she asked, pouting her fully lip-sticked mouth.

Edwin wrinkled his brow.

"I wasn't aware the murderer was after you, Miranda," he said politely. "I assumed he, or she, was after Peter Mallory."

"Is it officially a murder investigation?" asked Portia. "I thought the police were still trying to determine that."

Miranda ignored her.

"Well, you don't know about all the things that have been happening on the set up to this point," she said, holding onto Edwin's arm, delighted to have a new audience. "The car I was riding in broke down, a light panel almost fell on me, and a chair fell to pieces as soon as I sat down in it! What else am I supposed to think? Clearly someone is out to get me. Maybe they shot Peter by mistake."

Edwin nodded at her, but gave his mother a concerned glance.

"Miranda, that's ridiculous," said Julia as she entered the room. "You weren't even in the dueling scene."

"How would you know?" Miranda retorted. "You weren't even here. What kind of a producer doesn't even come to the set?"

Julia's eyes flashed, and she opened her mouth to speak, but before she could, Sir Frederick arrived in the Dining Room.

"What's all this?" he said, scanning the room. "What is it this time, Miranda?"

"You see?" Miranda hissed in Edwin's ear. "They're all out to get me. I can't trust any of them."

She clutched his arm. He patted her hand and led her back into the Drawing Room.

"Let me get you settled in here, away from the others, and I'll bring you a plate," he said soothingly. "Then we can talk."

Miranda gazed up at him, adoringly, batting her false eyelashes.

Anna knew what Edwin was doing. He couldn't possibly believe Miranda's story, and he probably wanted to do some investigating of his own. But she couldn't help but think how absurd it was to watch a woman flirt with a man who was young enough to be her son.

Her distaste must have shown on her face, because she caught a conspiratorial gleam in William's eye.

It's like he reads my mind, she thought, and the knowledge both thrilled and scared her. She wondered what he was learning in the interviews, and if he would share his information.

"Where's the crew?" asked Sir Frederick, blinking around the room.

"They already ate," Adrian answered, opening his button-eyes wide. "I think they wanted to keep away from the rest of us."

"Why?"

Adrian stood to leave.

"Maybe they suspect us all," he said.

Although his face held his usual blissful expression, Anna noticed the corners of his mouth were turned down, and his eyes showed crow's feet at the corners. She watched Adrian leave, wondering what he thought of all this. Was he worried about a practical joker gone too far? Or was he concerned about being caught?

That's ridiculous, she scolded herself. I can't think of everyone on set as a possible murderer.

"We have to think of everyone as a possible murderer," William said, his face serious. He was looking intently at Anna.

She caught her breath. They had escaped to the small vestibule off the Great Hall, the one William had told her used to be a chapel. It was smaller than the bedroom she was staying in, filled with odds and ends of furniture and old trunks. Despite the junk, Anna could see the beauty the room held, with its stained-glass windows depicting Bible scenes, and a carved wooden altar at the far end. When they entered, he pointed out the end of the secret passage that connected this room with the Tapestry Room and up to the Nursery. It was beside the fireplace on the inner wall. There was a semi-circle cleared in the dust on the floor from the swinging of the secret door.

William had told her he wanted to talk to her, away from prying ears.

Now, as she gazed into his blue eyes, she saw a mixture of emotions. She tried to read his mind like she felt he could read hers, but it was difficult. There was something hidden in him now, like a curtain had been closed that used to be open. What she did see was concern: concern for her, for the others, for the future of *Cavendish Manor*, perhaps? She knew he needed its success to pay his father's debts. But there was something else.

Fear, she thought, though he was trying to hide it. What would make Lord Somerville afraid?

"I know you don't want to think that way, suspecting everyone," he continued, "but we have to. Someone killed Peter, and we don't know why. And not knowing why makes me wonder if—"

"If what?" she asked, although she knew what he meant.

"If we knew why," he said, "we would know if it was an isolated incident."

"Or if we're all still in danger," she clarified. Her hazel eyes were grey as she stared steadily at his face.

"I want to talk to you about all the interviews," he said, "but I don't know if I'm allowed. I'm surprised Inspector Ferguson is letting me stay in the room, and I don't want to lose whatever trust he has in me. Sergeant Patel doesn't like me being there, I can tell."

"Yes, it does seem unusual," Anna said.

"No one has confessed, or anything like that," he said quickly, to ease her worries. "It's just, there are so many details. And I'm learning things about people I wouldn't have suspected."

"Like what?" she asked.

A gong sounded throughout the house. Anna jumped.

"The doorbell," William explained. "That would be the Inspector returning from lunch. I want to try to be in these afternoon interviews, as well, so I should probably join them. Maybe we can talk later?"

She nodded.

He put his hands on her shoulders, then slid them down her arms. Her skin prickled at his touch, even through her sweater. She looked up earnestly into his face.

"Be careful, Anna," he said. "Don't trust anyone."

Even you? she wondered as she watched him leave.

CHAPTER FIFTY

As he entered the Great Hall, William was surprised to see Jaime speaking with Inspector Ferguson near the fireplace. Jaime gave him one of her sly glances as she finished her conversation. William was puzzled by the smirk she gave him as she slipped quickly away toward the Drawing Room.

"Ah! Lord Somerville," said the Inspector, noticing him. "Will you be joining us this afternoon?"

"If you'll allow me," said William.

"Of course."

William was once again surprised by the Inspector's willingness to have him in the room for interviews, but Sergeant Patel maintained her obvious displeasure at her superior officer's decision. She scowled at William beneath her black brows as she watched him enter the Study. She had been adjusting the camera while Inspector Ferguson was speaking with Jaime Douglas in the Great Hall.

Inspector Ferguson closed the Study door, then turned to face William, who had settled himself in his spot in the corner.

"Before we begin our interviews, my lord, I wanted to speak with you about something," he said as he crossed to the desk. "If you don't mind?"

"Of course," said William, curiously.

"It has come to my attention that Peter Mallory was in Monte Carlo when your father died of an overdose. Is that true?"

"Yes," William said, surprised. He wondered who had told the Inspector. His mother seemed an unlikely candidate. Could it have been Anna? But why?

"And yet you neglected to mention this to me," the Inspector said stiffly.

"It didn't seem relevant to the case," said William.

Inspector Ferguson squinted at him for a moment.

"Your argument the other night was overheard more fully than originally thought," he explained, eyeing William carefully. "My informant says you were arguing about more than real estate. In short, you accused Peter Mallory of murdering your father."

William folded his arms over his chest and glared at his clean boots that were thrust out in front of him.

"Would you care to elaborate, my lord?" the Inspector urged.

William clenched his jaw.

"It was Peter who informed me my father had been taking sleeping pills in addition to his usual whisky," he blurted out. "That was how my father died. An overdose of sleeping pills."

"Do you have evidence that links Peter to your father's death?"

"No! Of course not, or I would have brought this to the police long ago. I have nothing to go on but a feeling."

"But you accused him of murder?"

"Not in so many words," said William. "When Peter was making his offer to buy Hampstead, he brought up the fact that things hadn't been going well for the estate, even after my father's death. Something about the way he said that, the look in his eye—" William's mind reflected back to Peter's sneering expression. "When I saw that look on his face, taunting me, like he had some kind of control over me—I couldn't help myself. I confronted him about it. I told him I blamed him for my father's death because I believed he was the one who gave my father the sleeping pills. He had never taken them before that trip."

"What did Peter say to that?" the Inspector asked.

William shook his head.

"He didn't admit to it, if that's what you're asking. He just kept mocking me with that look he gets. That's when I wanted to punch him."

Inspector Ferguson nodded.

"So, you lied to me," he said.

"No!" William cried. "I didn't lie! I just left that part of our conversation out. It was more to protect Peter than to protect myself. I didn't have proof he killed my father. I didn't think it was relevant. Especially now that he's dead."

"Those are very important words, Lord Somerville. 'Especially now that he's dead.'"

William sat rigidly in his chair.

"Are you accusing me of something, Inspector?" he asked, his voice like a razor.

"No one's accusing anyone, Lord Somerville. I merely question why you withheld the information."

"Again, I didn't think it was relevant to this case."

"In future, your lordship, let me decide what's relevant to the case or not."

Anna finished circling the rose garden and moved into the arched walkway on her way toward the Japanese bridge. The dark-eyed Sergeant had told her, in her cold and business-like way, the order of the next few interviews, and Anna was toward the end of the lineup. It made sense; she hadn't actually been in the dueling scene, and she wasn't one of the power people, like Sir Frederick or Julia. She had decided to take a walk in the garden while she waited her turn.

It was a grey day, the kind of day when the sun sends his understudy. The sky was a wash of immoveable clouds with no rain, and the temperature was sullen, withholding warmth but not cold enough for winter.

She had been considering what William had said: don't trust anyone. What did he mean by that, exactly? Did he really think they were all still in danger? She didn't want to believe that. She wanted it all to be behind them as quickly as possible. She especially didn't want to believe William had anything to do with Peter's death. She pushed those thoughts to the back of her mind. No, she told herself. I'm being silly. William's an earl, and he's helping the Inspector with the interviews. Besides that, he's on the right track, she realized. It was the *why* of the murder that was important. If murder is what it was. They still hadn't heard an official report from the police.

Why would someone want to kill Peter Mallory?

She asked herself the question as if it were an interview.

Well, she answered, *he was a despicable human being.* The kind of man who made a woman feel creepy just by looking at her. The kind of man who took advantage, who thought rape was a good way to teach someone a lesson. If she was honest with herself, *she* had an excellent motive for killing Peter Mallory.

Her phone rang from her pocket, and she took a deep breath before answering.

"Hello, Mother."

"I was beginning to think something happened to you," came her mother's curt reply.

Anna gripped the phone tightly.

"What would have happened to me?" she asked, breathless. Could the news have gotten out?

"I don't know," her mother replied, with an irritated tone. "Fallen and gotten amnesia or something. That would explain why you haven't called."

"Oh," said Anna, relieved. "Sorry about that. We've been very busy. How's Daddy?"

They chit-chatted for a few minutes. Anna realized she had to be careful what she said, She didn't want to get in trouble with the Studio, although she wondered how long they could hold out before Peter's death would be in the news. This was only day two.

"Mother, do you know if we're related to anyone in England?" she asked on a whim, remembering the portrait in the Gallery and hoping to steer her mother clear of *Cavendish Manor* news.

"I don't know right off-hand," said her mother. "Why?"

"I wondered who our relatives were," she replied. "Like, our ancestors. Did we come from England? From Surrey, in particular? That's where we're filming."

"Well," said her mother with a superior sniff, "many Americans have English in them somewhere. Yes, we're English on my father's side. I've got a whole photo album full of ancestors somewhere. In my office, I think. With information on them that my father started to put together before he died. I'll take a look. Surrey, you say? I'll definitely look into it. I'm glad you're starting to become interested in genealogy. Maybe it's something we can do together when you come home."

Anna rolled her eyes. *When I come home and stop playing actress,* she means.

"Oh, I almost forgot," said her mother. "I hope you haven't started anything with that Jake Rawlings character."

"Why?" asked Anna, puzzled.

"Well, I've been asking around, and guess what? The *Rawlings Furniture* Rawlings only have one son, and he's still in high school. A lot of daughters, but only one son. So he's an imposter!"

Anna rolled her eyes.

"He's not an imposter, Mother, he just isn't who people thought he was."

"Well, it's a good thing I found this out before—well, you know. Before anything romantic happened between you two."

Anna sighed.

"He's still a nice guy, even if he isn't a *Rawlings Furniture* Rawlings."

After finishing her call, Anna leaned her elbows against the wooden rail of the bridge and stared down into the murky water of the moat. A flash of orange reminded her there were giant goldfish in the dark waters. She thought about Jake.

He really is a nice guy, she reminded herself.

But the more she thought about him, the more she knew she could never think of him as more than a friend. Even without William to confuse her. Especially with William to confuse her.

Out of the corner of her eye, Anna saw a black shape emerge suddenly out of one of the garden rooms further down the path, toward the lake. She turned her head; Jaime was standing there, in the middle of the path, staring at her, her draping black clothes blowing in what little wind was stirring, and her colorless hair streaming back from her face. Anna straightened, gripping the wooden rail with both hands. She felt sadness emanating down the yew lane, and thought she saw the shimmer of tears in the woman's eyes.

Anna sensed a quivering in the air as she locked eyes with the Scottish woman, and there was a rumbling sound in her ears. The distance between she and Jaime closed in an instant, and Anna found herself face to face with her.

But it wasn't really Jaime, she realized. At least, not the Jaime of right now. It was the Jaime from her dreams, the poor relation, and as she watched, that Jaime's eyes bore into hers, as if she were trying to convey a message. Help? Was that the message? Or was it I'm sorry? It was in her eyes for a fleeting moment, then gone. Jaime closed her silver, slanting, Scottish eyes and leaned her head back, giving the impression that she was sleeping, hanging in mid-air like a levitating witch, her black clothes floating around her like a funeral pall.

And then the vision was gone. Anna was back on the bridge, and Jaime was still a hundred yards away. The props master tore her gaze from Anna and disappeared into the yew hedge on the other side of the path.

Before Anna had fully recovered from her dizzying vision, Jake appeared on the path.   Anna gasped at the look of disgust on his face as he stared after Jaime. His head snapped in Anna's direction at the sound of her gasp, and his face cleared. He hesitated, glancing back to where Jaime had disappeared into the yew hedge. Then, as if he had made up his mind, he walked quickly down the path toward Anna.

"Did you see Jaime?" he asked as he approached.

"Yes," Anna answered cautiously. She took long, slow breaths to calm her racing heart. She didn't want to explain the recent vision to Jake.

Jake shook his head, a look of exasperation crossing his handsome features.

"I hate having to do that," he admitted, running a nervous hand through his blond hair. "I had to be blunt with her. She just wouldn't take no for an answer."

"Answer to what?" asked Anna.

He wrapped her in his arms.

"Apparently, she likes me," he said. "She's jealous of you, and told me her feelings just now. I had to let her know, once and for all, I'm not interested, that someone else had my heart."

He leaned his forehead against hers, and Anna could feel traces of cold sweat transfer from his skin to hers.

She pulled back to look at him.

"But surely you knew that," she said. "It was obvious she had feelings for you. At least to me."

He rolled his eyes.

"Okay, maybe I knew it. But I hoped she would just get over it. After she and Peter broke up, I noticed a change in her toward me. I just thought she'd figure it out, once you and I got together."

"How long have you known each other?" asked Anna curiously.

He shrugged.

"About two years," he said. "We met on the set of *Love and Loss*."

"Isn't that the movie Miranda mentioned? When Jaime dated Peter?"

"Yeah," he said. "I was in that film, too. Did you see it?"

Anna shook her head.

He grinned.

"You didn't miss anything," he admitted.

"If Jaime is Peter's ex, I'm surprised she went to Windsor with both of you," Anna said, her brow furrowed. "I don't think I could have done it with my ex-boyfriend."

"Maybe she was hoping to make him angry by flirting with me," he suggested.

"Maybe," Anna agreed. "She looked sad, just now."

He nodded. Then he shrugged.

"I can't help it that I don't have feelings for her," he said, pulling Anna closer. He leaned in to kiss her, but Anna moved back. Jake looked at her questioningly.

"Jake, we need to talk," she said. It was unfortunate timing, but she couldn't keep his hopes up forever.

"Don't do this, Anna," he said, guessing her intentions. "Not right now. I need you more than ever."

She looked up into his concerned face.

"I like you, Jake," she said, sighing. "I really do. But—"

"It's William, isn't it?" he asked, dejectedly, dropping his embrace. "I get it. You two have more in common. I'm just a poor boy from Little Rock."

He tried to give her one of his grins, but it fell short.

"Jake," she said. "please don't see this as a class thing." She felt horrible, disappointing him like this. She rubbed the sides of his arms, as if she were infusing strength into him. "I was already having feelings for William before I knew he was the Earl. I like you both."

"But you like him more?"

She sighed. "You are a wonderful man that any woman would be honored to have."

"But not you," he said, tears forming in his eyes. He swiped at them angrily, looking away.

She didn't answer.

"Does he feel the same?" he asked quietly.

"I haven't told him how I feel," she admitted.

"Do you—trust him?" he asked, hesitantly.

"What do you mean? Because he lied about his identity? So did you," Anna reminded him with a smile.

"That's not what bothers me," he said, scowling slightly. "It's how much he hated Peter. It just makes me wonder—"

He shook his head.

"Nevermind. Don't listen to me." Jake grabbed her hands. "Just give me some time," he begged. "Don't break things off completely. Let me prove myself worthy of you."

Anna was torn. She didn't believe her feelings would change, but she hated hurting Jake, especially after he had made such a stand with Jaime. Maybe he needed time to adjust to this new reality. Maybe she should let him back out gently, instead of being as blunt as he had to be with Jaime.

She nodded.

"Okay," she said. "But I don't think—"

He stopped her speech with a passionate kiss. Anna almost regretted her decision to break things off. But a memory of William's warm lips on hers came to her mind, and she gently pulled back from Jake.

"Just a little time," she said, breathlessly. He held her close and buried his face in her hair.

CHAPTER FIFTY-ONE

"What was your opinion of Peter Mallory?" Inspector Ferguson asked Sir Frederick.

The plump director was wedged in the leather chair in front of the desk like an apprehensive Tweedle Dee.

"He was a good actor," said Sir Frederick regretfully. "He will be missed."

"What about as a person?" the Inspector clarified. "Did you like him?"

Sir Frederick hesitated.

"Well," he said, "I wouldn't want to speak ill of the dead."

Inspector Ferguson leaned back in his chair.

"This is a police investigation, Sir Frederick. I'm looking for honesty."

The director frowned.

"He was a clown," he said, his eyebrows lowering. "Peter was the kind of guy who always had a joke, even if it was at someone else's expense. Especially if it was at someone else's expense."

"Did he joke with you?" asked the Inspector. "Or about you?"

"No. At least, not that I'm aware of. It was more that he took away time with jokes and making fun. Made filming longer because he wouldn't just say the lines. He always had to make a comment. Be the center of attention. Wouldn't you agree, William?"

William shifted uncomfortably in his chair, but didn't answer.

"I can see how that could make you angry," said the Inspector, shifting the attention back to him.

"Not really angry," Sir Frederick back-pedaled, eyeing the Inspector warily. "Just annoyed."

"She is so unbelievably annoying!" said Edwin Sterling to his mother.

Anna and Jake stopped in the doorway of the Drawing Room. They were entering the house from the garden through the French doors when Edwin made the statement, and Anna was afraid they were eavesdropping.

"Come in, Anna. Jake," said Portia, motioning to them. "Edwin was just complaining about Miranda."

Edwin was pacing the room. He pulled both his hands through his light brown curls, standing them on end.

"See," whispered Portia, pointing to her son. "She stressed him out. He always pulls on his hair when he's stressed."

Anna could feel the urge to smirk, but she controlled it. It wouldn't do to laugh at *the* Edwin Sterling.

"What did Miranda do?" asked Jake.

Edwin snorted.

"She claims to believe she's the intended victim in all of this," said Edwin, shaking his head in disbelief. "I'm not sure if she's delusional or self-aggrandizing."

"Surely she can't be serious?" said Anna, shocked.

Edwin collapsed into a chair.

"It was mentally exhausting, having to keep a pleasant look on my face while that woman prattled on like a martyr," he said, closing his eyes and leaning his head against the back of the gilded chair.

Jake sat on a nearby sofa, frowning thoughtfully.

"I hope it's not a self-fulfilling prophecy," he said, his brow furrowed.

"Don't say that!" said Anna, alarmed.

"My best friend is dead," he said hollowly. "It all seems senseless. Meaningless. If someone would kill Peter, why wouldn't he kill any one of us?"

"Or she," added Portia, her blue eyes serious.

Anna lowered herself into a chair, defeated. Jake was right. Nothing made sense. And the longer they went on, not knowing, the less safe she felt.

"Oh!" cried Edwin, sitting up suddenly, a gleam in his eye.

Anna and Jake both jumped, staring at the actor.

"What if it wasn't murder at all?" he asked, gazing at each one of them in turn.

"You mean, an accident?" asked his mother.

"No. I think it was intentional," he said, "but what if Peter himself put the lead ball in the pistol?"

"Suicide?" Anna asked.

"Exactly," Edwin answered.

The room was silent for a few moments as everyone considered the possibility.

"Is Peter the type to have committed suicide?" asked Portia.

"Is there a type?" asked Edwin. "You've all told me he was having diffi-culties in his love-life, and there was the attack on Anna, something he could be facing charges for. Maybe he couldn't face the consequences of his actions."

Jake shook his head.

"I can't see it," he said. "Besides, Anna wasn't going to press charges."

"How do you know?" Anna asked, giving him a cold stare. He stared back, surprised. "And even if I hadn't, William would have."

"Did he say that?" Jake asked.

She hesitated.

"He was very concerned."

She could feel Portia's sharp eyes on her. Had she overheard William the morning of the duel?

"Did anyone see Peter at the props table before the dueling scene?" asked Portia. "Maybe he picked up one of the lead balls when no one was looking."

Anna thought back in her mind.

"Yes," she said. "He was there right before Brian handed him the gun."

"Could he have popped the lead ball in the barrel without being seen?" Portia asked.

Jake shook his head.

"I don't think so," he said. "With everyone's eyes on him? Besides, it was my gun that had the bullet, not his. He would have had to somehow steal a lead ball, then get it into the barrel of my pistol without anyone seeing, including me. I don't think it's feasible."

The room grew silent again. Anna replayed the day of the duel in her mind. The props table had been bustling with activity that morning. Brian was loading the guns; Jaime was there as well. And Jake and Peter were standing at the table waiting for their weapons. But that wasn't all. Anna dug deeper into her memory. Perry was there, too. She could see his eager face as Brian handed the pistols to the actors. And William. She remembered being surprised that he was standing near the table, since he wouldn't be receiving a weapon.

"Miranda mentioned something to me that I wanted to ask you about, Jake," said Edwin, turning to the other actor.

Jake didn't answer. He was staring into space, like he was daydreaming.

"Jake?" Anna called. "Edwin wanted to ask you something."

Jake blinked a few times, as if coming awake.

"Sorry," he said. "I have a lot on my mind." He smiled at Edwin. "What did you want to ask?"

"When I was talking with Miranda, or actually, when she was talking to me," said Edwin with a roll of his eyes, "she said you and Peter had an argument. She was trying to insinuate that no one could be trusted, not even 'nice guys' like you."

Jake frowned, as if trying to remember.

"When was this?" he asked.

"On Monday night, she said. The night before the duel," Edwin explained. "Of course, I don't know how reliable she is as a witness. She said it was just after dinner. She had eaten in her room that night because it was lightning and catering had moved indoors. She said she didn't want to associate with 'the riff-raff'. Sorry. Her words. She was about to put her tray in the hall for the staff to pick up, when she heard another door open. According to her, you were standing at the door, and Peter was leaving your room, smirking. Miranda said you looked angry. Peter said something like 'Calm down, friend,' and you said 'Don't call me that again!' and slammed the door."

Jake wiped his face with his hands, and Anna was alarmed at how pale he had become. He shook his head, tears forming in his eyes.

"We would have made up," he said, beseechingly. "I would have forgiven him."

Edwin watched him, waiting, but didn't ask him any more questions.

Jake sighed, looking down at his hands. After a few moments, he looked up at Edwin, his eyes bright.

"He had insulted Anna," he said, not looking in her direction. "He blamed her for Corinne's sudden coldness toward him. He thought Anna was a bad influence, making Corinne into a prude. His words," he said, turning to Anna. "I never thought that!"

"I know," she said soothingly. It was all the things Peter would accuse her of to her face later that night in a drunken rage.

"I told him he was being ridiculous, that Anna wasn't coming between he and Corinne. That's when he told me he thought Perry was coming between them, that he thought Corinne was spending time with Perry, and Peter was jealous. Anyway, he said some vile things about the woman I cared about, and then laughed about it, like it was my problem for getting upset. I didn't want to be his friend anymore," he said, angrily wiping a tear from his cheek. "But it would have blown over. He would have eventually apologized. If there'd been time."

Edwin nodded.

"I'm sorry to bring up a bad memory," he said. "For all I knew, Miranda had made the whole thing up."

"Do you think she'll mention it to the Inspector?" Jake asked.

Edwin shrugged.

"Then I guess I should assume my interview isn't over," said Jake grimly.

"One more question," Inspector Ferguson said as Sir Frederick made a motion to rise from his chair. "What is the financial status of *Cavendish Manor*? Is it operating in the black?"

"Is any film operating in the black?" asked Sir Frederick with a brittle laugh. "You make a budget, and you hope to abide by it, but chances are, something will come up to throw everything out of whack."

"Like a death on set?"

"Yes," said the director, rubbing his chin. "With everything else going on, I really couldn't afford that. Julia—I mean, the Studio—gave me such a low budget, I had to put up my own money just to make things work. With every setback, it was money out of my pocket."

"What else was going on?" asked the Inspector, leaning forward across the desk.

"Well," said Sir Frederick, blinking behind his glasses, "the practical jokes, for one thing."

Sir Frederick explained to the Inspector what had been happening on the set.

"Any idea who was responsible?" asked Inspector Ferguson.

"None at all," said Sir Frederick. "And then to have Miranda and Adrian constantly questioning whether or not I was cutting corners with the budget, it made me feel like they were somehow blaming *me* for what was happening. As if it could all be explained by shoddy workmanship or inefficient lighting poles."

The director had difficulty hiding his irritation.

"Do you think Peter's death could have been a practical joke gone wrong?" asked the Inspector, squinting at the director.

"A morbid thought," said Sir Frederick. "I guess it's possible, but it seems a bit far-fetched, don't you think?"

"It does seem very theatrical," commented Inspector Ferguson, his squint shifting to William's corner.

"But it does show that you have experience with weapons. Why did you leave the Army?"

"I served my time," said Perry simply. "It wasn't for me."

"Then why did you join?"

"My dad was Army," Perry explained simply.

William listened, amazed at how many of the cast and crew had previous experience with guns. He wondered what Inspector Ferguson would think of his own experience. One thing the Eighth Earl had insisted upon was his son's knowledge of hunting. William glanced across at Sergeant Patel, hoping the dark-eyed officer couldn't read his thoughts.

"When you were previously asked about Peter having any enemies," the Inspector continued, "you mentioned William. Is that correct?"

Perry glanced back nervously at William.

"I only meant that they didn't get along," he explained quickly. "They had that fight and all."

"Do you know the subject of the argument?" asked the Inspector, squinting at him.

"Nah," he said, shrugging. "All I heard was Peter saying not to punch him because he was William's bread and butter."

"And what did you think he meant by that statement?"

"It didn't make sense to me," admitted Perry. "I guess I thought he might have gotten William the job as Sir Frederick's assistant. That always confused me."

"You mean, William's role in the production?"

"Yeah," said Perry. "I knew Sir Frederick was looking for an assistant after Sam left for California, but I never saw him interview anyone. Then all of a sudden, there was William. Makes sense now, of course. Should have known he was pretending."

Perry returned to the Drawing Room after his interview, quiet and withdrawn. Corinne, who had arrived in the room a few minutes before, stood up, and they exchanged apprehensive glances.

"How'd it go?" asked Jake.

Perry shrugged.

"Okay, I guess," he answered, pouring himself a glass of water from a pitcher on a side table. He gulped it down quickly.

CHAPTER FIFTY-TWO

◆—◆◇◆—◆

"What does a production assistant do, exactly?"

Perry sat very upright in the chair across from Inspector Ferguson.

"You name it, I do it," he answered.

"Including gun handling?" asked the Inspector, squinting at him across the desk.

Perry swallowed hard.

"Just that day," he said.

"Why did you have possession of the pistol box on that day? Did someone ask you to retrieve them?"

Perry shook his head.

"When I saw they weren't on the props table, I remembered William, I mean, Lord Somerville, had put the pistol box back in the Drawing Room, so I went to get it before Sir Frederick lost it on someone. He can be very particular about things."

The Inspector nodded.

"And was anyone in or around the Drawing Room when you were fetching the pistols?"

"No," said Perry. "I mean, William was, but only after I brought them out. He gave me a ride back to the dueling field."

Sergeant Patel flashed a suspicious glance at William.

If she could, she would already have me behind bars, thought William rue- fully. He tried to ignore her, paying attention again to what Perry was saying.

"Would your duties include loading the pistols?" asked the Inspector, glancing down at his notes.

"No, of course not," Perry answered, puzzled. "That's Brian's job."

"But you do know how to load a gun."

"I—what do you mean?" asked Perry, stalling.

"According to my notes, you were in the infantry of the British Army until three years ago."

Perry eyed him warily.

"Yes, I was, but what has that got to do with this?"

"Probably nothing," said Inspector Ferguson, flipping his hands over.

"What did they ask you?" asked Corinne.

"About my experience with guns," he said, frowning. "They knew about my time in the Army."

Corinne put a comforting hand on his arm.

"They asked me about hunting with my dad," she said compassionately.

"How can serving your country be suspicious?" asked Jake. "You'd think that would exonerate you."

Perry shrugged.

"How long did you serve?" asked Edwin.

"Four years," he said.

"Why did you leave?" Edwin asked.

"I served my time," he said. "I was ready for something new. My dad was Army, and he thinks I'm an idiot for getting out. He and my brothers are still Reservists. It just wasn't for me. But I did love shooting." He glanced around furtively. "Probably shouldn't admit that out loud, but it's true. I still go skeet shooting on the weekends every now and then. And air soft."

Corinne gasped.

"You have *got* to take my daddy skeet shooting," she said, clapping her hands together. "It's just the thing for him! He used to go hunting, until Mama forbade him."

Anna watched her with a smile.

She's acting just like the old Corinne, she thought. Before Peter's death.

"Why did your mother forbid him to hunt?" Perry asked, his brown eyes lighting up at her attention.

"Well, the last time he went, he brought home a buck. We ate venison for three years straight. After that, Mama told him he could only walk around in the woods with his friends, but he couldn't shoot anything. He told her what's the point."

Portia laughed.

"I don't blame her," she said, chuckling.

"I would love to take your father skeet shooting," said Perry, drawing himself to his full height. "If I have the honor of meeting him someday."

Corinne blushed, looking up at him through her lashes.

Anna smiled, watching them, but her smile quickly changed to a frown.

I hope they get that opportunity, she thought. I hope neither of them used their knowledge of guns to kill Peter.

Inspector Ferguson glanced up from his notes. Sitting across from him, Alan Potts sat rigid. William wondered what the script supervisor was thinking behind his quiet facade. He had never been an easy one to read.

"I've been told by Sarah Stern," the Inspector began, "and also by the cinematographer, that Peter is the one who had been doing practical jokes on the set. Is that true?" asked the Inspector.

Alan eyed him warily.

"Someone was doing practical jokes," he agreed slowly. "I know Jim and Sarah thought it was Peter."

"You don't agree?" the Inspector asked.

Alan shrugged.

"As far as I know, they didn't get a confession out of him," he said.

The Inspector nodded non-committally.

"I was informed that there were some files missing," he continued, "and that you were being blamed for their loss. Do you think Peter was the one who deleted the files?"

"No," said Alan, sitting up even straighter in his chair. "Peter may have done the other things. I don't know. But he didn't delete those files."

"How do you know that for sure?" the Inspector asked.

"Because I did."

Inspector Ferguson placed the pen he'd been twirling in his fingers back onto the desk.

"*You* deleted the daily files?" he reiterated.

"Yes," Alan repeated, his expression serious.

William leaned forward. This was a strange confession.

The Inspector leaned back in his chair, making a gesture with his hands to encourage Alan to elaborate.

Alan ran his tongue over dry lips.

"On Saturday, when we were filming the attempted rape scene, Peter asked me to delete that day's dailies. I told him no. Didn't want to put my job in jeopardy."

"What made you reconsider?"

Alan sighed.

"I felt I had to," he explained.

"And why is that, exactly, Mr. Potts?"

Alan looked directly into Inspector Ferguson's eyes.

CHAPTER FIFTY-THREE

———◆◆◆———

Anna sat on the edge of her chair, attempting to calm her nerves. *Why was she nervous?* She hadn't done anything. Yet, to sit in front of a police officer, answering questions, with a camera recording her every word, made her feel like a suspect.

"Actually," she realized, "I guess I *am* a suspect."

We all are.

She looked back at William sitting in the corner. He gave her an encouraging smile. Taking a deep breath, she faced the Inspector.

"Miss McKay," he began, surveying his notes, "I see that you are originally from Nashville, Tennessee. Is that correct?"

"Yes, sir," she answered.

"In your statement, you said you did not see anything unusual in the duel scene, except Peter Mallory falling when he wasn't supposed to."

"Yes."

"You're somewhat of a gun expert. Do you think there could have been a mixup when Brian Elliston loaded the pistol?"

"Well, I wouldn't say I'm a gun expert, but—"

"Oh, no?" interrupted Inspector Ferguson. "It says here that you were on the rifle team at your school. Harpeth Hall, isn't it?"

Out of the corner of her eye, Anna saw William lean forward in his chair, waiting for her response.

"Yes," she replied, her cheeks burning unexpectedly. "I was on the rifle team."

"The rifle team that won the National Championship three years in a row while you were a member?" the Inspector clarified.

Why did he make it sound like a crime? she wondered irritably.

"Yes, we were very good. Better than the boys' school in town," she snapped. "What does that have to do with anything?"

Inspector Ferguson lifted his hands innocently.

"I was merely pointing out that you know a lot about weapons," he explained. "You know, for instance, how to load a gun."

She scowled at him.

"I think you already know, Inspector," he answered, indicating the notes on the desk.

Inspector Ferguson gave a brief nod.

William furrowed his brow. What did the Inspector already know? Inspector Ferguson glanced at his Sergeant, who seemed just as eager for information.

"Peter Mallory had somehow found out that this is not Alan Potts, but Alan Chaney," he explained.

Alan nodded solemnly.

"And Alan Chaney, as it turns out, has an arrest record. For petty theft."

"You can see how it was for me," Alan answered, his hands clenched in his lap. "I've been clean for ten years. That's why I was stealing in the first place. And this is a good job. And I'm good at it. Always have been good at details. And here's this chump trying to wreck everything by threatening to go to Sir Frederick with the truth. I said no, at first, but the longer I held out, the more uncomfortable he made it for me. I figured I could just move the files and pretend they were deleted, and then, if things got tough for me, I could find them again."

"So they aren't deleted?" asked the Inspector.

"Nah. I moved them onto a thumb drive. I figured, when the time came, I could just put them back and rename them. Say I found them them 'cause they'd been misnamed or something. But I should'a known he wouldn't stop at one thing."

"Did he ask you to do something else?"

"Not anything as bad as stealing files. Not yet, anyway. But he was holding it all over my head. That's why I agreed to do the whole 'seconds' thing," he said, glancing back at William. "Peter made it sound like he would squeal if I didn't go along with it."

"That must have made you feel cornered," the Inspector said, squinting his eyes. "Like there was no way out."

"Yeah," Alan agreed, then stopped himself, looking warily at the Inspector. "But I didn't kill him, if that's what you're trying to say. I never want to go to prison again. I would risk being fired by Sir Frederick and starting my career all over again rather than go back for something like murder."

"I know how to load a *rifle*," she said curtly. "Dueling pistols are different. Brian had to show me how to load those."

"So Mr. Elliston showed you how to load the guns?" the Inspector asked with interest, making a note on a pad in front of him.

William closed his eyes. He could tell the Inspector was using her own words against her, and it was making him angry. He wished he could stop him. He wished he could tell Anna not to answer the questions, to keep the Inspector from turning an innocent, after-school activity into evidence against her. But he was afraid that would make things worse.

Anna clenched her jaw, her face even more flushed than before.

Why did she feel accused? It wasn't a crime to be good at sharpshooting.

"Back to my original question," Inspector Ferguson said. "Do you think it possible for Brian Elliston to have made a mistake?"

Anna furrowed her brow, thinking about that morning. Her mind had been so occupied with her own thoughts that day, with Peter's attack the previous night and what to do about it. She thought back to Brian Elliston and the props table.

She replayed it in her mind: William and Perry brought the pistols to Brian. The sun was about to come up, so they were in a hurry. Could Brian have been careless, rushing to beat the sun? Could he have put a lead ball into one of the pistols?

"I can't say for sure," she said finally, and was sorry about it. She didn't want Brian to have made a mistake, but she couldn't rule it out. "I wasn't at the props table, so I didn't see the actual loading."

"Do you remember who was?"

"Jaime and Brian, obviously," she answered. "Peter and Jake. And William and Perry, too."

The Inspector's right eyebrow raised slightly.

"Thank you," he said. "Would you say that you and Peter Mallory were friends?" he asked, changing subjects.

"No," she said honestly.

"Were you enemies?"

She reddened again.

"Peter was difficult to like," she said.

"What do you mean by that?"

She hesitated.

"What she means is, Peter Mallory tried to rape her the night before the duel," said William, refusing to keep silent any longer.

Anna stared back at him, surprised.

"Is this true, Miss McKay?" the Inspector asked. Sergeant Patel's body stiffened. She definitely reminded William of a cobra now, coiled and ready to strike.

"He didn't rape me," she said quickly. "I don't know if he would have or not. He was drunk, and he was threatening me and acting like he was going to, but—"

"I need the whole story," the Inspector said, looking from Anna to William.

Between them, they told the Inspector about the attack and the decision to wait until after the duel to decide what to do.

The Inspector looked grave.

"Why didn't you mention this before?" he asked, lowering his brows.

Anna sighed.

"I thought I should keep it to myself, since he was dead," she explained. "Jake and I agreed that it would just be ruining Peter's reputation for no reason. When you first questioned me, I thought Peter's death was an accident."

"Is it being considered murder?" asked William.

Sergeant Patel scowled across at him.

Inspector Ferguson clenched his jaw.

"It is definitely a suspicious death," he admitted.

"Anna's story matches with the autopsy report," Inspector Ferguson said to Sergeant Patel after Anna left the room. "There was still a large amount of alcohol in Peter's system at his death. And also cocaine."

"Cocaine?" asked William, surprised.

"Some people use it to counteract the feeling of drunkenness," the Inspector explained. "It's an upper."

William grew thoughtful. Peter's lifestyle was worse than he realized.

"I shouldn't be surprised," he said to himself. It explained his ups and downs, his extreme mood swings. He must have used cocaine that morning to sober up for the scene.

"Inspector!"

William jumped, then turned toward the speaker. Miranda Vogel posed dramatically in the doorway of the Study.

"This woman said you didn't need to take another statement from me," she said, indicating a scowling Sergeant Patel. "But I told her that as a victim, I—"

William blinked at the older actress, surprised at her audacity.

"I wonder if she's on something," he thought.

"Ms. Vogel, do come in," the Inspector said with a smile, although his eyes continued their usual squint.

"Thank you," Miranda breathed, settling herself in the leather chair in front of the desk. She spread the skirt of her dress over her knees and folded her hands primly in her lap.

Sergeant Patel rolled her eyes, her jaw tightly clenched.

"We do have your previous statement, Ms. Vogel," began the Inspector politely, "in which you outlined your concerns for your safety."

"Oh, please call me Miranda, Inspector," said Miranda, flashing him a winning smile.

The Inspector squinted in reply.

"Do you have anything to add?" he asked. "Anything you failed to tell us in our first interview?"

"Well, no," she admitted. "I just wanted to see if there have been any developments in the case. Are you considering Peter's death an accident? Or murder? It does make such a difference, you know, in my peace of mind."

"Difficult to say," said the Inspector. "What is your opinion?"

Miranda batted her lashes, preening under his attentiveness.

"I think it's murder!" she said with a satisfied smirk.

"You think Peter's death was murder?" Inspector Ferguson repeated.

"It's all been leading up to this," said Miranda, melodramatically dropping her voice an octave. "We've all been living in fear for the past three weeks. Ever since the first lighting rig fell down on top of us."

"I understood no one was in the room at the time?" the Inspector said.

"But what if I had been?" said Miranda, undaunted. "And then William, with his curse. That's when I knew," she said, nodding her head sagely.

"Knew what?"

"That we were all doomed."

"Oh, come on!" muttered William, exasperated.

Miranda straightened in her chair, refusing to look in his direction.

"William uttered *the name*," she continued, "and it was then that I knew something bad was going to happen."

"The name?" questioned Inspector Ferguson.

"I said the name of Mac—the Scottish play, and everyone freaked out," William explained with an irritated tone.

"Ah," the Inspector nodded. "I've heard of this superstition."

"Have you?" asked William, surprised. "I hadn't."

"You believe Peter's death was the result of Lord Somerville's *faux pas*?" the Inspector clarified, squinting at Miranda.

"Nobody believed me at the time," she sniffed. "But I've been justified now."

"I'm not sure how a curse, however viable, could cause Peter Mallory's death," Inspector Ferguson countered.

Sergeant Patel snorted her agreement.

Miranda's eyes widened and she leaned forward, placing her hands on the desk.

"How do you know Peter was the intended victim?" she asked, cocking her head at the Inspector. "It could have been any of us. What if Peter picked up the wrong gun, and Jake was supposed to die?"

Inspector Ferguson frowned.

"What if it should have been William?" Miranda continued. "He stood in the middle of the duel. Maybe *he* should have been shot instead of Peter. I mean, it was his curse."

William wiped his face with his hand, then leaned his head against it.

Surely the Inspector knows this is rubbish, he thought, irritated. No one is trying to kill me.

A brief memory went through his mind: Anna comparing dream-Peter's motives to real-life Peter. Would Peter have been desperate enough to buy Hampstead Hall that he would have killed him, too? If he killed the Eighth Earl, what would stop him from killing the Ninth?

He mentally shook the thoughts from his mind.

"What about you, Ms. Vogel?" asked the Inspector, squinting at the actress. "You keep mentioning that you feel threatened."

Miranda sat up straight in her chair again and sighed voluminously.

"What is my life?" she asked, her eyes on the bookshelf behind the Inspector's head. "A mere ripple on the waters. If my time has come, then it has come. My only concern is for the safety of the cast and crew."

"It's good to know we have the same intentions," said the Inspector with a tired smile.

CHAPTER FIFTY-FOUR

Without catering or a filming schedule, Hampstead Hall resumed its usual mealtimes, including tea at four o'clock. The Inspector was delighted to have a cup, and even sat with the cast and crew in the Drawing Room.

Sheila made sure there was coffee in addition to tea for the Americans, and she offered an assortment of finger sandwiches, like roast beef, smoked salmon, and egg salad to go with the sweet things: scones and cake.

Anna smiled to herself as she glanced around the room. It was a mish-mash of cultures and styles. Instead of *Downton Abbey* finery, most wore jeans or shorts, with the exception of Miranda, who was still dressed to impress. Little groups formed around the large room, and some gathered around the dining table in the next room, since balancing a tea cup and plate were not skills taught in American schools. Also, Anna suspected, they were avoiding sitting with the police, who had settled in next to Portia Valentine and Edwin Sterling.

Anna couldn't tear her eyes away from the spectacle of Jim Anderson, sprawled in a Queen Anne chair, attempting to manage a delicate, china tea-cup. She was sure it would topple to the floor and break into a thousand pieces. But maybe the priceless Oriental rug would break its fall.

She sat near Portia and Edwin, but with her back to them, and far enough out of the circle to avoid being part of their conversation. It enabled her to eavesdrop without being asked any more questions. After today's interview, she was tired of being questioned. It seemed to only bring more questions rather than answers.

William had disappeared after the last interview, although she noticed Lady Diane holding court across the room next to Sir Frederick. She wondered if William felt the same as she did, sick of questions. But he had some of the answers. At least, that's what he seemed to be indicating when they talked in the Chapel earlier. She hoped he would trust her with what he had gleaned. Maybe, if they put their heads together, they could figure all of this out. Then everyone could get back to normal again. The new normal, post-murder.

Jake entered the room, obviously looking for her. She gave him a tentative smile. He grabbed a cup of coffee and a plate of food, then seated himself next to her.

"How did your interview go?" he asked.

She shrugged.

"Not as well as I'd hoped," she admitted, lowering her voice. Jake leaned in closer, causing Anna to feel a slight twinge of attraction again. She pushed it out of her mind.

"The Inspector is very thorough," she told Jake. "He found out I was on my high school rifle team, and that made things awkward."

"He brought up my hunting, and the fact that Peter and I went to a gun range a few times," said Jake, sympathetically. "Don't let him get in your head."

"And then William told him about Peter's attack," she said. "So now he'll probably think of me as a suspect with a motive."

Jake's expression darkened.

"I wish William hadn't done that," he said hotly.

Anna was surprised at his anger. Then she remembered he was being protective of her, and she found it sweet.

He shook his head, smiling again.

"Don't worry about it," he encouraged. "You may have had a motive, but you didn't have opportunity. You weren't anywhere near the guns that day."

He took her hand and squeezed it. She smiled.

"I arrived the day after Peter's death," Edwin said to the Inspector. "My mother asked me to come down."

Anna glanced his direction, and was struck by how debonair the famous actor looked. He was at ease, wearing the perfect "casual afternoon tea" outfit, although his light-brown curls showed signs he had recently run his hands through them, as she'd witnessed earlier.

"And why is that, Ms. Valentine?" asked the Inspector, squinting at the seasoned actress. "Why did you ask your son to come down?"

She rewarded him with a glorious smile.

"I knew Edwin's soothing manner would be a balm to us all," she said, squeezing her son's hand. Edwin cocked his head and smiled genially at his parent.

"You brought him in for moral support?" the Inspector clarified, unconvinced.

"He's wonderful to have around in a crisis," said Portia.

Jake and Anna exchanged glances. Obviously, Edwin and Portia were keeping their crime-solving motives to themselves.

"And what about you?" asked the Inspector, turning to Julia Shrewsbury, who was seated beside Edwin. "When did you arrive at Hampstead Hall?"

"Me?" asked Julia, surprised. "I believe I already told your Sergeant that I arrived in the afternoon," she said, nodding at Sergeant Patel. "Sarah called me and told me what happened, and I came immediately. I don't know when I would have been notified by the *director*," she said snidely, rolling her eyes in Sir Frederick's direction. Her jab went unnoticed by the director in question, who was giggling at something Lady Diane said.

"You came directly from London?" Inspector Ferguson clarified.

"Well, no," said Julia, looking down. "I came from the Studio. In Hertfordshire. It's about an hour from here. Of course, I had to put a few thing together, first."

"Interesting," said the Inspector. "You're sure you arrived in the afternoon on Tuesday?"

"Yes," she said, irritated. "I arrived around lunch-time, but I had a difficult time finding Freddie, at first, to make my presence known. Perry saw me, though, as soon as I arrived."

"Hmm," the Inspector commented, furrowing his brow. "I understood from the staff of the Runnymede on Thames that you actually arrived in Surrey on Monday evening. The evening before the dueling scene took place."

Turning her head, Anna watched as Julia's face reddened. Her breathing came in shallow gulps. Sergeant Patel's sharp, black eyes were watching, too.

"Perhaps you were mistaken, Ms. Shrewsbury," suggested Inspector Ferguson.

Anna and Jake exchanged a conspiratorial glance as they eavesdropped. Clearly, Jake was just as interested in the Inspector's line of questioning as she was.

"Ah, yes," Julia stammered. "Perhaps I was. Now that I think about it, I *was* at the Runnymede on Thames when I got the call," she said, gaining confidence. "The stress of this murder has confused my timeline."

Inspector Ferguson flipped his hands.

"It happens," he said. "And why were you in the area?"

Julia's face darkened.

"I was coming to see about Freddie," she said, her lips pursed in anger. "I received a call from Miranda Vogel suggesting things were not being done properly. Corners being cut. Practical jokes causing setbacks. I came to see for myself."

"Is it usual for a producer to remain off-site?" he asked.

"No," she admitted. "I knew I shouldn't have given Freddie so much lee-way, but with our past personal relationship, I figured it would be less stressful for everyone if I monitored things from the Studio. Maybe drop in a time or two to make sure things were going nicely."

"And why did you wait several hours before coming to Hampstead Hall after you received the call from Sarah?"

She shrugged.

"I thought it would look suspicious, my already being in the area, since it was a surprise visit on my part. If it had been anyone else, I would have…"

"But it was Peter Mallory," added the Inspector.

"You know our previous history, I take it?" Julia asked.

"I know Peter Mallory sued you for firing him from a job four years ago," he said. "Claiming he was let go for breach of contract. But the claim was eventually dropped."

"Peter Mallory was a scoundrel and a liar!" said Julia, lowering her voice. "I fired him because he was coming to the set drunk or high. Or both."

"Then why was the claim dropped?"

She shifted in her seat.

"Because…because Peter and I had been…I was in a fragile emotional state!" she insisted. "Freddie and I had just divorced. Peter was younger than me, I admit, but he made me feel beautiful again. At least, for awhile."

"And then?" the Inspector prompted.

"And then, when things weren't going so well between us, he started acting defiant," she said. "He wouldn't obey the rules on the set, he wouldn't follow the director. He took up with one of the makeup artist's assistants, a girl barely out of school. Just to rub it in my face. And all the time, laughing. Laughing at me. Laughing at all of us. It was infuriating. I felt I had no choice, as the producer, but to let him go. Then he sued me and the Studio claiming it was a breach of contract. He would have claimed I fired him because I was jealous of his new relationship. The suit was dropped because I didn't want to drag my reputation through the courts. He agreed to drop the suit if we agreed to bring him back to the film. So we did. Not that it mattered. It was a flop, anyway."

Anna glanced at Jake, wondering what his reaction was to this information about his friend. Peter was proving to be more and more despicable. It made Jake's friendship with him even more of a puzzle. But Jake's face was impassive, and his eyes were on his coffee cup.

"It's understandable that you would be cautious, considering your past dealings with Peter," Edwin said to Julia. "Right, Inspector?"

Anna could hear sympathy in Edwin's voice. He reminded her of a judge, ready to make a pronouncement on the guilty. Anna wondered if he had known Peter, and what his opinion of him had been. It was clearly not favorable now.

"It was a difficult position to be in, certainly," the Inspector agreed vaguely.

"I can't imagine how you must have felt when Freddie cast Peter in the show," said Portia. "Was that the real reason you stayed away?"

Julia nodded, her eyes flashing.

"My ex-husband and my ex-lover on the same set," she said, angrily. "What could go wrong?"

After tea, Jake and Anna moved to the Great Hall and seated themselves on the windowseat. The same windowseat where they had shared a kiss, Anna remembered. She fingered the bracelet he had given her.

"That was quite a revelation," said Jake, his jaw clenched.

"Yes," Anna agreed cautiously. Did he believe Julia's story? Did he already know it?

"It explains why Julia stayed away during filming," she said.

"Peter told me about suing the Studio," he admitted, "but he said it was because Julia had a thing for him, and when he turned her down, she kicked him off the film."

"Why would Julia lie about something so embarrassing as having a fling with a younger guy and then being dumped by him?"

Jake shook his head.

"I don't know what to believe anymore," he said, staring out the window. The sun was just beginning to set, giving the sky a pinkish hue.

"Well, if it's true," Anna said, "it gives her a clear motive for killing him, although it has been a few years. Maybe he had brought it up again, and was threatening to expose her. But I don't know that she had opportunity. Someone would have seen her."

Jake nodded, absently.

He's obviously got a lot to think about, Anna thought, but there was one more question she wanted to ask him.

"Why were you and Peter friends?"

"Hmm?" he asked, coming out of his reverie.

"You're so different," she pointed out. "The more information that comes out about him, the more surprised I am that you were friends."

Jake nodded, running his hand through his hair in his familiar way.

"He wasn't all bad," he said with a sigh. "We met on the set of *Love and Loss*, and we just hit it off. Had a lot of laughs, a lot of fun. He offered me a room for a while, when I decided to stay in England. He became like a brother."

His eyes reddened, and there were tears that pooled on his lower lids.

He took her hand and looked intently into her eyes.

"Sometimes, you're there for someone because they need you, not because you need them," he said. "I think you know what I mean."

Anna nodded, swallowing hard.

"Anna, can I talk to you?"

Anna pulled her hand out of Jake's at the sound of William's voice. She hadn't realized he'd come into the room.

"Yes," she said, attempting to read his expression, but he kept it veiled. Jake's, however, was unmistakeable.

"Talk to you later," he said, rising quickly and heading toward the stairs without acknowledging William.

William smiled down at her, ignoring the other man, and offered his hand.

"I want to show you something."

CHAPTER FIFTY-FIVE

"We have to hurry," said William, pulling Anna across the courtyard. "The sun is going down."

She quickened her pace, attempting to keep up with William's long strides, and hoping he couldn't tell how exhilarating it was for her to be holding his hand.

He led her to the stables where his four-wheeler sat under the watchful eye of a large, black stallion, who whinnied at them from over the door of his stall as they approached. William patted the horse's nose.

"I promise, I'll have time for riding soon," he told it. The horse snorted and turned away.

"Here, put this on," William said to Anna, taking off his jacket. "I was in such a hurry, I forgot you would need a coat."

Anna snuggled into the down of William's jacket, breathing in his scent. It wasn't his field jacket, but a thicker one with a black nylon outer shell. Winter was on its way.

"Hop in," he said, climbing into the four-wheeler.

Anna hopped, but as they drove out of the back of the stable and onto a rutted road through the field, she wasn't sure she should have. There didn't seem to be any seatbelts or hand-holds. She clung to the seat with both hands and prayed she wouldn't be thrown out with the next bump in the road. It was a two-seater, with a small space in the back to carry equipment, although it was currently empty.

They headed west, away from the field where the duel had taken place. In front of her, Anna watched as the sun sank closer and closer to the horizon, casting wide fingers of orange, pink, and purple across the cloudless sky. She could see tufts of white dotting a hillside as they passed.

"Sheep!" she cried out. "I didn't know you had any!"

"It *is* England," he replied with a grin.

After a few minutes of silence, he turned to her.

"I hope you didn't mind my telling the Inspector about Peter's attack," he said.

She rolled her eyes.

"It was bound to come out," she answered. "But he probably considers me a suspect, now."

"I think he considered you a suspect when he found out you were a champion rifle-shooter," said William, flicking her an amused glance.

She sighed.

"But don't worry," he added. "You weren't the only one with gun experience."

He told her about Jake's and Corinne's hunting, and Perry's army days.

"Wow," said Anna. "That's a lot of people with gun knowledge, if you count Brian Elliston. And I guess Jaime knows how to at least load the weapons, since she's the props master, though I can't see her shooting anything."

"Even my own mother can shoot," said William, musing. "I hope the Inspector doesn't interview her. She's likely to say something incriminating simply out of spite."

Finally, William pulled to a stop alongside a wooden fence. Row upon green row extended toward a fence-line in the distance, and Anna could see another field beyond it, like a great red sea. The sun bowed its head toward the ground, spreading a halo of golden light over the scene.

"This field has winter wheat," William announced proudly in answer to Anna's look. "And that's crimson clover in the other field. It helps replenish the soil for the spring crops."

"How do you take care of it all?"

"I have a farm manager," he explained. "But I'm very hands-on, as well. At least, usually. When I'm not assisting and acting."

He gave her a sideways smile. She smiled back.

He climbed out of the vehicle and leaned his elbows against the fence. A gust of wind blew his black curls from his forehead. As Anna joined him, she smiled at the look of pleasure and pride on his face as he gazed fondly across his fields.

"This is a gigantic farm," she murmured, looking out at the vastness of the view. To the right and left were more fields, some with crops and some containing only tall grass, flattened by the icy wind.

William shivered.

"I'm sorry," said Anna. "I have your coat. You'll freeze!"

He pulled her close to him, wrapping his arms around her body underneath the jacket. Anna lay her head on his chest and embraced him back.

William felt himself shudder, and wasn't sure if it was from the chill of the wind or the warmth of her body against his.

"I will not kiss her," he told himself as he held her close. He could feel her heart beating against his ribcage.

"I was thinking of planting lavender," he said quietly, nestling her head under his chin. "It's becoming quite a popular crop. Plus, it will look and smell heavenly."

"Yes, it will," Anna agreed.

Suddenly, the immensity of William's land felt like a weight. This was not a small farm, with a quaint, little thatched cottage. There was no smiling, plump mother waiting to cook William dinner after a long day in the fields. This was acres and acres, with a farm manager, and who knows how many other employees. And Lady Diane was elegant and aloof and formidable. A frown formed across Anna's brow as she squinted her eyes at the setting sun.

A pinging sound came from the pocket of William's coat. She pulled out his cell phone.

"Sorry," he said, glancing at the screen as she handed it to him. "Apparently, my mother would like a word with me."

He closed his eyes.

What could she need now? Or did she instinctively know he was with Anna and wanted to interrupt? The text reminded him of something that had been nagging in his mind for days.

"I'm sorry I didn't answer your text the other night," he said, sheepishly. "I was angry with you for running away again after we kissed at the lake."

Anna blushed, looking away.

"I'm sorry I ran away," she said, avoiding eye contact. "I needed time to think."

"What did you want to say to me?" he asked. "I was afraid you just wanted to tell me off once and for all."

"No!" She turned toward him. "That wasn't it at all."

He waited expectantly.

Anna glanced again at the vast fields, and thought of Hampstead Hall, and Mr. Barnaby, and Lady Diane.

What was I thinking? she thought, suddenly feeling small and insignificant. She realized William was right. They weren't equals. It was all right when he was William the assistant who wanted to be a little farm boy someday. But this? And wouldn't it be playing right into her mother's expectations? Not the heir to the Rawlings Furniture Company, but a British Earl. She could hear her mother bragging to her friends at the Belle Meade Country Club already.

She racked her brain for a plausible explanation, sensing William's questioning gaze.

"I just wanted to apologize for running away," she said, her attention on her hands. "You surprised me, and I needed to think. I wasn't angry."

"You said 'you needed to think' twice now," said William, turning her toward him. "What did you need to think about?"

He had lowered his voice to a gravelly whisper, his eyes staring longingly into hers, and it was all Anna could do not to leap into his arms and kiss him. But it would never do. He was too far above her. Too different.

"It doesn't matter what I was thinking then," she told him, tearing her eyes from his. "It only matters what I'm thinking now. And what I'm thinking now is that people like you aren't like the rest of us."

"What's that supposed to mean?"

"It means, you are aristocracy. I am not."

"Anna! Don't be ridiculous."

"I'm not! You said it yourself. I am a commoner, no matter how wealthy my parents might be in America. And look at this," she said, waving her hand toward the fields.

"So, because I destroyed your illusion of William the assistant, barely getting by, now I'm not worthy of you?"

She snorted her annoyance.

"I'm simply explaining to you why we are not suited for one another," she said.

"Let me guess," he said, folding his arms across his chest. "You're suited for Jake."

"No," she said, shaking her head. "I don't feel for Jake what I—Jake and I are just friends again. Nothing more. This doesn't have anything to do with him."

William felt conflicting emotions. On the one hand, she was dismissing him because of his money and family name. Not a new feeling. He had felt it on numerous occasions: at school, at parties, even in the Surrey County agricultural meetings with other farmers. They treated him like wealth was a disease, like being born into an aristocratic family was a mark against him that he could never scrub away. Not all of them treated him like that, but enough to make him always on his guard. They were polite, sometimes even obsequious, but there were those with whom he never felt equal, not because he felt like he was above them, but because they felt superior for not being an aristocrat. Somehow, his wealth and status put him under their working-class feet.

Now Anna was doing it. But at the same time, she wasn't running to Jake. Did he hear her correctly? She and Jake are "just friends again"? And what did she mean by that comment about her feelings? He couldn't let any of this dissuade him from pursuing her. He had allowed another man to stand in the way, but if Jake wasn't the man she wanted, then he had to keep up the fight for her heart.

"We should get back before it gets too dark," he said coolly, climbing back into the four-wheeler. "And I have my mother to contend with."

Anna sulkily climbed in beside him.

That was it? she wondered, disappointed. No comment? No desperate plea for her affection?

No last kiss?

After they safely returned the vehicle to the stable, Anna pulled off William's coat and gave it to him.

"Thank you for this," she said. "For the coat, and for showing me the farm."

William shrugged, staring at the toe of his boot.

"I wanted you to know more about me," he said, his eyes full of half-hidden pain. "I wanted you to see what I love."

Her heart sank under his gaze.

"Well, good night," she said, wrapping her arms around herself.

"Wait," he called after her. "I had something I wanted to ask you."

She paused, turning back.

"I spoke with Inspector Ferguson, and he said it would be okay if we left Hampstead Hall tomorrow. Just for the day. I wanted to take you to Windsor. Show you the castle. I thought we could use a break from all this."

He looked at her wistfully.

She shook her head. Alone in Windsor? There was no way she could resist him. And she had to resist him.

"I don't think that would be a good idea," she said, backing away toward the house. "But thank you."

William's face twitched in a brief smile that returned to melancholy when her back was turned.

"Old King Coal," he whispered to the black stallion who was nuzzling him, hoping for a treat. "I wish I were a poor man."

Old King Coal whinnied his irritation.

"Yeah, I know," answered William, grabbing a carrot from a nearby basket and offering it to the horse. "Then she'd want a rich man."

CHAPTER FIFTY-SIX

The lights were on in the Drawing Room as Anna approached the house. The heavy brocade curtains had yet to be drawn for the evening, allowing her to see Edwin and Portia conversing together. There didn't appear to be anyone else in the room. As she entered through the French doors, she heard Portia say:

"I just can't help feeling that it's smoke and mirrors."

Edwin nodded, speculatively.

"Is everything all right, Anna?" asked Portia in a motherly tone as Anna sank into a nearby chair. "Has something happened?"

"No, nothing's happened," she answered dejectedly. "William was showing me his farm fields, that's all."

"Ah," said Portia with a knowing smile. "That was nice of him."

Anna shrugged, frowning at the ground.

"Smoke and mirrors," Edwin repeated slowly. He had been deep in thought and seemed oblivious to Anna's melancholy. "Is that how it feels to you, Anna? Like this whole thing is smoke and mirrors?"

"I don't know what you mean," she said, puzzled. "Are you talking about Peter's death?"

"Yes," he said, his brow furrowed, "but more than that, I think."

"Smoke and mirrors, like a magic trick?" she asked. He didn't seem to be making sense.

Portia's face was thoughtful as well.

"In a way," said the older actress. "But it's more like an illusion. Like what is real is being camouflaged."

Anna nodded. It did feel like that. Like it wasn't real. Was Peter really dead? He had to be. They took away the body. But he shouldn't be. The bullets were blanks. At least, they should have been. And the practical jokes Peter was playing—what was he trying to accomplish? Was it just to be funny or annoying? Was he sabotaging the show? Or was there a more sinister purpose?

"Peter's practical jokes," she said aloud. "I guess he was trying to sabotage the show so that William would be forced to sell Hampstead Hall to cover his debts."

Edwin eyed her thoughtfully.

"Why did that come to mind when I said 'smoke and mirrors'?" he asked.

"I wondered if there was more to it," she admitted. "In my dream, Lord Mallory was responsible for William's father's death. He would have inherited Hampstead Hall, with William and his father out of the way. So if Lord Mallory had lived, dream-William would have been in danger."

"You think present-day William was in danger, also?" asked Portia.

Anna nodded, lowering her voice. "He thinks Peter gave Lord Somerville the sleeping pills that caused the overdose. It's nothing he could prove, but it's what he believes. All I can think is, if Peter hadn't died, would he have killed William? Was that what all of this was leading up to?"

"That's a serious charge, Anna," warned Portia.

"With serious implications," Edwin added.

"I know," said Anna, grabbing the sides of her head. "Everything is so complicated."

Portia shook her head decisively.

"No," she said. "That's what I meant by 'smoke and mirrors.' It looks complicated, but it's really quite simple, I believe. If you look at things the right way."

William buried his icy hands into the pockets of his coat. He had decided to walk to his mother's cottage near the front gates. He needed space to think, and a brisk walk down the long lane to the Dower House felt like the perfect opportunity to do so. At least at the time. Now he was regretting it. The wind was colder now than it had been before the sun finished setting, and he could feel his cheeks reddening under its harsh treatment.

The lights of Lady Diane's cottage gave a welcoming glow as he approached, and he was thankful for an even warmer welcome from his mother's faithful housekeeper, Franny.

"Lord Somerville!" she scolded, pulling him into the warmth of the hall. "What are you doing, walking? You'll catch your death!"

"Franny, how many times do I have to tell you to call me William?" he chastised her, kissing her wrinkled cheek and handing her his coat. "And I needed the walk this evening."

"Well, Master William, her Ladyship is in the Parlor, but I don't like you walking around after dark, with a murderer still on the loose."

"It could be an accident, not a murder," William suggested. "And it's William."

Franny pursed her lips in disapproval as she returned to the kitchen.

Lady Diane looked elegant as she reclined on a chintz sofa. The walls of the room were painted a delicate rose, and everywhere William looked, there were pillows in varying shades of pink, red, and green.

"Finally," she declared as he entered the room. "I was beginning to think you were ignoring me."

She swung her feet onto the floor, then noticed the pinkness of his windblown cheeks.

"You didn't walk here, did you?" she asked, scandalized. "Franny, please bring us tea. William has been frolicking about the grounds."

She pressed the back of her hand against William's cheek and forehead, belying her true concern. William rolled his eyes. Lady Diane might put up a cool veneer, but underneath, she was a tender-hearted mother.

"I'm not ill, Mother," he complained good-naturedly. "I'm just a little cold. Tea will be nice."

"I was already on it," said Franny as she reappeared with a tray. "I knew he'd need it."

"Have they arrested anyone, yet?" asked Lady Diane, raising a manicured brow. Franny paused, her nose quivering with excitement, like the White Rabbit from *Alice in Wonderland.*

"Not yet," said William. "But there were interviews all day."

"Any prime suspects?" asked his mother.

William shrugged.

"At this point, everyone and no one."

"That doesn't even make any sense, William," his mother scolded.

"You're right," he agreed. "None of it really makes any sense."

Lady Diane waited until Franny left the room before she brought up the reason for William's summoning.

"I wanted to ask you about that girl," she said, raising her chin and looking down her nose at her tea cup.

"What girl are you referring to?" William asked, knowing the answer.

"You know who I'm speaking of," she replied. "The red-head. The one who looks so astonishingly like Lady Anna Somer."

"You noticed that?"

"How could I not? It's as if she had come to life off the wall of our Gallery. Which is suspicious, don't you think? Like she did it on purpose."

"I don't understand. Why would Anna impersonate one of our relatives?"

"To lure you in, of course," said his mother, giving him a pitying glance. "So that she could get her hooks into you without you suspecting anything. Those American actresses are always coming over here, trying to marry our men."

"That's absurd," he said, shaking his head at her. "Especially since she didn't even know I was the Earl until after Peter's death."

"Why on earth not?" asked Lady Diane, shocked. "Is she barmy?"

William attempted to explain his reasons for keeping his identity a secret. He had hoped to avoid the explanation, since Lady Diane arrived after the Inspector required him to identify himself.

"I'm surprised Mr. Barnaby agreed to it," she responded. "But I'm not surprised that Freddie went along. He's always loved play-acting."

William smiled inwardly. His mother had just reduced the accomplishments of the Oscar-winning director to "play-acting."

"What did you want to ask me about Anna McKay?" he prodded.

"I wanted to make sure you weren't having feelings for this girl," Lady Diane said, setting her tea cup on the low table in front of her. "It's one thing to have a little fling, but I trust you don't have any serious intentions toward her?"

"A *fling*?" William nearly spit out his tea. "I'm twenty-eight years old, and you want me to have a *fling* instead of a serious relationship?"

"She's not the right one for you, William," said his mother, petulantly playing with the tassel of a pillow.

"You have no way of knowing that," answered William, gritting his teeth. "You've barely met her. And under very trying circumstances."

Lady Diane pulled herself up straight with a regal air.

"William, we don't marry actor-people," she said with disdain. "It just isn't done. Yes, I know Prince Harry just did it, but that doesn't mean I approve of the practice! And Sir Thomas Sterling's marriage seems to have worked all these years, but she's *Portia Valentine*. I mean, *everyone* wanted to marry Portia Valentine. I heard she turned down the prince of some foreign country before she met Sir Thomas. But *you*—you don't get that luxury."

CHAPTER FIFTY-SEVEN

Anna stared at the empty chair at the head of the dining table. William had not appeared for dinner, and she had a sinking suspicion that she was the cause. What was the protocol for breaking an Earl's heart?

Don't be silly, she told herself. William doesn't really care about me. Letting him go only hurts me. But despite her best efforts, images of his blue eyes kept playing through her mind like a bad dream: despair, sorrow, regret, pain. Did he really feel those things? Or was he just acting?

Like the rest of us.

Inspector Ferguson and Sergeant Patel had left for the day, to the relief of the cast and crew, although Anna could still sense tension in the air. The Inspector had yet to give a definitive verdict of murder or accidental death, which left everyone on edge. Was someone among them a murderer? Or was it just a senseless accident?

"You're looking a bit more alive this evening, Brian," Sir Frederick said genially to the stunt coordinator.

"Freddie!" Julia whispered savagely. "Watch how you word things!"

Sir Frederick appeared frustrated.

"I just meant that he seems more lively than he did immediately after—well, you know."

Corinne sighed, dejectedly shoving a forkful of food into her mouth.

She's fallen back into her reverie, Anna thought, concerned.

She glanced at Brian Elliston. He did appear more at ease than he had before. More confident, Anna felt. Less apologetic.

"Thank you, Sir Frederick," Brian said, nodding at the director. "I do feel better today. I've gone over it and over it in my mind, and I simply can't fault myself for what happened. I'm positive I checked the barrels before I loaded them, and I'm positive I loaded blanks. So whatever happened…"

He trailed off.

"Whatever happened was murder," finished Jake. He laid his fork down on his plate, as if he'd lost his appetite.

"It's what I've been saying all along!" Miranda cried out.

Edwin Sterling put out his hands.

"Let's not jump to conclusions," he said calmly. "Just because Brian wasn't negligent doesn't mean it wasn't some kind of accident."

While several opinions were offered and discussed, Anna was distracted by Jaime, who was sitting across from Jake; she was looking at him intently, trying to make eye-contact, but he didn't raise his eyes to hers. Instead, he took Anna's hand and pressed it to his lips. Anna froze, unsure what to do. Did Jake realize how cruel that action was? To flaunt their relationship to the woman he had scorned? She searched his face. He gave her a ghost of a smile before releasing her fingers. Jaime scooted her chair back from the table, and Jake jerked his head up in surprise.

"Excuse me," Jaime mumbled to Adrian as she squeezed past his chair to leave the room.

"Of course," he said, sympathetically. "This whole thing has been difficult for all of us."

Anna was sure Adrian hadn't noticed what had just transpired. She hoped no one had, but looking down the table, she saw Portia eyeing her speculatively.

"Nothing escapes her," Anna thought, and blushed, ashamed at being an unwilling participant in another's pain.

"We can't figure it all out ourselves," Julia piped up in an irritated voice. "So let's stop quibbling about it and let the police do their job."

"Speaking of jobs," said Sir Frederick, beaming, "we may be able to continue the show after all. Alan found Saturday's dailies!"

His glasses shone with excitement as he gazed happily around the table.

"Is that true?" asked Sarah, stunned, turning to the script supervisor. Alan nodded.

"Where did you find them?" Jim asked, amazed.

"They were mis-labeled!" Sir Frederick declared.

"Really?" asked Portia, exchanging a glance with her son. "That's a miraculous discovery."

Alan simply nodded again.

"Isn't it, though?" Sir Frederick agreed. "It solves all our problems. With those dailies, we should be able to continue where we left off. With a few adjustments, of course."

"You think we can continue filming?" Jim clarified, his brow furrowed.

"Yes," said Sir Frederick. "So if everyone will stick around a little longer while we wait for the police to wrap up their investigation, we should be able to finish up in the next few weeks."

Corinne stared at him, her expression blank. Perry looked apprehensively at Corinne.

"You know, Sir Frederick," Edwin spoke up, "for the police to wrap up their investigation, they will probably have to make an arrest for murder."

"Yes, yes, of course," said the director impatiently, waving the suggestion away with one hand.

Edwin leaned his elbows on the table and settled his chin on his fists.

"They will have to arrest one of you," he continued, lowering his chin and looking pointedly across the table at Sir Frederick, who paled under his gaze.

"Right," he agreed quietly, then rallied. "Unless it's ruled an accident!" he said hopefully.

"Oh, Freddie!" Julia muttered with disgust.

After dinner, Mr. Barnaby pushed back the mahogany pocket doors to the Drawing Room. He had set up games and cards for the cast and crew, to ease the boredom of their voluntary confinement.

Miranda disappeared upstairs, complaining of a headache, but Adrian joined Jim, Sarah, and Alan for a game of cards. Perry and Corinne were choosing a board game, and Brian and Sir Frederick seemed eager to join them. Julia wandered off, talking on her cell phone.

Anna hesitated at the pocket doors. She had a lot to think about, a lot to process. Should she go to her room? Or would the others find that rude? She couldn't seem to muster up the energy to play a game.

She could feel Jake hovering nearby.

"He's probably waiting to see what I'm doing," she thought with a sigh. She wasn't sure she had the strength to handle him, either.

"Anna," said Portia from behind her. Anna turned around. "Edwin and I are going to the little Parlor on the other side of the Great Hall. Would you care to join us?"

"Yes, of course," she agreed with relief. Portia and Edwin meant peace, and she definitely needed peace.

Jake made an awkward movement.

"And you, too, Jake," Portia added with a smile at the handsome actor.

Jake gave Anna a questioning glance, as if asking for permission. She gave him a brief nod and a partial smile.

"At least I won't be alone with him," she thought, as her mind wondered where William had disappeared to.

Lady Diane had invited her son to dine with her, and as he walked home down the long drive, William was regretting for the second time his decision to walk to his mother's cottage. The cold night air burned in his lungs; he buried his hands in his pockets and wished he had worn a knit cap.

But, he reasoned, it gave him time to think, something he desperately needed to do. As his feet crunched on the pea gravel, his thoughts went immediately to Anna. She frustrated him. She angered him. She bewildered him. She enchanted him.

Her refusal to go with him to Windsor surprised him. He replayed her words: "People like you aren't like the rest of us." She was echoing the feelings of others he'd encountered. It disappointed him. He hoped she'd be different, that any discrepancies between their upbringing wouldn't matter. Then his own words dropped into his conscious mind: "We felt like equals," he had said to her after she found out his true identity, "and I didn't want to ruin it."

"Stupid!" he said out loud, pounding his forehead with the heel of his ungloved hand. "William Langley, you're an idiot. You made her feel inadequate. Less than."

He scowled inwardly at himself, hunching his shoulders against the wind. No wonder she saw herself as vastly different. Because he had told her she was. He made her feel like he towered above her, and she was only good enough for him when he was William the assistant.

"I'm such a fool," he told himself, shaking his head. Somehow, he had to tell her he didn't care about that stuff, although his own words revealed that perhaps it mattered to him a little more than he believed. He had convinced himself that he wasn't like the other men of his rank. But one red-headed actress had just proven otherwise. He cringed at his own hypocrisy.

"I completely forgot about this little room," Anna said, gazing appreciatively around her. With windows that faced the front and west of the house, it would be a bright, sunny room when the sun was shining. She promised herself a visit in the morning. The walls were a lovely shade of blue, and birds featured prominently in the decor. The curtains on the French windows had birds intertwined with flowers, and there were ceramic birds on the shelves of the bookcases that flanked a white marble fireplace.

Anna wandered about the room, taking in each detail.

"If I lived here," she thought, "I would spend a lot of time in this room."

She frowned at the memory of William's hurt expression when she turned down his invitation to Windsor. But what did he expect?

Jake's voice near her ear startled her.

"Where did William take you today?" he asked. He gave her a serene smile that Anna knew cost him a lot.

"Just to see his farm fields," she said, trying to sound nonchalant as she pushed William's blue eyes to the back of her mind.

"Why?" he asked, wrinkling his brow.

Anna shrugged.

"Did William tell you anything about the interviews today?" asked Edwin from his seat on a chintz-covered sofa. He threw one arm over the back of it. Anna wished she felt as relaxed as he appeared to be.

"No," she admitted. "I don't know if the Inspector would want him to."

Edwin made a face.

"Maybe not," he said. "But I'd still love to know the details."

"He did say that no one had confessed," she said, moving to an armchair. Jake seated himself on a velveteen settee next to Portia, but kept to the edge, like he was prepared to take flight. Anna could feel his eyes on her, and wondered what he was thinking.

"And he said a lot of us have previous gun experience," she continued, remembering their conversation.

"Really?" said Edwin, perking up.

"Besides me?" Jake asked with a sideways smile.

Anna nodded.

"Me, Jake, Perry. Even Corinne," Anna explained. "And of course, Brian. But what does that prove? William said even he and his mother know how to shoot."

"It means the Inspector has his work cut out for him," said Portia, nodding.

"The Inspector questioned Julia fairly sharply this afternoon," Edwin reminded them. "It was good of her to come clean, since he already seemed to know her whereabouts."

"Odd of her to lie," Portia agreed.

"If she lied about where she was," suggested Anna, "maybe she lied about other things."

"Like her relationship with Peter?" asked Jake.

Anna nodded.

"And maybe she really *is* the one who sabotaged the car," she said.

"Wait, what?" asked Jake, puzzled.

"We were discussing who would have sabotaged the car that Perry was driving," Portia explained. "The one that would only go backward."

"You think it was sabotaged?" Jake asked. "I guess that makes sense, now that I think about it. I just thought it was car trouble."

"We thought it might be the beginning of the practical jokes," Anna explained.

"But Sarah and Jim said they thought Peter was responsible for those," Jake reminded her. "And he was in the car."

"Maybe Peter and Julia were still an item," Edwin suggested. "They were sabotaging the show together, but Peter started something with Corinne, and Julia was jealous."

Portia pursed her lips and shook her head at her son.

"Why would the producer want to sabotage her own show?" she asked, skeptically. "What would she gain from it?"

"True," Edwin admitted. "That's the true test. What would someone gain by Peter's death? Who benefits? Of course!" he said, sitting up. "Who gets Peter's money? That's something none of us has asked. I wonder if the Inspector knows?"

"I know, actually," said Jake.

All eyes turned to him.

"He told me after his parents passed away that he was willing his money to a charity organization. They dig wells for people in Africa. He didn't have any other close relatives."

There was a stunned silence.

"I have to say, I'm surprised," Edwin said. His mother nodded in agreement.

"That seems out of character for Peter," said Anna, then blushed when Jake looked her way. It was his best friend, after all. Don't speak ill of the dead, she reminded herself, although she couldn't help *thinking* ill of him. She didn't trust Peter to have actually given his money away to charity.

"Well, maybe we can ask the Inspector," suggested Edwin. "Just to be sure.

For now, I guess we should look for another motive other than direct financial gain."

They sat in silence, contemplating the possibilities.

"If Peter was responsible for the practical jokes on set," Edwin mused, "would that be something worth killing him over?"

He glanced questioningly around the room.

"Jim and Sarah were pretty hot about it," Jake ventured. Anna agreed.

"And Miranda," Portia pointed out. "She felt it was a personal attack."

"The car incident made Perry look bad and caused Miranda and Adrian to be angry with him," Anna suggested. "But would he have been angry enough to kill Peter over it?"

"Maybe that, plus the fact that he wanted Corinne," said Jake, then shook his head. "I hate this," he said. "Looking at our friends as possible murderers!"

Anna nodded sympathetically.

Edwin leaned forward toward him, leaning his elbows on his knees.

"It's difficult," he agreed, looking intently at Jake, "but necessary. We can't get away from the fact that Peter did die, and if so, someone—one of you— killed him. I don't for a moment believe it was an accident. A lead ball was in the barrel of the gun. Someone put it there. Maybe it was Peter himself, but more likely, it was someone else, someone who had access to that gun. Someone on the set at the time. Whether the rest of you knew it or not."

"Like Julia," said Anna. "If she was in the village the night before, she could have snuck onto the set somehow."

Edwin shrugged, returning to his original relaxed position on the sofa.

Jake rubbed his face with his hands, letting one hand swipe through his blond hair.

"I'll be glad when this is over," he said, "even if—even if I hate the result. At least we'll know."

He glanced nervously at Anna.

"In that case," said Portia, gently, "I can think of another person who might have been angered by Peter's practical jokes." She looked apologetically at Jake. "And that's Jaime."

He swallowed and nodded, his lips a thin line.

"I know," he admitted. "I've thought of that. She was very upset about the chair being tampered with. And then, with their previous relationship—"

"But she told you she didn't care about him anymore," Anna reminded him.

Jake shrugged.

"Maybe she lied," he said. "Maybe she cared more than she wanted to admit, and his relationship with Corinne was too much for her to take. Or maybe she really did hate him, like Miranda said."

Edwin squinted his eyes in thought.

"It's possible," he said. "She does seem like someone who would keep her feelings bound up inside, which can be very dangerous when those feelings are suddenly released."

Jake looked down for a moment, then looked up at Anna with a sorrowful expression.

"I think I need to go talk to her," he said. "I may have inadvertently hurt her feelings at dinner."

Anna nodded that she understood. She was glad he felt the need to apologize.

"But Jake," warned Portia as he stood to leave, "don't tell her of this discussion. I hope there isn't any truth to our speculations about her, but if there is, you could be putting yourself in danger."

Jake smiled his appreciation. He took her hand and gave it a squeeze.

"I won't mention it," he promised. "And thank you for looking out for me. For all of us," he added, with a backward glance at Anna.

CHAPTER FIFTY-EIGHT

The walk back to Hampstead Hall seemed to take forever. It was two miles from his mother's cottage at the gates to the main house, but to William it felt like two hundred. There was an eerie stillness in the air, not helped by the fact that there was no moon to illuminate the driveway. He kept glancing from left to right, and listening intently for stealthy footsteps in the dark.

He gazed upward at the myriad of stars above his head and blew out a long breath that lingered in an icy mist. He was reminded how beautiful his home was, and how much he didn't want to lose it. Staring vacantly up at the black hulk of the house outlined against the starry sky, he hoped Peter's death hadn't killed his dreams of keeping it.

There was a light on in the little Parlor, he noticed with surprise. His mother's favorite room. The curtains were drawn, but there were chinks of light filtering out into the night, giving him inexplicable hope.

William wondered what Anna was doing in his absence. Was she spending time with Jake? He couldn't blame her. Why would she want to spend an entire day with him in Windsor, he thought bitterly, when he made her feel like she couldn't measure up? Could he ever make it up to her? Would she forgive him? Or was it too late?

Sighing with relief, he finally drew closer to the lights of his home. The front of the house and the circle drive were illuminated by landscape lighting, and William couldn't wait to be safely within their glow. He was almost there when he heard a shuffling of gravel to his left. William stumbled to his right, his hands raised.

"Who's there?" he said sharply into the blackness.

"Just me, your lordship," said a voice.

Adrian Reed stepped into the circle drive; his face, lit from below by the landscape lights, gave the spooky appearance of a storyteller around a campfire, holding a flashlight to his chin.

"Sorry I startled you," Adrian said, his face wearing a guilty expression. William noticed he was hiding something behind his back, and for some reason, he smelled a faint waft of watermelon.

"What are you doing out here?" he asked, keeping on his guard. What if Adrian had a weapon?

Adrian rolled his eyes, pulling his hand from behind him. William stepped back, his arms protecting his face; then he saw what the actor was holding in his hand.

It was a vape pen.

"Oh," said William, feeling silly as he lowered his arms.

"I would appreciate it if you wouldn't mention this to anyone," said the actor sheepishly, his eyebrows raised to his hairline, and his lips pursed.

"Okay," William replied, "but why not? Smoking and vaping aren't allowed inside, but I have no rules about doing it outside. I know Jim Anderson has been vaping the whole time he's been here."

"Yes," said Adrian, "but Jim Anderson isn't the face of the 'No Smoking' campaign to UK youth."

"Ah," William said. "That would be a problem. Well, no one will hear it from me," he assured him.

"Thanks," Adrian said, breathing a sigh of relief.

"It's cold," said William, shivering. "Are you coming in?"

"Not yet," said Adrian, indicating the device. "Just a few more minutes."

"Mr. Barnaby locks the doors at ten. Just so you know."

"Thank you," said Adrian. "I'm well aware. This isn't the first time I've been out here."

William gave him a curt nod as he strode quickly to the door. His sudden fright, added to the cold air, made him anxious to get indoors.

As he entered the Great Hall through the front doors, he nearly ran into Jake, who was just exiting the Parlor.

Jake hesitated, then pointed back to the room he had just left.

"Anna's in there," he said, "if you're looking for her."

William glanced at the partially-open pocket doors to the Parlor. He could see Anna seated on a chair, her back to the doors.

He shook his head, meeting his rival's eyes. The two men stood for a few seconds, eyes locked, as if in limbo. Finally, Jake made an impatient movement and shifted his gaze to the stairs.

"I'm on my way to Jaime's room," he explained. "I did something at dinner that upset her, so I'm going to apologize."

William nodded.

"Always good to do that," he agreed. "Women can hold grudges a long time."

Jake gave him a curious glance before disappearing into the stairwell.

William paused in the Great Hall, giving Jake time to ascend, to avoid any more awkwardness. He glanced one more time at the back of Anna's head. Her auburn hair glowed with gold highlights as he watched her push a strand behind her ear. He took a step toward the door, but then he heard Portia Valentine's voice, and he stopped.

Shaking his head, he turned away.

"So," Portia said to Anna once Jake left the room, "tell us about your farm visit with William."

Anna sighed. Portia was looking at her like a matchmaking grandmother, and she hated to disappoint her.

"He just showed me some of his fields," she said vaguely. "He has a lot of acreage. It was really quite amazing."

"Can you see yourself living here?" asked Portia. "Being mistress of this estate?"

"Mother!" Edwin reprimanded. "Please excuse her," he said to Anna. "She has a habit of poking her nose in when she smells romance."

Anna smiled and shrugged.

"I hate to disappoint you," she said to Portia, "but I don't think I'll ever be 'mistress' of this estate."

"Why? What has William done this time?"

"It's not William, it's me," Anna explained. "He was very sweet. He said he wanted to show me the farm because he wanted to show me what he loved. And he asked me to go with him to Windsor tomorrow, as a break from all of this. Inspector Ferguson gave him permission. I'm not stupid. I know he was thinking about the two of us, wanting to be alone together."

"Are you going to go?" asked Portia.

"Of course not. How could I? It would give him false hope, because it would never work between us. He's too far above me, and I think I've learned my lesson about dating someone with a different background."

"Did you tell him that?" asked Portia, frowning.

"I told him we were too different," Anna explained, tears forming in her eyes. "I reminded him that he was aristocracy, and I wasn't. Of course, he thought it was because I still had feelings for Jake."

"Do you?" asked Edwin. "Because clearly, he—"

"No!" she said, adamantly. "I thought I did, at first. But it's always been William. At least, when I thought he was Sir Frederick's assistant."

She wiped a tear from her cheek.

Portia continued to frown. When Anna glanced at Edwin, he was also frowning. She suddenly felt self-conscious.

"I don't see what else I could have done," she insisted.

"You have feelings for William," said Portia, "and he obviously has feelings for you, but you won't give him a chance because he's wealthy?" She raised her eyebrows at Anna.

"You make it sound like I'm a snob or something," Anna said defensively. "Shouldn't it be the other way around? Shouldn't the rich guy be the snob?"

Edwin shrugged.

"Anyone can think more highly of himself than he ought," he said. "Or herself. Can you honestly say you didn't reconsider your feelings for him once you found out he was the Earl?"

"If he had remained Sir Frederick's assistant, would you be running away from him?" asked his mother.

Anna pounded her fist against the seat of her chair, her tears increasing to sobs.

"I *am* a snob," she admitted.

Edwin handed her a clean handkerchief from his pocket. Anna thanked him, wiping her face, silently amazed that anyone, especially a famous actor, still carried an actual handkerchief in his pocket.

"All through college, I felt like I had to defend myself for my family's wealth," she explained once her sobs subsided. "When I met new people, or when they found out where I went to school and the friends I had growing up. As if I had to prove myself worthy of being a normal person just because my parents had money. Like somehow being wealthy was bad, something to be ashamed of. As if I had any control over it!"

Portia Valentine gave her a knowing look.

"That's what I just did to William, isn't it?" Anna said tearfully. "I made him feel ashamed for being who he is!"

William sat in his favorite chair in the Tapestry Room, staring listlessly into the fire. He had his feet warming on a stool, and a glass of wine was at his elbow. It was midnight, or thereabouts, he guessed. When Mr. Barnaby brought him his wine, it was almost ten, so William had warned him to watch out for Adrian Reed when locking up. He didn't want the actor locked out in the cold. The house manager seemed well aware of Adrian's habits, however. It never ceased to amaze William how in control that silvery gentleman always seemed to be.

Unlike himself.

Just when he thought he had it all together, things began to unravel. Like *Cavendish Manor*. It should have been an easy fix to his cash-flow problem; the only snag should have been his own irritation at having a film company on his property. And now, here he was, in the middle of a murder investigation. Probably even a suspect.

"I should have had Mr. Barnaby handle all of it," he thought irritably. "And taken myself off to France with my mother. Then it would be Mr. Barnaby handling all these details. And I would never have met—"

He stopped himself. Would that have been better? To have never met her? He scowled as fragments of a quotation about having loved and lost went through his mind.

The door opened noisily behind him, and William jumped to his feet to face the intruder.

Anna stood there in her night clothes, her hair disheveled, as if she'd suddenly gotten out of bed for the sole purpose of interrupting his solitude. He watched her, speechless, fearing she was an apparition that would disappear if he made a sound.

She took a deep breath, then pointed her finger at William.

"Yes," she said. "I will go to Windsor."

She turned on her heel and left as quickly as she had appeared, closing the door behind her.

William sat down again in his chair, stunned. Then he chuckled to himself as he picked up his wine glass.

"Red-heads!" he said, and raised his glass to the fire.

As Anna neared her bedroom door, she saw Corinne exiting the bathroom in the hall. Their eyes met. Corinne started to turn away, then she paused, glancing timidly back at Anna.

"How are you doing?" Anna asked, sympathy in her voice.

Corinne swallowed hard and nodded her head.

"I'm okay," she said. "I've been thinking about a lot of stuff and I couldn't sleep," she explained, wrinkling her brow. Anna noticed Corinne's eyes, without makeup, showed dark circles underneath, and she looked like she'd lost ten pounds in the last few days.

"What kind of things?" Anna asked.

Corinne shrugged. "Just things that don't make sense," she said. "Couldn't sleep, either?" she asked.

"Yeah," Anna admitted. "William invited me to go to Windsor with him tomorrow. To get away from here. I turned him down before, but Portia and Edwin thought I should go. I couldn't sleep, so I got up to tell him."

"Is he in the Tapestry Room?" she asked.

"It seems to be his favorite room in the evenings," Anna answered with a small smile.

"That'll be good, to get out of here," Corinne encouraged. "This place feels like a tomb."

She picked at her fingernail.

"I know it's been hard for you," Anna sympathized. "You and Peter were close."

Corinne snorted.

"You were right about him," she confessed. "I barely knew him. I thought he cared about me, but…"

"Maybe he did," Anna suggested.

Corinne shook her head.

"No. He only cared about himself. And he scared me, Anna," she said, grabbing Anna's hand. "I should have known what he was capable of."

"How could you have known he would attack me?" she asked.

"Because I feared he would do it to me," she explained. "He was starting to get rough with me, when we were alone. Then, during the rape scene, the look on his face." She shuddered, closing her eyes. "It was like a different person. Like he changed while I was watching him. And I was scared, Anna," she said, gripping her hand. "I was scared of him. And I wouldn't let him near me after that. And because I did that, he turned on you. If only I'd let him in that night. Then he wouldn't have attacked you. I'm so sorry!"

The heavy tears in Corinne's eyes spilled down onto her cheeks.

"Corinne, don't," Anna said. "He would have attacked *you* that night. He was so drunk and out of it."

"That would have been better," said Corinne.

Anna stared at her friend.

"What do you mean?" she asked. "Better?"

"Because I deserve to be treated like a slut, but you don't," she said. "That's how men always treat me. I don't know why I thought it would be different this time. And you're right," she continued, pushing away Anna's protests. "I jumped into things too fast. I deserved what he tried to do to you."

Anna grabbed Corinne's shoulders and leveled her gaze at her.

"Stop right now," she said with authority.

Corinne held her gaze, too surprised to look away.

"No one ever deserves to be treated like you were treated," she said. "Everyone is worthy of respect. Just because some idiot didn't realize how valuable you are, doesn't mean you aren't valuable."

Corinne closed her eyes, shaking her head.

"Look at me," Anna demanded. Corinne looked up. "You are beautiful, and talented, and worth so much," she said, tears streaming down her own face. "Don't ever let me hear you talk like this again. Peter was a jerk. And now he's dead and can't harm you ever again. And those other guys, whoever they are, they're in the past. Forget them. Somewhere out there is a man who truly values you for who you are, not what you can give him. Someone who sees you for the wonderful woman you are. Someone," Anna said with a sly smile, "who already sees your worth, and is sleeping on the third floor right now."

"Do you really think Perry likes me?" asked Corinne in a whisper, looking like a fragile little girl.

"I know he does," Anna answered, smiling.

Corinne wiped her tears with her hands and smiled as well.

"Thanks, Anna," she said, giving her a hug. "You're a good friend. A better friend than I've been to you."

"No more of that," said Anna. "Get some rest, and tomorrow, let Perry get to know the real Corinne."

"That's hard," said Corinne, biting her lip. "I'm not sure I can do that. I'm so used to showing people what they want to see."

"Trusting is hard," Anna said, "but if it's the right person, it's so worth it."

As she watched Corinne go back into her room, Anna's smile dropped. As she walked slowly into her own bedroom, she fiddled with the heart bracelet around her wrist. The one Jake had given her. Then, making a decision, she pulled it over her hand and laid it on the dresser.

Trust, she thought. *Who am I to give advice on trust?* Then another thought chased after the first.

I hope Corinne didn't kill Peter.

CHAPTER FIFTY-NINE

Anna hadn't realized how much she needed the escape until she and William drove out of the massive stone gates of Hampstead Hall. It felt like skipping school, like breaking the rules.

It was a perfect day for an outing. The sky was pale, the color of river rocks, but the sun was bright and clear, giving a freshness to the cold, winter air. William's Range Rover had a sunroof which gave the feel of a convertible without the cold, biting, November wind.

Anna peeked at him as he drove. She noticed he had long forearms and long fingers that he rested casually on the steering wheel. His face had relaxed once he left Hampstead Hall. The past few days, his jawline had been continually tense, but now his face was peaceful, and it made him look younger, like a boy. She wondered what he had been like as a boy. Had he been difficult for his parents to manage? Had he been carefree and imaginative, or sullen and serious? For some reason, she imagined him always out-of-doors, roaming around the property, climbing trees, even when he was supposed to be dressed for some aristocratic event.

William glanced over at Anna seated beside him. She had been studying him, but she focused her sight out the window at the passing landscape when he turned his head. He smiled, settling himself into the leather seat as he drove. He felt different somehow, outside the gates, like a weight had lifted. He felt content for the first time in a long time, and he suspected Anna had something to do with it. The light coming in through the sunroof exposed a sprinkling of pale-colored freckles across her nose, and he noticed her eyes were a golden amber this morning. He sighed, smiling at the pub on the corner as he passed it, and at the Sainsbury's grocery store, and at St. Mary's Church. Everything looked beautiful and alive to him, even the brown-tinged grass and the barren gardens. He felt alive again, after so many years of death.

That's what it had felt like, he realized. Years of death. The death of his father had only been one kind of death; Geoffrey, the Eighth Earl of Somerville may have died physically a few years ago, but his soul had died long before. He had been a different man—a partial man—for years, and it had taken part of William's mother's life as well. And of his own. He had lived under the shadow of death for over a decade, when he should have been in his prime. Was it too late?

No. There were sparks of life in the auburn hair beside him, and in the pale freckles on her skin, and in the pinkness of her lips. There was life in the chameleon color of her eyes and the clear honesty of her gaze. She had given life back to him, and he knew in the depths of his heart that it was a sacred gift, something to treasure, like his own soul.

After parking the Range Rover, William and Anna passed under a bridge to enter the main thoroughfare. As they entered the High Street, Anna's mouth dropped open.

"Impressive, isn't it?" said William, gazing up at Windsor Castle.

"It's right here!" Anna exclaimed.

William was puzzled.

"I mean, the castle is right across the street from us!" she explained with awe in her voice. "I guess I expected it to be high on a hill somewhere. Not so close to the city streets."

She gazed across at the thick stone walls that almost began at the edge of the sidewalk, where people milled about, seemingly unimpressed by the fact that an ancient castle was within reach of their hand.

"It looks like I could just climb over that wall," said Anna, smiling. "It's amazing!"

William laughed.

"Well, the walls are taller than you realize," he said, "but even if you did succeed in scaling the wall, I think you'd be immediately greeted by the guards. Especially today. Look, see that flag flying on top of the tower? It has a lion on it."

Anna nodded, shading her eyes.

"That means the Queen is in residence today. When she leaves, they'll fly the Union Jack."

"Will we get to see her?" Anna asked.

William shook his head.

"Visitors aren't allowed in her part of the castle."

Inside the castle walls, William and Anna did the self-guided walking tour, aided by headphone sets that explained each area and its significance. Even if don't do anything of significance in the government. I'm a farmer. Really and truly."

He gazed down at her, wondering if this would diminish him in her mind, or make her feel more comfortable.

"I know," she said, studying him, "I saw your fields."

William insisted that Anna had to see the changing of the guard. As they headed in that direction, Anna peeked over a wall.

"What's this?" she asked.

"It used to be the moat," William explained. "But now it's a garden."

Although it wasn't green and flowering now, Anna could tell that the garden would be beautiful in the spring and summer months. There were paths and benches that wound through flower beds, with a fountain or a pond in strategic locations. Trees and bushes crept up the hill toward a stone tower in the center.

"I'm assuming we aren't allowed in," Anna said as she peered over the wall, trying to see as much as she could of the secluded spot. Leaning on her arms, she pushed herself up further on the stones that pressed against her stomach and left her slightly breathless. Gazing down into the dark waters of the fountain below, she suddenly became dizzy. For a brief moment, she felt panic, a fear of falling over the wall and down into the garden and onto the deep-red bricks of the path. She felt hands pressing against her shoulder and pulling on her arm. Was someone pushing her over? She let out a scream.

William steadied her with his hands once her feet were on the ground, watching her curiously. She stared up into his eyes.

"The guards were looking this way," he explained, releasing her arm. "I thought you should get down. Did I frighten you?"

Anna shook her head.

"Of course not," she lied, shaking off the dark feelings of a moment before. "I almost lost my balance, that's all."

Anna enjoyed the spectacle of the changing of the guards. She was surprised that there was a band to accompany them, and even more surprised to see that each band member carried a large knife attached to his or her belt, the same large knife on the belts of the guards who carried guns.

"Don't mess with the band," she commented to William, who laughed.

they couldn't visit the part of the castle the Queen lived in, Anna realized, there was still plenty of castle to explore.

"This looks and feels just like a castle should," she commented, looking appreciatively at the stone turrets, the narrow slits in the walls for shooting arrows at the enemy, and gargoyle heads guarding the tops of towers and windows. It reminded her of Hume-Fogg High School in downtown Nashville. The designer must have had Windsor in mind when it was built in 1925.

She learned quickly that Windsor Castle was considerably older than 1925. It was originally built by William the Conqueror in the 11th century, and expanded considerably over time. It was massive and impressive, with bold colors on the walls of the rooms and intricate details in all the woodwork, stone, and marble. She found herself staring at the ceilings; she had never seen so much detail above her head, and it made her wonder if people in previous centuries spent a good deal of time lying around on the floor, looking up.

Every room revealed art Anna had only seen in books. It took her breath away to see famous paintings face-to-face. She saw several portraits of Henry VIII and Elizabeth I, and immediately thought of Hampstead Hall. What must it be like for William, she thought, to live in a place where royalty once lived? To know that your ancestors knew the kings and queens of old, fraternized with them, fought beside or against them?

"Have you met the Queen?" she asked suddenly.

They were standing in St. George's Hall, a large banqueting hall that seemed ten times the size of the Great Hall at Hampstead.

William nodded slowly, almost sheepishly.

"I've been here to the castle for a number of charity events," he said with a shrug. "I met the Queen in this very room."

Anna's eyes widened, glowing amber.

"Of course, our conversation was very short and polite," he insisted. "Lasted about ninety seconds. I've had more conversations with Prince Charles and Prince William. Nice guys."

Anna laughed at how easily William rolled royalty off his tongue. She'd never met the President of the United States, and wasn't likely to. She'd met the Governor of Tennessee at a political event with her parents, but it was a far cry from kings and queens.

He noticed her awe, and rolled his eyes.

"I'm not important," he reminded her. "I'm not in the House of Lords. I

Afterward, they entered nearby St. George's Chapel.

"More like a cathedral than a chapel," Anna murmured, marveling at the rich golden color of the stone, and the massive columns holding up the ceiling.

William agreed.

They weren't allowed to take pictures, so Anna tried to memorize every detail.

"I'm so amazed at how delicate and lacy the ceiling looks, even though it's made of stone," she commented.

In the Quire, where the choir sits during services, the room was flanked on either side with ancient wooden seats, elaborately carved. Above each one was a coat of arms, signifying a family from the Order of the Garter.

In the center of the room, Anna side-stepped a large, rectangular plaque in the floor.

"Don't step on Henry," William scolded with a laugh.

"Henry?" she asked, reading the plaque.

It told her that the bones of Henry VIII were buried beneath the floor.

"This is where Prince Harry and Meghan Markle got married," Anna remembered. "I mean, right here, in this Quire. They must have stood on Henry!"

William nodded, amused.

"How weird that would be," she continued, "to walk on your ancestors every time you came to church."

"I do it all the time," William admitted. "In the village church, some of my ancestors are buried beneath the floor."

"Is that where you'll be buried?" asked Anna.

He shook his head.

"It's against the law to be buried in the walls or floors of a church nowadays. For health reasons."

He pinched his nose with his fingers to indicate his meaning.

"Oh!" said Anna, as it dawned on her. "The smell!"

"I can only imagine what the air around a decaying body smelled like, especially in the summer," he said, grimacing.

Anna shuddered.

Then she thought of Peter. Glancing at William, she could tell he was thinking of him as well.

"Do you think there will be a funeral for Peter?" she asked. She knew his parents were dead, and he had been an only child. Who was there to arrange a funeral? Who was there who would actually mourn his passing?

William shrugged.

"They haven't released the body, yet," he said. "I guess we'll find out when his will is read. Surely someone is his executor. Maybe his solicitor."

"Would you go to his funeral?" Anna asked.

William paused. Would he go to the funeral of the man who almost raped Anna? Who helped kill his father and might have killed him if he was desperate enough for his land?

"Yes," he said simply.

"Why?"

He looked into her eyes.

"Because every life counts," he said. "Every life has meaning, even if we don't see it."

On their way out of the castle grounds, William grabbed her arm, pulling her through the glass door of a shop.

"This should be a familiar place," he said.

The aroma of coffee hit Anna in the face.

"Starbucks!" she said, grinning.

After ordering their drinks, they sat at a small table near the window. Anna couldn't contain her amazement.

"We have to take a selfie here," she said. "To show how close we are to the castle, even from inside this Starbucks."

William acquiesced, resting his hand lightly on her shoulder as they huddled close together to take the photograph. Behind them, through the Starbuck's window, loomed one of the massive castle towers.

"My friends won't believe how close it is," she explained.

William breathed in the scent of her hair and hoped she couldn't feel the tingling that went through his arm when he touched her. He knew he couldn't linger like this, in a pseudo-embrace. He wanted to earn her trust again, to prove to her that they weren't that different, after all.

Anna hoped William couldn't tell how nervous he made her feel when he touched her. She reminded herself that this was just a selfie between friends; it meant nothing. Yet, for some reason, she could feel some sort of—she wasn't sure what to call it. Magic? Energy? He pulled his arm away and smiled a very friend-ish smile, and she pushed down her disappointment. Maybe he had already moved on, no longer had feelings for her. She couldn't blame him. She had done nothing but push him away, even last night. She gave him a flicker of a smile and concentrated on her tea.

"By the way," said William, "I found the journal. The one Sir Frederick was looking for. It was in the bedside table in my parents' old room. My mother left most of my father's things when she moved to her cottage."

"Did you find the story?" Anna asked. "The one Sir Frederick was looking for?"

"I haven't had a chance to look through it, yet," he admitted. "Maybe we can do that when we get back."

"Sir Frederick will be happy to see it," said Anna. "Maybe he'll be able to finish the show, after all. Everything seems to be working out in his favor, now that Peter's dead."

"What do you mean?"

"Well, last night, Sir Frederick told us that Alan found the missing daily files. Apparently, they were just mis-labeled."

"Ah," William commented, not wanting to share Alan's secret.

"And with this journal, maybe Sir Frederick will be able to figure out how to make *Cavendish Manor* work."

"It's hard to know what he'll do," said William. "I know how much this project means to him, and I think he'll do everything he can to finish it. But with Peter's death—"

Anna nodded.

"Kind of hard to finish it without a lead character," she agreed.

"Who knows," William added. "Maybe Sir Frederick has enough material to make it work. If he changes the script."

"Yes," said Anna. "It's possible, if he writes in the death of Lord Netherington and adjusts the future scripts. That is, if everyone agrees to stay. I'm surprised Miranda and Adrian haven't demanded to be released already, and Jake said he wasn't sure he could continue, either. For emotional reasons."

"I think Miranda and Adrian secretly love the drama of all this," William said wryly. "Despite all of her supposed concerns for her safety, I don't believe Miranda would leave, even if she were released by the police. She wants to be the center of attention, which is hard to do alone in your flat."

"True," said Anna.

"What about you?" he asked, a look of concern crossing his face. "Will you stay if *Cavendish Manor* continues?"

She sighed.

"I think so," she said. "I mean, I wouldn't want to be the cause of more difficulties for Sir Frederick. I want the show to succeed. And I hope this doesn't sound heartless, but I need this job. It's my first break, and I was hoping it would lead to future things in my career. I don't want to go home a failure."

"It wouldn't be your fault," William reminded her. "If there's no show, it shouldn't reflect on you or your abilities."

"But it will mean that to my mother," she said, grimacing. "It will be evidence that acting isn't what I should be doing. My parents think our family is above acting. What's funny is, if they met a famous actor, they would fall all over themselves and brag to all their friends. As long as he or she isn't a member of their own family."

"That sounds familiar," murmured William.

"On the one hand, I don't want to come home in disgrace. But on the other hand, I'm beginning to wonder if they were right. Maybe this isn't what I should be doing. I mean, this hasn't gone very well, so far."

It felt good to unburden her family situation. William, she realized, was a good listener. Deep in his crystal-blue eyes she could read that he was truly interested in what she had to say, and there was something else. Was it compassion? Or something more?

"But *you've* been doing well," he encouraged. "I may not be an actor myself, but I've watched a lot of movies in my time," he said with a smile, "and the scenes you've done are really, really good, Anna. You have a talent, a gift. I hope you won't throw it away because of a few setbacks. Although, admittedly, murder on the set is a little more than most actresses have to deal with."

She smiled, and then blushed at his compliment. Did he really think she was good? He actually thought she should stick with it, not give it up as a ridiculous dream? Derrick had always complimented her after each role in her college productions, but the day she told him she wanted to make her acting dream a reality, she had felt something change in him. Like a door had closed. She should have known then that their lives would take different courses. He probably knew. It took her until after graduation to realize his heart wasn't really hers. And now she knew it never was, never should have been. Looking across the coffeehouse table, she was glad. Derrick needed someone whose dreams matched his, and she needed—

"I met Jake last night when I came home from my mother's house," said William, trying to appear disinterested. "He said he was going to apologize to Jaime for something he said at dinner."

"Yes," said Anna, frowning. "I think he hurt her feelings."

"What did he say?"

"It wasn't what he said," Anna stalled. Should she tell him? Maneuvering between two men felt dangerous.

She told William about meeting Jake in the garden after his meeting with Jaime, and how she'd taken that opportunity to tell him she didn't think they were suited for one another. She omitted the part about Jake wanting more time to prove himself to her. Then she explained Jake's actions at dinner the night before that had resulted in Jaime leaving the table.

William scowled.

"That was just cruel," he said, angrily.

"I really don't think he realized she was watching," Anna defended.

"He knew," said William. "Why do you think he felt the need to apologize?"

Anna shrugged. She hoped he was wrong, that it was just jealousy that made him question Jake's motives.

"Anyway," she said, "I'm glad he went to apologize."

"What do you think of Jaime?" William asked suddenly.

"She seems nice," Anna answered carefully. "Keeps to herself. She's good at her job."

"Yeah, but don't you get a weird vibe from her?" he asked. "Something—I don't know—dark? Like she's a—"

"Like she's a witch?"

"Exactly!"

William marveled that Anna would choose that word. It was the word he was about to say, and the best word to describe the props master.

"Whenever she smiles at me," said Anna, "I get the impression that she doesn't mean it, like she really hates me."

"Yes!"

"But then, a moment later, that feeling goes away, and I end up thinking I made the whole thing up. That she really is exactly what she seems to be."

"I get that feeling, too," said William. "Like she's plotting evil, and then I feel guilty for thinking that. But what if she really is evil?"

"What do you mean?"

"What if Miranda's right, and she hated Peter? One of his practical jokes used her prop chair. Peter was a jerk, remember. He probably did it on purpose, to make Jaime look bad, and she knew it. Maybe she killed him, to get back at him for it."

"We were talking about this last night in the parlor," Anna said. "Before Jake left. Jake suggested that she could still have had feelings for Peter, and was jealous of Peter and Corinne."

"But then she wouldn't have been after Jake," William reminded her. "Why would she be jealous of you and Jake if she still had feelings for Peter?"

Anna frowned. William was right; it did seem unlikely that she would be in love with both Peter and Jake. At least, not at the same time, she thought, pushing down the hypocritical thoughts of her own feelings for two men.

"I think it would be easier for me to believe she hated Peter than that she still loved him," William speculated. "It would make more sense to me that she wanted Peter out of the way so she could have his friend all to herself. But it backfired on her. Jake doesn't want her."

"No, he doesn't," Anna said with a note of sadness. It would help if he did, she thought. It would ease her own conscience if Jake had someone else. But was her own peace of mind worth putting Jake with witchy Jaime? She shuddered at the thought.

"We should probably be getting back," said William, fruitlessly patting his pockets. "What time is it? I must have left my mobile at home. It's getting dark, so I'm guessing it's after four."

Anna pulled her phone out of her purse.

"It's nearly four-thirty already," she said, surprised at how quickly time had gone by. "And I have a cryptic message from Portia Valentine."

"What does it say?" he asked, throwing away his paper cup.

"She just says, 'Come back soon. New development. Be prepared.' What do you think she means? Be prepared for what?"

William shrugged.

"I guess we have to be prepared for anything right now."

CHAPTER SIXTY

They walked back to the car in silence, both feeling a certain solemnity. Windsor had been an escape, and returning to Hampstead Hall meant a return to the serious business of murder. Anna found it ironic that going back to *Cavendish Manor* was going back to reality.

She glanced at William out of the corner of her eye. He seemed relaxed, but Anna could see that his jawline was tight again, and there was a sharpness in his eyes that hadn't been there before. She wished they could stay away, not go back to the suspicion and the watchfulness.

William opened her door for her.

"Thank you for agreeing to come," he said. "Eventually."

He gave her a shy smile as she looked up at him, and suddenly, Anna knew at least one way to lighten his load. If she wasn't too late.

"The night I texted you," she said, her eyes shining green and gold in the afternoon sun. "After I ran away from you at the lake."

"Yes?" asked William curiously, his hand on the door.

"I wanted to tell you something. In person. But you didn't answer."

"No," said William, looking down.

"I'd been thinking," Anna continued, "like Portia told me, about the why, not just the what. She said it was the *why* of something that was important. And I realized then why I was so protective of my relationship with Jake. It was because it wasn't real. It's not that it was fake. I don't mean that. But, our relationship was kind of like a Disney princess movie, where the guy and the girl meet, and the next day they plan their wedding. It had no foundation, no real friendship. It was just—just the icing, without the cake. And I figured out why I kept pushing you away."

William stepped closer.

"Why?" he asked, afraid to breathe.

"Because I knew we were real," she answered. "Because when you suddenly appeared at the lake, I'd been thinking about you, and I wanted you to come, and when you came, I knew I never wanted you to go away again. Because I love you."

William's mouth prevented her from further speech. He kissed her, pulling her close to him, and she wrapped her arms around his neck and tangled her fingers in his hair.

When they parted, he leaned his head against her forehead.

"But you've only known me as long as you've known Jake," he reminded her, kissing her lips again. "What if we're only the icing?"

She shook her head.

"I feel like I've known you—"

"Forever?" he asked. She nodded.

"Yeah," he agreed. "Me, too."

The drive back to Hampstead was painfully short. They took the long way home, but it was still only twenty minutes. Anna could have sat beside William for hours, especially when he reached over and held her hand, adeptly maneuvering the car with only one.

When they pulled into the long drive to Hampstead Hall, they saw police vehicles up ahead, their blue lights flickering in the darkness against the stone and brick of the house.

William frowned. Something felt wrong. There were too many vehicles for it to just be more evidence-gathering.

"Why are there so many?" Anna asked.

"I don't know," said William, kissing her hand. "This must be what Portia meant by 'be prepared.'"

He stopped the vehicle in the circle drive as Inspector Ferguson and Sergeant Patel exited the house through the front doors. Light from the Great Hall spilled out onto the pea-gravel drive, but failed to dispel William's dark foreboding. He had the feeling the officers had been waiting for their arrival. Sergeant Patel looked like a cobra who had swallowed a canary.

"Lord Somerville," Inspector Ferguson said with a squint. "Did you have a pleasant day?"

William reached for Anna's hand as they stood beside the Land Rover, holding it tightly.

"Yes, Inspector," he said warily. "Thank you for your permission to go."

The Inspector shrugged.

"A free man doesn't need my permission," he said. "But I was concerned you wouldn't return."

"Why wouldn't I return to my own house?" asked William, his blue eyes flashing.

"Leave him alone!" shouted Lady Diane, rushing out onto the drive. Her face showed evidence of tears. "William, don't say anything!"

William eyed his mother oddly, then looked back at the Inspector.

"Has something happened?" he asked. "Why are there so many police vehicles here?"

"Yes, you could say something's happened," the Inspector nodded.

"What is it?" Anna demanded. She was clutching William's hand like a lifeline, a sense of dread weighing on her heart.

"You'll know everything in good time, Ms. McKay," said the Inspector. "But for now, William Langley, I need to bring you in to the station to ask you a few questions."

William eyed both officers warily. Inspector Ferguson was frowning, and Sergeant Patel wore a look of triumph.

"Why to the station?" asked William slowly, focusing his suspicious glance at the Inspector. "Why can't you ask them here? Is it about Peter's death?"

"Not entirely, my lord," the Inspector squinted at him. "It's about the murder of Jaime Douglas."

CHAPTER SIXTY-ONE

The fire in the grate shifted uneasily, sending sparks up the blackened chimney. There was a faint scratching at the door; a blonde head appeared around the edge of it.

"I didna' want to disturb you, milady."

"You're not disturbing me, Newberry," said Lady Anna languidly, watching the sparks vanish into whiffs of smoke. "Come in."

Lady Anna huddled in the Library in one of the chairs by the fire. She watched with disinterest as Newberry laid a silver tea tray on a table by the window. As she began to pull back the drapes, Lady Anna stopped her.

"Leave them!" she said, cringing at the brightness of the day. The maid obediently pulled the room back into darkness.

It had been a nightmare of a night. Lady Anna's eyes filled with tears as her mind replayed the scene of Mr. Langley—her Mr. Langley—being taken away by the detective, Mr. Ferguson, claiming he needed to ask him questions about the death of her cousin, Jaime. How could he think he had done it? It wasn't true. It couldn't be.

Newberry interrupted her thoughts by handing her a cup of tea.

"Thank you, Newberry," she said politely, setting the cup and saucer on the small table beside her without tasting it. "You may go now."

Newberry curtsied, but as she headed for the open door, she paused, looking back.

"Milady?" she asked in a quiet voice.

"Yes?" Lady Anna answered, pulling her attention back from her brooding thoughts.

"I wondered...I was thinking about that day, the day of the duel."

"Yes?"

"I was remembering something, and I was wondering what you thought about it, if you thought I should tell the detective—"

"My dear, here you are."

Lord Somerville and Sir John Rawlings stood in the doorway. Lord Somerville swept past Newberry and crossed the room, taking his daughter's hands in his.

Sir John stood awkwardly in the doorway, as if asking permission to enter.

"Wait, Father," said Lady Anna, "Newberry was asking me about something."

Newberry shook her head, her face pale.

"It can wait," she said, bobbing a curtsy and scurrying out the door.

Sir John watched her go, then stepped further into the room.

"Please, sit," said Lady Anna irritably to the two men hovering above her. "I'm not an invalid. I don't want people fussing around me."

They sat, Lord Somerville in the opposite armchair and Sir John in a straight-backed chair he pulled from the corner. Both men watched her anxiously.

Lady Anna swiped at her eyes with a lace handkerchief.

"Is there any news?" she asked.

"Nothing yet, my lady," Sir John answered in an apologetic tone.

"Surely they can't keep him there if they haven't charged him," she demanded.

The two men exchanged a glance.

"There does seem to be evidence against him," Sir John said.

"What evidence?" she asked. "Jaime took too much laudenum to help her sleep. It was an accident."

"Like the duel?" Sir John asked in a low tone.

Lady Anna glared at him.

"Get out!" she demanded imperially, pointing her finger at the door.

Sir John's face reddened, but he gave her a curt nod and left the room.

"Anna," her father gently reprimanded, "don't take your anger out on poor Sir John. He's been nothing but a gentleman throughout this whole ordeal. It was his friend who was shot, remember."

"You don't believe it was Mr. Langley, do you, Father?" Lady Anna asked tearfully. "He couldn't have killed Lord Mallory. And he couldn't have killed Jaime!"

"I don't know what to think," said her father. "He deceived us before."

"But this is different," she insisted. "This isn't keeping his identity a secret. This is murder!"

Lord Somerville sighed.

"I hope he's innocent, my dear," he said. "I like the man. And it will cause me a great deal of trouble to lose him. If he's convicted, he'll be hung."

"No!"

"And that will be a great deal of trouble to me. I'll lose a fine secretary, but more importantly, I'll have to go with heir number three. Which maybe, all things considering, wouldn't be such a bad idea."

"Father!" Lady Anna scowled at her parent's heartless and self-centered statement. How could he think of his own discomfort when poor Mr. Langley's life was at stake! Then she furrowed her brow.

"Who is heir number three?" she asked.

"Anna?"

Anna jerked awake. She had been dreaming, and it took her a few seconds to remember where she was. The Library at Hampstead Hall. And William was being held at the station. "Questioned" for the deaths of Jaime Douglas and Peter Mallory.

"Am I disturbing you?"

Jake stood in the doorway, as if asking permission to enter.

"No," she answered, waving at the chair in front of her.

"How are you holding up?" he asked sympathetically, sitting on the edge of the chair and leaning forward, his elbows on his knees.

Anna shrugged.

"How should I be?" she asked irritably, then remembered that Jake had just lost another close friend. Even if he wasn't in love with her, Jaime had been an important part of his life.

"How are you?" she asked.

He nodded, swallowing hard, his eyes red around the rims.

"I'm sorry it was you who found her," she said.

"Me, too," he said, sweeping his hand through his hair as he sat up again. "I was also the last one to see her alive, apparently. Except for her killer. I'm surprised it's not me down at the station being questioned."

"Is there any news this morning?"

Jake shook his head.

"Only what they told us last night. William's not under arrest, but they're holding him for questioning."

"How long can they hold him without charging him?"

"A couple of days, I've heard," Jake said, shrugging his shoulders. "Anna," he continued, taking her hands, "I think you need to prepare yourself for the worst."

"No!" she cried, jerking her hands away. "He didn't kill Jaime. Or Peter. He couldn't have!"

Jake sighed, leaning back in his chair, turning his attention to the fire.

Anna closed her eyes. She didn't want to believe William was capable of killing two people. She would solve this herself, she decided. Find the real murderer. For his sake.

And for hers.

"Tell me everything that happened yesterday," she said, taking a deep breath. "Portia tried to tell me, but my mind had trouble focusing."

"Are you sure that's what you want?" he asked.

She nodded.

"Start with the night before," she said. "When you apologized. How did that go?"

Jake shifted in his chair.

"It went well," he said, swallowing hard. "We talked it out, and we left as friends. I thought it could all be put behind us, you know. Starting fresh, as friends." He leaned forward on his elbows and pushed his hair back with both hands. "And now she's gone."

"At least you have that consolation," Anna said. "You were reconciled."

Jake looked up at her gratefully. He sat up again in his chair.

"As far as yesterday, everything seemed normal that morning," he began, "at least, what normal has become. Except Jaime was late coming downstairs. Nobody thought anything of it. There's no schedule. Nobody was really looking for her. William had opened up his media room to us, since we're all stuck here, so everyone was watching the crew play a game in there. Around eleven or so I began to wonder where Jaime was, if anyone had seen her. I looked for you—but you had gone to Windsor with William. Why didn't you tell me you were going?"

"I didn't know I was going," she explained. "I decided at the last minute."

"You could have been—" he began, then stopped himself. Anna noticed his fist was clenched at his side. "Anyway," he continued, "I'm glad you're back safe. I went up to her room and knocked, but she didn't answer, and I had a bad feeling. The door was locked, so I found Mr. Barnaby, and we opened it."

He wiped his eyes with his hand, as if wiping away the memory. Anna reached forward and squeezed his hand.

"Two deaths, and both my friends," he said in a monotone. "It's almost as if someone deliberately..." he trailed off.

Anna released his hand and sat back. Jake glanced at her apologetically, then continued.

"She looked peaceful," he said. "Like she was sleeping. There was a wine-glass by her bed that the police took away. Later they told us it had also contained a combination of valium and oxycodone."

"Which is why they talked to Miranda first?" asked Anna.

"It seemed logical. And she couldn't tell them for sure if any of her medication was missing. After we found Jaime, Mr. Barnaby went out to the policeman on guard, the one that was stationed out in the drive. He called in Inspector Ferguson. He kept the rest of us in the Drawing Room so we wouldn't talk to each other or text anyone. I couldn't even tell you, or check on you. It was a long, torturous day. Inspector Ferguson took Miranda into the Study, to interview her. That's when she told him about overhearing William talking to you at the dueling field."

"How do you know what she told the police?"

He shrugged.

"Miranda bragged to all of us about it afterward."

"What did she hear William say?" Anna asked, though she could guess.

"She said he grabbed your arm and said, 'Something needs to be done about Peter Mallory, and if you don't press charges, I'll take matters into my own hands.'"

Anna paled.

"She told us that when William said that, she didn't know what he was talking about," Jake continued, "but later, someone told her that Peter had attacked you the night before the duel."

"Great!" Anna said. "Now everyone knows."

"I wish I knew who leaked it," Jake said gravely.

"Maybe more people overheard it that night than we realized," Anna suggested.

Jake looked steadily at Anna.

"Did William say that?" he asked. "Was Miranda telling the truth?"

"Yes," she breathed, "but he didn't mean murder! He only meant he would report Peter's attack."

"Are you sure of that?" asked Jake, his eyebrows raised challengingly. "Do you really know what his intentions were?"

Anna stood suddenly and went to the window, gripping the sill.

CHAPTER SIXTY-TWO

❖

"How long are you planning to keep me here?"

William sat sullenly in the hard, metal chair across the table from Inspector Ferguson. Sitting beside him was the family solicitor, Sir James Prawn. Sir James was small, shriveled, and slightly pink, and William was reminded, as he always was when forced to be in the solicitor's presence, that Sir James looked exactly like his surname. Which didn't give William peace of mind, especially during a murder investigation.

The Inspector flipped his hands.

"That depends on you, my lord," he said casually.

Sir James cleared his ancient throat.

"My client has done nothing deserving incarceration," he said in a voice that resembled whistling through seaweed, "and I insist on his being released immediately."

Inspector Ferguson shifted in his chair.

"I'm allowed to keep His Lordship under my care for up to ninety-six hours, if I feel the necessity," the Inspector explained. "As you well know, Sir James."

The solicitor shriveled a bit more in his rumpled suit. William sighed heavily.

I'm going to be here another night, he thought bitterly. He stole a glance around the closet-like interrogation room, with its peeling, bile-colored walls and metal, nailed-to-the-floor furniture. A dusty rectangle of fluorescent lights hung precariously above their heads, and William's eye twitched as one of the long, fluorescent tubes flickered with an inconsistent rhythm. He wondered how his mother was faring in the lobby of the police station. Sir James had told him she refused to leave without her son, so the officers had pointed her in the direction of the sparsely furnished front room. He imagined she was not a quiet inhabitant, and wondered if the Inspector would release him to get her off the property, and not because he thought William was innocent of the crimes.

"Now," said Inspector Ferguson, glancing up at the camera mounted in the corner of the room, "tell me again your movements on Wednesday evening."

"They haven't changed since you asked me the first time," William insisted.

Of course, he didn't mean murder, she thought. Not William. Not the man she loved.

"I'm sorry, Anna," said Jake. He had risen as well and stood beside her at the window. "I'm not accusing him, but I would understand if he took matters into his own hands to protect you."

He looked at her with such sorrow, Anna had to look away.

"We're talking about Peter's death, not Jaime's," she said in a tired voice. "Why would William kill Jaime? And how do we know she didn't kill herself?"

"First of all, there was no note, which doesn't prove it wasn't suicide, I guess," he said. "Edwin Sterling asked the same question, and the Inspector said that Jaime had already given evidence that she overheard William and Peter arguing about buying Hampstead Hall. You remember. She told us about it after her interview."

Anna nodded.

"So the Inspector figured that maybe Jaime also overheard William on the dueling field, like Miranda, and had said something to him about it," Jake continued. "Maybe even tried to blackmail him. She died because she knew too much."

"Maybe she died because *she* killed Peter?" Anna said spitefully. "Maybe she killed herself because she had a guilty conscience?"

"Anna! Don't be ridiculous!"

"I'm not being ridiculous!" she said, sobbing and hitting his chest with both hands. "*You're* being ridiculous!"

Jake grabbed her hands to stop her from pounding on him, then pulled her into his embrace. Anna clung to him, her tears soaking his shirt.

"I'm sorry," he whispered, smoothing her hair. "I didn't mean to upset you. Maybe we shouldn't speculate. It isn't helping anything."

Anna pulled back from him, wiping her face with a kleenex from a box on a nearby table.

"It's nearly lunchtime," Jake said. "Would you like me to have Sheila bring yours to your room?"

She nodded, giving him the ghost of a smile.

"Anna?" he said, pausing at the door. "I know you care more for William than you do for me," he began, waving away her protest, "but I want you to know that, whatever happens, I'll always be here for you. If things don't go as you hope they will, I'll be here."

"Nevertheless, my lord," said the Inspector, squinting at him. "Humor me."

William sighed.

"After tea, I took Anna to see my farm fields. When we returned, I walked to my mother's cottage."

"You said she summoned you?"

"Yes. She wanted to ask me some questions about my guests."

"Any guests in particular?"

"You already know the answer," said William, irritated.

"Just answer the question, my lord."

"Yes, she wanted more information about Anna McKay. She was concerned I was having a romantic relationship with her."

"And were you?"

"I already told you. I have feelings for her, but she had rejected me that night."

"How long were you at your mother's cottage?"

"A couple of hours. We had dinner."

"Why didn't you have dinner with your guests?" asked the Inspector.

"I was not in the habit of eating with my guests," William explained. "And I didn't think she wanted to see me right then."

"You mean Miss McKay?"

"Who else?"

"Please continue."

"I left my mother's cottage and walked back to the house."

"It was a cold night. Why would you choose to walk?"

"I needed to think," said William. "And I didn't realize how cold it was until I was walking in it."

"Lady Diane says you left her cottage shortly after nine. Is that correct?"

William nodded.

"It was nine-fifteen or so, I think."

"Did you meet anyone else in the grounds?"

"Yes, as I told you before, I saw Adrian Reed. He was taking a smoke break but didn't want anyone to know."

"Approximately what time did you meet Mr. Reed?"

"It was a quarter to ten, because I glanced at my mobile. I told him Mr. Barnaby locks the doors at ten. I didn't want him to be locked out."

Inspector Ferguson nodded.

"Did you meet anyone in the house when you returned?"

"I met Jake Rawlings in the Great Hall when I entered the house. He told me he was going upstairs to apologize to Jaime."

"And what was he apologizing for?"

"He didn't confide in me, as I told you before," William insisted, "but Anna said he and Jaime were at odds, and that he had done something at dinner that he knew had upset her. I told him it's always good to apologize, and he went on his way upstairs."

"What had he done at dinner?"

"Why don't you ask Jake?"

"I have," said the Inspector with a slight smile. "And according to Jake Rawlings, Jaime Douglas was alive when he left her room around eleven o'clock."

William folded his arms and leaned back against the metal slats of the chair.

"So Jake went upstairs," the Inspector continued, "but you remained downstairs."

"For a few minutes," said William. "To let him go on ahead."

"Why is that?"

William sighed.

"Because Jake and I like the same girl," he explained. "He had already pointed out that Anna was in the Parlor if I was looking for her, which I wasn't, but—anyway, I thought it would be awkward if we both went up the stairs together. Not much to say to one another. So I waited until he had gone up."

"But you say you didn't go into the Parlor and join Miss McKay?"

"No. I looked in, saw her sitting there. But there were others in the room, and I didn't feel like socializing, especially when she'd turned down my invitation to Windsor. There wasn't anything more to say."

"Who else was in the room with her?"

"Portia Valentine and Edwin Sterling," said William. "I didn't go in, so I can't be sure no one else was there, but it didn't seem like it."

"After looking into the Parlor, what did you do?"

"I went upstairs to the Tapestry Room. I called Mr. Barnaby and asked for a bottle of wine and a glass."

"What time would you say Mr. Barnaby brought your wine?"

"I don't know. Shortly before ten?"

"Was anyone else in the Tapestry Room with you?"

"No."

"Why wine, my lord?"

"What do you mean?"

"Why not whiskey? Tea? Coffee?"

"I wanted wine."

"Are you aware that Jaime Douglas also had a glass of wine that night?"

"No. What does that have to do with me?"

"That's what we're trying to determine."

Sir James cleared the seaweed from his throat.

"My client does not have to answer your insinuating questions," he said.

William patted the old man's arm.

"It's all right, Sir James," he said. "The Inspector is just doing his job, right Inspector? You're not charging me, are you?"

"Not yet, my lord," the Inspector squinted.

William raised his eyebrows questioningly.

"Did you speak with anyone else that night?" Inspector Ferguson continued, ignoring William's eyebrows.

"Only Mr. Barnaby when he brought the wine. I let him know Adrian Reed might still be in the grounds," said William. "Then no one else until close to midnight, when Anna walked in and told me she would go to Windsor after all."

"And that surprised you?"

"Of course it did."

"Why? You'd invited her to go."

"But she'd already turned me down, as I told you already. You act like it's important, or suspicious or something. When a woman turns you down, you don't expect her to jump out of bed in the middle of the night and accept your invitation."

"Perhaps you'd already made other plans," suggested the Inspector. "Perhaps her acceptance threw a wrench in those plans."

"What plans?" William asked. "I wouldn't have gone to Windsor without her. I've been there before. I wanted to share it with her. I had no other plans."

"No plans with Jaime Douglas?"

"None whatsoever. I barely ever spoke to Jaime Douglas."

"Perhaps you wanted to share a glass of wine with her."

"No."

William folded his arms.

"And what time did you say you left the Tapestry Room?" asked the Inspector, unruffled.

"It was around two," William admitted. "Just before, I think. I sat down again after Anna left, and fell asleep in the chair. I woke up because I heard something."

"What did you hear?"

"A rustling sound. I thought I dreamed it, at first. Then I heard it again. Sounded like it was in the fireplace. I was concerned that a bird had gotten in there, though I should have known it would be unlikely at this time of year, with the fires burning most of the time."

"Did you figure out what was causing the noise?"

"No. Like I said before, I went over to the fireplace and listened, but I didn't hear it again. So I went to my rooms. Now that I've had time to think about it, it was probably someone in the secret passage. It goes up along the fireplace."

"Someone *was* in the secret passage," the Inspector agreed. "*Your* finger-prints were found in there. How do you explain that?"

William gave out a mirthless laugh.

"It's my house," he said. "I used to play in those passages as a boy. I think the last time I was in that passage was when my father died. I did a thorough examination of the state of the place at that time. Were there any other finger-prints in the passage?"

Inspector Ferguson smoothed his tongue over his front teeth.

"And you say you left the house the next morning around eight?" he asked, changing the subject.

William sighed.

"Yes. We wanted an early start."

"Did you see anyone in the house before you left?"

"At that hour, we only saw Mr. Barnaby and Sheila. Everyone else was still in bed."

"And no one else accompanied you to Windsor?" asked the Inspector.

"No," said William, rolling his eyes. "As I told you before, we were alone."

CHAPTER SIXTY-THREE

Eating lunch alone was helpful, but by afternoon, Anna began to feel isolated. Plus, she wanted to find out any news about William. She knew that only good news would trickle up to her; if there was bad news, she would have to actively find out.

When she arrived downstairs, she found Edwin and Portia once again in the Drawing Room. They seemed to have taken it over as their favorite spot. Anna wondered if it was out of convenience, or if they found it a good way to investigate without being obvious. It was the best gathering place, especially now that catering was gone.

She paused before entering the room to observe Edwin Sterling. Now that she was past her initial fanaticism over the famous actor, she began to see him as a man. How weird must it be, she wondered, to have people—even those you work with—see you as special, as larger than life, as not quite real. She had to admit she had felt that. On television and the movie screen, he was perfect. Always put together. Flawless, unless the character called for otherwise. Yet, looking across at him lounging in a corner of the sofa, she could see he wasn't perfect. He was just like everyone else. His light brown curls waved in a million directions; it wasn't perfectly coiffed like in the movies or red-carpet photographs because he had a habit of pulling it straight up when he was upset or thinking deeply. He had a tendency to stress out over irritating people, like Miranda. Yet, he was a dutiful son, and Anna could see a sharpness in his blue eyes that foretold a keen intellect. His mother had called him in as soon as Peter was killed, with cryptic remarks about his ability to solve problems. Obviously, Portia thought he could help the situation.

Maybe Edwin Sterling could help William.

Anna took a deep breath, then plunged into the room.

Portia and Edwin weren't the only occupants. Although the crew was absent, most of the cast were there. Corinne and Perry were seated together, and Jake was standing at the French windows, staring out at the grey drizzle. Sir Frederick was seated near Portia, and was sipping coffee, but Anna saw no sign of Lady Diane.

She's probably with William, she thought, wishing she could be there as well. Inspector Ferguson had made it clear that he didn't want an onslaught of actors descending upon his police station. Not that they'd be allowed to see him, anyway.

Anna was surprised to see Julia in the room. She could tell that the producer could only take a limited amount of time with her ex-husband. Adrian was chatting on the phone in the corner, and it sounded like business. Anna wondered if he was lining up his next job.

If William was arrested, would *Cavendish Manor* have to find a new home?

"Anna, my dear, how are you feeling?" Portia asked, waving her over.

Anna seated herself on the sofa next to Edwin. Jake turned at Portia's greeting, and Anna could feel him watching her with anxious eyes.

"Is there any news?" she asked, gazing into each face for signs that they were keeping something from her.

"Nothing yet, dear," Portia answered sympathetically.

Julia threw up exasperated hands.

"I wish they'd do *something*," she exclaimed. "Arrest him for murder or release him. I don't care. Just get on with it and let the rest of us go."

Jake made an involuntary disgruntled sound and gave Julia a sharp look before pulling a chair into the circle and sitting down.

Adrian, finished with his call, walked over.

"I heard you went with him to Windsor, Anna," he said, giving her his high-eyebrow look. "You must feel lucky to be back safe and sound."

"Excuse me?" Anna asked, spearing Adrian with a piercing gaze.

"Well, you were alone together," he continued, his button-eyes wide. "You could have had an accident, and there would have been no one there to save you."

"That's uncalled for, man," Jake said defensively, rising from his chair. Adrian merely threw up his hands.

"Well, it's finally happened!" cooed Miranda, nearly dancing into the room, her cheeks pink and her eyes bright.

All eyes turned to her.

"*What's* happened, Miranda?" asked an irritated Julia.

"The press has finally found out about the murders, and they're lined up outside the gates."

"Oh, no," Sir Frederick murmured, leaning his head on his hand.

Julia stood angrily.

"Who told them?" she demanded. "It's expressly against your contracts!"

"Nobody told them, Julia," said Edwin calmly. "The Earl of Somerville was hauled off for questioning in a murder investigation. What do you expect? The news was bound to get out eventually."

"Well, they can't stay camped out in front of the gates," she said. "What if one of them climbs a wall or something?"

"Oh, don't worry," said Miranda, grinning oddly. "The police made them move."

"How do you know?" asked Jake, eyeing her suspiciously.

"I was taking a walk," Miranda began. "I was!" she demanded, catching the doubtful glances of the others. "And I happened to walk down to the gate, and there were all these reporters."

"The gate is almost two miles from the house!" Anna commented.

"It was a long walk," Miranda countered.

"What about the police?" asked Edwin. "I thought there was an officer stationed outside in a car to watch the house?"

Miranda gave an impish grin.

"There's a path through the woods," she said. "It returns to the drive further down, although he saw me eventually. He's the one who made the reporters move along."

Julia huffed.

"You didn't speak to them, did you?" she asked. "The press, I mean?"

"Not about the case," Miranda answered, batting innocent eyes.

"Oh dear Lord," muttered the producer, grabbing her phone. "Freddie! Come with me. We've got to do damage control."

"Yes, dear," said Sir Frederick obediently. "I mean, yes, Julia."

"Great!" said Jake, frowning as he lowered himself back into his chair. "My publicist is going to love this."

"I'm sorry," said Anna sympathetically.

"No, really," said Jake. "I'm not being sarcastic. He's going to love this. It's the kind of thing he loves to take advantage of."

Edwin nodded.

"You're right, he'll love it," he said.

Jake looked at him questioningly.

"We have the same publicist, don't we?" asked Edwin. "David Wiseman?"

Jake nodded, surprised.

"He's a devious one, that's for sure," Edwin continued. "I would almost blame the murders on David, if I didn't think he'd be too protective of his own skin."

Miranda flounced into a chair, smoothing her hair into place with a heavily-ringed hand. Adrian gave himself a quick once-over in a nearby mirror, as if expecting the press to come breaking into the Drawing Room at any moment.

Anna looked away from them, trying to keep her face from showing the disgust she felt. It was a show to them, she realized, an opportunity to grab attention for themselves. She glanced across the room to find Corinne's eyes on her. Her blonde hair was swept up in a messy ponytail, and she was wearing jeans and a sweater, with only a trace of makeup.

This is the real Corinne, Anna thought. A compassionate Corinne, who was a little bit fearful and not afraid to show it. She liked this Corinne better. Looking down, Anna noticed that Corinne was holding hands with Perry, and it made her smile softly. She must have taken her advice and talked with Perry.

Corinne was looking at her as if she was trying to communicate something. Anna hoped they'd have time to talk later, when no one else was around.

"So," said Miranda, interrupting Anna's thoughts, "it was the Earl the whole time. I knew there was something sinister about him the first time I met him. I never trusted him," she said, turning to Adrian, her hand on her heart. Adrian nodded sagely.

Edwin stood to his feet and began pacing the room, pulling both hands through his curls, then leaving them there, fingers entwined on top of his head, as if they were taken prisoner. His mother watched him, then patted Anna's hand.

"Don't worry, my dear," she soothed. "Edwin is thinking."

"You don't think William did it, do you, Portia?" Anna asked, irritated by the cracking of her own voice. She didn't want to show vulnerability to these people. *Don't trust anyone,* William had warned her. But surely he didn't mean for her to include Portia? Or himself?

"Of course not," Portia said decisively. "Do you think I would have encouraged you to go to Windsor with him if I did? No, my dear. It was what I feared would happen, of course. His arrest. Which is why I brought Edwin here in the first place."

She beamed affectionately at her son, who had released his fingers but still paced erratically in front of one of the marble fireplaces, deep in thought.

He was her last hope, Anna realized, and her heart sank. She was entrusting William's future, and her own, in the hands of an actor. No matter how talented or handsome he was, he was still just that. Not a policeman. Not a private detective.

An actor.

Anna collapsed against the back of the sofa, sighing mournfully.

"I don't know how we're going to continue filming now," Miranda offered. "With one lead actor gone and now the props master. *Cavendish Manor* was doomed from the start. Maybe William said the name of the Scottish play on purpose," she speculated. "He cursed us. He cursed Peter and he cursed Jaime."

"Isn't it usually that the person who says the name curses himself?" Adrian reminded her.

Miranda waved away his comment.

"I guess it backfired on him," she said. "That's why he didn't get away with it."

"He took quite a risk, if he's guilty," Jake said. He had been silent so long, Anna had almost forgotten he was still in the room.

"What do you mean?" asked Perry.

"His history with Peter isn't a secret, although the fact he thought Peter killed his father was. Anyone could see they weren't friends."

"Which is why he lied to us and told us he was Sir Frederick's assistant," said Miranda, triumphantly. "That way we wouldn't know the connection between them."

"But Sir Frederick knew who he was," Anna reminded her. "And Portia. And he couldn't have hidden that from the police. And he didn't."

"It was still a risk," Jake continued. "To load a lead ball into my gun without anyone seeing it? Including me?" He glanced around at the others' faces. "What if one of us had seen him do it? What if Jaime did?"

"I don't believe he could have done it," said Perry. "I was there at the table the whole time. I would have noticed."

"There was a time I thought he might have," said Corinne, glancing timidly at Anna, "to get back at Peter for Anna's sake. But the more I think about it, the more it doesn't make sense. I would have seen him, too. I could see the props table from where I was standing."

Jake eyed her sharply.

"I thought you were behind the trees?" said Jake. "How could you have seen anything?"

"I sort of went back and forth," she admitted. "It was cold, and it seemed to be taking forever for the sun to rise. I only went behind the trees for good after Jaime dropped the bullets."

"Jaime," said Edwin. He stopped pacing and was staring at Corinne with wide eyes. "Jaime dropped bullets?"

"Yes," said Corinne, eyeing him curiously.

"That's right, she did," Portia nodded.

"Maybe Jaime killed Peter and then William killed Jaime for revenge!" said Miranda, her finger raised for emphasis.

There was an uproar, everyone speaking at once.

"That doesn't even make sense, Miranda," said Perry above the rest. "We just said William didn't like Peter. Why would he want revenge on his killer?"

Miranda pouted.

"Back to Jaime dropping bullets," said Edwin, waving his hands to silence the protests. "When did this happen? Before or after the guns were loaded?"

"After," said Anna, thinking carefully. "I remember Sir Frederick was frustrated because the scene was about to start."

"It made a big racket," said Corinne. "Everyone looked to see what happened."

"So Jaime couldn't have added a bullet at that point," Perry pointed out. "She didn't have the guns in her hand. And even if she did have the guns, everyone was looking at her."

"Hmm," said Edwin, frowning. He began pacing again, his hands clasped behind his back.

Anna remembered that his character, Dr. Hanover, did that same thing when he was solving a crime.

He must have picked up the habit from his character, she thought, and smiled inwardly. Or Dr. Hanover and Edwin Sterling are more alike than she realized.

"I still don't understand why Inspector Ferguson thinks William killed Jaime," she said. "We weren't even here. We left early."

"They're saying the time of death was around two in the morning," Corinne said, looking at her sadly. "So we were all still here."

"Mr. Barnaby brought William a bottle of wine in the Tapestry Room that night around ten," said Perry, "and William said something to him about locking up. So William was still up at least that late."

Anna noticed Adrian's button-eyes blink rapidly a few times before he turned away from the group and examined a porcelain vase on the mantelpiece.

"He was in the Tapestry Room around midnight," Anna volunteered. "I spoke to him then."

"For how long?" asked Jake.

"Not long," she admitted. "I just told him I'd go to Windsor with him. And he seemed fine," she added, looking defiant. "He didn't seem nervous or agitated, or like he was about to commit a murder."

"Did you know there was a secret passage between the Tapestry Room and the Nursery where Jaime was staying?" asked Edwin, pausing again in his pacing to look pointedly at Anna.

"Yes," she admitted. "Although I never went in it. How did you know it was there?"

"Jake told the Inspector about it," said Edwin, nodding his head in Jake's direction.

Jake reddened under Anna's scrutiny.

"Jaime showed me," he pleaded. "She found it by accident. She said she thought she could hear voices sometimes near the chimney, then she figured out there was a passageway down to the Tapestry Room."

"So Inspector Ferguson thinks that William used that to sneak up into Jaime's room while she was sleeping and drug her," said Miranda, watching for a reaction from Anna, a smirk playing across her carefully-painted lips. "Anyone could have stolen from my prescriptions," she went on. "I keep some in my trailer, and some in my room, and some in my handbag. I never know when a palpitation will come on me." She pressed her hand to her heart, like she was checking her pulse rate. "William could have easily borrowed from my stash, put it in a glass of wine, and taken it up to Jaime's room without anyone knowing."

Anna scowled.

"Just because he knew about the secret passage doesn't mean he used it," she said angrily. "I don't know why you chose to bring it up, Jake!" she added, aiming her animosity at him and ignoring Miranda's challenging looks.

"The latches had been wiped clean of fingerprints," Edwin continued, "but they did find William's prints on the walls inside the secret stairs."

"Of course, his fingerprints would be there," Anna insisted. "It's his house.

He's probably been in those passages a thousand times. He showed me some of the others."

Everyone looked at Anna curiously. She bit her lip. She needed to be more careful what information she gave out, she realized. William's ability to stealthily navigate his home wasn't helping his image right now.

"Wouldn't Jaime have to drink the sleeping stuff?" she asked, moving the subject from secret passages. "How would William know she'd drink a random glass of wine left on her bedside table?"

The others were silent, contemplating the problem.

"Maybe William and Jaime were secret lovers!" Miranda offered. "They were drinking wine together!"

"Oh, Miranda! You make everything into a soap opera!" Portia chided, shaking her head.

Anna sat up straighter, remembering something.

"The secret passage goes down another floor!" she announced, clasping her hands together as if pleading for mercy. "It goes down to the Chapel that's next to the Ballroom. Maybe someone else knew about the passage and entered it through there."

Glancing up, she found Jake giving her a sympathetic look.

He feels sorry for me, she thought, and blushed. The silly girl who doesn't want to believe William's a killer. Who looks for anything that could clear him.

I would do anything to clear him, because he's innocent, she told herself, setting her jaw. Isn't he? She glanced timidly around the room at her friends and co-workers.

But if William didn't kill Jaime, who did?

CHAPTER SIXTY-FOUR

The Inspector squinted across the table at William, his head on one side.

"Have you ever used oxycodone?" he asked.

"I may have, at some point in my life," William admitted, shifting in his uncomfortable chair in the interrogation room.

"Perhaps three years ago, when you hurt your shoulder playing rugby with friends, for instance?"

"Yes," William said, impressed with the Inspector's thoroughness. "I probably used it then."

"We did not find the bottle in your medicine cabinet," the Inspector admitted, a look of disappointment crossing his face.

"I either used it all, or threw away the rest," said William. "I'm not in the habit of keeping old prescriptions."

"Ever used valium?"

"No," said William. "I can definitely say I've never used that. And never will," he added firmly.

The Inspector blinked at him, then leaned forward.

"Your fingerprints were found on the bottle of wine we retrieved from the Tapestry Room," he said. "And on the glass on the table."

William grinned.

"Not surprising," he said, "since I already told you I ordered the bottle from Mr. Barnaby and freely admit to drinking a glass or two from it."

"Did you also offer some to Jaime Douglas?"

"No," said William. "As I mentioned, I barely knew Jaime Douglas."

"So you wouldn't have put a lethal dose of oxycodone and valium into her wine, hoping she would sleep away what she knew about you?"

"What did she know about me?" William demanded. The interrogation was beginning to wear on his patience.

"That you were going to take matters into your own hands if Anna McKay didn't press charges against Peter Mallory."

"Don't answer that!" wheezed Sir James, the few hairs left on his head rising like antennae under the heat of the fluorescent lights.

"I didn't mean I would murder him!" William growled, losing his temper.

"I meant that I would press charges myself!"

"Don't answer!"

Sir James' eyes were beginning to protrude in a ghastly manner. William thought it best to be silent, if only to calm the old man.

I wouldn't want to be accused of causing another death, he thought angrily.

The subject in the Drawing Room moved from the murders back to the news media at the gates. Edwin Sterling seemed to have very decided opinions on the paparazzi, and was debating with Miranda on the ethics of popular culture and the public's insatiable appetite for intimate details about celebrities' lives. It sounded like he had personal experience with the downside of fame.

Anna stood up and headed for the door. She was in search of a cup of tea, and she knew Sheila would give her one. She also might need a comforting friend, now that her employer was being questioned about Jaime's death. Did Sheila think William was capable of murder? It couldn't hurt to ask.

Before she could leave the room, she felt a slight pull on her arm. It was Corinne.

"Hey," she said, quietly, "Can we talk?"

"Sure," Anna said, pausing at the door. "Is it about Perry? Things seem to be going well between you."

Corinne smiled shyly.

"No, it's not about Perry," she said. "I have something I wanted to ask you about."

"What is it?"

Corinne glanced furtively around before answering.

"There's something I've been thinking about," she said. "From the day of the duel. Something that doesn't make sense."

Anna looked more closely at her friend. She seemed agitated, nervous. And this was sounding familiar. Hadn't Newberry said something similar in her dream that morning?

"Anna, please don't be mad at me," said Jake, coming up from behind Corinne and breaking into their conversation. "I told the Inspector about the secret passageway because I thought someone could have used it to get to Jaime's room without being seen. I didn't do it to implicate William. How would I know he was in the Tapestry Room that night?"

Anna nodded impatiently at him.

"Wait, Jake," she said, putting up one hand. "Corinne was about to tell me something."

Corinne shook her head, her lips pursed. She seemed pale, Anna noticed, and she was staring over Anna's shoulder at someone in the hall.

"It's okay," Corinne said quickly. "It's nothing, anyway."

She scooted away into the Great Hall toward the stairs, passing Sir Frederick as he returned from dealing with the media fiasco.

The director turned for a moment, watching her go.

"Is Corinne all right?" he asked.

"Yes," Anna answered. "I'm sure she's fine."

Inwardly, she wondered about Corinne's sudden change of mind. Was she afraid of Sir Frederick? She watched the plump director as he crossed the room and settled himself happily next to Portia Valentine.

He doesn't seem threatening to me, she thought. Just a little callous and self-absorbed.

She shrugged off Sir Frederick and concentrated on Jake's pleading brown eyes.

"Do you forgive me?" he asked.

She sighed.

"Yes, I forgive you," she said. "I just hate all the evidence that seems to be piling up against William."

"Have you considered that he might be guilty?" he asked.

"No!" she said, defiantly. "And if you keep suggesting that, I really won't forgive you."

Jake nodded, his expression serious.

"Just be careful, Anna," he said. "If they release him, don't be alone with him. For my peace of mind."

The kitchen was warm and smelled of gingerbread.

"It's funny," Anna thought to herself, "how smells trigger memories."

Gingerbread immediately transported Anna to her grandmother's kitchen at Christmas, where she would help decorate by piping royal icing onto the fat, brown cookies. Sheila wasn't making gingerbread men, though. She was making gingerbread, a dark cake, heavy with molasses.

Sheila cut Anna a square of it and dolloped cream on top. Although it was similar to the flavor of gingerbread cookies, Anna found the heaviness of the molasses a bit too much for her taste. But cream, she found, makes anything edible.

Sheila cut herself a slice and joined Anna at the wooden kitchen table.

"I just needed a bit of comfort food," she explained, bobbing her stiff helmet of hair. "With His Lordship hauled off to gaol. First, murder on the estate, and now this!" She dabbed at her eyes with the corner of her apron.

Anna marveled that, like Edwin's handkerchief, she was watching someone actually use the edge of her white apron to wipe her tears. It was like living in a novel.

"You don't believe William murdered anyone, do you?" she asked the cook.

Sheila stiffened, a haughty expression hardening her kind face.

"No, indeed, I don't," she said with a huff. "And that Inspector better let him go, or he'll have me to deal with. Not to mention Lady Diane, who Mr. Barnaby tells me hasn't left the police station this whole time. Raising all kinds of ruckus, I'm guessin'. And rightly so."

She chuckled low in her chest. Anna smiled at the thought of Lady Diane interacting with the local constabulary.

"Her Ladyship probably has them running her errands for her, and fetching her food from restaurants and such," Sheila added, her face softening. "If they haven't charged him, they'll send him home soon," she said, patting Anna's hand. "He's in God's hands."

Anna clenched her jaw to keep from bursting into tears. William either had blindly-loyal employees, or he was an innocent man.

"Oh, did we tell you?" asked Sheila. "Mr. Barnaby found a bottle of wine was missing from his Butler's Pantry. And a wine glass. He thought it might be what the murderer used to put the drugs in."

Anna's eyes widened.

"Did he tell the police?" she asked, hope surging through her. A stolen bottle of wine? This had to be good news. William wouldn't have stolen it. He already had a bottle with him in the Tapestry Room. If she could find the missing bottle, maybe she could find the killer.

And she knew just where she would look first.

Anna crept into the Dining Room through the Butler's Pantry, hoping she wouldn't be noticed. She wanted to investigate alone. There were still people gathered in the Drawing Room. She straightened her shoulders and strode confidently across the Dining Room and into the Great Hall, pretending she had something important she was doing. Something that shouldn't be interrupted. No one called out to her, and she thought she was free and clear, until her phone rang in her pocket. In her frantic efforts to silence it, she accidentally answered it. With a deep sigh, Anna put the phone to her ear.

"Hello, Mother," she said, trying to sound bright and cheery.

"Anna, what is going on?" her mother demanded.

"I don't know what you mean," Anna said, cringing.

"It's all over the news. Two deaths? And you haven't called me once to let me know you were okay?"

"We aren't supposed to talk about it," Anna attempted to explain. "We signed confidentiality agreements, and the Studio said—"

"I don't care what you signed," her mother interrupted. "I'm your mother, and if there's some kind of murderer on the loose on your set, then you should at least have had the decency to call me."

"But don't you see? You didn't know about it, so you weren't worried."

"That's no excuse. I want you on the first plane out of there. Your father is looking for tickets as we speak."

"No."

"What?"

Anna was surprised, even at herself. When Peter was shot, and everything was crazy, the thought had crossed her mind to give up and go home. Back to safety, and to her family. Away from whatever danger lurked in Hampstead Hall. But now, though there was a second death, she had an inexplicable desire to stay. Well, perhaps not so inexplicable. A vision of William sitting alone in a holding cell played through her mind.

"I can't go home right now," she said with determination. "I'm needed here, and I'm staying. One of the deaths was an accident on the set, and the other seems to be an overdose of sleeping pills. You know how some of these film people can be," she said, hoping to downplay the murders in her mother's mind. "I'm not in danger, and the police are handling things. Until filming for *Cavendish Manor* is canceled, I need to stay here."

There was silence on the phone. Anna wondered if they'd been disconnected, or if her mother had hung up.

"Okay." Her mother's voice sounded strangely acquiescent. "If you're sure you're all right."

"Yes, Mother," said Anna. "I'm fine."

"I still don't like it," said her mother. "I just wish I was there with you," she added tearfully.

"Did you find out anything about our British ancestors?" Anna asked quickly, hoping to get her mother's mind off the subject of murder.

"Oh," she said. "Yes, actually. It's quite amazing. I found the most incredible photograph. It seems to be of a portrait hanging somewhere, like a museum. I'll text you a picture of it. You really won't believe it until you see it. And the funny thing is, the family is from Surrey, just like you asked. The Earls of Somerville, with a family crest and everything. One of the younger sons came to America, sometime after the first World War. One that wasn't in line to become the Earl. Seems he fell in love with an American nurse during the war, and they both came back to Nashville. Just a minute and I'll text you that picture I was talking about."

Anna opened her text messages and pulled up the picture her mother sent. Then she expanded it with her fingers, her jaw dropping.

She was once again looking into the eyes of Lady Anna Somer, the exact portrait that hung in the Gallery upstairs.

"Isn't that amazing?" she heard her mother's voice faintly squawking from the phone she was holding at arm's length. "I don't know her name, but she looks just like you!"

CHAPTER SIXTY-FIVE

William looked up as Sergeant Patel approached his holding cell. He had been absent-mindedly stirring some kind of stew on a plastic, partitioned tray with a white, plastic spoon, and thinking about Anna. What was she doing while he was being questioned? What did she think? Did she believe he was guilty of these crimes?

"How's your dinner?" asked the Sergeant, standing across from his cell, her arms folded smugly across her starched, white blouse.

"It's delicious," William smiled, spooning a huge bite into his mouth and hoping he wouldn't gag.

"Get used to it," she commented. "You won't be getting your fancy food in here."

"I thought you liked my fancy food," William said, all politeness. "You certainly drank enough of my tea the other day."

She approached the cell, her black eyes flashing.

"You thought you were smart, didn't you?" she asked. "Sitting in on the interviews? You thought you'd stay one step ahead of us. But the Inspector suspected you from the start. I thought he was crazy at first, letting you sit there all day, but now I know he was baiting you the whole time. Watching you. Waiting for you to slip up. And you did."

"Are you letting me go?" asked William, his smile fading. "Because you haven't actually charged me with a crime."

Sergeant Patel snorted.

"Hardly," she said. "Wouldn't want you endangering someone else, now would we? Wouldn't want you sneaking around in any other secret passages."

A thought occurred to William.

"You know that passage goes all the way to the ground floor, right?" he asked.

"What do you mean?" asked the Sergeant, her eyes narrowing.

"There's a door," he explained. "In the passage at the Tapestry Room level. It closes off the stairs that lead to the Chapel below. If it's closed, it looks like a dead end. A wall."

He watched as Sergeant Patel's mind calculated the truth of what he claimed.

"We got your handprint off the wall in the passage," she said, eyeing him.

"Right in the center, probably," he agreed, "because I would have been pushing on it.   It's really a door.   There's a latch up above it, behind one of the ceiling beams.   There's a room behind the door.   Some kind of old hidey-hole.   And the stairs lead on from that room to the Chapel below."

Sergeant Patel swirled her tongue around her mouth, like the canary she had swallowed had left a bad taste in her mouth.

"We'll check into it," she said as she turned to leave. "Enjoy your dinner."

Anna couldn't steal away by herself until after dinner.   The crew reappeared, loud and boisterous, and ravenously hungry, having missed the afternoon tea that Sheila had provided.   They had been holed up in William's Media Room playing computer games all afternoon, and now they were dominating the Dining Room and the conversation.   She was surprised to see Brian Elliston and Alan Potts with the group, but they seemed to have enjoyed themselves as much as the others.

Another not-unexpected match seemed to have been made during the gaming tournament; Jim and Sarah kept casting sheepish looks at each other across the dinner table.   Anna was glad they were together, although what the assistant director saw in the unkempt, lanky cinematographer, she didn't know.   She could only conclude that there was someone for everyone.

Watching them during dinner, she briefly entertained the idea that one of them, angered by Peter's practical jokes, had done in the actor.   But somehow, that didn't seem plausible.   Would practical jokes be enough of a motive to commit murder?   And how would either of them get the lead ball into the gun?   She dismissed them as suspects in her mind.   At least for the time being.

Sheila's gingerbread made an appearance as dessert.   Anna passed on it, choosing instead a chocolate tart.   Corinne, on the other hand, seemed to really enjoy the heavy dessert.

"It's just like my Mama makes at home," she commented, with a smile Anna hadn't seen on the pretty blonde since Peter's death.

Anna chose the pandemonium that always ensued after dinner to slip away.   It was when groups formed for talking or games, or slipping off to their rooms, and she knew if she could make a quiet exit, she wouldn't be missed for a while.   She slid silently into the Chapel and closed the door behind her.   Upstairs, caution tape cordoned off the Tapestry Room and the Nursery, but around at the piled up boxes and old furniture. "You think this room might be a likely hiding place?"

"It's a place to start," she said with a shrug. "He would have—or she—come back down these stairs, and wouldn't have wanted to carry a wine bottle through the house."

"True," Edwin agreed. "First, let's examine the dust," he said, motioning her to stay still.

"The dust?"

"Yes," he murmured, staring avidly at the floor, then at the piles of odds and ends. "Look for places where the dust has been disturbed."

"Oh! That makes sense," Anna said, joining the search. She stared at the floor in front of the fireplace, then gazed up at the wood-carved mantelpiece.

"Look!" she said. "It's barely hidden!"

Edwin followed her pointing finger to a row of old bottles in the far corner of the mantel. Tucked in behind the dust-covered glass was a new, un-dusty, bottle of wine.

"Well, what do you know," he said, grinning at Anna. "Not very inventive, our murderer."

"Probably in a hurry," Anna said. "He looked for the quickest spot, figuring no one would look in this room. At least not right away."

"Now we definitely have to call the Inspector," Edwin said, rubbing his chin. "We'd better leave the bottle where it is. Not touch it. Although, my guess is it's been wiped clean. Same with the latch on this end of the secret passage."

"So it doesn't really help William at all," said Anna, disheartened. "It doesn't give us another suspect."

"Perhaps not," Edwin agreed. He put his hands on her shoulders and looked intently into her eyes. "Listen to me, Anna," he said somberly. "I know you don't know me very well, and I seem like an odd kind of—I don't know—detective, but I promise you, I will do everything in my power to find this killer. It seems like a strange thing to ask of you," he said with a sideways smile, "but I'm asking you to trust this actor who plays a detective on TV. I'm asking you to trust me to keep an innocent man from being charged with a crime he didn't commit. Can you do that?"

Anna took a deep breath. Somewhere in the depths of his crystal-blue eyes, she saw truth. And justice. And besides that, he was all she had to trust.

since the police didn't know about the second entrance into the secret passage, the Chapel was free from restraints.

It didn't occur to her that the light in the Chapel was already on until a curly head popped up from where it had been bending down near the fireplace.

"Oh, Hello," said Edwin, giving her an embarrassed grin. "Looks like we had the same idea."

"What idea is that?" asked Anna, recovering from her near-heart attack.

"To examine the other end of the secret passage," said Edwin, pointing at the floor. "I suppose we'll need to tell the police about this," he added. "But maybe not yet." He grinned. "Gives us a little uncaution-taped time."

Anna nodded.

"You can clearly see the door has been opened recently," Edwin added.

"See the semi-circle path in the dust?"

"Yes," she replied. "I remembered it from when William brought me in here a few days ago. I didn't think anything of it at the time, but that's what I remembered when we were talking about the secret passage today. This room is rarely used, so if no one had been using that door in the fireplace, the dust wouldn't be disturbed."

"Exactly," Edwin agreed, frowning at the pattern in the floor.

"Why did William bring you in here?" he asked.

"For privacy," she admitted. "It was during the interviews, and I think he was wanting to fill me in, but the Inspector arrived back from lunch before he could say much."

Edwin nodded, seemingly satisfied.

"I actually came here for something else," Anna admitted. "Sheila the cook just told me that Mr. Barnaby noticed a missing wine bottle in his Butler's Pantry. And a wine glass."

"Someone stole a bottle of wine?"

"Apparently. Which makes sense, because how else would Jaime have had a glass? Mr. Barnaby didn't bring it to her, and no one has left the house. Except for me and William, and we didn't buy any wine."

"And it was after Jaime's death, anyway."

"Oh. Yeah, right. So, I was thinking, if they didn't find a bottle of wine in Jaime's room, it has to be somewhere else."

"Yes," said Edwin, thoughtfully. "The murderer's not likely to hide it in his or her bedroom. And the police searched all our rooms, anyway." He glanced

He was her last hope.

"Yes," she said with a brief nod. "Yes, I trust you."

"But I don't," said Sergeant Patel from the Chapel door.

CHAPTER SIXTY-SIX

Anna was thankful to finally be in her bed. After she and Edwin explained their reasons for being in the Chapel, pointing out the wine bottle they'd found, Sergeant Patel and her forensics team went to work, searching for physical evidence, like fingerprints and DNA. They explored that end of the secret passage, as well. The Sergeant was angry with them for investigating on their own instead of calling the Surrey police. Everyone was questioned again; Anna felt the accusing eyes of the cast and crew as each one went through yet another round of interviews.

"At least this one was relatively short," she consoled herself. It mainly consisted of "do you know anything about this wine bottle?" and "have you ever been in the Chapel?" Of course, she was one of the only ones who had to truthfully answer yes to the last question, which made her feel like a suspect all over again. Especially when Sergeant Patel kept looking at her as if she'd been found out. Anna had felt the Sergeant's unspoken suspicion, and noticed how she evaded every question Anna asked about William.

Maybe the police think I'm his accomplice, she thought.

That started her mind racing. The whole time, she'd been thinking of Peter's death as single-handed, the act of one man. Or woman. But what if it wasn't? What if more than one person was involved? Like Sarah and Jim, for instance, although she still didn't find them likely suspects. But what about Corinne and Perry? Could they have planned Peter's death together?

No, she said to her brain. She had to stop thinking of her friends as murderers. It couldn't be healthy. Instead, she said a prayer for William, still sitting in a cell somewhere, and for Edwin, whose mind, she hoped, was still working to solve the crimes, even if hers wasn't.

Just as she was drifting off to sleep, she remembered the journal William had found. They'd never had a chance to look through it, since William was hauled off for questioning as soon as they returned from Windsor. She made a mental note to look for it the next day. Maybe there was a clue in the journal. Maybe it explained everything. She shrugged the day off her mind as she settled into her lacy sheets. There would be time for solving the murders in the morning.

"Miss! Miss! My lady!"

Lady Anna groaned, pulling the sheets over her head. Someone was shaking her, and she didn't appreciate it. And the voice wasn't Newberry's.

"My lady! Please wake up! Not you, too!"

There was a sudden burst of light into the room as someone rudely pulled the curtains back on the breaking day.

Lady Anna growled and opened her eyes, focusing them sleepily on a familiar face.

"Perry?"

Finally, she thought. It's about time he appeared. And as some kind of man servant, based on his outfit. Is he a butler?

"Lady Anna! Thank God you're all right!" said Adrian Reed from the window. "Prince and I were concerned."

Lady Anna scowled at him as the culprit behind the curtains being opened. Adrian is the butler, she remembered. Reed, I suppose he's called. So Perry must be something lower. Maybe a footman? Valet? Prince is his last name. How odd that must be in the servants' quarters, to have a Prince as a footman?

"You must come, Lady Anna!" Prince said urgently, ending her speculations.

"We mustn't ask that of her," said Reed, joining him at her bedside.

"Why? What's happened?" Lady Anna asked, realizing by the men's faces that something serious had occurred. Perry's was tear-streaked, though he was clearly attempting to keep himself stoic for her sake, and for his job.

"It's Corinne," he blurted out. "Newberry," he corrected, receiving a look of reproof from Reed. "She won't wake up."

Lady Anna threw off her sheets and stuffed her feet into her slippers.

"Where is she?" she asked as she grabbed her robe.

Prince and Reed led her to the third floor where the servants lived.

"She didn't get up at her normal time to do her duties, milady," said Prince as they hurried through the halls. "And when Vogel went to see what was keeping her, she couldn't wake her."

"Where's Vogel now?" asked Lady Anna. "Why didn't she come to me instead of you?"

Reed and Prince exchanged a glance.

"Vogel is indisposed, my lady," said Reed. "She found the experience too taxing for her nerves, and is lying down in her room."

They reached Newberry's tiny bedroom, and Lady Anna rushed to her side. The maid was in bed, her sleeping cap on her head. There was a glass of water on the bedside table and a bottle of laudanum beside it, half full.

"Newberry!" Lady Anna cried, shaking the woman. "Newberry, wake up!" There was no response. She desperately felt for a pulse in her lifeless wrist, and leaned down to her blue lips hoping to feel a breath. "Corinne!" she called. "Please, Corinne, wake up! Wake up!"

She turned to the men behind her.

"Call the doctor!" she ordered, and Reed scurried away, but even as he did, she knew it was too late.

She stared helplessly down at the beautiful face, so peaceful in sleep. Forever sleep.

"Oh, Corinne!" she moaned softly. "Why? Why did you do it?"

Behind her, she heard Prince cry out mournfully and fall to his knees.

"No!"

Anna sat straight up in bed. Her scream echoed in her mind, and she had the distinct feeling that it had echoed through Hampstead Hall, as well.

"No!" she said again, quieter now. Her breathing came in gulps and her heart raced.

It was a dream, she told herself. A dream.

But a dream of death. Corinne's death.

She threw off the sheets, pulled on her robe and stuffed her feet in slippers. It may have only been a dream, she told herself. But what if it wasn't? What if Corinne was really dead? She had to check on her.

When she opened the door of her bedroom and ran out into the hall, she saw Jake standing in his bedroom doorway, his hand pulling through his bed-tousled hair.

"What's going on?" he asked her sleepily. "I heard you scream."

"It's Corinne," Anna said, rushing to her friend's door which was between hers and Jake's.

"What about her?" he asked sharply.

"I had a dream that she was—I just want to check on her. It's probably nothing."

She knocked on Corinne's door. Jake joined her, eyeing her suspiciously.

"She's not answering!" Anna said.

"She's probably just asleep," Jake assured her. "Knock louder."

Anna did.

"Corinne?" she called, her mouth close to the door. "It's me, Anna."

There was still no response. Jake glanced uneasily at Anna.

"Corinne!" he called out loudly. His fist on the door reverberated through the hall. Anna could hear others stirring in their rooms, disturbed by the noise.

"I'll get Mr. Barnaby!" said Jake calmly, but beads of sweat appeared on his forehead. Anna could tell he was just as concerned as she was. And this was the second time he'd had to get Mr. Barnaby to open a door. Anna put her hands on her head, as if keeping it from exploding.

Hurry, Jake, her mind pleaded.

As Jake raced off to the west wing, faces began appearing at bedroom doors.

"What's going on?" Jim demanded irritably, pushing an eye mask up on his forehead. He had come from around the corner where there was another hallway of bedrooms.

"I can't get Corinne to open her door," Anna gulped.

"Maybe she doesn't want to open her door," Jim suggested with a leer. "Maybe Perry's in there."

There was a clatter on the stairs, and Perry appeared hurriedly in the hall.

"What's all the racket?" he asked, looking intently at Anna as his most reliable source. "I heard you calling Corinne's name. Has something happened?"

Anna could see his face was pale as he came down the hall toward her. She remembered the scene in her dream, and her heart sank.

"I can't get Corinne to answer her door," she whispered. Her throat didn't seem to work anymore.

"No," Perry muttered, adding his fist to the pounding on the door. "Corinne!" he shouted, then he grabbed the doorknob. "It's not locked!" he cried, pushing the door open and flipping on the light switch.

Why hadn't she thought of checking the door? Anna wondered. How much precious time had been wasted waiting for the key to an unlocked door?

Corinne lay serenely in her bed, like a sleeping beauty. Anna grabbed the doorframe for support. It was exactly how Corinne had looked in her dream, minus the nightcap. She'd looked down at a sleeping beauty. A dead beauty.

"She's still alive!" shouted Perry from the bedside. "Get help! Get a doctor! Call 999!"

"I'm on it," said Jim, pulling off his eye mask, all serious now. He moved out into the hall to make the call.

Anna breathed, then realized she hadn't been breathing before. She felt herself floating; little black specks were crowding out her vision.

"Don't faint."

Edwin Sterling held her up by the shoulders.

"I need you not to faint," he said, coming around in front of her and looking into her eyes, holding her gaze until the room stopped being hazy. "You've had a shock."

Anna gulped a few breaths, then slowed her breathing, staring into Edwin's eyes as she forced herself to be calm.

When she nodded that she was all right, he turned from her and took a quick assessment of the room.

"Don't touch anything, Perry," he warned calmly. Perry nodded. He was sitting on Corinne's bed, rubbing her hair back from her face and holding her unresponsive hands in his.   Every now and then, he quietly called her name, asking her not to leave him. He looked like agony itself.

Jake appeared suddenly in the doorway with Mr. Barnaby, who was wearing a shiny, black robe over steel-grey pajamas.

Even in a crisis, he's perfectly dressed, thought Anna.

"I need everyone to stay out of here," Edwin ordered. "Corinne is sick and we've called 999."

Mr. Barnaby gave the actor a quick nod, and turned to the others who had gathered in the hall, assuring them that everything was under control.

"I'll alert the police guard," he told Edwin.

Jake's anxious face peeked through the doorway.

"You, too, Jake," Edwin said. "At least for now."

Jake nodded.

Edwin closed the door and turned to Anna.

"Listen to me," he said, speaking low. "We need to take in every detail before the police arrive and tape this off."

He was businesslike, matter-of-fact. How could he detach himself when a woman lay lifeless in front of him?

"Anna," he said again, quietly in her ear. "Help me. Help Corinne." Anna nodded at him dumbly. "What do you see?" he asked.

Help him. Help Corinne.

Anna narrowed in on the bedside table.

"Pills and empty capsule casings on the bedside table," she said.

"And?"

"And a glass of water."

"Good. What else?" He waved his hand around the room.

"The fire is still going strong," she said, "even though it's late. Usually I let mine die down at night."

"Yes. Interesting. Maybe she hasn't been in bed long. What else?"

Anna stepped closer to the fireplace where, like her room, a couple of chairs stood with a small table in between.

"There's a plate on this table," she said. "And a fork. It looks like gingerbread. She didn't finish it all."

Anna puzzled over that. Gingerbread was served as dessert, but she knew Corinne had eaten hers. How did she get another slice? Had she asked for one from Sheila?

Edwin leaned into her ear once again.

"And the door wasn't locked," he whispered.

The door swung open suddenly, and the officer on duty rushed in. A clattering in the Great Hall downstairs told them the paramedics weren't far behind.

"We need to clear the area," the officer shouted to Edwin and Anna. They obediently exited the room, joining the others in the hall. As the officer began CPR, Perry hovered behind him, his arms folded protectively over his chest. Anna wondered if it was to keep his heart from exploding.

CHAPTER SIXTY-SEVEN

———◆•◆———

Anna awoke, hours later, huddled on the sofa in the Drawing Room. Someone had covered her with a blanket, and she could hear muffled voices nearby. She yawned, rubbing her eyes, and sat up, blinking at the pinkish-grey dawn stealing in through the French doors.

"There she is," said Sheila as she entered carrying a tray of tea. She was wearing a flowered robe and slippers.

"What time is it?" Anna asked sleepily.

"Just after seven," Sheila said. "I need to go get changed, I suppose. Been up since the police got here. Some people never went to bed."

She nodded her head to the corner, where Edwin Sterling and his mother sat, deep in conversation. They were both still wearing their nightclothes, but somehow still carried themselves like royalty. The only thing that seemed out of place was the state of Edwin's hair.

"Is there any news about Corinne?" asked Anna, afraid of the answer.

Sheila shook her head.

"All we know is she was alive when they left here with her," she said solemnly, "and barely that."

Anna nodded. She remembered Perry had insisted on going with Corinne in the ambulance, and she was glad. Corinne needed someone to be there for her when she woke up.

Or if she didn't.

"I'll be getting breakfast out, shortly," said Sheila. "And then I'll be taking a nice long nap!"

As Sheila bustled off, Anna poured herself a cup of tea, trying to remember all of the details of last night. The Inspector had come. And the Sergeant. And their team. Everyone was roused from their beds, even those who hadn't already been awakened by the commotion. The interrogations went on for hours, and the police searched the bedrooms and the house. The Inspector wanted to make sure everyone was accounted for, he had said. Anna wondered if he wanted to make sure everyone was still alive.

She remembered that Miranda had a fainting attack and insisted on having a second ambulance called to take her to the hospital for shock. So now three cast members were at the hospital. And one was presumably still at the Surrey police station in a holding cell. Who was left?

She glanced to her left and found Jake asleep in a chair, his feet on an otto-man. He was snuggled under a blanket, with only his closed eyes and tousled blond hair showing. Anna sighed. He was a handsome man, she admitted. And his actions lately had caused her to wonder if she'd been wrong about him. Maybe he did care about her. Maybe she had misread the look in his eyes that seemed so vacant of love. She could feel compassion welling up inside of her. Jake had lost two friends, and here was a third member of *Cavendish Manor* whose life was in jeopardy, possibly already gone. It was a lot to handle. The fact that he was also sleeping in the Drawing Room probably meant he was just as nervous about sleeping in his own room as she had been.

"Anna," Portia called softly to her from across the room, then motioned her over.

Anna joined her and Edwin, seating herself in a nearby chair and wrapping her robe around herself.

"How are you doing?" asked Portia in a motherly tone. "It was a long night for you."

"It was a long night for everyone," Anna agreed. "And I'm okay, I guess. I'm anxious to hear how Corinne is doing."

"The fact that she was still alive when you found her is a good sign, I hope," Portia said. "It was fortunate you came to her room when you did."

"Why did you go to her room?" asked Edwin.

"I had a dream," Anna admitted. "But in the dream, she died."

Anna explained the details of her dream, while Portia and Edwin leaned in to listen.

"So, when you got to Newberry in your dream, she was already dead?" Edwin clarified.

Anna nodded.

"I guess it's because it was already morning," she said. "More time had gone by since she'd taken the sleeping medicine."

"It was your quick action that probably saved Corinne's life," said Portia. "It looks like your dream this time was a warning. And the fact that she was still alive when you got to her may mean that your dreams aren't just re-enact-ing the past. The outcome can be changed. If you hadn't gone to Corinne's room when you did, if you'd brushed it off until the morning, she would have died. But instead, she's alive. And we hope she stays that way."

"Maybe it would have been better if I hadn't," said Anna tearfully. "The Inspector found the extra oxycodone and valium in the drawer of her bedside table. She must have killed Peter and Jaime, and couldn't stand the guilt anymore. I don't want to see her in prison for life!"

Edwin pressed his lips together, giving a skeptical look.

"You remember what was on the bedside table, right?" he asked.

Anna nodded, her brow furrowed.

"A glass of water and some pills," she said.

"Why were they there?"

"The pills? I guess because she put a bunch on the table and just started taking them. And there were some left over."

"There were also some empty capsules. Why were those on the table?"

Anna eyed him dubiously. Where was he going with his odd questions?

"She must have opened them and put them in the glass. To drink them dissolved rather than take them as pills."

"Why would she do that?" asked Edwin, raising his eyebrows at her.

"I don't know," she answered. "Maybe it was easier to take them that way."

"So she randomly took some of the pills with the water, and some of them dissolved into the water."

"I guess."

"Then why was there still a glass of water?" he asked, smiling at her triumphantly.

Anna stared at him. Had the famous Dr. Hanover gone crazy? Or was he sleep-deprived? She couldn't make any sense out of his questions at all.

"There was no note," he reminded her. "If she killed herself out of guilt for committing murder, wouldn't she have left a note?"

"Maybe we just haven't found it yet," Anna said. "The police took away her computer and her phone. Maybe she left the note on one of those."

Edwin twisted his face around as if considering it.

"Maybe," he said. "Did she say or do anything unusual yesterday?" he asked. "Anything that would indicate she was contemplating suicide, or that she had a guilty conscience?"

"She was wanting to tell me something," Anna remembered. "The night before, when I was coming back from telling William I would go to Windsor, I saw her in the hall, and she said she was up because she had been thinking about things. But we started talking about something else, so she never said what she was thinking about. Then yesterday after tea she said she wanted to ask me about something. Something that didn't make sense about the duel. But Sir Frederick came in, and she stopped. She looked—afraid," Anna said, trying to conjure up Corinne's face. "She said it didn't matter, and kind of ran away."

"So she never told you what it was that puzzled her?" asked Portia.

"No."

"A pity," she said. "It may have saved her life if she had."

"But it may have put Anna's in danger," her son reminded her.

"Hello," said Sir Frederick as he bustled into the room. "Who's in here? Who's up?"

Jake jerked awake and attempted to sit up in his chair.

"Just a few of us, Sir Frederick," said Edwin.

"Oh. Well, I have news from the hospital," said the director. "I called down there, and Corinne is alive, but still in a coma. They don't know if she'll ever come out of it. The nurse told me she should be awake by now, that the medications should have worn off. But then, she also said these things affect people in different ways. Some people are more sensitive to drugs than others. It's still a waiting game."

Anna sighed. It didn't sound good for Corinne.

"How's Perry?" she asked.

"I don't know," said Sir Frederick. "He's still down there, is all I know. And Miranda is kicking up a fuss with the nurses. I won't be surprised if they send her packing as soon as possible. Meanwhile, Jaime Douglas' sister has arrived from Scotland. Julia is meeting her at her hotel to give our condolences."

"Will there be a funeral?" asked Jake huskily. His blanket was protectively wrapped around his shoulders.

"I'm sure Julia will let us know of any arrangements," said Sir Frederick. He frowned. "I suppose Peter will have to have a funeral or something, too. And that takes time away from the show."

Anna closed her eyes at the plump director's insensitivity.

"If there still is a show," Portia reminded him.

"That reminds me," said Anna. "William found that journal you were looking for. We were going to bring it to you the night he was taken in for questioning."

Sir Frederick clapped his hands together.

"Where is it?" he asked.

"I'm not sure," Anna said, wrinkling her brow. "I'll have to ask Mr. Barnaby."

Her head suddenly felt light, and she steadied herself with the arm of the chair.

"But right now, you're going to go upstairs to bed," said Portia. "You're exhausted."

Anna glanced nervously at her. Portia patted her hand.

"Lock your door," she said, leaning forward confidentially. "And don't let anyone in." She held on to Anna's hand in a firm grasp. "No one," she repeated, giving her a stern look.

CHAPTER SIXTY-EIGHT

Safely behind her locked bedroom door, Anna wept.

She wept for Corinne, for William locked up somewhere, for herself, and even for witchy Jaime, whose silvery eyes were closed forever.

Curling up on the bed, Anna clutched the blankets in her fists, pulling them tightly up under her chin as she lay on her side staring emptily at the tree just outside her windows. She hadn't wanted to close the drapes; the light brought comfort. There was too much darkness in her life right now. And too many things that happened under the cover of it.

Her thoughts drifted to Corinne.

Inspector Ferguson had made a big deal about finding little baggies of pills in Corinne's bedside table. Did he believe Corinne was the one who drugged Jaime? Could she have snuck up the secret stairs into Jaime's room with a bottle of wine, pretending to be her friend, and then killed her? And if so, why? Does that mean she also put the lead ball into the gun that killed Peter?

"Actually," Anna thought, "Corinne killing Peter is more believable."

She thought about their dysfunctional relationship, and Peter's jealousy. And Corinne's statements the other night about being afraid of him. Could his attack have pushed Corinne over the edge? Did she feel he had to be stopped?

Maybe all her talk about seeing something that puzzled her was to throw me off, she thought. Maybe she kept coming out from the trees to make sure her plan was in place.

An even more outrageous thought occurred to Anna.

What if Corinne and Jaime were in it together? What if they conspired to kill Peter? Jaime clearly hated him from their previous relationship, and Corinne admitted being afraid of him. Maybe they both wanted him gone, and planned his murder together. Then they had a falling out, or Jaime was going to confess, and Corinne killed Jaime? But the guilt she felt was too much, so she took her own life. Or attempted to. She still might succeed.

Anna covered her face with the blankets. It was too much to think about. She didn't want to speculate on the guilt or innocence of her friends. She just wanted it to all go away.

Lady Anna stared unseeingly out the French doors of the Drawing Room. She was dressed in a long, black gown, with a shawl of black lace around her shoulders that did little to keep at bay the chilly fingers of air that reached toward her from under the doors.

She was lost in her own thoughts until she felt the gentle pressure of warm, masculine hands rubbing down her shoulders and onto her upper arms.

Mr. Langley? she thought, hope surging through her as she turned to face the man who touched her so intimately.

But it was not Mr. Langley. It was Sir John.

She attempted to hide her disappointment, but she wasn't fast enough to fool him.

He bowed his head as he stood beside her, his hands discreetly clasped behind his back.

"I know you hoped it was someone else," he said softly, watching a blackbird pecking fruitlessly at the frozen ground beyond the terrace.

She made a movement as if to correct him, then stopped herself.

"Is there any word?" she asked, gazing up at him. "Have they released him?"

"Not yet," said Sir John. "But even if they do, can you trust him? I don't. Not after three deaths."

"But Mr. Langley couldn't have killed Newberry," Lady Anna insisted. "He wasn't even here."

"Perhaps he didn't kill her himself," he agreed, "but he still could have caused her death. Perhaps they were in it together, and she couldn't handle the guilt," Sir John suggested.

"Newberry and Mr. Langley? But why?"

Sir John shrugged.

"Men are often beguiled by a pretty face," he said, glancing at her, then looking away. "Langley could have loaded a bullet in my gun, and then pretended he only loaded blanks, like I had asked. It was a risk, but he must have been a gambler, like his father."

"How did you know his father was a gambler?"

"Lord Mallory must have mentioned it. I think, unfortunately, I was mistaken in my choice of friends. I believe Lord Mallory did kill Langley's father, and in turn, Langley killed him to revenge his father's death. And also to defend your honor."

He looked pointedly at her, and she glanced away quickly.

"But where would Newberry come into it?" she asked. "And my cousin, Jaime?"

"Either one of them could have been his accomplice. Or they knew something that caused him to fear being found out, so he killed them. When you've killed once, it's easier to do it again. But I must say, Newberry's death seems most like a suicide. The laudanum was there on her bedside table. The same thing that killed Miss Douglas."

Lady Anna sighed deeply and wiped a tear from her cheek. She couldn't help but feel responsible for the death of her maid. It was the real reason she was in mourning. Not for Jaime Douglas. And certainly not for Lord Mallory.

"Lady Anna," said Sir John, turning toward her. "I know I wasn't your first choice, but if Mr. Langley turns out to be—" He paused to compose himself. "If things don't go as you hope, I hope you can consider me a worthy second choice."

His brown eyes pleaded with hers, and she suddenly found that tears were flowing down her cheeks. She took his hand, noticing that it shook with emotion, carefully concealed.

"I've always found you worthy," she said, looking boldly into his eyes.

He took a step toward her.

Reed the butler entered the room, clearing his throat to announce his presence. Lady Anna stepped back, dropping Sir John's hand and turning her attention back to the wintry scene outside. Reed busied himself clearing tea cups and straightening pillows.

"We're always watched," murmured Sir John.

"Yes," she agreed. "And I wish I knew who to trust and who to fear."

"My dear, there you are," said Lord Somerville, entering the room and waving his glasses in the air. "I've been looking for you."

There was a crash as Lord Somerville blindly walked into a small table.

"Oh, dear!" he muttered. "Reed? Who put this table here?"

Reed maintained a pleasant, high-eyebrow expression as he returned the table to its upright position.

"Anna, my dear. Are you in there? I've been looking for you."

It was Sir Frederick's voice on the other side of her bedroom door. He knocked again.

Anna awoke from her dream to find tears on her cheeks. She wiped them away quickly as she went to the door.

She paused, her fingers on the lock.

Portia had told her not to let anyone in.

"No one," she had adamantly insisted.

Anna took a deep breath and opened the door.

"Sir Frederick?" said Anna as she exited her room. The director took a surprised step backward as she came out into the hall.

"Oh," he said, then recovered himself. "Yes. I was going to go in, but you came out. I was looking for you. I had Mr. Barnaby get the journal from William's room. I thought we could look at it together."

"Yes, I'd like that," she agreed. "We should join the others. Are they still in the Drawing Room?"

"Oh," said Sir Frederick vaguely. "Probably. That's where they always seem to be anymore."

Anna heard a text message ding on her phone that was still on her bedside table.

Probably my Mom, she thought. Portia's warning about not letting anyone in echoed in her ears. Better to leave the phone, she decided, than come back in the room and allow Sir Frederick to follow her in.

The director begrudgingly followed Anna down the stairs and into the Drawing Room. Glancing at the grandfather clock in the hall, Anna realized it was nearly tea time, and she'd slept through lunch. Her stomach growled, letting her know its displeasure.

The Drawing Room was full, in expectation of a mid-afternoon snack. The crew, as well as the remaining cast members, was there waiting. Edwin stood conversing with Julia, obviously returned from discussing funeral arrangements with Jaime's sister. She wondered, for a brief moment, if Jaime's death would fall under workman's comp, and if Julia's real reason for meeting with the sister was to keep her from filing a costly claim on the Studio.

She shook her head. Not everyone had mercenary motivations.

Did they?

Glancing in the Dining Room, Anna saw that Mr. Barnaby was assisting Sheila to set up the food and drinks. Most of the crew, including Sarah and Jim, were standing near the doors, ready to be the first in line. Instead of boisterous talking, everyone spoke in hushed tones, like a funeral. Anna could only hope there wouldn't be a third funeral that had to be planned. But then, would that mean Corinne would spend the rest of her life behind bars?

Brian Elliston caught her eye; he gave her a nod and a look of sympathy. She smiled back her appreciation.

I must be a topic of conversation, she realized. For finding Corinne. Then a thought struck her.

"Is there any news from the hospital?" she asked. She had slept so long, Corinne could have died, and she would be the last to know.

"Nothing new," said Edwin, looking up from his conversation with Julia. "How are you?"

He moved closer and lowered his voice.

"Anything new to report?" he asked. "Any dreams?"

"Yes," she said, "but I don't know how helpful it was. I'm not sure it revealed anything new. Before I fell asleep, I was speculating about Corinne," she admitted, glancing around her to make sure no one was listening. "About motives, or possible accomplices. I wondered if she and Jaime planned Peter's murder together."

"Together?" asked Edwin, surprised.

"Yes," she said. "I realized I'd been looking at this as one possible murderer. But what if it was two? What if they both wanted him dead, and they planned it together? Then something went wrong, and Corinne felt she had to kill Jaime. When the guilt was too much, she tried to kill herself."

Anna stopped speaking, realizing Edwin was staring into space. She wasn't sure he'd even heard the last part of her theory.

"An accomplice," he repeated in a whisper, his eyes wide. Suddenly, they focused again, and he looked at her with a look of excitement.

"Thank you, Anna," he said, grabbing her face and kissing her dramatically on the forehead. "You may have just solved the case."

Anna staggered, gingerly touching her forehead where she could still feel the imprint of his lips.

She watched as Edwin ran out of the Drawing Room doors; Anna could hear his footsteps mounting the stairs.

"What was that all about?" asked Jake, his lips twisted sardonically.

"Edwin Sterling kissed me," she breathed.

Jake stared jealously at the door Edwin had run through.

"Anna!" Sir Frederick called. "Let's look at this journal."

Anna shook off her fanaticism and moved closer to the director. He had settled himself on a sofa. Portia, who had been watching the proceedings, walked over and sat down.

"What's this?" she asked.

"Sir Frederick has the journal he was looking for," Anna explained. "The one with the story on which he based *Cavendish Manor*."

"Oh? That's interesting," said Jake, joining them and standing behind Sir Frederick. "I didn't know it was based on a true story."

"Well, I don't know how true it is," Sir Frederick commented. "Sometimes people like to enhance their own history. But it is written down. I was hoping to find it again. Especially now that I'll need to rewrite a few things. Can't very well continue as we intended, now that—well…"

He mumbled off, and Anna shook her head. Sir Frederick seemed so unfazed by the deaths. Annoyed, but unfazed. Like they were setbacks to the success of the show, not lives lost.

"It's in here somewhere," muttered Sir Frederick, flipping through the yellowed pages.

"I don't know how you expect to resurrect this show," said Julia haughtily. "It's not only a heartless proposition, it's impossible from a storyline perspective. Or a budget perspective."

Sir Frederick looked up, blinking behind his glasses.

"No, not really," he said. "Not impossible. I'll just have to kill off Lord Netherington in the duel after all. He died in the real story."

"He did?" asked Anna.

"Oh, yes, my dear," said Sir Frederick, smiling. "But I didn't want to kill off one of my main characters so soon in the series. I was going to wait and kill him off later. Make a real splash. But even with all the setbacks, my most important character is still alive and well."

He beamed across at Anna.

"Who do you mean?" she asked, puzzled.

"Why, you, of course," said the director. "Daphne Thomson is the real star of the show."

"She is?" asked Anna, shocked. "The poor relation?"

"Oh, yes. She's the actual villain."

"What?"

"That's why I chose you," he continued, flapping a plump hand. "You're the strongest actress, by far. Of the younger generation, of course," he said, patting Portia's arm. "With all of the behind-the-scenes manipulation that Miss Thomson would be doing, I knew you could pull it off. A regular Lady Mac—well, you know. The Scottish woman."

"Tea is served."

Mr. Barnaby, doing his best butler impression, stood at the Dining Room doors. He nodded at each person who entered, and even endured the good-natured punch on the shoulder from Jim, with only a hint of irritation showing on his impassive face.

Sir Frederick leaped to his feet, clearly feeling tea took precedence over adjusting his script.

Anna stood still as the cast and crew headed toward the Dining Room, like a stone standing alone in the middle of a stream. Sir Frederick's revelation had shocked her. She was the bad guy? She needed to get away to think about it. Something was nagging at the back of her mind, and she felt it was important. When no one was looking, she stole silently out of the French doors and into the darkening afternoon.

CHAPTER SIXTY-NINE

As her feet crunched on the frozen pea gravel, Anna's thoughts raced. She regretted not stealing the journal while everyone was occupied. Then she could have read the true account for herself.

Maybe not in this light, she realized, looking up. The sun, never bright in winter, was already sliding behind Hampstead Hall.

What was it about Sir Frederick's revelation that disturbed her so much? She didn't mind being the villain. She could already tell that her character, Daphne Thomson, was devious and manipulative. No, it wasn't the role that bothered her. It was the implication. Because it was all connected. One and the same, like William had said, so long ago now, about her dreams. If Daphne Thomson was the villain in *Cavendish Manor*, and if Sir Frederick had gotten the story from real life, that's why the show and her dreams were so similar. Her dreams were re-enacting actual events that took place at Hampstead Hall. So if her character was the villain, that meant—what did it mean?

She wandered aimlessly over the Japanese bridge and down the path toward the lake. As the darkness increased, so did the fog that rolled up from the lake and the nearby river. It was already creeping toward her, forming a cloud-wall that blocked the path. Somewhere in the distance a fox cried out, like a banshee.

Anna glanced to the side. Seeing a bench in one of the garden rooms, she headed off the main path and into the more secluded space that was currently clear of the haze.

A footstep behind her caused Anna to whirl around.

"It's just me," said Jake sheepishly, waving his fingers at her.

Anna visibly relaxed.

"I saw you leave, and I didn't want you to be alone out here," he said. He shivered, and wrapped his arms around himself. "Aren't you cold?"

Anna sighed. She had been so determined to get away, she'd forgotten she was coatless. She hadn't noticed the chilly temperature until Jake mentioned it.

"Just a little," she admitted. "I needed to get away to think."

He nodded.

"I was as surprised as you to find out Sir F made you the villain," he said.

"Did that bother you? I thought it was a compliment."

She smiled.

"Yes, I think it is a compliment," she agreed. "But that's not what bothered me. There's something I'm missing, something about Daphne Thomson being the villain that means something. But I can't seem to put my finger on it, yet. I wish William was here to help me think it through."

A twist of emotion crossed Jake's handsome features. Anna could see his jealousy, even in the fading light.

"I'm sorry," she said. "I didn't mean—he just always helped me figure things out that puzzled me."

"Speaking of puzzling," said Jake. "Did Corinne ever tell you what she was concerned about? She seemed like she wanted to talk to you last night."

"No," said Anna. "When Sir Frederick walked up, she stopped talking, and she never told me. I have to think it was important, especially since she either tried to commit suicide, or someone tried to kill her."

"Here's my theory," said Jake, sitting down on the stone bench in front of her. "I think she and William killed Peter together. They both thought he deserved it. And I've been wondering if there wasn't something between the two of them."

"William and Corinne?" asked Anna, her stomach twisting. "What makes you say that?"

"I saw them talking together a few times. Didn't you?"

An unbidden image passed through her mind of William and Corinne in the courtyard. She was laughing and touching his arm, and he smiled down at her. And covert eye-signals at the dinner table. Had there been something between them? Something they kept secret?

"And after they killed him," Jake continued, "Jaime either saw something or knew something, and they found out about it and thought she was a threat. I don't know which one of them did it. Probably William, since he was already in the Tapestry Room and could easily access the secret passage. They used what was readily available: Miranda's stash of pills. Or maybe Corinne had her own. She isn't exactly the most stable person I've ever seen. She and Peter were drinking almost every night. Maybe she already had those pills. And when William was taken in for questioning, she was afraid he would give her up. There's no death penalty in England. She tried to kill herself rather than face a life in jail."

Anna stared at the ground. Her thoughts swirled and floated, dipped and disappeared into the murkiness of her mind, like the fog that had made its way up the path and was pouring like a slow waterfall over the tall yew hedges.

Smoke and mirrors.

The phrase that Portia Valentine had said. Smoke and mirrors. Like a magic trick. Or an illusion.

Anna frowned.

"What makes me the angriest about all of it," Jake continued, cutting through the fog of Anna's thoughts, "is the fact that William used me."

"What do you mean?" she asked, focusing on him again.

"I was his weapon," he explained, pulling his hand through his hair in his familiar gesture. "He used me to kill Peter. He was the one who put the lead ball in the gun, but he had me pull the trigger. He made me kill my own best friend! What kind of person would do that?"

Anna closed her eyes. She thought about Jake's gesture of pulling his hand through his hair. He did it often, and it meant something. Something subconscious. Like Edwin pulling his curls straight up when he was thinking.

"I'm surprised he took that kind of a risk," she said, stalling for time, waiting for her thoughts to solidify.

"Anyone could have seen him," Jake agreed.

"Well, yes," said Anna, "but I meant that the lead ball wasn't packed into the gun like a real bullet would have been. He had to move fast, and push it in the barrel without any wadding to keep it secure. It's a good thing you held your gun pointing at the sky, or it would have rolled out. I remember Peter had his pointed at the ground until it was time to fire."

Jake was silent. Anna could see his face appearing and disappearing as the fog swirled past his head.

And then she knew. She knew what Jake's gesture meant. And she knew what Corinne had seen.

"Ah, beautiful Anna," Jake said finally. "I wish you hadn't said that."

CHAPTER SEVENTY

William waved to his mother as she drove away, back to her cottage at the front gates. All he wanted was to take a shower and change, but his first thoughts were of Anna. He had texted her as soon as he was released, but she hadn't answered. Then he'd called and left a message. It was strange to have no response from her. Surely she didn't actually suspect him? He had to find her and make sure.

He hadn't been given a reason for his release. He assumed it was because they didn't have enough evidence to keep him. Either way, he was glad to be a free man again. At least for the present.

As he entered the Great Hall, he could hear talking in the direction of the Drawing Room. It was tea time, he realized, and he was looking forward to a good cup and something decent to eat. The meals he had been served the past few days sat like a rock in his gut.

He hesitated in the hall, listening. Sir Frederick was talking, and it sounded like he was proposing changes for the script. William rolled his eyes. Didn't the director have any sense of decency? Two members of his team dead, and all he can think about is his precious show?

William stepped cautiously into the room. At first no one noticed him. All attention was on Sir Frederick and his script. Then Portia Valentine, who was seated near the door, looked up and saw him. Her face lit up with a smile, and she immediately rose to greet him.

"William," she said, quietly, giving him a much-needed hug. "I'm so glad to see you home."

"Thank you," he said.

"Have you heard about Corinne?" she asked with a serious expression. "She's been drugged. She's at the hospital now. They aren't sure she'll make it."

"No! They didn't tell me," he said, shocked. "Maybe that's why they released me. I couldn't very well drug someone from a holding cell."

"William, my boy!" Sir Frederick called out. "They've let you go?"

"Yes," said William, moving closer to the group, searching for Anna's face in the crowd.

"You're just in time," said the director. "I need your help as my assistant.

We're trying to come up with a solution to the script rewrite."

"Don't listen to him, William," said Julia snidely. "I haven't approved the continuation of this project yet."

"Julia, I told you, it's very simple," Sir Frederick pleaded. "If we kill off Lord Netherington in the duel, then we can just go with the real story, the one that's in the journal."

"What was the real story?" asked Sarah.

"I should have gone with it in the first place, but I didn't want to kill off a main character that early. Plus, I was trying to be respectful of the family. Wasn't sure William would want his dark family history on national television."

William furrowed his brow.

My dark family history?

"What history are you referring to?" he asked.

"The murders, of course. Back in the eighteen-hundreds. They wrote it all down here," he said, indicating the journal. "I was going to include the murders, just mix it up a bit. Make it slightly different from the real story."

Edwin strode into the room.

"Ah! William! I was told you were on the way," he said. "Is the Inspector with you?"

"No," said William. "My mother drove me home."

"Instead of killing Lord Netherington," Sir Frederick continued, as if there hadn't been an interruption, "I injured Jake's character, Lord Waverly, in the duel. Had Lady Margaret fawn all over him, to heighten the drama with Lord Netherington. Jealousy between the best friends, and all that. Then in Episode Five, I was going to have the two of them kill Lord Netherington with poison or something."

"The two of them?" asked William. "Who do you mean? Lord Waverly and Lady Margaret?"

"Oh, no. Not Lady Margaret. Lord Waverly and Daphne Thomson, of course. Just like the real story."

"The best friend and the poor relation?" asked Adrian, his eyebrows raised.

"Yes," said Sir Frederick, thrilled by the undivided attention. "I was going to have a sensational murder to end Season One, hoping that people would want to know 'who dunnit' and we would get a Season Two."

"Oh, Lord, Freddie," said Julia, rolling her eyes.

"Where's Jake?" asked Edwin, glancing anxiously around the room.

"Then I could have Lord Waverly kill off Daphne Thomson sometime in Season Two," Sir Frederick continued. "Keep people guessing."

"So in the actual, historical events," Julia clarified, "a man killed his best friend, then killed off his accomplice, who was also his lover?"

"Yes," said Sir Frederick. "She was the real mastermind. She had her first lover kill off her second lover, his best friend, and all in hopes of one of them inheriting the estate and marrying her. Both men were in line for it, so when the first one spurned her, she went after the next, and convinced him to kill off his friend. But afterward, he felt so guilty, he turned against her and killed off his Lady Macbeth. Don't think she expected that. Oops! I've said the name! Does it count if it's the female?"

William stood staring at the director. Pieces of the puzzle were beginning to fly together into a completed picture. He felt if he waited long enough, the final piece would click into place.

Edwin grabbed William's arm.

"What Sir Frederick is saying is that, in *Cavendish Manor*, it was Jake's and Anna's characters, Lord Waverly and Daphne Thomson, who murdered Peter's character. That means, in Anna's dreams it would have been Sir John and the poor relation, Jaime."

Jaime. Something was connecting in William's mind.

"If Jaime is dead in the present-day," he said, turning to stare at Edwin, "that means she must have been the mastermind. The one killed by her lover."

Edwin nodded, his grip tightening on William's arm.

"Which makes the murderer—" Edwin prompted.

"Where's Anna?" William cried out.

"Dear, beautiful Anna," said Jake, rising from the bench and moving slowly toward her.

Anna backed away, staring incredulously at the man in front of her. Handsome, like a movie star, with a smile that dazzled.

"You put the lead ball in the gun," she said. "You did it. When Jaime dropped the bullets, and everyone looked, you slipped it in the barrel."

Jake was smiling at her, a mirthless grin swirling in and out of the fog.

"You thought no one saw, because we were all looking at Jaime," Anna continued. "But Corinne saw. She stepped out of the trees and saw you do it. But she didn't know what she saw. Not at first."

"She was supposed to stay behind the trees," said Jake, still moving toward her. "Why didn't she just stay behind the trees, like she was supposed to? She'd still be alive."

Anna felt branches brush against her back and arms, sharp twigs poking into her skin. She had backed into the yew hedge wall. She could go no further.

"If Jaime was your accomplice, why did you kill her?" asked Anna, stalling for time.

Jake stopped in front of her. He reached out his hand and brushed her cheek with the edge of his fingers. Cold fingers. Deadly fingers.

"She made me do it," he said simply. "She made me kill my best friend. He was better than a thousand of her, that manipulating witch!"

His mouth curled in a snarl, the darkness causing his usually soft brown eyes to look black and soul-less.

"And I do mean witch," he said with a sharp laugh. "Always looking at me with those evil eyes, like she could see through me. Like she could control me. But she couldn't. Not in the end."

"She made you kill Peter?" asked Anna, urging him to talk. Maybe she could distract him. She could feel that her life depended on it. "How did she do that?"

"We made a deal together, the three of us," he explained. "They were no longer lovers, and Pete said he didn't care if I had her. The three of us were going to buy Hampstead Hall. Pete said he could get William to sell it for cheap. He'd already killed William's father. She made him do it."

He wiped his face with both hands. Anna noticed he was sweating, despite the cold air around them.

"Jaime made Peter kill Lord Somerville?" she asked.

"Yeah," he said. "Pete said that when Lord Somerville died, he would leave William in so much debt, he'd be ready to sell to get out from under it. He said the old Earl wouldn't last much longer, as much as he drank. But Jaime got impatient. She wanted him dead sooner. So Pete gave him an overdose of sleeping pills."

"Just like William thought," said Anna.

Jake shrugged.

"He was an old man. An old drunk, half-dead already. But when William started paying off his father's debts, and Sir Frederick decided to film here,

Jaime told Pete she wanted him to kill William. But Pete said no. For all his faults, he didn't like death on his conscience. I think that's why he started drinking more. So we decided to sabotage the show, instead. Little accidents, so the show would fail, and William wouldn't be able to pay his debts. Then he'd be desperate."

"You knew who William was, then?" Anna clarified. "You knew he wasn't Sir Frederick's assistant."

Jake grinned.

"We just played along," he admitted. "We knew he couldn't keep it up forever."

"But why, Jake?" Anna asked. "Why was getting Hampstead Hall so important? It's just a house."

"You have no idea!" he yelled, leaning close to her face. Then he calmed himself, pulling back. "You have no idea what it's like to be poor," he said, smiling at her. "To scrape by, to be made fun of for your clothes. I deserve better. When people started thinking I was a *Rawlings Furniture* Rawlings, it was like coming home. That was who I should be. Who I deserved to be. When I met Pete, the Viscount, I knew he could make me rich. We made this fake company and started buying property, claiming it was for charity, hiding some of the money. But he was going to double-cross us." His face crumpled, and Anna thought he would burst into tears, but he smoothed out the lines again.

"Peter double-crossed you?" she asked.

"Jaime heard Pete and William talking in the Tapestry Room," he explained. "He was trying to make a deal with William without us. Without us! Jaime said Pete had to go, that I needed to get rid of him. She said I could take his place, do what he does. Better than he could, she said. People trust me. They believe me. I told her no, at first. Kill my best friend? Take his place? I tried talking to him, but he just laughed it off. And then he attacked you. He would have raped you, if I hadn't stopped him. Jaime said that should prove it—he had to go. So I made him go."

"That's understandable," said Anna, pressing herself against the yew hedge. "Anyone would do what you did."

"Would they, Anna?" he sneered. "Would anyone kill their best friend? No, that witch made me do it. And when I cried over him, she called me weak. She laughed in my face. You saw us, after we had a fight. Right here," he said, gazing around. "I might have killed her then, but there you were, on the path, beautiful as ever," he said, his eyes focusing on her face. "So I waited until that night. Borrowed a few pills from Miranda, not that she'd notice. And I got rid of Lady Macbeth."

He laughed then, horrible in its sincerity.

"William with his Macbeth curse!" he chuckled. "I totally used that. I don't believe in that superstitious stuff, but it sure helped with the sabotaging. I kept playing up the curse. Miranda was so helpful, with her melodramatic antics. I couldn't have scripted anything better."

He laughed again, wiping his eyes. Anna made a movement sideways, but Jake was too quick. He grabbed her arms, pinning her to the yew hedge.

"No, beautiful Anna," he said, his face inches from hers, no more laughter in his eyes. "I can't have you running away. I thought we could have a future together, if you believed me. If you'd just left it alone, and believed what I told you. But no, you had to think. You had to question everything, and figure it all out. And I'm very sorry about that. I think we could have been happy together."

"Has anyone seen Anna?"

William's voice was desperate, searching each face in the room, but only receiving blank stares.

"I wasn't in the room," Edwin admitted. "I just came back in."

"She was here before tea," offered Brian.

"I was talking to her when Mr. Barnaby announced that tea was ready," offered Sir Frederick, blinking rapidly. "I had just told her she was the star of my show. The villain."

"Jake's not here, either," said Edwin in an urgent tone. "We have to find them."

Where would she go?

William's mind clouded, swirls of hazy thoughts drifting in and out like the fog he watched wafting past the French doors outside.

"Check the bedrooms!" he said to Edwin. "I'm going to check the garden!"

"We could still be happy together, Jake!" said Anna, trying not to cringe at his touch.

"I'm not stupid, Anna," he said. "If Corinne lives, and they believe her, I've got to start a new life for myself. Make myself into something new. I can't have you as a liability. You could turn on me. Turn me in. No, you'll have to go."

He reached up and pulled her hair tie out, allowing her red hair to tumble down over her shoulders. He tenderly pushed a strand from her face, and she trembled, closing her eyes.

He kissed her lips, pulling her close with his hand at the back of her head, his fingers tangled in her hair. She made a muffled sound in her throat.

"Why are you crying?" he asked, pulling back. "You know I can't leave you alive. It wouldn't make sense."

She looked into his eyes, hoping for mercy, but finding only darkness.

"You said it bothered you, the killing," she reminded him. "You didn't want to kill Peter. You didn't want to kill Corinne. You don't want to kill me. Isn't my life worth something to you?"

"Life?" He spat out the word. "Life is but a walking shadow," he said angrily, his fingers tracing her cheekbone, then her lips. "A poor player that struts and frets his hour upon the stage and then is heard no more." He gripped her chin with one powerful hand, his other hand on her back, pressing her against him. "It's a tale, Anna," he breathed into her ear, "told by an idiot, full of sound and fury, and—" His hand on her chin moved down to her throat, "and signifying nothing!"

William ran through the rose garden, pausing on the Japanese bridge to listen. He thought he heard voices in the fog, swirling past from an unknown direction. He tried to steady his breathing, which sounded deafening in his own ears. He gripped the wooden rail of the bridge with one hand, something solid in the ethereal darkness. Yes! It was voices. Or at least one voice. A man, sounding like he was reciting a play. He ran toward the sound.

Anna tried to scream, but Jake's hands on her throat stifled all sound except a rasping gurgle. She pulled desperately at his fingers, her legs kicking at him, but only in a feeble attempt, since the yew hedge folded her in its embrace, giving little resistance.

Jake's face faded in and out of the fog, and suddenly Anna realized it had changed to another Jake, or rather, to Sir John; she could see his starched, white shirt and cravat that covered his throat. Her legs floundered in her skirt, and her hands pulled against Sir John's velvet coat sleeves, slipping on the smooth material. She gasped for breath, black specks clouding her vision, but this time she couldn't stop herself from fainting. This time, it was the very life fading out of her, darkness in spots that joined with other dark spots. Darkness that covered everything, that she couldn't stop. Darkness that took away life.

"Lady Anna!"

She heard her name being called. Was it God? Was she dead already? She felt a breath on her face. Or was it the wind? Something rushed past her, and the darkness stopped its progress. She crumpled against the yew hedge, then onto the cold ground. Her head hit something hard, and she saw sparks of light. Someone was twirling in the fog. No, it was two people. One was punching the other one. She could see Mr. Langley. Or was it William? One and the same. He was struggling with Sir John. The two men staggered in the fog. One was running away, but the other ran after him. Down, two men on the ground.

Lady Anna tried to concentrate on breathing. A funny thing, breath. Easy to take for granted. You shouldn't have to think about each breath, she thought. It's supposed to be automatic. It's not supposed to hurt. She could hear her throat make gurgling sounds as the breath came. No. It wasn't her own throat making the sounds.

She pulled herself onto her knees, which was no small feat in a long skirt. Her eyes focused on the two men fighting. One was sitting on top of the other, his hands around the other's throat, and the gurgling sound came from between his fingers.

"Mr. Langley!" she called. It was only a whisper, but the man on top turned his head at the sound. "Don't! Every life counts!" she wheezed.

The man sat back, releasing his hands. The man under him gasped and coughed.

The effort to speak took more breath than Lady Anna had within her, and she collapsed under the strain.

She heard running feet, and men's voices, shouting orders.

"Lady Anna?"

Someone turned her over, gently and carefully, smoothing her hair back from her face. His face leaned close to hers, black hair falling over his forehead. Mr. Langley! She could see the broad shoulders of his coat and the starched white cravat, rumpled and untied around his throat. She had an overwhelming urge to giggle; she always seemed to find him with his cravat undone. He hated the restraints of it, she knew. If he could, he would throw it off completely.

"Anna?"

It was a question. Mist hid his face for a moment, wet and cold. Then his face reappeared. His cravat faded away before her eyes, and the sharp edges of his coat softened into a down jacket. Flashlights played across the garden room, light filtering through the wisps of fog. There was a crowd of people in the corner of her vision, but above her? She could see glimpses of his eyes, worried and haunted, looking down at her.

"William!"

Her voice croaked through her fragile throat, but it was the most beautiful sound William had ever heard. He gasped for breath himself, falling on top of her, his kisses raining down upon her face, mixing with his tears.

"William," she said again. "I can't breathe."

"I know," he said. "The paramedics are coming."

"No," she said. "You're on top of my chest."

"Oh. Sorry," he said, raising up.

She laughed. Or tried to. It came out in a wheeze and a cough, but she was smiling. Then just as suddenly, she was crying, sobbing with dry heaves under the weight of her experience. He pulled her into a sitting position and held her close.

"I'm here," he whispered into her hair. "And I always will be."

CHAPTER SEVENTY-ONE

"I don't want to leave!" said Miranda, actual tears on her face. "I've grown to love all of you so much!"

The Drawing Room was full of people, and Miranda had a captive audience. Anna exchanged glances with Corinne. They both smiled politely at the older actress, who was striking a pose in front of the Drawing Room fire. Corinne and Miranda had just returned from the hospital that morning. Corinne, newly awakened from her coma the afternoon before, was looking rested and happy, especially sitting next to Perry.

"Well, the good news is, we'll all be back together in the spring," said Sir Frederick, beaming at her. "Julia approved us to finish out the season. Gives me time to do some rewrites to the script, and we'll be right back at it come spring."

"Thank you, Julia," said Portia.

Julia waved her hand like a benevolent queen.

"And now, I'm off," Julia said. "Now that this dreadful business is finished, I can finally go home."

She exited the Drawing Room with a regal salute, pulling her suitcase behind her.

"This whole time, I've been wanting to go home," said Miranda, "and now that we can leave, I want to stay." She dabbed her eyes with a kleenex.

Adrian pursed his lips and nodded sympathetically.

"But Corinne and I missed all the excitement," Miranda pouted. "You have to fill us in. Anna, you're looking well. I heard you were almost the next victim."

Anna fingered her turtleneck sweater that hid most of the bruising from her brush with death.

"Anna is lucky to be alive," said Edwin.

"Oh, Edwin!" said Miranda, batting her false lashes at him. "Why don't you tell us what happened? I heard you were the hero who figured it all out."

"Several of us figured it out, all at the same time," he admitted. "I wouldn't call me a hero. I'm sure Anna would say William was the hero for saving her life." He gave her a brotherly smile and a wink.

"Where is William?" asked Portia, glancing around the room.

"He had to see to his farm," Anna explained. "He'll be back soon."

"What I want to know is how you figured out that William wasn't the murderer," said Miranda, gathering the attention to herself again. "I mean, I was sure he was the guilty party."

"To be honest with you," said Edwin, "everything finally made sense when Anna suggested there could be two murderers, not just one. I hadn't considered an accomplice until then. After that, the pieces just fell into place. Just in time, too."

"Yes," Anna said. "Thank you for calling the police when you did. They were already on the way when Jake followed me outside."

"They'd already released William when I phoned them," said Edwin, "for lack of evidence. Also Corinne had awakened, and told the Inspector what she'd seen. I was horrified when I came back in the room, and Jake wasn't there. I'm sorry I put you in danger, Anna."

Anna shook her head.

"It was my fault for leaving the house," she said. "When Sir Frederick said I was the villain on the show, I knew it was important. That it had something to do with the murders. I just couldn't immediately figure out why. I wanted to think. I didn't realize how foolish I was, separating myself from the group."

"You're the villain?" Miranda said in a shocked voice. "Edwin, tell me about it all from the beginning."

Edwin bowed slightly, then took a stance in front of the fireplace. Anna could tell he was taking on the role of the detective in a novel. Miranda took a seat.

"Mother was sure the police would arrest William," he began, "and she was right. It's why she called me down here. When Peter was shot, she was sure William would be used as a scapegoat because of the accusation that he had caused a curse on the show."

"I'm glad *I* never thought there was a silly curse," Miranda said, her hand to her heart.

"Oh, really?" said Sir Frederick, but was silenced by a look from Portia.

"Anyway," Edwin continued, "even though William had a motive for killing Peter, both because of his suspicions that Peter was responsible for his father's death, and the fact that Peter had attacked Anna the night before the duel, I knew his sense of duty too well. After all his hard work to save Hampstead

Hall, I couldn't imagine him putting it all at risk, even for a scoundrel like Peter. But the crime puzzled me. It had aspects of premeditation and of spur-of-the-moment passion."

"Did you ever suspect Jake?" asked Anna, her eyes filling with tears. Jake may be a cold-blooded killer, she thought, but she had been fond of him once. It was hard not to feel sorry for him, at least in part.

"I have to say, Jake is a superb actor," Edwin admitted. "To kill a man, and then immediately act like you think he's faking his death? Genius. None of us ever doubted the sincerity of his grief. And part of the reason was it was sincere grief, as he admitted to Anna, and again to the police, last night. Peter was his best friend. He grieved his loss. He even regretted killing him. And so, he turned on the person he blamed for making him do it."

"Jaime," Anna breathed. Witchy Jaime, with her *an da shealladh* eyes. *Lady Macbeth.*

"I still don't see how she could have made him do anything he didn't want to do," Adrian complained. "She didn't hold a gun to his head. Oh. Sorry for the reference."

"Jaime, like Lady Macbeth, used a man's own pride against him," Portia explained. "With Peter, she convinced him to kill off poor Geoffrey Langley instead of waiting for him to die naturally, which at the rate he was drinking, would have been soon. She played on his greed, the fact that he wanted Hampstead Hall. All Peter had to do was put a large dose of sleep medication into Geoffrey's drink. With the alcohol, it was a deadly combination, and something William couldn't prove. I think Peter convinced himself that Geoffrey's death was inevitable, and didn't feel too guilty about it. But when she wanted him to kill William—"

"That's when he put his foot down," said Edwin. "An old, drunk Earl was one thing. A young Earl was quite another. And his death would have been more noticeable to the police."

"So, even though he was no longer her boyfriend, Jaime still had some kind of hold over him?" asked Jim, incredulous.

"Apparently so," Edwin said. "Probably Geoffrey Langley's death. She stayed connected to him because they were in business together. And Jake, as well. The police found papers in the lining of Jake's suitcase that outlined their business arrangements. They had a company that claimed to be a charity on paper, but in reality, they used it to buy property. Their latest plan was to buy

Hampstead Hall for cheap, betting on William's desperation. But *Cavendish Manor* was helping William cover his father's debts. He wasn't interested in selling."

Anna thought back to the papers on Jake's desk, the ones he hid from her and that Jaime had been annoyed to see. She had assumed he was hiding his messy room, when in reality, the papers would have revealed his business association with Peter and Jaime.

"So the anonymous practical joker was actually three people?" clarified Jim. "Peter and Jaime and Jake?"

"They wanted to sabotage my show!" said Sir Frederick, offended.

"I'm afraid so," said Edwin. "It started with messing with the car, and then the lighting rig."

"I knew it wasn't my fault," said Tim, his mustache bristling.

"The chair was a brilliant idea," added Edwin. "Sabotaging the chair simultaneously upset Miranda and made it look like someone was out to make Jaime look bad. In actuality, it was Jaime who cut through the leg of the chair."

"So devious," Corinne commented.

"So clever," said Edwin.

"That must have been the loud bangs in the night," Anna offered. "It was them bringing the chair down from the third floor."

"Probably," Edwin agreed. "They would have had to set it up when no one was around so the broken leg wouldn't be noticed."

"But if they were in business together," said Adrian, "why would they want to kill Peter? Just because he refused to kill William?"

"No," said Anna. "Peter was double-crossing them."

"What did Jake tell you about it?" asked Portia.

"He said that Jaime overheard William and Peter arguing in the Tapestry Room. She and Jake didn't know William until *Cavendish Manor*, although they'd seen pictures of him, but Peter knew him well. They had been neighbors. He'd been to Hampstead Hall many times. When Jaime heard voices in the Tapestry Room, she snuck down into the secret passage that Peter had told her about. She overheard Peter trying to convince William to sell Hampstead Hall directly to him. He was cutting Jake and Jaime out of the deal. But William wouldn't sell. Jaime told Jake about Peter double-crossing them, and she told him Peter needed to die."

"I think she hated him," said Edwin, "and was looking for any excuse to get rid of him, but she needed him to help make the deal because of his connection to William. When he double-crossed her, she calculated that Peter's death, blamed on William, would accomplish her purposes just as well. It would still stop the show and keep Hampstead Hall in debt."

"That little witch," said Jim, scowling. "I don't care how good of a props master she was."

"I don't know if she would have succeeded in convincing Jake to kill Peter," Anna speculated. "It was Peter's attack on me that settled it in his mind."

"When we thought about the morning of the duel," Edwin continued, "we all focused on who had access to the lead ball. Who was at the props table? Who had access to the guns *before* they were handed to the actors? When I found out Jaime had dropped bullets right before filming began, I knew it was significant, but I couldn't figure out why. She couldn't have put the lead ball in the gun then because the gun was already in Jake's hand. I should have realized the obvious. *The man who shot Peter was the man who intended to shoot Peter.* Jake already had the lead ball concealed in his pocket. Jaime's dropping bullets was the distraction: it gave Jake time to slip the lead ball out of his pocket and into his own gun while everyone else was staring at Jaime. Everyone, that is, except Corinne."

Perry kissed Corinne on the cheek.

"You're lucky to be alive, my girl," he said.

"I know," she said, squeezing his hand. "I feel so stupid. I shouldn't have let him in that night, but he seemed so sincere. He came to my door with a piece of gingerbread, saying he wanted to talk to me about Anna. His feelings for her, whether she had feelings for him or for William. He looked so sad, and he kept saying he thought William was the murderer, and that he feared for Anna's life if William was released. I was still trying to figure out exactly what I saw. He seemed so sincere, talking about Anna. It made me doubt myself. I guess I didn't want to believe that Jake did it. He was such a nice guy."

Anna grimaced.

Jake was a nice guy. At least, he acted like a nice guy.

"Jake tried to make it look like Corinne had attempted suicide, but the glass of water was the giveaway," explained Edwin with a wink at Anna. "If you're trying to make it look like someone took an overdose with a glass of water, don't leave a full glass of water! The drugs were actually put in the gingerbread."

"Oh! Of course!" said Anna, finally understanding.

"And he killed Jaime because he regretted killing Peter, just like in the real story in the journal," said Sir Frederick. "He killed off his Lady Macbeth."

"Yep," said Edwin, rubbing his jaw. "They were pretending not to have a romantic relationship, to keep people from linking them together. It's also possible that Jake had tired of her and was moving on."

He glanced at Anna, who blushed.

"He stole a bottle of wine, and snuck up the secret passage from the Chapel," said Edwin. "I would imagine he had used that passage many times before that for secret rendezvous with Jaime."

"Yes," said Anna, crinkling her brow in thought. "I remember catching him trying to go in the Tapestry Room once, and he looked guilty about it. At the time, he claimed he was looking for me, but he must have been surprised to see me there since it was supposed to be an off-limits room."

Edwin nodded.

"He probably started entering from the Chapel after that," he said, "to avoid being seen. The night he killed Jaime, he began his little drama by making a big show of going to apologize to her earlier in the evening. It was early enough that he was cleared of giving her the overdose. But he went back later that night."

"He must have pretended to make up with her earlier," Anna speculated, "promising to come back when no one was looking."

"I think the show started even earlier," Portia piped up. "At dinner. I think Jake purposely hurt Jaime's feelings to give him an excuse to apologize later. It would explain any of his DNA being present in her room."

"I believe you're right," Edwin said to his mother. "When he came back the second time, the two of them had a glass of wine, and she went to sleep. He hid the bottle in the Chapel, where we found it the next day."

"Last night, when he followed me outside," Anna said, "he tried to convince me that Corinne and William had killed Peter together. And when Jaime suspected them, they killed her. He tried to convince me that you were unstable," she said, turning to Corinne beside her. "That you were abusing prescription medication, and that's why you had the pills."

"What a jerk!" Corinne said. "He obviously didn't think I would survive to tell on him."

"He tried to make me believe there was something between you and

William," Anna added. "Romantically, I mean."

"You didn't believe him, I hope?" asked Corinne. "Every chance I got, I tried to convince William to make a move on you. But he was so stubborn. He kept telling me he didn't want to get between you and Jake."

She folded her arms, clearly still annoyed her matchmaking schemes hadn't worked.

The truth of Corinne and William's secret conversations dawned on Anna. She bit her lip, embarrassed by her own jealousy.

"And then he said William used him as a weapon to kill Peter," Anna continued. "When he said it, he pulled his hand through his hair, and I remembered that he does that a lot. It's a gesture he does subconsciously, and I started thinking that it must mean something, like when people fidget when they're nervous, or when Edwin pulls his hair straight up when he's thinking."

Edwin paused, quickly pulling his fingers out of his curls, grinning sheepishly.

"And suddenly, I knew," she said. "I knew he did that every time he lied. And if that was true, then he was lying to me right then."

"So you had to die, as well," said Edwin.

Anna nodded.

"But William saved you," announced Sir Frederick with excitement, "just like the first William Langley in the real story. I couldn't write a better ending to this."

"Oh, Freddie! I hope you're not going to make my son do any more acting!" announced Lady Diane from the doorway. She was back to her impeccably coiffed self now that her son was out of danger.

Sir Frederick paled, then blushed.

"My dear, of course not," he bleated, "unless he wants to?"

Sir Frederick beamed at William, who had followed his mother into the room. William gave him a decisive shake of the head.

"No, Sir Frederick," he said, "my acting days are over."

Anna's heart did a somersault at the sight of William. He bore only a few bruises and scrapes from last night's rescue, and somehow it only made him look more handsome and masculine. Or maybe it was the fact that he'd saved her life. Or that he had told her, over and over again, that he loved her.

With Jake arrested, William was welcomed warmly back into the company, even by Miranda, who had apparently forgiven him for his curse. He stood behind Anna's chair, his hands resting protectively on her shoulders.

"So, this is goodbye," said Lady Diane, sweeping across the room to Sir Frederick. "At least, for now. William tells me you are all released to go home."

She beamed a smile on them reminiscent of an indulgent nursery school teacher sending her pupils home with their parents.

"Yes," Sir Frederick agreed, "but only for now. I do hope you'll join us in the spring to watch the filming."

"Mmm," was Lady Diane's incoherent response, her perfectly-manicured brows raised. She turned an aloof smile to Anna, as if Sir Frederick's comment reminded her of something.

"Anna, I hear you're staying with us for a time," she said coolly.

"Yes, Lady Diane," Anna answered nervously, fidgeting with her hands. William squeezed her shoulders.

"Through Christmas, I understand," said Lady Diane. "William has invited me up from my cottage to be a sort-of chaperone, I presume. And your parents are joining us?"

"If that's all right," said Anna. She had a momentary vision of her mother and Lady Diane meeting for the first time, and inwardly cringed.

"It's William's house," Lady Diane reminded her in a flippant tone, her nose in the air. "He is free to invite whomever he chooses." Then she smiled graciously down on her. "I understand we are kin. I look forward to meeting the rest of our family," she said, warmth radiating in her glance for a moment before resuming her detached air.

Anna smiled back at her, sighing with relief. It was a glimpse of what was to come, she knew. Lady Diane's exterior was only a veneer; on the inside was a warm and caring person, carefully concealed.

CHAPTER SEVENTY-TWO

The Drawing Room felt strangely empty in the afternoon. Most of the cast had left or were packing to leave. The last of them would be gone by tomorrow. The crew was busy dismantling the equipment that hadn't been already packed away, and base camp was no more. *Cavendish Manor* had disappeared; Hampstead Hall had returned.

At least until spring, Anna thought to herself.

She would miss Corinne, she realized with a smile. The two had parted as dear friends, sisters almost.

Bound together by death, Anna sighed. Then she shook her head as she stared out the French doors into the rose garden. The light was fading fast, casting an orange glow over the tangled vines.

"No," she told herself. "Not death, only."

Life lingered beneath the surface, just like it coursed through the now-brown stems of the roses, twining over the arbor, and in the grey leaves of the lavender around the sundial. In the spring, they would turn green again. Leaves would form on the rose vines, followed by flowers in profusion. The lavender, she knew from experience in her mother's garden, would flush green from the ground outward to the tips, making what looked dead come to life again.

What was nearly taken from Corinne had been restored. Would continue to be restored. And what Anna almost lost—

"I thought I'd find you in here," said William from the doorway.

Anna couldn't stop the smile that lit up her face.

William gathered her in his arms, pushing down the fear that rose in his chest.

There's no more Jake, he reminded himself. No golden-boy actor to steal her heart. Or her life. He kissed her, holding her close. She's in my arms, not running away. Not fading like a ghost. Or a dream.

She laughed, and the sound of it brought tears to his eyes that he hoped he could hide away. Then he laughed at himself, and let them fall, allowing her to wipe them away with her gentle fingers.

"I can't believe I have Peter to thank for my life," said William when they had settled themselves on a sofa.

"Ironic, isn't it?" Anna agreed, snuggling against his chest. "Whatever the reason, self-preservation or not, I'm glad he decided he couldn't kill you."

William wrapped his arms tighter around her.

"I suspected there was something between Jake and Jaime," he said gently, hoping it was the right time. "The first day they arrived, I saw them in the garden. They seemed to be more than friends, but I couldn't prove it."

"You didn't tell me that," she said, sitting up.

He shrugged.

"I didn't want to hurt you," he said, tucking her hair behind her ear. "You two were getting friendly, and it would have seemed like I was just trying to break you up."

She nodded. He was right. That's exactly what she would have thought.

"I figured it would come out, if it were true," he said, "and then I wouldn't be the one to blame."

"There were times I wondered about their relationship," she admitted with a sigh. "Even when he and I were—whatever we were. And then he told me Jaime admitted having feelings for him, but he told her he didn't care about her that way." She shuddered. "That was the day I saw them arguing in the garden, and he looked at her with so much hatred. He killed her that night!"

William's face was solemn.

"He must have lied about what they argued about," he speculated. "They must have actually fought about Peter's death, his guilty feelings."

"With that tell-tale swipe through his hair," she said, remembering. "I should have known."

She frowned, tears forming in her eyes.

William pulled her into his arms again.

"How could you have known?" he assured her. "He was a first-class liar. An actor who made you believe what he wanted you to believe."

"Do you think he cared about me at all?" she asked, pulling back to look him in the face again. "Or do you think that was a lie, too?"

William leaned his head against hers.

"I don't know if he did at first," he said, honestly. "I think he may have started something with you to keep people from thinking he and Jaime were together. It's probably why you felt her animosity. But after a while, I think—he seemed genuinely jealous of me. I can't imagine it was all acting on his part."

"But to be able to turn on me so quickly," she said. "To kill me? To kill Jaime before that? I think he must have only really loved one person. Himself."

"I can't argue with that," said William, kissing her. "Real love sacrifices, puts the other person first. All he ever did was protect his own interests, and his own life."

"Thank you," said Anna, looking up at him. "I owe you my life."

He gazed intently down into her amber eyes.

"I would have given mine for yours," he said.

CHAPTER SEVENTY-THREE

The next morning, Anna stood at the Tapestry Room window, gazing out at the frozen garden below. Frost had crept in overnight, and the morning sun had yet to warm the evergreen yew leaves and the brown blades of grass enough to melt its rime. She took a deep breath, staring at the iron window handle.

Were the dreams over now? she wondered. Or would Anna always be plagued with the continuation of their story, William Langley and Lady Anna? Had Lady Anna accomplished her purpose?

According to the journal, Mr. Langley and Lady Anna had married, raising their family at Hampstead Hall. After the death of Lady Anna's father, Lord Somerville, the title had been given to Mr. Langley, who became the Fourth Earl of Somerville. Somewhere along the way, one of their descendants sailed to America. Anna was sure her mother would waste no time figuring out every detail of the connection so she could discuss it with Lady Diane when she arrived in a few weeks.

Anna had read the journal herself now, and found that although her subconscious mind had changed some of the names, her dreams had revealed the true story of what happened so long ago. His name may not have been Sir John Rawlings, but the man he represented—third in line to the title—had killed his best friend, Peter's ancestor, and his Lady Macbeth. Unfortunately, Lady Anna's real lady's maid had not survived the drug overdose. Anna was sobered by the fact that her quick action had saved Corinne from a similar fate.

Although the dreams and visions had been alarming, and sometimes terrifying, Anna was thankful for them. Without those visions of the past, the present would have remained in the fog, and in one instance at least, her dreams had changed the future. *An da shealladh.* Second sight. She hadn't had it when she arrived. Would she always have it? From now on? She shuddered at the thought. But she had to know for sure.

Closing her eyes, she reached out her trembling hand and touched the window handle. In the distance, she heard the sound of horse hooves on hard-packed ground, and opening her eyes, she watched a black horse and its rider galloping toward the archway that lead into the garden. She stared, mesmerized, until the horse and rider came to a stop outside the window.

"Mr. Langley," she whispered, clutching the window handle.

But this time, instead of a top hat, he was wearing s Stetson. A cowboy hat. She wrinkled her brow and looked closer. And a stained field jacket, she realized. And muddy boots.

He looked up at her and whipped off his hat, a mischievous grin on his lips and a twinkle in his blue eyes.

William!

Anna pushed open the window, and leaned out, a smile lighting her face.

"Lady Anna!" he called.

"Yes?" she answered with a flirtatious aloofness.

"Would you care to join me for a ride in the park?"

She nodded, grinning broadly.

As she closed the window, she realized something important: the handle had never hummed.

Anna grabbed her jacket and raced down the stairs, through the Great Hall, into the Drawing Room, and out the French doors into the garden. As she passed through, she shouted something.

"Well!" said Portia, rising from her seat to peer out the window after her. "All's well that ends well."

She smiled a motherly smile as William dismounted, and after twirling her in an embrace, walked beside Anna toward the stables, leading his horse.

Portia's son joined her at the window.

"What did she say?" he asked.

"She said, 'It didn't hum.'"

"Hmm," mumbled Edwin, raising his brows. "I suppose it's time for us to be going."

"For now," said his mother. "I'm so glad you agreed to come back in the spring. Sir Frederick will need you to fill in his cast."

Edwin rolled his eyes.

"I should have known you'd rope me in," he said.

Portia smiled.

"I was right, roping you in to help," she said proudly.

"The police would have gotten there," he said with a shrug.

"But not in time," she reminded him. "Anna could have been killed."

Edwin scowled, staring at the garden.

"Mother," he said. "Remember when you said Istanbul was a test run?"

"I never said that," she said, moving away from the window. "*You* said it. What *I* said was that this was an opportunity to be a real-life hero. Not just one on TV. That is what you want, isn't it?"

She gave her son an arched look. He sighed.

"I don't need to be a hero," he said. "I just want to be real. To help in real situations."

"And you have," said Portia. "Saving someone's life is as real as it gets."

Edwin gave his mother an affectionate look. Then he hugged her close.

"Let's go home," he said.

"We made a good team, didn't we, dear?" she asked as they headed toward the Great Hall.

"We did," he admitted. "A regular Sherlock and Watson."

"I was thinking Miss Marple, and…oh dear. She didn't have a sidekick."

Edwin's laugh echoed across the stone floor of the Great Hall. He ducked his head as he followed his mother through the wicket door and out into the frosty morning.

THE END

ACKNOWLEDGEMENTS

Although writing a novel is a solitary pursuit, it can never come into printed form without the input and help of many. With that in mind, I'd like to thank my Inkwell partners, Joanne and Joshua, for their friendship and expertise; Sarah Siegand, my designer, for her ability to make a professional product out of a pdf; George and Kim at Vincent Creative Group for marketing help, and my cousin, Pat Evans, for his cover artwork—you outdid yourself on this one! Special thanks to Brian Allison from Andrew Jackson's The Hermitage for his dueling expertise, and to Christin Loera, whom I dragged along with me to "The Duel" reenactment to hear Brian's expertise! Thank you to Kenda Benward and D. Scott Graham for valuable input about the backstage of a film set. I'd also like to thank Marisa, Shea, Greg, Jessica, Joanne, and Anna for assuring me that this book is worth reading, and to my Pretty in Ink ladies for their constant friendship, encouragement, and love. And lastly, I'd like to thank my family for their support and patience while I pursue my calling. Thank you!

ABOUT THE AUTHOR

Ashley Sargeant Hagan has the mind of Agatha Christie with the soul of Mark Twain. She writes mysteries with a literary twist, and sometimes something completely different! Originally from Lakeland, Florida, she is a long-time resident of Nashville, where she lives with her musician husband and three children. She loves cats, mysteries, history, and tea, and when she's not writing, you'll find her involved with Historic Nashville and volunteering for the Land Trust for Tennessee's Glen Leven Farm.

ALSO FROM
ASHLEY SARGEANT HAGAN

Available at
AshleySHagan.com

CPSIA information can be obtained
at www.ICGtesting.com
Printed in the USA
LVHW110413051219
639508LV00001B/118/P